LAND OF THE GOLDEN CLOUDS

Archie Weller was born in 1957 and was brought up on a farm in the south-west of Western Australia. His first novel, *The Day of the Dog*, was shortlisted for the *Australian*/Vogel Literary Award and won the fiction award in the literature section of the prestigious West Australian Week Awards. In 1991 *The Day of the Dog* was made into the film *Blackfellas* which won two AFI awards. Archie has also published *Going Home*, a critically acclaimed collection of short stories, plays and poems, and he is a regular contributor of short stories to various publications.

Land of the Golden Clouds

Archie Weller

ALLEN & UNWIN

I would like to thank the Austalia Council for financial help with the making of this book which took seven years of writing altogether.

First published in 1998 by
Allen & Unwin
9 Atchison Street
St Leonards NSW 2065
Australia
Phone: (61 2) 9901 4088
Fax: (61 2) 9906 2218
E-mail: frontdesk@allen-unwin.com.au
Web: http://www.allen-unwin.com.au

National Library of Australia
Cataloguing-in-Publication entry:

Weller, Archie.
    Land of the golden clouds.

    ISBN 1 86448 338 5.

    I. Title.

A823.3

Set in 11/12pt Plantin Light by DOCUPRO
Printed and bound by Australian Print Group, Maryborough, Victoria

10 9 8 7 6 5 4 3 2 1

Acknowledgments

The book used for the quotes of poetry was *Bartlett's Familiar Quotations*, (fourteenth edition) by John Bartlett, published by MacMillan Press, 1977. The songs from Bob Marley were from various records but mostly *Legend* and *Exodus*. Lyrics reproduced with permission from Polygram Music Publishing are from *Wake up and Live* (Marley/Davis), *Babylon System* (Marley), *Ride Natty Ride* (Marley), *Top Rankin'* (Marley), *Survival* (Marley) and *Ambush in the Night* (Marley). The quote about Babylon is from *A Dictionary of World Mythology* (p.20) by Arthur Cotterell, published by G. P. Putman and Sons, New York, and other quotes are from the Bible. The books I used for the Gypsy language are *The Romany Rye* (1914), *The Gypsies of Spain* (1923), and *Lavengro* (1851)—all by George Borrow and published by John Murray of London. I used *Names for Girls and Boys* by Carole Boyer, published by Mayflower (1974) to get my Hebrew names and their meanings. I used references from *Dictionary of Jamaican English* by Professors F. G. Cassidy and R. B. Le Page, published by Oxford University Press, for the Jamaican language and referred to *A Handbook of Jamaican History*. As always, I relied upon *Brewster's Book of Fact and Fiction* for many of my descriptions.

Every effort has been made to contact the copyright holders of material used in this book. However, where an omission has occurred, the author and publisher will gladly include acknowledgement in any future editions.

I dedicate this book to Claire-Louise, who put up with the writer's temperament and kept me company during the hard times, and to James Ricketson, in whose house I first thought of the idea and where the waves of Palm Beach helped formulate those ideas.

Contents

Note on the use of language

I have used several different styles of language for my various characters. There are Nyoongah words from the south-west of Western Australia and also Koori words from New South Wales. There are Gypsy words and Spanish words and I experimented with a type of Hebrew using first names such as Evadne, Jothaim, Eve, Simeon as a language in itself. The four West Indians speak, therefore, a type of hybrid English. I understand that this, of course, is not how they would normally speak on their Island home in this day and age. I only use my writer's licence to portray what that language might be like in three thousand years time. I have many West Indian friends and do not wish to offend them by presenting what may appear to be a ridiculous sentence structure and conversation. I hope this explanation is satisfactory.

The characters

In the Land of the Purple Plains

Ilgar, soon to be known as Red Mond Star Light Moon-talker
Ilki, his cousin
Kareen, his cousin and Earth Mother
Violet Lynx Foot, his uncle and clan Chief
Kala, his mother, who is sister to Violet Lynx Foot

Other members of the clan Violet Lynx Foot, of the Tribe Elk

Rabit-the-White, prophet
Yellow Eyes, warrior
Grey Fur, hunter
Magpie, sister of Grey Fur
Ensee, lover of Grey Fur
Joda, young boy
Oka, young boy
Roan, farmer
Kiki, Roan's son
Orange Horse, stableman
Dark Carmine
Cimarron Rose
Grey Wolf of the Yellow Plains, the oldest living clansman
Akar Black Head, warrior
Culvato, of the Gypsy Race
Lynx Kitten, now known as Blue Berry or Durrilau, Culvato's younger
    half-brother
Baba, the clan's collector of stories

In the Land of the People of the Caves

S'shony, a young girl from the People of the Caves
Willum, a member of the Sun People
Radi, his younger brother
Olbeno, a healer among the Sun People
The Secret-maker, a Beacon
The Creeper, a Beacon

From the Island of Springs

Nanny, Captain, a Maroon Warrior
Port Rial, of the Buccaneer cult
Surrey Anne, healer, cook, and Port Rial's lover
Cudjo Accompong, Maroon Warrior, Ras Tafarian
The Baptist, deceased
The Syrian, deceased
Saint Catherine, deceased
Clarendon Jon Cannu, deceased
Porky, deceased

From the Keepers of the Trees

Mungart, warrior of the Kawar, Purple-Crowned Lorikeet People, from the Parrot Totem
Weerluk, his twin brother
Dongkarak, their younger sister
Koobeaku, their mother
Kwila, their grandfather
Nolku, his brother, a warrior lawman
Kwoola, his brother, a dancer
Billah, his brother, a painter
Mumboyet, the youngest brother
Yabini, great-grandson of Mumboyet

Pemul, of the Platypus People
Muraong, his wife
Gurrewe, his daughter
Twiuga, his son
Arakui, his brother

In the Silver City

Shimona, leader of the Twelve Virgins from the House of Willows
Ruth, their healer
Bethesda, from the House of Willows
Naomi, from the House of Willows
Zillah, from the House of Willows
Carmela, from the House of Willows
Clemence, from the House of Willows
Vida, from the House of Willows
Abigail, from the House of Willows

Elihu, Highest of the Prophets
Jothaim, grace of the Lord, Prophet
Arainias, God is perfect, Prophet
Joash, loved by God, Prophet

Hiram, God is exalted, Prophet
Absalom, God is peace, Prophet
Girvan, the Lord's grace, Prophet
Tobias, God's goodness, Prophet
Johanan, favoured of God, Prophet
Janan, grace of the Lord, Prophet
Danette, the Lord judges me, wife of Janan
Jessamine, God is, wife of Jothaim

Obadiah, servant of God, Scribe
Beniah, son of the Lord, Scribe
Zachariah, God has remembered, Scribe
Adriel, from the Lord's Kingdom, Scribe

Elia Melchoir Solomon the twenty-third, King of Kings
Zoheletha, the serpent of the stone
Evadne, her assistant
Sarah, her assistant

Israel, a soldier
Darkon, a soldier
Elon, a soldier
Gabriel, the Gatekeeper
Jarebb, a soldier

Siddon, a fisherman
Ithnan, a fisherman
Meras, younger sister to Ithnan
Simeon, once known as Rockstone
Ivy, his twin sister
Gilead, once known as Sastra, Gypsy warrior
Jaala, once known as Ambról, Daughter of Delilah, his younger sister
Lothario, also known as Boshomengro, their father
Pacuaro, their mother
Phenice, once known as Juva, their older sister
Tamara, once known as Sinerella, their older sister

In the Desert and in the Mountains

Laelia, devoted to the Lord, wife of a Prophet
Prince Michael of the Ants, a poet and singer of songs
Leef, warrior leader of a band of Outsiders
Leef-shadow, his young companion
Red Fin, a dwarf among the Outsiders
Wunda, Sister Earth
Jynni, her young friend, Sister Sun
Aybee, member of the Cricketeers' cult, guardians of the mountains

In the City of Bones

Fu-Hsi, Emperor of the Children of the Moon
Han-Shan, Imperial Poet of the Children of the Moon
Hu-Hsien-Ku, female warrior of the Children of the Moon
Yi, famous bowman of the Children of the Moon

In the caverns of the Caves

The King of the Bats, King of the Crooked Cross, leader of all the People
of the Caves

Book One

The Purple Plains

CHAPTER ONE

It was soon to be the night of the dead moon and the people of the Ilkari Nations all knew what that meant. It meant the time of the Nightstalkers. So the men of the clans gathered together their spears and pikes, swords and daggers . . . and magic . . . while the women gathered enough food for the brief time of peril, and they all moved into their stockades to wait out the danger.

But it was Ilgar's misfortune to be caught out on the open plain with his cousin-brothers Rabit-the-White, Grey Fur, and Yellow Eyes, who had all been through their story and so were Travellers now, with their hair in the Traveller's braids. Only young Ilki who, like Ilgar, had not had a story told about him yet, wore his hair long and flowing. As with Ilgar's hair it caught the dying glow of the sun with an added crimson flame, for these two were true cousins and they both had their family's deep flaming red hair.

They were late home on this fateful night because Ilgar had been talking to the moon high up on the roof of the world where he had been born. He had been there for a week in a semi-trance. It was said by some that he had such powerful visions that he would be as strong a priest as his great-grandfather, Ralgar Moonstreak. Ilgar in turn had tried to teach Ilki some of the lesser laws about moon-talking but the boy was sixteen and had more important things to dream of: not least that, in two years time, he could choose the woman of his desires: then, after another six months, if she so wished, they would tie their hair together and be as one. So he had wandered away down the mountainside and joined his cousin-brothers in swimming or fishing in the sacred blue waterhole this huge hill protected, or whiled away his time with the others in the idleness the people of the Ilkari enjoyed most of all. Summer was always an easy time and as the summers grew longer and longer it seemed so did the indolent life of these Desert People. Indeed, their only true worry (apart from the constant attacks from Nightstalkers) appeared to be the rapid drying up of their river that was almost a God, so precious had water become.

So the four of them played and laughed and whittled away the sunny days in hunting and fishing while they waited for Ilgar. Where this clan lived was on the far outskirts of Ilkari country, on the edge of the Purple Plains—the dead country where no one ever ventured and where only a few hardy Keepers of the Trees resided. So hunting was good in such an out-of-the-way area with many water-buffalo, pigs, rabbits or feral cats to catch and eat as well as the occasional big cat or bear or wild dog pack for Ilki to have a chance to make his story.

The other three related *their* stories around the fire one special night of storytelling. Even if they had heard it one hundred times, the listeners would always be surprised by one small detail for it was the teller's prerogative to slightly change or add onto his story every time he told it. The art of storytelling was much admired by the Ilkari for his story was the most important part of a man's life. The women, too, had their tales passed down from mother to daughter since the Old Time. It was a man's story that was his very heart and soul and made him different from any other Ilkari.

On the fifth night Ilgar came down from the mountain and they set off for home.

'What stories did the moon tell you, cousin-brother?' Rabit-the-White wished to know.

'I saw a shadow cross the moon in the shape of a flying dog. I saw a falling star that changed path to kiss the Mother Star. The red star died at the caress of the moon. But I saw much rain for this coming season and the birth of two new babies—one that is strange to our clan.'

The clansmen all wondered at these signs. Yellow Eyes rather wished Rabit-the-White had kept silent. He pondered with typical warrior's foreboding on the magic of these things. A flying dog was a bad omen indeed but the other two signs had to do with love and—possibly—marriage. None of the young men were married. Yellow Eyes had a passionate lover in the form of Kareen. But he had no desire to marry, wishing instead to serve his stockade as a warrior, the same as Ilgar's father had done.

Grey Fur, with his quick and sharp mind, would have asked Rabit-the-White for his opinion of those signs, as it was known the slight blond youth was as much a religious man as Ilgar. Perhaps then the signs would read differently and more favourably. After all, Rabit-the-White was closer to Sister Earth than the Moon-talker and things in the sky often lied. Just look at Sister Sun and the devious schemes she had perpetrated. But before he could form his thoughts into a question, Ilgar's sharp eyes caught sight of something on the slowly darkening horizon.

'Keepers of the Trees come.'

'We will make a fire,' Ilki said eagerly.

He enjoyed the company of these quiet, dark people who walked the land all over. It was known by every Ilkari that the Keepers of the Trees had sprung from this land like the rocks and rivers and trees themselves. They were a part of this country—every grain of it—and they knew all

4

its secrets. They kept out of the way of the white people and their ways, for it had been the white people who had annoyed the spirits and caused the High Ones to walk upon this earth, bringing not sustenance but destruction. So they kept to themselves, these remnants of the oldest Tribe, with their own language, laws and customs.

But because the Ilkari lived the closest to the dead country, sometimes these quiet people would trade with the wild unruly clans. So it was that many of the Ilkari could speak a smattering of the language and even believed in many of the Keepers' stories.

Sometimes, though it was strictly forbidden by the Keepers' laws, an Ilkari woman would give herself to one of the Keeper men and thus there were Ilkari who had a Keeper ancestor. But never would a dark Keeper woman give herself to a white man. Their race was much too pure and regal for that.

But they could be a friendly people, like the Ilkari, and enjoyed jokes and dancing and the telling of stories as much as they. And, being such inveterate travellers, they had some fine tales to tell.

Still, Grey Fur was worried.

'The moon, he dies. Soon is the time of the Nightstalkers and we are far from home.'

Four pairs of blue and one of brown eyes studied the sky.

'There is time yet. Besides, are we afraid of the Nightstalkers?' Yellow Eyes snarled. 'I myself have killed three. Perhaps it is the time for Ilki or Ilgar to make their story.' He punched the dreamy Ilki playfully on the shoulder. 'Perhaps you will kill five or ten Nightstalkers and become a great warrior like your cousin-uncle, Ilgar's father!' he laughed.

'Remember the omens,' Rabit-the-White warned.

'The omens were for love. There is nothing to love about the Nightstalkers,' Yellow Eyes reasoned.

'And the flying dog?' Grey Fur asked.

'Tell them, cous-cous,' Yellow Eyes said to Rabit-the-White. 'A flying dog across the moon is truly not a good sign of love. It can be sign of cowardice as well as death. And the death can be by disease as easily as by Nightstalkers. They don't breathe death as we all know. I am not afraid of the flying dog!'

'It's too late anyway. They have seen us. It would be rude to keep going now,' Ilki said.

It was true. If they snubbed the Keepers of the Trees, who knew what misfortunes the magic of these people would cause to their clan? For the Keepers never forgot that the Ilkari were also from the white Tribes that had shattered the earth with their strange, unbelievable weapons and cruelty.

So the five set about making a camp and building a fire. The day before yesterday Grey Fur had hunted down a young pig and this carcase was placed upon the coals in readiness for their guests.

There was quite a large crowd for these people, who mostly travelled in smaller family groups: three or four old men (or men in their forties—old for these hard times) and three old women. Several young men and women in couples, some eight girls and ten boys and twelve little children made up the rest. Through sign language and the smattering of words that they knew, the Ilkari learnt they were on their way to a big corroboree out in the desert.

The dark Tribe had several kangaroo carcases, goannas and a rare emu which they shared with the Ilkari. None of the old people ate of the pig as they believed it was one of the white man's animals, and thus tainted. But they allowed the young mothers to give some of the crackling to their children as a special gift. This family lived on the dead lands and so had much to do with the Ilkari and felt safe in their company. After all, were not Ilkari almost Keepers of the Trees, they reasoned. Look at that one there, the one that was supposed to talk to the moon. Look at his deep-brown eyes! Were they not the eyes of our Race? And his skin was darker than the others, while some of his hand movements were shadows of our own. There was nothing anyone could hide from a Keeper of the Trees.

So it was that the two clans shared their food and their stories. The young men put on a dance for the Ilkari and then the Ilkari danced in celebration of the Earth Mother whose children they were, led on by Grey Fur's wolf-skin drum and Ilki's lilting flute.

And then the five were alone once more upon the plain and their saviour the moon was dead. How many would die a death along with the moon tonight?

It was during the period that the Old Time ended and the Gods walked upon the earth that the Nightstalkers were born. They were called by many names—Nightstalkers, Deathshades, Prowlers, Night Bats—for there were many more cultures than the Ilkari upon this land.

The Keepers of the Trees, who were the Nightstalkers' especial enemies, called them Djanaks and were greatly affected by their murderous ways. There was not one family who had not lost a member to this evil Race. But, to one and all, they were known as the People of the Caves and their leader, whom no one ever saw but of whom everyone had heard, was called the King of the Bats.

It was in this time—the Old Time—when the sky fell down and all the land shook to the footfalls of angry Gods—that Devils and monstrosities were born too, to scuttle like curs or grotesque beetles at the High Ones' feet and to partake in the destruction of the known world.

One of the breed of monsters, as every Ilkari knew, was the bats who were neither bird nor animal, but a mutation of each lurking in the darkness of the caves. The People of the Caves were not mutations, as anyone lucky enough to survive seeing them could tell. They were the same as other humans. But their skin was as white as no ordinary humans could possibly be and cold to touch. It was a sickly white, like the poisonous fungi that also grew in the caves, and their eyes were as black as the caves' darkness and not like human eyes at all but rather like a snake's—all black and completely devoid of emotion. Their Devils were everyone else's Gods and Goddesses and this alone made them evil.

But the People of the Caves were wicked in many ways. They had developed a love for human meat and every night, when the moon died and the earth was cast in gloomy shadow, they would pour forth and attack whole villages, carrying away entire families, kicking and screaming out their death songs. To look upon the sun was instant and agonising death, everyone knew that. That is why there were no qualms about killing those above. Even though they looked the same they weren't, for the simple reason that those above, who bathed in the dreaded sunlight all day long, were already dead and there was no shame or cruelty in eating ghosts.

The People of the Caves had developed powerful arms and strong hands to claw away at the soil and rock, so their Kingdom was a crisscross of tunnels and shafts across the entire country. They could pop out from anywhere on these deadly nights of the empty sky. Living all their life in the darkness of their world they had acquired a fear of any light, including the moon. Their eyes and skin were so sensitive that they could barely stand the light of the myriad of stars that shone when the moon was down. And this was all that saved the people from above ground from being completely wiped out. For there were many Nightstalkers and their appetites were insatiable.

Her name was S'shony and, upon this joyous night when the hated moon was beheaded by the black arms of the night, she was eighteen stones. It should have been a joyous time for her too, for tonight was her sonaflite when she became a woman. As her nearest and oldest kin (in S'shony's case an uncle) had dropped the eighteenth white stone into her soul urn, then so had she dropped the veil of childhood. The next rock to be placed in the urn would be black and this would be done by herself from now on until she died. Then the oldest in her immediate family would place a red rock in her urn and smash it, thus returning rocks and soul back to Father Earth.

As soon as every boy or girl turned eighteen stones they were led up and out, upon the next moonless night, into that magical yet fearful outside world. It was on this night that they would kill their first Upsider. In the cleansing ritual they would drink the warm blood of their victim and wash their hair in the dying, writhing person's blood. Incanting the sacred words, they would devour the still beating heart, then skin the victim to make their wings. So it was that they became true members of their Race.

It was the most important night of her life and she should have been happy. Yet S'shony squatted in a hidden dark corner with her braided hair gathering in coils around her, like a collection of black snakes protecting her secret. For she squatted there and shed silent tears. It was a sin to cry and anyone caught doing so faced immediate strangulation with their own hair. She had seen it done not two weeks ago to a friend of hers. She did not weep for her friend though. She cried for someone who had shown her that tears were natural enough.

It was also a sin to have a lover before one's first sonaflite and any girl who did so could be tossed into the Hunger Pits to starve there amongst the rotting bones of other wrongdoers. Mostly, depending on the whim of the King, or the Beacon who caught her, she would be spared because, as a woman's only purpose was to procreate, no woman belonged to any one man. Of course, if the girl was foolish enough to fall pregnant then it was instant death for her and the unborn abomination.

As with all her Race before her, she would soon become a true bat and would wear her wings with pride. But right now S'shony was naked and her body shaved of any hair, except the hair on her head that was her only clothing and fell to her knees in thin neat braids. She hugged her hair about her and sank into her nudity as she recalled the events of only recently.

Like all people from the caves S'shony's skin was translucent white. So white one could see every blue vein on her body that carried her life's blood. Even the parts of her body that normally would have been darker, like her nipples and lips, were pale, while her fingernails were silver tips on slender white fingers. Like all her people her hair and eyes were a beautiful jet black, as black as the cockroaches that were their chief sustenance or the hidden secret pools of water in the deep dark caverns, or as black as the bats' eyes. White were the luminous mushrooms or fungi that was the only light they could face or the little white pebbles that signified innocence. So it had always been. Black and white the colours of the caves, the sacred colours.

Often, however, a throwback from the old days was born, a child with red or yellow hair and blue, green, brown or grey eyes. They were called Sun Children because of these hated colours from Upside where the evil sun ruled supreme. After killing the woman who had born this frightful abomination, the squalling child was taken to the pantry—a huge cave where children were kept as special meals for special people (usually the King of the Bats, who was said to wear a necklace of baby skulls). If these children survived they became slaves without a soul and could be killed at anytime by anyone—often as practice by those about to go out on their first sonaflite. They did not live long.

S'shony had often joined in the hunting down of one of these dreaded Sun Children and then watched the beating that would eventually kill the freak. Once she herself had killed a whimpering Sun girl who had turned her ugly blue eyes to her in pain and fear as she lay in her own blood and vomit. S'shony had been careful not to let the yellow hair touch her skin for it would surely burn her. She had beaten the girl's head in with a stone club and exulted that this was how it would be on her first sonaflite.

But a little before the seventeenth white stone was tossed into her soul urn, something had happened.

She had been in a different part of the tunnels than she was used to. Although no one part of the tunnels belonged to a particular family or group, most people stayed around the place where they were born. They felt safer in old company and with proven friends; with a Beacon that they knew and trusted. But this day S'shony had gone exploring, a habit she had fallen into, being curious about life. Now she was far from home. There was always the chance a strange man would come out of the shadows, bend her over and have her. It had happened before and would happen again, no doubt. But this was a risk worth taking if she could discover some new and exciting cave or an old, unused tunnel or—best of all—a hidden lake, whose cool, pristine waters could charm her mind and soothe her body with its black, cold silkiness. For she was a dreamer and, in this respect, much different from the rest of her kind. She asked questions to herself about why was this and what was that and how could this thing be? To have thoughts like these was almost as dangerous as being born with pale hair or eyes in this murky world of conformity.

So she was climbing up the slippery grey walls of a cavern, her eyes, used to the dark, perusing the rock wall for cracks or small ledges for her to get a grip on. Like the rest of her people she was extremely dexterous. They could cling like lizards upon the great rock walls and roofs of the bubbles floating underground, caught forever in the soil's clammy hands.

This cave was underneath an underground river or lake. Or perhaps she had travelled so far that she was under the land of water that every now and then her people inadvertently wandered into. So, digging upwards in search of prey, the last thing they ever saw was a wet silver tongue licking down at them and a happy gurgling as the salty water claimed yet another victim. That is how her father and older brother had died. Not many survived and there were salty rivers now where once there had been tunnel towns. The mouths of these tunnels were blocked up but she still thought she could hear the ghosts of the drowned, calling out in water-soft voices whenever she passed one of the sad empty tunnels.

The walls of this cavern were covered in a green luminous type of moss and were treacherously slippery from the water that trickled down all around, and made a murmuring, eerie song as background to her gasps of exertion as she climbed. She was halfway to the top when her fingers failed to find the crack she needed when her foot slipped and down she tumbled, her single cry an echo in the black emptiness. But the dilemma that faced her was that she had fallen into a cleft in the floor. This had been made by the constant trickle of water, that had smoothed the sides as if they were the jewel glass that was still sometimes found. She was wedged in the narrow space, the hardened soles of her feet against one wall and her naked back against the other. But they were cold, unrelenting walls and she gradually felt herself slipping. She could sense with her highly developed mind, that was used as a third eye by the People of the Caves, and hear with her extremely finely tuned ears that below her there was a massive evil void. She would fall—perhaps to the middle of the earth; perhaps right through to the other side and out into the Never World of Demons most hideous to comprehend. Even if she survived the fall, no one would hear her cries in this unknown cavern and she would die alone . . . a non person. No one would eat her flesh, then crush her bones and bury them into the all-enveloping earth. They would bleach white and naked like those of the worst criminals hurled into the Hunger Pits to die slowly as they contemplated their sins.

Then her sensitive ears caught a faint rustling sound from up above that was neither bat nor rat nor giant cockroach. The faint form of a pale face peered over the side at her for a moment, then withdrew just as quickly, so she wondered if it had been a dream.

But a second later a long thin object came over the lip of the chasm and edged its way down towards her. At first she thought it was a snake, and she was much afraid, for everyone knew snakes were Devils in disguise and should be avoided at all costs. Then it touched her bare shoulder and she felt the rough caress. She wondered what manner of person would carry the image of a snake with them.

'Wrap it around your body several times and then hold onto the end tightly,' came a soft sibilant whisper.

This she did with some difficulty and much trepidation as she wondered what being was above her. Was it some Demon toying with her before tearing her heart out of her mouth and eating it before her terrified, dying eyes?

'Now hold on tightly and let go of your hold on the wall,' the voice ordered.

She was so scared her whole body trembled but what else could she do than trust the strange disjointed voice? She dropped about six times the length of her own body until the snake ghost clamped itself around her midriff, cutting off her breath abruptly and leaving her swinging in the black air, feeling the cold breath of ghosts below gathering around her feet.

10

Her hands were cut raw by the pull of the snake that seemed to be made from some type of hair. She, who had never known fear before, knew it now.

Then, at last, she was up on the top and dragged sprawling onto the floor, safe and free from the horror that had grabbed at her ankles before. But when she saw her rescuers she wished she was dancing with the Demons in the Never World. A new type of fear overtook her now.

There were three: one not much older than herself. The youngest one, a lad of perhaps fifteen stones, had black hair but his eyes were a bright and fierce green, burning into her soul. The woman had skin whiter than white, if that was possible, so she seemed transparent. Even her hair was white although she was only a few stones older than S'shony, while her eyes were blue with pink whites—the eyes of a Demon indeed. The youth who held the rope was also older and had hair as orange and red as a monster's. Even in this dark world it seemed to glow like a luminous mushroom with a type of evil beauty. He only had one eye, the other being an empty red socket, but the one that gazed at her now flared like that of his younger companion with a green fire amongst the brown.

And they had touched her: were touching her even now! Why, then, did she not burn?

One-eye smiled at her.

'It is lucky for you we were out picking mushrooms. This is one of the best fields for them. We did not know the black ones had found this place yet, but now it seems we shall have to lose another treasure.' He gave a rueful laugh.

'Kill her now. See how the ungrateful being cringes at our touch,' the green-eyed youngster scowled.

'I shall show her a touch,' purred the white-haired, red-eyed Demon and moved up close to a trembling S'shony. A parody of a smile fluttered across the Demon's hard pale face, then she put her arms around S'shony and, ever so gently, kissed her full on the lips.

Never, in her whole short life, had the girl been so terrified. Why did they play games with her? It was better they killed her quickly than let her die a lingering death. But, it seemed, they must have their fun first.

She felt the hot breath of the Demon on her face and waited for her skin to peel off and the pain to begin. She felt the warm wet tongue of the Demon lick her face and she closed her eyes and waited for the long, slow, burning death to begin.

She heard One-eye laugh softly as he gently pulled the woman away. They spoke in the old language—the language only the Sun People remembered—that sounded like the squeaking of rats and bats and the clicking of cockroaches. Then One-eye turned to her again.

'You see, now you are dead,' he smiled. 'We cannot let you go back for you would lead the enemy to us and we three have lived too long to die by a mistake. My baby brother would have you killed but I say we have lost one treasure and found another.' He laughed again. 'Let them think you are a ghost just as we are,' he then murmured, touching her skin. 'For indeed you are beautiful for a black one.' His fingers traced the shape of her nose and mouth. 'Only a ghost could be so glorious.'

Never had she known such gentleness. It was as alien to her as the sun's rays that these Sun People represented. She stayed because she was fascinated by this One-eye's very gentleness and strangeness. His name, she learnt, was Willum. His younger brother was called Radi and he stayed close to her side, watching her with fierce, suspicious eyes. Their mother had been a healer and had loved their father well. It was not just his bravery and beautiful green eyes she had loved but his joy and wisdom too. Together they had looked after the little band of outcasts and together they had died in this cruel world that so despised them. But they had left behind two wonderful sons.

The woman's name was Olbeno. The snake was called rope and was made of human hair. It was the invention of the Sun People and was remarkable for its dexterity. It could be used to scale inaccessible parts of the cave world and to catch the most succulent though cunning rat, even when it was some distance away.

S'shony was to learn the art of knot tying and how to make a noose so she, too, could trap rats and climb the smoothest walls with ease. Most important of all, she learned to love and laugh like her strange companions and let the cold lack of feeling into which she had been born melt away at each chuckle or joke of these people. She questioned her own beliefs as she lived with these outcasts who were not Demons at all but humans, the same as she. How could she believe what her Beacons had been teaching her all her life, now she knew that at least this part of it was untrue?

Willum took her to other secret places deep within the breast of the earth where his people survived. Of course if they fell and broke a leg then they would die a long and lingering death since most Sun People travelled alone. It was quicker and safer that way. But even that death was preferable to living up in the caves and tunnels where every moment was fraught with danger.

Willum seemed unafraid of any danger. He was several stones older than S'shony which, if he hadn't been cursed, would have made him a true bat—possibly a Beacon, for he was fearless and brave as only a Beacon could be. As it was he knew more about the caves than any other person she had known. He also had done his share of killing: the snake rope's unrelenting hold had not only strangled the life from rats, and the short, sharp flint knife he had tied to his side had tasted more than animal blood. His body was covered in the scars of countless fights, all of which by necessity he had won. But he was not a violent man as so many of the People of the Caves were and he also allowed himself time to dream. His eye would soften as he gazed upon her and his hands were gentle on her face and body. When he took her to him he wasn't having her but loving her. And his strange, squeaking language taught her that word—love—so she was never the same again.

Olbeno was known as a doctor amongst her kind and many was the time some Sun person came staggering, crawling or limping into the cave to be soothed or healed by her magic potions. It made S'shony very sad to see the horrendous wounds some of these people carried, because they had been inflicted by her own kin. But Olbeno forgave the murderous black-hair-and-eyed ones because she loved all the world and devoted her entire time to her baby daughter and to the art of healing. The white woman loved S'shony as well in her quiet way, just as she loved Willum. There was no room for jealousy in her make up. In fact there were no negative thoughts about her at all. She certainly taught S'shony a lot about human nature.

At first the Sun People were wary and afraid of this all-too-well-known threat living amongst them. But gradually they came to trust her and share their life with her. S'shony took to wearing a snake around her waist just like every other Sun person and thus she was identified as one of them. It was as though she had fallen through that vast chasm that day long ago and ended up in a land of ghosts. But not the Demons of the Never World or upside-in-the-sun. No! These ghosts were kind and gentle and full of laughter. The People of the Caves used laughter as a type of war-cry but these Sun Children used laughter to wash away the sorrows of life. It was a type of song for them and they sang it every day, bringing together families and close friends in warm companionship. She learnt to smile and laugh too. Then she truly was beautiful.

The longer she stayed with her new-found friends the less she wished to see her own kind again. She felt deeply ashamed—another new emotion for her—at the memory of her killing of the golden-haired, sky-eyed Sun girl and went out of her way to befriend the Sun People of that colour. Sometimes she would see her people crawling about and, once, she saw her uncle, the famous Beacon. Only now she knew him to be a pathetic man who clung to senseless laws and obeyed a ridiculous regime led by a cowardly King. But she had a new life now and wanted nothing to do with the violence of before. She did not join in the killings that sometimes happened when one of her kind wandered into the Sun People's world.

As well as learning she was able to teach the Sun People and she dedicated herself to this task.

Over the three thousand years they had lived in this cramped, dark world, the People of the Caves had developed a complex telepathic control. So advanced it was that they could now read minds and pass on silent messages to one another via thought power. At the same time, as a protection, they could set up shields against prying minds and thus keep their own thoughts to themselves. Also, they had developed a radar-like sensitivity which enabled them to detect and pin-point movement some distance away. A mind message sent towards such movement which failed to bring a response alerted them at once that aliens were in the vicinity. It was the one skill that made the People of the Caves different and more powerful than anyone else in this land and they kept its secret jealously. But the Sun Children, being outcast, had not developed this intricate method of communication.

Their secret was old paths and tunnels through the People of the Caves' world. These were as old as the beginning itself and had been forgotten when new tunnels were forged along with a new lifestyle. Over the centuries they lay unused until they had faded from everyone's memory—everyone except the Sun People, who used them as a refuge and haven. They were cleverly hidden with special doorways and they honeycombed the entire Kingdom, it was said. The People of the Caves could mind read movement in these tunnels but could not find and destroy the Sun People because often they were just above or below the existing tunnel—so it seemed that they were using the same tunnels as the black ones.

Once, Willum had taken S'shony a long long way. They had travelled many miles when they came onto a ledge high above the black smooth walls of a huge canyon. Far below, figures only as big as giant rats could be seen to be men and women.

'This is the cave of the King of Bats,' Willum whispered and she had peeped over the ridge, incredulous, trying to see the famed and feared figure. But he was too far away.

It seemed unbelievable that the Sun Children could view their hated enemy right within his own stronghold. For Willum to show her this meant he trusted her completely. She laid a hand in his beautiful red hair and smiled at him.

On a special day Willum took her to his special place. He would not tell her where they were going as they clambered over rocks and wended their way down valleys in the caves' floors. This part of the Kingdom was riddled with caves, some as huge as the King of Bats' own domain and others scarcely large enough to hide a rat. There was little need to make tunnels. Rats and cockroaches were everywhere, while flocks of every conceivable type of bat whirled and twirled overhead. Luminous algae and all kinds of fungi grew here in abundance because it was a place more fertile than any other in the caves. Some of the fungi were as big as small trees and glowed with a blue light.

The girl was bewitched by all this beauty. But this was not what Willum wished to show her. He took her hand in his and squeezed it softly while he gave her a quiet smile.

'Behold, the jewels of Nimbelyung for the jewel of my eye,' he whispered.

Everyone had heard of the fabulous treasures belonging to the mystic wizard of the rocks, Nimbelyung, who was said to have turned his entire

14

Kingdom into jewel statues wondrous to see. Even his beloved wife, sons and daughters had been turned into jewels so they would be with him for always—and not follow the rest of the world up into the sun to die.

Now Willum led her, trembling and awe-struck, through the black entrance guarded by two massive, twisted, slimy, black rocks that must have once been monsters most hideous to behold. And they stood in his magic Kingdom.

It was cold here. The air seemed permeated by the breath of the dead and the walls were damp from unseen water. Huge clumps of moss and luminous algae, shining with phosphorescent light, clung to the walls, or hung down like curtains or the web of some strange spider. It was their light that lit up the incredible world before her. Some of the jewels hung like bats from the ceiling, twisting down to meet others that writhed upwards to meet them. Occasionally they had already done so and huge columns were dotted about the cave. The jewels were of every shape and size, including some that resembled human forms right down to facial features. That was quite eerie to study. But others were sharp and thin, fat and squat, some small, others huge, and most in colours she had never seen before. They shone with inner lights of oranges, reds, pinks, purples, greens, blues that were indescribable, while the bulk of them were covered with an electric blue or brilliant white over-glow. These colours were intermingled with the throbbing glow of the plant life to form a dazzling kaleidoscope of colours that any black-hair-and-eyed one would have been horrified to observe.

Her legs became so weak at the sheer splendour of it all that she had to sit down. Here her black hair and black eyes—once deemed a sign of great beauty—became dull and flat. Her pale fingers reached out and tentatively touched a jewel. It was as smooth as glass yet was more alive than her tapering fingers. The side was wet and cool and the green inner lights danced for her within the prism with a warmth that was matched only by the green light in Willum's eye. She sighed, awe-struck. It was not every day one could touch a God.

'So, it was true. The wizard exists. Where is Nimbelyung?' she asked, glancing around.

'He is here. He is everywhere,' Willum laughed.

'How long have you known of this place?'

'It has been here forever.'

Forever was when the Gods walked upon the earth and banished the people to the homes of their only allies, the bats. It was when the sun fell from the sky and all of the Gods' creations were destroyed. Forever was like the Never World, a scary and unwanted place.

She shivered and he put an arm around her.

'It is truly a magical place, this Kingdom of Nimbelyung. It is the heart of the earth. It is the place for me to tell you I wish you to be my queen and live with me forever.'

There! He used that word again. She looked at him and around him as he smiled at her in the eerie glow. Was it some sign? And was it a good sign? Her dark eyes clouded over in worry but he laughed out loud so the laughter rolled amongst the towering jewelled people of Nimbelyung and joined with the constant drip-drip-drip of water that was the song from the soul of the cave and the only sound usually heard here.

Her worries evaporated and it was in this magical place she told Willum the secret she had kept for him. She, too, had a jewel to give him—their child now nestled in her womb.

So it was in great joy they walked hand in hand back to the caves they knew so well. Their plan was to gather up the Sun People and move to the fertile plain within the caves. With her skills at setting up mind shields they would never be found. They would start their own small Kingdom in this far away place and bring up their children in a world of peace.

As they arrived at the entrance to their home S'shony's sharp hearing and mental wave lengths sensed something wrong. There was too much stillness for this cave of activity. She went to rest a warning hand on Willum's shoulder when, from out of the dark recess, a white figure ran. In the gloom Olbeno seemed to float above the ground, her thin waving hands and flowing hair stark against the black of the cavern. She called out in the old language but S'shony could not understand.

Willum did, however. He was brutally torn from his dreaming and, quick as a cornered rat, he spun around. 'It's a trap! We are surrounded!'

Three things happened in rapid succession. Too quick for S'shony, who was still in a glow at all the things she had seen that day. Besides, she was not used to violence anymore.

Firstly, there was a piercing shriek like a rat in pain and Radi, with several others, leapt down to stand beside their leader. Secondly, Olbeno gave a croaking cry and sank to the ground. Lastly, Willum unwrapped his precious rope from around his waist and pressed it into S'shony's hands.

'Quick! You must go now! If you are caught with us, vile things will happen to you. You would not die fast and clean. Use this rope to help escape, along with your own. You know the way back to your people?'

She began to protest just as a javelin threw one of the Sun People backwards, gasping in death. Further on there were screams and cries as the women and children were found cowering in their hiding places. It had taken a long time but, at last, her people had found the retreat of the Sun People and they did not come with love in their hearts.

'Go,' yelled Radi, his green eyes alive with hate. 'Go before I kill you myself.'

She knew he had children back in the caves. She wondered what had become of the daughter of Olbeno. She also realised it was people of her own family that were tumbling towards them, like an avalanche to crush out the lives of the friends she knew and loved. For an instant she stood there, then Willum pushed her gently towards a murky hole that was one of their own tunnels.

'Go, lovely one. Remember the life of our unborn child,' he said urgently.

This was what decided her. Their child could not be harmed. S'shony set off even as the first of the fleeing women and children burst from the cave, followed by her leaping, shrieking cousins in the grip of a blood-crazed frenzy of violence.

She twisted and turned along devious passageways she knew better than anyone. But she did not go far. She hurled Willum's snake up onto a jagged rock and climbed to safety. She huddled into a dark corner and waited. She heard cries of fear and rage and death drifting up the tunnel and, once, the sound of footsteps as someone rushed away. She could sense the smell of fear emanating in sonic rays from the body as it flew past. But no one followed.

At last it was all over. She could hear the emptiness that was the lack of life in the tunnels and caves. It was like the emptiness of the cavern below her the first time she had met these strange people. But there really were Demons now—waiting. As ghosts, the Sun People would walk this land, unburied and unrevered, killed by Demons who called themselves humans. They would become hideous in their agony.

Gone. Gone. All gone. She walked amongst the strewn bodies of her comrades, flung where death had abandoned their bodies while stealing their souls. Men, women and children. There lay Olbeno, her body now red with her blood, and there were the twin girls of Radi with their mother, who had died curled up trying to protect them. There was one who had made her laugh at his many jokes and another who had, of all the camp, been the best and most cunning hunter of rats. There lay a woman who had, most patiently, taught her the old language of the Sun People.

There were others not here and these were the ones she felt sorry for. They would be dragged upwards into her cruel world to be played with and tortured until gradually they would become food for the King and his Beacons.

There lay Willum.

Her vicious cousins had not killed him straight away but had torn out his one eye with a javelin and then prodded and poked him as he stumbled about blindly. But he had died with his knife in his hand and there was blood upon the broken blade.

She cradled his battered head in her lap and smoothed back the matted hair made redder by his precious blood. His sightless sockets stared back at her and his smashed mouth hung open in a parody of the smile he had always kept for her. She cradled his head in her lap and wept as she had never wept before.

That had been three spans ago. In the depths of S'shony's underworld, there was no night or day. The highly developed senses of the People of the Caves however had induced what they called spans which, had they known of such things, would have been twenty-four hours. Seven spans made a time and fifty-one times made a stone. As with their incredible hearing that could 'hear' emotions and their amazing mind powers, this sense of spanning was absolutely accurate.

She had lived amongst the Sun Children for a little longer than a stone. She knew this because she had watched her uncle the Beacon drop her final white stone in her urn. In all that time she had seen only kindness and love from these hitherto despised Race. She had taught them the lost gift of sonar shields and they had taught her many things, like love and caring and the use of their only true weapon—the ropes made from the hair of slain enemies.

Now she covered her nudity with her long dark hair and her seething thoughts with a shield. She would go Upside tonight and kill a stranger. She would be no better off than others of her Race who had killed the gentle Sun Children. The Sun Children who killed fellow human beings only to survive—not for the fun of it. Possibly those going with her on her sonaflite were some who had participated in the massacre of her companions. Maybe one who had tormented Willum; perhaps even killed him.

Beside her, in coils like her hair, she carried the snakes of Willum and her own. When questioned by the suspicious Beacons she had answered she had defeated two Sun Children in a fierce, gruesome fight and decided to keep them as trophies. Not happy at the close proximity of the dreaded Snake Gods, the Beacons had at least understood and relished the violence of the story and allowed her the use of them. The lie and her sense of betrayal however only brought more pain.

But now she would get her wings and, with her wings, womanhood, and a certain amount of respect. From the knowledge she had learnt from Olbeno she could become a healer or even a rare female warrior. All the secrets of the Sun Children were hers to use and she would use them to destroy the hated King who had ordered the brutal deaths of her lover and friends. Then she would have her alien baby in peace. Just before the baby was born she would disappear and live in the Kingdom of Nimbelyung and survive as best she could in a world she now hated. She would bring up her child to hate those who had killed his father and so she would end her days, a loner among her own people.

She heard the hollow booming of the stone drum summoning those whose sonaflite it was to go to their appointed places.

They gathered at the tunnel to the night, which was known as a chimney. These chimneys dotted the Kingdom and were blocked off with special stones upon which was engraved a coiled snake, to remind everyone of danger, two bats that represented the people and a human skull amidst the coils. The stones were guarded all the time by a priest, for these chimneys were the only channel between the two worlds—Upside and Cave—and religious powers were needed constantly to keep the dreaded moon or sunlight from entering their Kingdom. Of course, after a cave person received their wings they could tunnel up anywhere on the night of the dead moon and kill however many and whatever they pleased. But on this sacred night their bodies had to be cleansed and protected from the outside by the chimney so it was up this ascent they would go.

There were two other females and four males waiting by the sacred rocks. They gathered together while the Priest muttered incantations and sprinkled them with coal dust, that precious gem that only the Priests, the King and certain Beacons were allowed to use. This dust would make them strong and invisible. The youngsters eyed with reverence the two Beacons who would lead them on this night's raid.

S'shony knew one of them because he had been the first man to have her several stones ago. In the cave people's height he was a giant, being some two arms high. (Or, in the old measurement, about five and a half feet tall.) The muscles on his arms bulged like boulders and he had many scars on his hairless white chest and muscle-ridged back. He wore a rat-skin belt in which his famous ironstone sword was held. The sword—called 'Whispering Death'—had slain many a creature in its day for he was an old warrior in the cave people's estimate, being just over forty stones, and he was known as 'The Secret-maker' because every killing he performed was a secret to whoever was about to die.

The other Beacon was no less famous although he was much younger. Unlike many of the People of the Caves whose body hair was rubbed off by constant friction as they crawled through the narrow tunnels of their homes, his body was covered in a thick curly coat of black hair, because as a true warrior he spent most of his time above ground hunting. It was rumoured he even went Upside when the moon was but a sliver of light in the sky—but a light all the same. His eyes certainly held a madness that only the light of the moon could have given him. His warrior Beacon's name was 'The Creeper' and the weapon he held in his hairy white hands was a huge, glass-jewel-bedecked club known as 'The Tearer'.

So it was that these nine set forth on a ritual that had occurred many times a year for centuries. Little did anyone know that on this dark and silent night a new moon would rise that would herald the beginning of a new enlightened era.

CHAPTER TWO

The dying light of the fire, that was a gift to the Ilkari from the Keepers of the Trees, threw shadows around the sleeping forms of Ilki, Grey Fur and Rabit-the-White. It kept them warm from the cold night air that crept in from the dead plains. Ilgar himself lay sleepless as he brooded over the omens he had read in the sky. What did they mean? The moon had spoken to him and now he must interpret the messages, yet he could not understand what had been spoken. Was that an omen in itself? He listened to Grey Fur's murmured endearments to Ensee, the girl he adored, as he dreamed of her . . . and Rabit-the-White's whimperings as he lived a nightmare in his sleep. Perhaps he was dreaming the meaning of the omens for was he not a sacred person too? Two signs of love—a falling star kissing the Mother Star was very good indeed and he wondered who in the clan would be blessed by this. The ill-fated red star dying in the light of the moon was good as well and probably meant the birth of a rare child to the clan. But a falling star could mean misfortune too, and the red star always meant cunning and deviousness and a trickster. The shadow of the dog was not good. Death by disease—and the High Ones knew there was enough of that on this poisoned earth. Most people died in their early forties in these days of the New Time. It was said in the Old Time that people had lived into their eighties or nineties—even into their hundreds if that could be believed! That was two lifetimes. Ilgar's own ancestor's mother, Ayelee, had lived to be sixty-seven and the stories of her wisdom were told today—but that sort of age was rare indeed.

Most people succumbed to the kiss of Melanoma, the daughter of Sister Sun, whose kisses and caresses left a body covered in ugly sores to die a painful, slow death, cooked alive by her hot love. Others breathed in the poisoned air the Gods had left behind as a legacy and slowly died as well, their insides rotting and their hair falling out as they sank towards death. But it was what people were used to in this dry, hard land, as was dying a thousand ways from wild creatures, too numerous to name, that roamed this world as Devils left behind by the High Ones, so no one would ever forget the stupidity and greed of their distant ancestors who had caused the wrath to fall upon them. Cowardice was a form of death, too, when someone's courage waned like the light of the moon at Sister Sun's rising.

Over against the edge of the firelight, Yellow Eyes glared out into the night and gnawed on a kangaroo bone left over from the feast. He rubbed his tawny hair with one hand while his spear lay at his side.

All was quiet.

But only for this last moment.

Suddenly, there was a shrieking, chilling to hear, and a series of laughing screams that froze the blood. From out of the darkness, like pieces of darkness they came. Nine forms: seven naked and two with human skins flapping around their shoulders, all covered with soot to hide their ghostly whiteness. Shrieking and screeching with maniacal laughter they came, intent on murder as they leapt into the faint glow of the almost dead fire. And now, in Ilgar's terrified mind, the omen of the leaping dog shadow became abundantly clear. Death stared him and his cousin-kin right in the face.

Yellow Eyes leapt to meet one figure and, jabbing the small body with his spear, hurled it back into the gloom from whence it had come. He was the only one to have seen these monsters before and so the shock wore off more quickly for him. Rabit-the-White awoke from one nightmare into another and he was still shocked as he struggled to his feet. He wore the shocked expression into death as a huge club smashed his rib bones into his heart. The hairy one who had killed the young blond mystic spun around to attack Grey Fur but the wolf killer was too clever for him and ducked out of the way slashing him across the arm with his knife.

Yellow Eyes killed another with the ease of a hero and yelled for the others to gather around him as it was their only hope of survival. Ilgar saw his young cousin close with another of the Nightstalkers, the peaceful glow of the fire reflecting the fear in the youngster's eyes. Ilki was about to thrust forwards into the white heaving belly in front of him when he stopped and confusion flooded his vision.

'It—she is a woman—' he began hesitantly.

To the Ilkari, women were special. Not only were they the Mothers of Sister Earth and the collectors of water but they carried the gift of fertility in their body. There was no such crime as rape amongst the Ilkari. To murder any female would be unthinkable.

'Kill her! Kill her! She is but a monster!' Yellow Eyes cried.

Then the woman leapt forward to cut off Ilki's head and send his body, blood spurting in a horrible fountain, into the coals, scattering them and so blacking out the terrible tableau. Although not before Ilgar saw the ducking, weaving Grey Fur, using all the savagery and cunning of his old foe from his story, fell the killer of his cousin-brother and one other.

Ilgar twisted at a hissing sound behind his back and faced a silent attacker, the coal-streaked face etched in white. He came out of his fright and mortification and crouched to defend himself, although he was not a warrior of any description. He would avenge his beloved cousin's death. It was his fault the boy had come out here in the first place. To this desolate plain that sprouted flowers of death.

He had never killed a human being before. Every time he had killed a beast to eat of its flesh he had blessed the animal and asked its forgiveness. He was a Moon-talker, a mystic. Not a warrior like Yellow Eyes who, even now, gave a cry of rage as The Whispering Death slid between his ribs and found his heart, where it stuck as he staggered backwards. But in the warrior's dying breath he pulled the sword from his body and with cut and bleeding hands he made sure the blade found The Secret-maker's throat.

Ilgar saw this and saw his cousin-brother sink to his knees. He could sense all was lost now. The omens had been wrong. There was no love for any of them: for wild Yellow Eyes, huge in his living, or gentle Rabit-the-White, and for Ilki, innocent in his tender years, with quiet thoughts of his darling Magpie, there was only the cold embrace of cruel death.

His brown eyes blazed with an anger he had never felt before and from his lips there issued forth an alien cry—a roar of hate and rage for the dancing ethereal form in front of him, whose people had caused his kin's untimely deaths.

He leapt forwards and the knife in his hand was a blur. He felt a sharp bite of pain as his opponent's knife slashed into his shoulder and he wondered for a brief second if it was true that all their weapons were poisoned. But he didn't care anymore about dying. If he must die, he would make sure he took his enemy with him into the lands of no return.

His knife dug deep and almost jarred from his hand. Warm wet blood ran onto his arm and the light of life blurred from his victim's bleak black eyes.

Why, they are not monsters but humans, the same as us, he thought, and can die just as easily.

He spun around again, the bloody knife dripping in his hand. He saw from the corner of his eye a form coming towards him from the other side of the fire: a female, he could tell by her bouncing breasts and the shape of her hips. He would not be tricked like poor Ilki. He would kill this female as well. He would kill all of them and forsake forever the oath of the moon. Yes, he and Grey Fur would kill them all so none could eat of his clansmen's proud flesh nor skin their bodies nor tear out their hearts. This much he owed them for leading them into death.

Then he watched in horror as, while Grey Fur disposed of one of the two Nightstalkers, the other brought his huge club crashing down upon his unruly, brown, curled head.

'Oooh, nooo!' he groaned and knew he was lost now. He wondered what death would be like. He turned to face the charging club man and the female. *They* would know how he died, at least. This would be the story of Ilgar the dreamer, the Moon-talker who was told of his last night by his father the moon, but had not understood it. Not a very impressive story, but there would be no one to tell it, anyway. He would just disappear as so many of his people did and possibly only his mother and sisters would mourn him.

Then his eyes widened in surprise for a rope had appeared in the Nightstalker female's hands but it was not destined for him. No! It was around the club man's neck that the rope went and she jerked back on it so it was *his* turn to be surprised as he somersaulted over, almost losing his club.

For a second 'The Creeper' was confused, then the squat hairy man leaped up and ran at the female, thus loosening the noose around his neck. He swung his club and she ducked out of the way, lunging with her sword, but he twisted away, trying to get the noose off with one hand while he swung his club in the other.

Ilgar could not understand why these two were fighting each other. Perhaps the female wanted to kill him herself. He could not follow their reasoning but it had been the female who had attempted to save him from the club man's murderous charge and now she was under attack herself. The man had killed Rabit-the-White and Grey Fur. Ilgar would help the female dispose of him and then decide afterwards what to do. After all, he had nothing to lose except his life.

He ran forwards to slash the monster's hairy back but he was heard and the Nightstalker rolled away so he slashed only empty air. However, every time he faced Ilgar the female would pull on the snake around his neck, and every time he faced her he would be harried by the youth. The fight was not short and all three sustained wounds but at last even this mighty Beacon dropped to his knees, exhausted, his great club dragging in the dirt beside him. Then he turned his eyes onto the female and watched her while, with cool deliberation, she strangled the life from him. He watched in confusion as all the laws and rules he had ever known were being broken.

He, the mighty Creeper, was being killed by a mere female; a girl out on her sonaflite what is more. And he could not think of a single reason why she should kill him. He kept his black eyes upon her, as steady as a snake's. He would come back from the realms of the Never World and haunt this female. This was the last thought in his mind before everything burst white and a horrible, brilliant, evil red behind his eyes and he slid to the earth he had hated so.

S'shony gathered up her precious rope, then stood staring at Ilgar while he returned the stare warily. A great silence fell across the desert. Stars looked down, the Mother Star brightest of all. At last she pointed a finger at his long flowing hair and in a croaking, hoarse version of the language he spoke she hissed, 'Willum.'

He did not understand of course. He was not an all-knowing God—merely a Moon-talker from the wild, outcast Tribe Ilkari of the clan of Violet Lynx Foot. He could not see that the colour of his hair—his very build—had reminded her of someone and so saved his life. Thus had the prophecy of the Mother Star proved true for it was love's gentle emotion that had saved him.

But to him she was still a threat. He gripped his knife tighter as she moved forward and stepped back, keeping a close eye on the rope she held in her hand. He had seen how useful she was on that implement. Yet she seemed to lose interest in him in a moment.

She moved over to the fireside and gently picked up Ilki's severed head. She brushed the sand from his dead eyes and slack mouth then placed it close to the ruined body.

Ilgar had been about to leap at the naked back of the female for no one—and especially a hated Nightstalker—would touch his cousin-mine, except himself. But then he saw by her act these creatures must have the same beliefs the Ilkari had. That no spirit could travel if one part of the body was separated from another; that the body must be as near to each dismembered part as possible. He noticed the gentleness of her touch as she placed Ilki's head down beside his frail, limp body and he lost a little more of his wariness.

She rose then and black eyes scrutinised him carefully before she came towards him slowly. He tensed and raised his knife. It could still be a trick, he thought. S'shony, reading his thoughts, stopped and let her rope and knife drop to the ground.

She came towards him again and, even though his fear and caution were fast waning, he kept himself in a state of readiness. He had never seen one of these creatures before but they were the enemy of his people since the New Time began, probably even in the Old Time for all he knew. He had heard from some who had faced them and survived that their arms were as strong as any two men's and she could as easily strangle him as stab him.

It was only when her cool white fingers touched his cheek and ran through his hair in pleasurable motions that he completely relaxed. Here was a sign, not of hate or anger but, curiously, of affection. He could not know why, but only that it was so. The brief war was over.

He looked around at the dead bodies of his friends and family. He had grown up with these four. The echoes of their laughter reverberated in his mind. Many were the jokes they had played together. He turned away from the female (whom he now realised was little more than a girl). After all, it had been her Race that had brought about this destruction. Yet somehow he sensed she had nothing to do with any of the Ilkari's deaths.

He turned to her again and saw the look of concern for his sadness in her face. Then he noticed also the faint blue tinge in the sky. Soon it would be daylight and the birds would come. He must bury his kin before they devoured them, just as the Nightstalkers would have done.

But the girl touched his arm. When he looked down at her she pointed towards the faint glow and then covered her eyes, shrinking towards the ground. She looked at him to see if he had understood. He had, for he also knew of the belief that Sister Sun and her son Fire were the only two things that could surely kill these creatures.

He nodded and then made up his mind. He would take this girl back to the mountain he and his clansmen had left the night before. If they travelled quickly they would arrive in time and he would put her into the dark safety of the cave on top of the mountain that was his birthplace, while he returned to bury the dead. He would do this because he wished to know this strange girl better. She had saved his life and it could be that the omens of love spoke true. He could scarcely believe that not only were the omens for him but that they could involve a female alien to his culture; yet Father Moon could see all and knew all that was to happen from his lofty throne.

The book of the sky was strange reading sometimes.

For a while she walked beside him and they made a strange pair crossing the empty red plain: she shorter than him by a good three hand spans, naked except for her rope and her long, swinging braids of black hair. But the light was getting stronger now with a harshness to its touch and Ilgar knew they would never make it this way. So he scooped the small girl up in his arms, for she was light to carry, and he set off at a distance-consuming lope.

She smelt of the cold underground places he had never dared even to dream of and her body was cool against his skin. She snuggled closer to his hot, pounding chest and breathed in the rancid odours of his old sweat-stained cloak. For he was dressed in the clothes of the Ilkari which consisted of various wild-animal skins woven into jacket and breeches. At first she thought the cloak was a type of wing and she wondered if these people lived a similar life to her own, killing to obtain their wings.

She came out of her reverie to find they had reached a darker patch upon the earth. It was the shadow of the mountain stretching out purple fingers to cover her from the sun's brightening glare. All the sky was covered in red blood that was a fearsome sight for her. This was the first shadow she had ever seen and she marvelled at its wonder. This mountain, she knew, must be a powerful place. She remembered the towering, jewelled ghosts of Nimbelyung's Kingdom. Here was another towering ghost, bigger even than them and twice as eerie in its silence. She shivered a little as she read his mind and realised where they were going. She would be even closer to the dreaded sky, that vast unknown, as vast as the Never World that lurked below their feet. This sky was filled with

Demons just as that dark world was. They might lean down and pluck her from the earth, to hold her wriggling and vulnerable above gaping mouths.

Perhaps this crimson-haired stranger, who looked so much like Willum, had not read the signs of friendship Willum had taught her and which she had tried to show him. Perhaps, after all, it was his intention to leave her as a sacrifice to the ones he worshipped. Even when he kept her in the shadow of the mountain, while all around her was getting lighter, and he covered her head and as much of her body as he could, there was still that nagging doubt.

Only when they finally arrived at the top of the mountain and the cave that waited there, did she feel completely safe. He *had* read the signs and was prepared to be her friend.

Suddenly she heard the most glorious sound she had ever been lucky enough to hear: singing, soft and sweet. She cocked her head and peered about her, trying to find the source of the sound. Then she had it. In some huge fungi that grew on the mountain a flurry of wings sounded and a flock of tiny, brilliantly coloured bats flew off and headed for the deep purple that had washed away the blood from the sky.

Her face showed such amazement at this sight that the youth beside her laughed out loud. He pointed at the disappearing bats.

'Birds,' he said. 'Kittiupcowra.'

Although she could follow some of his language and thoughts—because he spoke in the old language of the Sun People—there were gaps her mind power could not fathom and this was one of them.

'Singing bats that eat the light and are in joy at the sun,' she said in awe, in her own language, so of course he could not understand. But he sensed her happiness and smiled down at her.

He took off his tattered and filthy cloak, sewn roughly together from the skins of three kangaroos, and used it to cover up the entrance of the cave. He gathered together some bushes and large rocks in the hope that their shadows and shapes would dilute the sunlight shining through. He touched her long black braids and pale white face with the tenderness she had shown him and gave a weary smile. Was the sacrifice of four of his clansmen—one his own young cousin—worth the saving of this woman's soul? What would the rest of the clan think? Yet he could not kill one who had saved his life.

But he must bury his clansmen before the birds got to them or, more pressingly, before their young bodies were embraced by Sister Sun for much longer. Birth and death were two sacred things to the Ilkari—the rituals of death were most often followed these days, since a birth was infrequent. There were several rules that had to be strictly adhered to if the dead person was to have everlasting peace. There were different rules for man or woman and it was up to Ilgar to make sure his cousin and cousin-brothers were protected.

For a dead man had no protection over his soul and, being kissed by Sister Sun, could be lured away from the love of Sister Earth to remain a sad and drifting shade, floating in the sky like a star and belonging to neither sun nor earth. Thus, whenever an Ilkari died it was preferable to cremate them. Fire was the sometimes destructive, sometimes useful son of Sister Sun. He was one of the few gifts given to man by her. And then there was wood from the trees that grew from Sister Earth's fertile heart, nurtured by her blood and tears. In this way, a man's body could be joined by the love of both sisters and, then, the ashes would be buried in the clan's burial ground to be looked after by the clan's spirits.

Sometimes, however, circumstances called for different rituals. This, unfortunately, was one of them. So, tired as he was, he set off back to the place of destruction. He, the only survivor, could not leave his clansmen alone like this and he knew what to do. Every Ilkari did, since death was an old friend of them all.

When he arrived the sun was creeping over the flat red horizon and the land was still an orangy-red hue while the sky was now a gentle pink.

The wind echoed his mournful thoughts as he stood looking at the carnage around him.

No time to waste. Already the sun rose higher, eager to kiss these four young men and swirl them away from Sister Earth's loving kindness. Baba wasn't here to say the sacred prayers so all Ilgar could do was to sing a solitary death chant, each verse praising one of the dead, while he sprinkled sand on each body and called upon the spirits of the clan to look after them while he threw the rest of the soil into the sky. Now he had secured their bodies for a while from Sister Sun's prying eyes.

He began digging a communal grave. Usually, their bodies would be devoured by Fire, the son of Sister Sun, and their ashes placed in the spot where the ashes of all their dead were lain. This especially applied to his cousin Ilki, whose hair Flowed Free and to whom no story had been told by Baba. So his Traveller's braid could not rest in the House of Baba. It took him most of the morning and a lonely sight he made out on the empty plain.

That he was not alone finally became apparent when he crawled out of the pit he had dug. Not forty steps away five Keepers of the Trees stood or squatted as still as trees.

There was an old old man, so old he even had snow-white hair and beard. Then there was a woman, also old for these times. He thought she could be the mother of the other three, two youths and a girl. They all had the same proud face and flashing eyes.

They were strangers in this part of the land. Their skin was a lighter hue than others who lived around here and their hair was more curly. There was a fierce light in their eyes and Ilgar sensed they came from parts seldom crossed by white men.

He must be careful then. The spears the men held were sharp and would bring down not only a kangaroo. The females' digging sticks were dangerous weapons as well. After a long silent moment Ilgar called out a greeting in the Keepers' language, although they had so many dialects he was not certain that he would be understood.

But one of the younger men answered back and the two brothers came forward, studying the dead bodies with eyes full of understanding. The old man, however, called out to them sharply and would not budge from his rigid stance and the two females crowded behind him.

When Ilgar saw the two youths close up he got another surprise—they were twins! Not only was this family of Keepers blessed with old age and the wisdom which that offered but were doubly blessed with this lucky sign. They were perhaps a little younger than him and all three touched each other in greeting and smiled. The only noticeable difference between the twins was their hairstyles: one being mop-headed while the other wore his hair in dreadlocks. The one with dreadlocks had a scar across his forehead, marring his handsome looks. Both had faint moustaches and straggly goatee beards. Like most of their Race they were a predominantly hairless people, except upon their heads where hair grew vigorously and wildly.

'Ngoonies noycha ngoorndiny,' the scarred one said, pointing to Ilgar's clansmen.

'Djanak!' the other spat on the body of The Secret-maker, which was already becoming black and shrivelled in the sun.

Through sign language Ilgar related the story, leaving out the part played by the Nightstalker girl. He said he himself had strangled the club man with his bare hands. He thought it better to keep her a secret from everyone, especially these people who didn't trust anything the white people did. He would wait until he saw Baba and find out what to do.

The twins decided to help Ilgar bury his dead. They were called Mungart and Weerluk, being the names, in their language, for Jam Tree and Salmon Gum. Their sister was called Dongkarak, the wattlebird, and their mother was Koobeeaku, the wise owl. Their grandfather was of the Water Totem and his name was Kwila, the shark. Ilgar in fact did not know what these creatures were nor had he seen the trees after which the brothers were named, but he was polite enough to pretend.

An important ceremony was taking place that required the presence of Keepers from everywhere to bring forth great magic. Only every five years did this event occur and it was a special time for the Keepers of this land. Especially for any young man lucky enough to be going through his initiation as it would enhance his powers.

That they told Ilgar this information indicated a trust in him. Perhaps they too, like the Old Ones of the night before, had seen something about him that told them he had been touched by one of their people and the ancient blood flowed through his veins. Once touched by that blood, the oldest blood in the world, there was no escape from recognition.

While Ilgar gathered the dead Ilkari and gently laid them in the grave, the Keepers gathered a collection of rocks and built a circle around it. Upon each rock they splashed a mark of red ochre to show that the dead lay here but they had been avenged, so the spirits could rest in peace. In the Ilkari law the rocks built a fence that kept the spirits within its confines and prevented them from wandering, lost and alone, upon the red plains so far from home.

From each he took one of their belongings. From Rabit-the-White his flute, from which gentle fingers had often woven beautiful songs. From Yellow Eyes his necklace of lion's teeth, in the hope that he, Ilgar, would carry the warrior's bravery with him until he died. From Grey Fur his wolf's-tooth ear-rings to give him the hearing of a wolf and also a wolf's cunning. From Ilki he cut a lock of the crimson hair that had never known the soft touch of his mother's fingers as they plaited his Traveller's braid while his story was being told. He would make a bracelet from the hair and this would be the most precious gift of all. His cousin would have no story now and his braid would never rest with others of his clan in the house of Baba, but whatever story became Ilgar's, then his cousin, in the form of this bangle, would be a part of the story as well. It was all he could do.

He cut the Traveller's braids from the other three and put them in his gathering bag. Their travelling days were over now and their hair must go to Baba so he could keep their stories in the clan.

After this the girl, Dongkarak, came over, shy and aloof, with a haunch of kangaroo meat. She gave some to her brothers then handed the rest to Ilgar while she appraised him with interested dark eyes. She had never seen a white person before and she was curious about this one. Her mop-haired brother said something too fast and low for Ilgar to follow and all three laughed. He burnt red with embarrassment and ducked his head, which only caused her to laugh more, then she walked back to the old people, wriggling her shapely buttocks for the pleasure of the pale man.

There was nothing else left to do now except leave this place of sadness—and, yet, a place where he had made two new friends. Such was the nature of this land where despair and joy rode close companions, Ilgar thought, as he watched the small proud family stalk away, the dust rising from their feet. And what of the Nightstalker girl? What could be the meaning of their intertwining destinies?

He wondered if she was now as dead as her Tribes-people were—withered black and red as an old, discarded leaf upon the ground. It was true that Sister Sun was no friend of these Nightstalkers. She was no friend to any of Sister Earth's children really. But she seemed to favour the night people least of all. Was that because even though the moon was dark when they came out he was still there, unblessed though he was by Sister Sun's light? Were perhaps these people moon worshippers and that is why Sister Sun hated them so? *There* was a mighty question to be answered, thought Ilgar the Moon-talker.

He leant down and picked up the weapons of the two fallen Beacons: 'The Whispering Death' that had killed Yellow Eyes and 'The Tearer' that had killed Rabit-the-White and Grey Fur and—almost—himself. Although not a lover of weapons he would keep these two that had taken the lives of his cousin-brothers.

So it was ensured that these gruesome weapons would live on in the hands of another who was dedicated to a life of peaceful meditation. And it was surely true that the pain and blood of those murdered etched upon their surface, was tainting the Moon-talker's mind for already he was having thoughts of revenge and war.

He went towards the mountain with never a backward glance at his companions' last resting place. In this time of short life and hardships the deaths of four young men of the clan would be a grievous burden to bear. Now that he was alone, he shed a silent tear for his cousin and friends. Water was sacred and no more so than the water that came from one's own body. Crying was only for special occasions and could not last long. He thought of the sorrow he must bring the womenfolk: Yellow Eyes' Kareen, with her bold grey eyes and wild tawny hair, the same as her lover's, whose bravery was matched by her lover's and whose outspoken views were second to none in the clan; Grey Fur's sister and Ilki's girlfriend, Magpie, whose only greater love above that of her dogs was for her brother and perhaps for the boy she thought she would marry; Grey Fur's beloved blonde-haired Ensee. Rabit-the-White's mother would cry for her only son, who would never become the great prophet the white rabbit had hinted at in his story. What his mother's sister would do when she learnt the fate of her youngest and most favourite child, Ilgar did not even want to think about.

He arrived at the top of the mountain just as Sister Sun once more kissed her sister's dusty lips with her hot red ones and then proceeded to die from shame in the time-old ritual the Ilkari knew best. That is how the story went—when love ceased to be and the High Ones walked upon the earth and Father Moon wept bitter tears for a long long time. Tears so bitter they burnt the flesh and killed the vegetation and brought misery to Sister Earth for they were the tears of death. When Sister Sun left her husband's—Father Moon's—side and took her sister in a sinful embrace so all the world turned hot and white; and everything that once had been melted into nothing.

Every Ilkari knew that and, if they forgot, Baba was there every morning when the sun pushed herself out of her sister's womb, covered in the blood of the sister that now had become her mother in the everlasting cycle of shame. From sister to mother and out of mother a sister is born. It is why sun and earth revolved around each other and why there could be neither one without the other. Baba was there to sing out the song of retribution every morning but also forgiveness for the earth's other children—the innocent ones made to suffer for a bygone folly.

When Ilgar got there he cried out softly and was surprised to find himself hoping to hear a reply. He was even more amazed to feel a warm elation rise in his heart when a soft answer did issue forth from the cave.

S'shony had spent a lonely day in the small cave. Her eyes had quickly become used to the gloom and she had explored the area. It was of an L shape she was to discover, for, as the day grew older, the light seeped through the skins and obstacles her new companion had laid across the cave mouth. But she was able to find some respite in the shorter, darker arm of her new home. With her immensely powerful fingers she was able to prise some rocks loose and make another wall at the shorter arm's entrance and so keep most of the sunlight out.

Yet she discovered another fact that was to prove her King and his Beacons wrong. The sunlight that seeped through carried no Demons, only a soft warmth she had never before experienced. And, even though it hurt her eyes after a while, this was no Hell upstairs. The ones who lived here were no Demons and she felt sad at the countless deaths her people had caused. She wondered if the red-headed one would cry for his friends, as she had when *her* lover and their comrades had been murdered.

At first she had thought him to be the spirit of Willum and had been so stunned she could take no part in the killing. She still was not entirely certain, as this man had two eyes and they were almost the same murky black colour as those of her people. But he had the red hair of her lover and, she could sense, her lover's gentle ways. If there was a place like the Never World, where ghouls and monsters of the worst description dwelt, then surely there was a place of beauty like the Kingdom of Nimbelyung where spirits lived in harmony. Who better to live there than the Sun People with their kind ways and gentle laughter? He even spoke a type of old language and every one of the dead had had eyes as blue as the sky—real Sun People's eyes. This is what her dreams that day told her. But could spirits die? She supposed they could. After all, the body was only like a spider's egg, a protection for the true life within. Once it was discarded it was useless but the young spiders were alive—vital and free yet still able to die. She had thought, at first, she would be sacrificed to the Sun Demon for this was the closest she had ever been to that particular monster. When she had sniffed the air of the small cave she had smelt no odour of her people and she had known she was the first of her kind to be here. That she was still alive, almost touching the sun, destroyed another myth in her mind.

When he called out to her in his strange—but gentle-sounding—language she answered back with gladness in her heart.

'I must wait until Sister Sun has gone from here. The light from her eyes will kill you as surely your brothers and sisters were killed,' Ilgar explained. 'I will light a fire away from the entrance so even her son's light cannot harm you.'

She could not follow all of this but she sensed he wanted to protect her. She listened to him sing softly in the purple aura the departing sun had left behind. Then came an unusual, sweet sound. It was Ilgar on Rabit-the-White's flute, performing a lullaby that was also a death dirge, as he serenaded his friends' first evening as spirits.

For Ilgar, this was always the magic time of day. He was glad to see the end of the oppressive sun for a while, although, these days, even the nights were often hot and musky. But, more than that, the night was the time of his father, the moon. He had been born here, on this spot, twenty-four winters ago, in the seventh moon, right in the cave where the alien girl now sat. Soon would be his twenty-fifth birthday and many would lament his childless existence. For children, to the poor Ilkari, were as rare as diamonds or the precious metal, iron. The Ilkari loved everyone and everything (except that which brought danger or death to the clans) but, most of all, they loved children.

But children were not to be a part of Ilgar's life, it seemed. He was, from the very beginning of his birth when Father Moon peered down at his pain-filled mother with his soft pale light, destined for greater things. He was born on an unlucky day—the fifteenth day. His mother Kala had known a child born on one of the three unlucky days was cursed for life, unless some great happening saved him from ignobility. Yet Baba had told her the moon would be full that night, so the unlucky number became lucky for him because Father Moon's silvery light became the boy's swaddling cloth as it encompassed him like his mother's afterbirth. The blue misty light bathed the mother as well and calmed her. The first thing the boy saw upon the roof of the world was the round pearly face of Father Moon staring down at his new son. There was no one else at the birth, since Ilkari women often birthed alone. On this unlucky day no one wanted to be present to witness her sadness if she failed to reach the mountain on time. The baby born might be a fallen star and that would be tragedy indeed.

But she had arrived on time and now she gave her baby the pure, clear, water-like fluid that was his first food for several days until milk would come. He would nuzzle her breast that was as creamy as the smiling moon. For a month she stayed there atop the mountain, living off the berries growing around the hidden spring that helped make this such a sacred place. She waited while the moon died and then was born again. When he saw his son was still alive (she related to Ilgar in the children's stories she would tell him) Father Moon smiled so brightly that she was able to take the dangerous journey home, safe, in his gentle white light, from any Nightstalkers.

As he grew older, on every full moon Ilgar would disappear from the camp. As often as he could he would go to his birthplace and communicate with his father. Later, he learnt to read the messages from the sky and when his messages started to come true, he was heeded as a Moon-talker and his life's path was mapped out for him.

As he prepared the haunch of kangaroo Dongkarak had given him, the appetising smell of cooked meat drifted slowly around him, and his eyes studied the stars and slowly awakening moon for any stories to be read in the purple-grey sky. But tonight the pages of the sky were empty.

He smiled to himself. He had his own story and his own beginning now.

The sky was an empty page and yet it was full of meanings, like when Baba would smooth out a piece of earth in preparation of telling a story, using symbols drawn with his finger or a piece of stick. Yet upon the smooth surface of the untold story, there would be tiny pebbles of exquisite colours or the tracks of a small insect or the minuscule ripples caused by a faint wind. Here, the pin pricks of a billion stars studded the darkness, each with their own story.

And it was with long hours of patience that he and the girl taught each other *their* story. They stayed together on the roof of the world for many days while the moon above slowly became alive once more and took away the beauty of the stars' light.

The first lesson S'shony learnt, that very first night, was the eating of cooked meat. The unknown scent of the roasting kangaroo meat frightened her. So when he opened the curtain of skins and left a portion of the food on the rocks for her, she would not touch it, but hid in her part of the cave where no light came.

But hunger won over suspicion and at last she ventured forth, sniffing, touching, licking, using all her developed senses including mind power to see what he was thinking. Finally she nibbled cautiously at the warm red meat. The meat she had always eaten was raw—and mostly rat meat. Spiders and cockroaches were not strictly speaking meat, and, after living with the Sun People, she hardly ate human meat at all. This meat was gamey and rich and a pure delight.

Spirit food! A gift from the Gods to her. With this simple act she knew that he would not harm her. When next his hand snaked through the curtains with a stone bowl of cool water and some berries from beside the spring, her hand clasped it in a sign of friendship. Her cool fingers ran along the length of his arm, claiming him. He did not pull away. In turn his fingers explored her arm and round, cold shoulder. Then he sat just outside the curtains and talked to her while the cold white stars revolved around the mountain like spokes on a gigantic wheel. His gentle murmuring was the last thing she heard before dreams overtook her.

It wasn't long before he came into her cave and they spent long hours teaching each other their languages and laws. They found each other not to be spirits at all but ordinary humans. Even though she spoke in the

33

harsh sibilant whisper of the caves, yet in a language he could understand, and he spoke in a guttural muttering with many hand gestures, they saw they feared the same Gods and Goddesses and enjoyed the same jokes. The only thing she did not tell him was of her powers of hearing, eyesight and—especially—mind reading. She could sense that he was from a people who lived uncomplicated lives and would not be able to comprehend these powers. He would think her a witch and lose trust in her and she wanted, most desperately, for him to trust her. She could sense he was a kind man just as the one who had died only a short time ago had changed her life with his gentility.

She learnt there were many different Tribes and clans of the Ilkari, who had lived all their life on the desert and around the one river that was their life-force. There were also many Tribes that Ilgar had heard about in story or song. Some were just as afraid of Sister Sun as her people were, but for different reasons. You could worship or even love a God or Goddess that you were afraid of. It was curious but true. In fact, the more in awe you were, often the greater your worship.

She learnt a few of the ways of the wandering Ilkari and their friends, the equally nomadic Keepers of the Trees. She learnt about trees and birds and various animals. She was told of the true things to fear, like giant scorpions or poisonous snakes or the bigger, wilder animals like bears or cats that sometimes roamed this desolate red wasteland.

She, in her turn, told of life amongst the craggy caverns and narrow tunnels. She spared him none of the evil or cruelty that her world thrived on. But then she told of the tranquil yet persecuted Sun People and a little of her lover, Willum One-eye.

Ilgar, not being foolish, realised the similarity between himself and this lover he would never meet and he began to look at her with compassionate eyes. He looked at her luscious black hair and her strange black eyes with their deep rich blackness that seemed to engulf him as they stared at him with a steady unblinking gaze, but this did not bother him at all. It was one of the things that enraptured him as was her cool white body that was the texture of the marble he had once seen decorating the outside of another clan Baba's house. Her body was the shape of a Goddess in the eyes of the lonely young man. For he *was* lonely. The girls in his clan were a little in awe at his moon-talking abilities because who, after all, wants to know the future before they are ready to live it?

Spending long hours inside her cave, Ilgar developed almost as good a night vision as S'shony. Of all the tales she told, the one he listened to most intently was the one about the King of Bats, who ruled with a fist of terror, who ate screaming, squirming babies and wore their skulls as a necklace. An idea began to form in his head.

It was not long before, on the darker nights—or when the waxing moon was covered by cloud—S'shony would venture from her cave and come and sit beside Ilgar. With the cave's walls no longer around her, wrapping her as if in a cocoon and keeping her safe, her senses were assaulted by an intensity of feelings which she had never known. She felt dizzy and disorientated, as though she had been pushed off a ledge and been expected to fly. The enormity of it all was frightening.

The young man sensed her near-panic and wrapped a protective arm around her.

'Some say the stars are the wandering souls of our unburied dead and in the power of Sister Sun. Some say they are the children she invented, like her son and daughter. If this is so, it is only right that while Sister Earth's children are alive with hopes and dreams and the gift to make more children, hers should be cold and empty like stars at the bottom of the river. Pretty to look at but that is all,' Ilgar told her.

'Am I pretty to look at?' she asked.

'I could look at you forever,' he smiled.

She remembered Willum also used this word and the uneasiness it had given her. Just before he died in the caves. 'What is forever?' she whispered.

'Forever began when the oldest rock was only a grain of sand and the whole world was only dust in the sky.'

She stared at him a long long time, savouring this monumental thought. This word frightened her almost as much as the huge empty space above and around her. 'When all the stars are dead, will the sky be black? Why does the moon die every four times? Where does Sister Sun go when the night comes down?'

'There are so many questions to answer, little black-hair,' he smiled at her again. 'We have much time to answer them because our forever has not come yet. This I know from the words the stars write. But even if we had all the time in the world we would never answer all our questions.'

S'shony hugged him closer and stared up into the sky with wrapt eyes. 'What else does the sky tell you?'

A dying star left a white streak across the sky and he pointed to it. 'See? There? The star falls into the claws of my own sign, the water dweller.'

'What does it mean?' she breathed.

He turned and stared down at her, solemn for once. His dark eyes were shy and he did not speak for a while. Then he breathed as well, awed by what might happen as a virgin would be awed at pure love.

'It means . . . a sign of true love for you and me.'

And as their eyes locked his head leant closer to hers and her arms gently encircled his burnt, brown back. She knew he was not an experienced lover for she read his tense mind but she, also, had only a brief period of loving to call on. Out on that ledge, watched over by the myriad of stars and the softly rustling berry bushes, she taught him how to make love and not just read it and he taught her that love existed for her once again.

He did not tell her that a falling star could also mean misfortune.

CHAPTER THREE

The Ilkari clan, of the Tribe Elk, whose leader was Violet Lynx Foot was luckier than most of its neighbours, because their wandering area, although it included quite a bit of hostile domain, also included part of the one remaining river in this parched land. As with everything, the clan shared the water with their less fortunate Tribes-folk. But it was nice to know it was their river and that they didn't have far to go to enjoy its cool waters and silver fish.

They were also lucky to have the remnants of a forest in their area, so firewood and housing timber was not yet a problem—items the other Tribes often had to barter for.

Children, in these infertile times, were a blessing on the woman who had them and pets were more friends than anything. There were always packs of dogs and aloof, arrogant cats in a camp, along with the more exotic pets like birds, ferrets, foxes, or marsupials of any kind. Although one of the poorer people in this land, the Ilkari were a contented Race with their simple beliefs, their water, their Baba and, of course, their stories.

In every clan the Baba's house was the only stone house amongst the raggle-taggle of tent-like structures. This one was two storeys high, a tower in any Ilkari's way of thinking and those of the clan Violet Lynx Foot were proud of it. The Baba was the clan's historian, law maker and, more importantly, the story giver. It was in his house that each and every Traveller's braid rested when the owner's travelling days were done. It was in Baba's mind that every one of their stories were stored and so he became the historian. The only one the old Baba ever taught was his young assistant who would take over when Baba died. Both these, the man and the boy, had shaven heads, the only Ilkari male to do so, and the blue, red and white striped staffs they carried. Also, of course, because they were the story keepers as well as the givers, they were the only Ilkari, man or woman, to have no story of their own.

Only a boy's nearest and dearest female relative could braid his hair while Baba told his story to the gathered clan. For this purpose each woman carried a special comb, mostly made of wood but sometimes of the jewel plastic or even metal. These were reverently handed down from mother to daughter, aunt to niece, sister to sister.

Every single family also had a tale as told to the daughter by the mother and only to be told to members of her immediate family. There were two exceptions to this secret: if someone was made a blood brother or sister they could be told the tale, or when a clan held a fiesta of tale telling (the last time this clan had one was ten years ago) the women were encouraged to tell their tales.

In the secrecy of their family home they would change the story subtly so as to have a slightly different meaning to the one the whole clan would know.

The tale was told secretly because it was considered to be the family's soul, keeping them together—making each family special. It kept them warm as the mother would speak her wise words to her children, and her eldest daughter would store it like banksia cones smouldering in her mind so the fire and flames of the tale would flicker away and mesmerise generations to come just as they had pleased generations before. It was said these tales came from the Old Time and it was true they were often about strange things the listener could only guess at and the meaning of which the teller did not know. So the tale was often interpreted as the family's omen.

As it was with the women so it was with the men, and each father would pass on to his oldest son the family skill that had also come from the Old Time, such as flute making, basket weaving, soap making or turning into jewellery the very rare gold or silver sometimes found on the Purple Plains.

Since there were only two real seasons—hot and warm—the people of the Ilkari would gather twice yearly in the dwindling shade of the forest beside the wide curving bend of the river for a great Trade Fair. Here the men of each family would sell or swap the secrets of their family for goods their clan did not make or have. Of course, other Tribesmen from other clans might have the same product but each family had a different technique that often made their goods much sought after. For instance, Violet Lynx Foot had a special way of adding crushed rose petals—very hard indeed to find—into his soaps so they were purplish coloured. It was one of the reasons his name colour was Violet.

It was a time of great festivity. They would gather at a Home Ground as their people had done since the beginning of the New Time three thousand years before.

And so it was now, as the Tribes and clans began trickling in, ready for the next full moon. With so many people on the move there was little fear of attack by the Nightstalkers and any attempted were mostly driven back. At the meeting place it would have been too bright for their sensitive eyes, with the hundreds of fires glowing everywhere, so wild unruly gangs of children ran about howling and laughing through the camps in pursuit of games, girlfriends, or boys, to love or tease.

Women gathered around their cooking fires and speculated on the men who wandered past, or told of their kinfolk's adventures.

It should have been a joyful time but Violet Lynx Foot and his clan were worried about the late return of their five clansmen.

Two were his blood nephews and he wondered where the red-headed pair had got to. How could this clan's future be determined without their Moon-talker? On the night of the full moon in just over a week's time the festival would reach its peak and every Moon-talker from every clan would join their magic and wisdom together to make a powerful seance. How could this clan hope to benefit and understand its future with no one present at this meeting? He could not look Kareen in the face. Whenever he walked past the yelping multi-coloured throng that surrounded the sedate Magpie, he could not look at her huge, wondering, brown eyes as she pondered on her brother's late arrival. Even the dogs that were her life would fall silent and stare after him and that in itself told a story as clear as the summer sky.

Now Violet Lynx Foot was so called because his story revolved around a fierce lynx cat who had tormented the clan for many days, killing their chickens or geese and even the odd lamb or two. The end came when the wild, spotted beast had spirited away a new-born baby. Violet Lynx Foot had only been eleven then but he had armed himself with a spear and gone in search of revenge. If the Ilkari could love with a passion as huge as life then they could hate too. The slain baby had been the boy's new cousin so hate burned deep indeed within his thin child's body.

It was not long before he found the killer. It was arrogant, as cats often are, and its caterwauling screams led him to it. The battle was short and violent. He would carry for always four scars across his chest where the lynx raked him. But he would carry the story as well. He was the youngest in living memory to have a proud mother braid his light-blond hair while Baba related the story.

He was also the youngest to become clan Chief five years later when his father was gouged by a rogue bull elephant that shared the plains with the Ilkari and was a constant threat to them.

Some of the older men had scorned such a youth to lead them and had left, taking their families. This was an almost unheard of thing to happen and the breaking up of the close-knit clan was distressing to many. But his two sisters and most of his blood cousins remained so the clan truly became a family unit. He was to prove a fierce leader and was wise beyond his years. But this strength and wisdom and good leadership exacted a price for he never married. So Violet Lynx Foot had led his clan for the ten years after his father's death and there were none who could fault him. Some of the older men who had left returned when it was seen his leadership was strong. Not a word was spoken about their desertion for all were happy to have them back.

Even though Violet Lynx Foot had no wife and children, the line of leadership must still go on, so he had adopted a baby boy from amongst the clan. The baby had been born from a wandering Gypsy woman, a woman known for her palm reading and fortune telling that some of the Ilkari believed in, and others feared. She had died, giving birth to the child, on the outskirts of Violet Lynx Foot's camp.

The child looked nothing like the dark people from the woman's Race. His curly hair was as blond as the Chief's himself and there was speculation among the women that the child was actually his. Why else would the wandering woman have stayed at their camp a whole year when her people were noted for their restless ways? If more proof was required just look at the baby's eyes—as blue as the sky! This was the talk of the women, but the truth was half their husbands had blue eyes and blond hair. The true secret of the boy's father was carried to the woman's grave and she left behind only her horse and wagon, the baby, and Culvato.

Culvato was a wiry child of some five summers with a thick mass of blue-black curls surrounding a lean, brown, hatchet-shaped face. Bright black eyes stared scornfully out over a hooked nose at the rest of the world.

It was Culvato who gave his half-brother his true name, for until then the baby was known as Lynx Kitten. Culvato called him Durrilau, which meant berry in the tongue of the boy's mother. It was said the Chief had picked the baby from a dying bush and given him life and the baby would give him pleasure just like a berry would.

Perhaps because the Gypsy did not believe in the awesome powers of Sister Sun and Sister Earth, the baby was born with a withered leg and a huge and ugly purple mark across his chest where Sister Sun had tried to claim him for her own by kissing the mother's womb. Children born like this were known as fallen stars and were loved and cared for by the whole clan. Just like the clan's pets, the fallen stars had one huge family until they died. They weren't usually given colours because they were only fallen stars and not really people, but because this baby was to be a Chief he was called Blue Berry and his foster aunt, Ilgar's mother, braided his fine blond hair when he turned eleven, the same age as when the Chief had had his story told. She braided his hair in the privacy of her home and his story was one she made up from her tale. So the child born from a secret had a secret story.

Blue Berry did not grow as others of his age group. Instead he remained frail and slight, weighing as much as a leaf on the berry bush he was named after.

But Culvato jealously looked after his brother and was never seen away from his side. When Durrilau was only a baby Culvato would let no one feed, clothe, bathe, or even touch him, except for Violet Lynx Foot and Ilgar's mother, Kala. This caused argument among the older men that, one day, their clan would be led by a virtual outsider, possibly not even of the Ilkari Race. What proof was there that the child was one of their own except that he had blond hair and blue eyes? Besides, another stranger was by his side constantly so the baby could not even learn the ways of the Ilkari. It was too bad that with all the beautiful women of their Race, their Chief had to choose the fatherless fallen star of a foreign wanderer. Who knew what spells she had placed upon their Chief? Or upon the soul of the baby her body had spewed out? Look at the baby's keeper, Culvato, as dark and mysterious as the Devil himself who, young as he was, practised his mother's arts! Who laughed openly at Baba's teachings and would have nothing to do with storytelling. He couldn't have a story told anyway because he had no womenfolk to comb and braid his hair. It was not from lack of the maidens trying to woo him. Culvato had grown into a dark and handsome youth, full of laughter and trickery, with a sharp questing mind that always got him into trouble. But there was still that certain aloofness and that scornful look in his eyes. He knew he was not of these people's blood and ways and he waited, wondering if people of his Race would ever come this way again. Then his wandering blood would awaken and he would leave, the dust dancing around his drifting feet and with peace in his wild, turbulent heart.

Today he was with his beloved half-brother, far from the crowded place by the river. They were at a smallish, muddy waterhole, a little way from the river, where, at certain times, the biggest catfish could be caught. It was their particular place and the only other person allowed there was Violet Lynx Foot.

A quiet place, with only the chirruping of crickets amongst the long green grass and the twittering of the small birds in the sweet-scented trees. On this day their waterhole was shared by a kingfisher whose blue-green feathers glinted in the sun in delightful colours. It sat stolidly on a dead tree branch, staring into the murky, muddy, black waters.

The boys stared up into the glaring blue sky that every day seemed to press more heavily upon them. There was a story that ages ago, after the first destructive meeting of the High Ones, another last God had walked upon the earth and had caused the waters to rise and the earth to shake and split open. The gift he had left with Sister Earth was that one day she would be embraced by Sister Sun once more. Only this time the embrace would be final and she would become, as Sister Sun, a barren, burning, empty woman. Everyone would be destroyed. Every one of Earth Mother's beautiful children. Culvato often wondered if the time was near. Would they witness the end of Sister Earth as they knew her to be?

'What are you thinking of, little Berry?' he asked. When they were alone like this the boys reverted to their mother's tongue.

'Today I dream of the coumlo chiricli.'

'And does the comely bird fly into your heart?' Culvato smiled.

'She is truly my kakkaratchi,' the blond youth murmured, his eyes closed and a dreamy smile appeared on his lips.

The older youth knew Durrilau was in love with Magpie in a hesitant fantasy kind of way. Like Durrilau, Magpie had a way with animals and this is what brought them together. He knew also that the boy's foster-cousin Ilki was in love with the chestnut-haired girl, but he sensed Ilki would bow gracefully out of the contest. It would help to allay the fears some of the clan held for Berry if he married into it now. Magpie's family was an old, respected one. Many of her ancestors' Traveller's braids decorated the halls of the house of Baba. When the next Chief-to-be was settled with a child-bearing wife, Culvato could set his mercurial feet upon the road that beckoned him with adventure. Then everything would be in its rightful place.

He closed his wild black eyes and let all thoughts slide out of his scheming mind. Today was a day for peaceful fishing. He heard the plop of heavy, lazy fish as they jumped from the water to catch insects. The chittering of crickets, cicada and other insects hammered at his ears while birds called to each other in the trees. He heard the moan of the wind in the leaves.

His drifting thoughts were jolted by the sudden remembrance. There *is* no wind today, he thought! He listened more carefully. The sound wasn't the whispering rustle of the wind but more of a drone—like a giant wasp!

His eyes sprang open, black and alert, and he looked around the sky while Berry snored softly beside him. What he saw was not a giant wasp, although he rather wished it had been. He could understand a giant wasp. What drifted through the air was a silver creature high up in the sky, sometimes turning a piercing golden colour when caressed by the sun, so it became a type of mini sun. It was not a falling star but it was definitely something that belonged from the sky. The only thing that lived in the sky were spirits so this must be a spirit. Perhaps it was a piece of the moon—or sun—coming down to visit the earth. It had the same colour as the sun and moon. And Culvato the unbeliever froze while his mind went numb at this inconceivable thought. His eyes watched the winking speck as it suddenly began to veer from its path and circle like an eagle or hawk. He saw it had wings.

If it had wings then it had eyes and if it had eyes it had seen the great gathering by the river. Who knew what flesh spirits enjoyed, but human flesh could be as good as any to the Gods and Goddesses that had used Humankind as their plaything for so long. Everyone knew how Sister Sun embraced many so their skin peeled from their living bodies before they died in burning agony. The mighty storms that erupted from the sky sometimes—they killed people too, as they were torn to pieces.

He shook Berry awake. 'Come, brother. We must run to warn the clans. Spirits arrive!'

Durrilau came awake just as, once more, the sun's rays touched the silver creature and it lit up in a glowing golden glow. His drowsy eyes cleared and filled with terror. 'A piece of the sun is falling to earth!' he cried, his blue eyes wide with fright. He clutched at Culvato with trembling hands. 'We are doomed, brother!'

Culvato hoisted the smaller youth onto his broad shoulders and, fishing gear forgotten in this emergency, set off at a loping run. Up above, the huge insect circled lower and lower.

They burst into the clan's campsite, yelling and shouting for the people to come and look. Men stopped their singing or storytelling or work, and women gathered at the doorways.

'An insect comes from the moon. Bigger than the biggest bird,' Culvato screamed.

'The sun is falling. I have seen it with my own eyes!' Durrilau cried.

Women gathered their children to them in fear while some of the men laughed nervously at what they thought was one of the wanderer's crazy jokes. But others muttered amongst themselves. It had been known the wandering woman had bought bad luck onto the clan. But bad luck of this proportion? If the sun was coming down to kiss her sister again they were all dead. That was the prophecy.

Then the lynx-hide curtain to the Chief's tent was swept aside and the young Chief strode forth.

'What talk is this, Culvato?' came his soft tones, yet his eyes were hard. 'An insect from the moon?'

'It calls like a wasp. It has wings and is silver like the moon in the daylight. Never have I seen a being like it. Even now it circles like an eagle before it swoops.'

'If you do not believe us, come and see. It was by the waterhole, cousin-father,' Durrilau said.

For a moment Violet Lynx Foot looked at his adopted son and then peered up into the sky. He knew Blue Berry could not pull a hoax like his brother.

'I see nothing,' he said softly. 'But that does not mean there is nothing there. Perhaps, like a ghost, this . . . this insect might turn invisible.' Then he began striding forth. 'Better we face this head on. Come, my family, let us go and see what is what! Come, Baba!' he called. 'Perhaps you will remember some story about this strange creature.'

They set off, most with reluctance and great foreboding, Culvato, with Durrilau upon his back, then the Chief and Baba with the rest of the clan creeping along behind.

As they passed the various campsites of the other clans and Tribes, shouts of curiosity followed them, for seldom was the march of a whole clan seen. The shouted queries were answered in whispers but the answers given made others come after in a huddled muttering mass to peer anxiously into the sky.

Here would be a story indeed if it were true. The men and young boys gripped their spears or swords. This would be a great chance to earn one's Traveller's braids by destroying a monster, they thought.

Beyond the river was a forest of dead, twisted, twirling trees that had been cursed by a Devil, because the trees were made of stone and no use to anyone. They cast grotesque shadows upon the cracked grey ground. In their death they had achieved a type of bewitching beauty, their thin white hands reaching out to one another and the whole forming a type of fossilised cobweb across the brilliant blue of the sky.

There were no birds in this dead forest, only a few crickets whose calls seemed unnaturally loud in the stillness of dried, twisted trunks and branches. Just as unnatural was the silence some two thousand normally loud and rowdy men, women and children maintained as they moved through the stone trees onto the plain beyond.

This plain stretched for many miles to reach a small range of purple hills hazy on the blue misty horizon. As the people poured forth on to the plain the thing from the sky came over the top of them with a low and mighty roar. It had come from the direction of the sun so no one had seen it until it was suddenly upon them.

Children screamed or clung to their mothers, while men threw themselves to the ground, emptying their bladders. The stench of fear was everywhere for never had they been so close to a High One before. Some of the younger, braver men hurled their weapons at the sleek silver body but they just bounced off. Violet Lynx Foot stood his ground with Baba beside him and Durrilau wailed piteously. Culvato also stood straight although his dark eyes dilated with fear. He felt the hot wind of the monster's passing ruffle his hair and touch his face. His people acknowledged a thing called fate and it seemed it was his fate to be the first to see this awesome creature. What else fate would bring as gifts—or burdens—to his life he could not know. But he would not fall down and cower in the dust as other lesser beings were doing. He would face fate head on as his mother had taught him.

The silver-winged thing from the sky had turned and now came back again. Some saw strange legs appearing as it swooped lower with a lessening roar.

'It is landing!' someone cried.

'What are we to do?' called another.

'It is Violet Lynx Foot's Home Ground. It is his decision,' said one of the guests and there was great relief at this reminder. Let one of Violet Lynx Foot's men go and make his story.

Violet Lynx Foot scrutinised the thing that crawled towards them on its funny black legs. It appeared to have two great eyes and a long thin nose. Its wings stayed outstretched, stiff and gleaming in the sun with two nodules on each wing. These seemed to be its nose, for hot air wafted from the openings and shimmered with a living presence in the already hot air. Its body was squat and heavy looking and huge, but its legs were thin, with great black paws. At the end of its body it had a tail a bit like a fish fin.

'Wait, my brothers. This is my land and my laws apply. We will see if this thing comes in peace. If it does not, then we must all die fighting,' he called, raising his hands in the sign of peace.

The Chief's word was law and could not be disputed but all fourteen men in the clan Lynx Foot wished it could be otherwise.

'Could he not have landed further down the river,' Roan whispered to his son Kiki.

Orange Horse gave one last scared glance at his new wife. Would he ever see her again, he thought, as his heavy feet dragged in the dust and he followed the others.

Only Culvato was glad as he laid Durrilau down on the earth gently. 'Wait, brother, Culvato will not be long.'

'I would come with you, brother.'

'No,' Culvato said kindly, 'you are the son of a Chief. I am only a wanderer's son who has no father. If anything happens to Violet Lynx Foot, then you are the leader. If anything happens to me, no one will weep.'

So saying, he strode forward. Straight away he broke one of the rules by striding to the front of the Chief and Baba, who was intoning religious verse to appease the monster. There were mutters of shock, but Culvato did not care. This was *his* monster and he would face it in his own way.

Violet Lynx Foot glanced once at Baba who shrugged his shoulders. It was not the first time the thin youth had broken time-honoured laws. He was a foreigner and had only one law. The law of his inner self.

The Chief caught up with Culvato and Baba was just behind. A way back, close as they could to obey the Chief's law, yet far enough behind to run if there was trouble, came the rest of the clansmen.

And then—when they were about eighty paces from it—a weird and terrifying thing occurred. In the side of the monster a mouth opened wide, black in the gleaming silver.

There was a hushed cry from the gathered hundreds and a slight shifting in the crowd as neighbour crept closer to neighbour in a subconscious seeking of comfort. But there was no other sound than this. The seventeen male members of the clan Lynx Foot froze—fingers nervously twisting weapons.

From the mouth a tongue protruded. It came down in stages until it licked the ground. There was a long pause, when the men were as still as the trees behind them and the only sound to be heard was that of persistent crickets, not caring that a monster had come to visit their home.

From out of the mouth and creeping down the tongue came four forms. One was enormous, like the giants of many of the women's tales, two were smaller than average and one was about the same size as other human beings. Their bodies were white and their feet big black paws. Their heads were huge and round with one large black eye in the front and no discernible mouth, nose or ears. In the hands of the enormous form was a curious stick, something like the Keepers of the Trees' musical sticks. But no one there was under any illusion it was a stick of peace. Not the way the giant held it and weapons again were tensed in sweat-slicked hands.

The four began speaking to one another. A muffled singsong lilt. They fanned out just as the warriors and older boys of Violet Lynx Foot's clan grouped together for a charge.

Culvato took no notice of this delicate dance between cultures. He was too busy studying the creature that approached him. He gave his mind over to his soul. It is in the cards, he heard his mother's voice. Life is held in our hands. Wherever the cards fall, thus will our path follow.

The creature that came up to within seven paces of Culvato was one of the smaller forms. There was something vaguely familiar about the way it walked, he thought. He sensed this was the leader of the Sun Children—for this is what he thought these beings to be. After all, there were Children of the Moon. Everyone knew who they were, even though none had seen that illusive Race. So these had to be Sun Children.

Now it was holding its hands out in the universal gesture of peace. It thinks I am the leader, Culvato thought somewhat ironically. Its eye scrutinised him. Then, slowly, it lifted up its arms to its head.

Here was the third surprise, for with a deft movement it twisted its head off and, lo!, it was not a head but a cocoon for a head. And the head that now smiled out at him was human-shaped. Its eyes were almond-shaped and alight with curiosity. Its wide, smiling mouth was full of fine white teeth. Its flat nose had two flaring nostrils, while masses of black hair fell in tangled coils down to its waist. But this was the blackest being any had ever seen—blacker even than the darkest Keeper and they knew this being was not of *that* Race. Large teeth glittered in the black as did the whites of the fiery eyes. Now Culvato knew what had seemed so familiar about its walk. This High One encased in its unusual skin of white was a mature female!

'They truly are from the sun,' whispered Violet Lynx Foot. 'See how their bodies have been charred by the sun, as her own son Fire does to the wood of Sister Earth.'

'Children, we are looking on the face of a High One. One who has come all the way from the womb of our Sister Sun. The womb we have thought was barren,' muttered Baba.

Then no one could say another thing for it was not every day one could look on the face of a living Goddess and live themselves.

And yet Culvato knew this Sun-child Goddess was smiling at *him*. He knew also what happened to mortals who became playthings for the whims of the High Ones. Yet his heart could not help but melt from the warmth of her mighty smile.

The others took their cocoons from their heads and it was seen they were all black as the sun had burned them as they had crawled from her womb. There were two men and two women. All, except the giant male, had huge bright smiles.

'We're the survivors, yes the black survival
We're the survivors like Shadrach, Meshach and Abednego
Thrown in the fire but never get burn,'

the Goddess sang out.

'I an' I irie Locksman. Jah lives. Ilie rah!' the giant called back. But he did not smile and he kept his hands on his stick.

The High Ones had arrived and nothing would ever be the same again.

CHAPTER FOUR

By the time Ilgar arrived home the Sun Children had been in the Ilkari's presence for a little over a week. The Trade Fair was all but forgotten as clan after clan, from all the different Tribes, came to look upon these Gods and Goddesses. The two females were as different from each other as the two males were. One had the most serene face with a glorious smile and warm brown eyes. The other—the leader—was thinner with a harder face and wary eyes. One male was little more than a youth, thin of build, with long legs and arms and a dancing energetic body. He wore a permanent grin and his laughter could be heard all over the camp. The big-framed male stayed near the insect that the Sun Children called a 'machine'. He would let no one touch it, keeping a silent vigil with no humour etched upon his stormy countenance. All of them wore their hair in flowing black braids that was similar to the Nightstalkers' hair. This was the cause of much discussion for there were those amongst the clans who said these were a type of Nightstalker. But nothing else about these four was the same as their hated enemy, so they were reluctantly made welcome.

As was only right for those who had come from Sister Sun's womb, the females were in command. Apart from the giant, the other three made themselves at home in a wary Violet Lynx Foot's tent. They stayed with him, Durrilau and Culvato in the tent and, all day, there would be a stream of people coming to stare at them or bring them gifts. It was discovered that although different accented and often not understood, many of the words these High Ones spoke were similar to the language of the Ilkari. This was hardly surprising for the Ilkari were children of the earth and these four—if not High Ones—were children of the sun and so were their blood cousins.

To Culvato the leader was a most wonderful Goddess. Never before had his heart been so ensnared. He would listen to her singsong voice, that was low for a female, as he drifted asleep in the smoky interior of the tent as she conversed with Violet Lynx Foot and Baba or other high officials from the other clans.

He had been the first to see them, so he had some status with the clan now. This was his story—even though he was not entitled to one and did not want one. Besides, this was too big for only one man's story.

In his mind, though, if he had first seen them, then they had first seen him and it was *he* they had come to see. Him *she* wanted to meet. And Culvato, the unbeliever, spent many long moments pondering on this.

When Ilgar returned from the roof of the world, he came on moonless nights to protect S'shony's eyes and skin which were still too tender to face light and probably always would be. It did not matter that it was dangerous, because he had a Nightstalker woman with him and she knew when her people were about. She cast some magic spell so, three times, he watched shadowy forms run past as he and the girl lay on the ground, not even being seen by them. If they *had* attacked he carried two mighty weapons of the enemy and the bravery and cunning of his dead clansmen. He strode like a Chief through the purple empty lands, the ghostly forms of trees and rocks standing like clansmen in the murky light of the stars. His Chieftainess scuttled beside him, affection shining in her dark, strange eyes.

Even from far off he could see the lights of many fires and he was surprised because he knew the Trade Fair should be over by now. It was not wise for so many Ilkari to be together for any length of time. They were happier in their family clans.

They stopped in a clump of boulders that offered deep shadow, not far from the camps. They could hear the muted sounds of a vast gathering: the tinkle of a loud laugh, the barks of dogs and yells of playing children, the cry of a hungry baby and the verse of some song sung in the joy of being alive. But S'shony trembled for she knew she was going into the world of her enemy. They had thought of a plan to present her to his kinfolk and she hoped it would work, but she was full of fear.

'You must wait here for a while, S'shony. I will see what is happening in my cousin-uncle's camp.'

'Do not leave me,' she said, afraid.

'We are bound together as one now,' he murmured. 'Never fear. When I leave you it shall be by death's cold hand.'

It was Akar Black Head who was the first of Ilgar's clan to see him. The tall, barrel-chested killer of the great black bear, which had but recently become his story so now he wore his Traveller's braids, was getting some peace and quiet from the campsite by sitting on a rock—as still as a rock as he kept an eye out for Nightstalkers. Although with such a crowd and, he thought wryly, with four children of their hated enemy—the sun—here, they would be foolish to come. So he saw the grey shadow of Ilgar before the youth saw him and leapt upon him, wrestling him to the ground. Then he let him get up, laughing in simple mirth at the surprise he had given him and joyous to see their Moon-talker back in the clan.

'Ho, cous-cous. We had all but given up hope for you. We thought the pretty women spirits of the Keepers had taken you all away. Back to their Dreamtime to dream of you.'

Ilgar could sense the big man, who was Rabit-The-White's uncle, looking over his shoulder for the others.

'There is only me, old cous-cous,' he sadly told him. 'We were attacked by Nightstalkers. But everyone fought well,' he reassured the silent man. 'When next we travel I will show our clan where lies the last resting place of our warriors so they may keep it clean and free of spirits for always,' he said gently.

Akar Black Head looked away and let a tear trickle from his deep blue eyes as he remembered his harmless nephew.

He sighed. People died every day and at least once a year someone in the clan succumbed to disease, accident or battle. Something of the magnitude that had occurred the week before, however, happened only once in a thousand lifetimes. So Akar Black Head told Ilgar the news, asking, 'Did you read about this in the sky? Some of the other Moon-talkers say *they* might have, but you are the Moon-talker of our clan! Is that why you have been so long gone?'

The plan that Ilgar had thought up was, coincidently, similar to the story the warrior had just told him about the amazing Sun Children. But now he was faced with the prospect of seeing real High Ones. Surely they would see through his lie. He could not stop now, though, so he took a deep breath and said, 'I have read of many things in the night's sky. Many wondrous things. While you have been visited by the children of Sister Sun, I have been visited by a daughter of Father Moon.'

Akar Black Head's face was a sight to see as he tried to take in this monumental news. Ilgar told himself this was not altogether untrue since it had been the reading of the moon that had indirectly led him to meet with the young woman from a different Race.

'Aaaah!' grunted Akar Black Head. 'I have heard of these Children of the Moon. They are yellow of skin like the moon at full and black of hair like the night he wears around him like a cloak.'

'No! She is white of skin like the pale moonbeam she came down upon—' Ilgar began.

'Like a Nightstalker, you mean!' the older man cried.

'She looks like a Nightstalker and, of course, because she is a child of Father Moon she cannot feel Sister Sun's cruel embrace who would be jealous and kill her. Or send her daughter, the evil Melanoma, to destroy her.'

'How can she look like a Nightstalker and yet not be a Nightstalker?' Akar Black Head's puzzled blue eyes peered into his face.

'You say the others are dead yet you still live—a Moon-talker! How can this be? Yellow Eyes and Grey Fur were great warriors yet you live.' He touched the great stone club in wonder, then stared at the ironstone sword. Ironstone could only be found deep below the earth's surface and no Ilkari had ever seen the likes of the purple-red rock before. Most of *their* weapons were wooden or the jewel plastic or, like Akar Black Head's great axe, the occasional metal that was so hard to get and was only traded by the Keepers who knew where it was.

'What weapons are these? Why does a Moon-talker even *carry* weapons? I fear you have been cursed and a spell placed upon you.'

'No, Akar Black Head. These weapons came from the moon itself,' Ilgar said, thinking fast. 'Much will be the weeping of our enemies when these fall among them.'

Akar Black Head ran his fingers once more over the club.

'Father Moon also bears the gifts of the glass jewels, the story goes. I did not know the children of Sister Earth had visited the moon. We are not all Moon-talkers, you know, and he has as little love for some of us as does his wife the Lady Sun,' the suspicious man said slowly.

'There is a story of one such man in the Old Time. His name was Strong Arm Kneels. It was he who was given the gift of the knowledge of glass. As he flew back to earth he scattered the precious jewel upon her surface in the joy at having visited his father, the moon. So these are the glass jewels of the moon. It was his gift to us,' Ilgar said. The story of Strong Arm Kneels was true anyway and the other made a good story any Ilkari might believe.

Akar Black Head grunted and turned away, but Ilgar sensed he was not yet convinced.

'Well, we have no need of your father's weapons. Already our deliverance has come, with no help from your "moon child", he said cynically. 'Even now Violet Lynx Foot talks to the burnt ones.' He eyed Ilgar craftily. 'If, as you allude, you have seen these Sun Children in the sky what do they look like?'

For Akar Black Head was a well-known unbeliever of Moon-talkers, getting into arguments with them all the time. He had more faith in his strength of arm and agile body and things he could see and touch. It was, after all, these things that had helped kill the great slavering, terrifying bear only two short months ago and given him a place in Baba's mind as his story was told.

Ilgar smiled. He liked this big, gruff, stubborn man, who was just a few years older than himself.

'The moon knew not the children he sired with Sister Sun, if sire them he did. Perhaps she *has* made these children herself as with her other children, Fire and Melanoma. But Father Moon can no more tell his children apart than a wolf can call a cub his own.'

Akar Black Head clapped a hand on the youth's shoulder, propelling him towards the campfires. 'Come,' he roared. 'There are many who will be glad to see you. Long will be the stories told this night.'

When Ilgar stepped through the lynx-skin curtain into Violet Lynx Foot's smoky, crowded tent, full of guests come to meet the Visitors, as they were now being called, this being a word both groups could understand, he caused quite a commotion. For the first time that week the Visitors were not the centre of attention as relatives enquired about the rest of his party and Culvato greeted his old friend with joyous hugs. In between passing on the sad news of his comrades' fate and telling of the arrival of the 'moon child', Ilgar was able to flick glances at the three Visitors. There was another, he learnt, a giant who was their warrior and kept watch on their insect called 'machine'.

When Ilgar saw the Visitors, he too thought they were Gods and Goddesses from another place. Not just because of their remarkable colour, although he had to admit it was the richest, deepest black he had ever seen. No, it was their beauty that transfixed him. Never had he seen such clear skin, unimpaired by the sores and scars that were so common to his kinfolk. Their huge almond eyes seemed to shine with the beauty of their souls and their mouths were wide and white in the charcoal ebony of their skin. Their bodies—both male and female—were balanced and agile and their muscles had been chiselled by a superb sculptor. He had never seen such perfect human beings and for this reason alone he knew they must be High Ones.

He could not help but feel the sharp intelligent gaze of the one they thought was the leader burning into his back. She studied every move he made and listened intently to every word, although she could probably only understand a little in the confusion and excitement. Everyone spoke at once and spoke fast in their agitation. He also noticed how the youth Culvato watched over this woman with as much care as he did his young brother. He knew the look that softened those dark scornful eyes because it had but recently replaced the dreamer's look in his own. So, he smiled to himself, female friendship had finally snared the wildest male in the clan as well as the quietest—and both of them adoring women from completely different worlds. Father Moon, who had fallen out of love with Sister Sun, to wander alone and bitter for eternity and helped cause all the disasters that now befell them, had told him of this. Would this impossible love be just as dangerous as his own?

Everyone wanted to see this new Goddess from Father Moon and it took all of Ilgar's expertise as a storyteller and mystic to dissuade them from coming en masse back to the frightened girl. He knew, as did she, that they would both be torn to pieces if it was seen she was a dreaded Nightstalker. Too many of them had lost loved ones to the Nightstalkers' cruel appetite while their skins flapped on pale white shoulders and their unhappy spirits drifted lost and alone on deserts made red by their blood.

At the very least her sensitive eyes would be blinded by careless people shoving light into her face for a better look.

So he held up his hands and spoke thus: 'She is not a child of the sun, as these are here. She is a special moon child sent down from her father to me. She is shy, like her father, and must never be seen by Sister Sun or any of her children.' Here he looked at the three Visitors briefly. 'She has come to make peace with Sister Sun through her children but any light must surely kill her so we must make a dome for her tonight. Great is the kindness of the High Ones who have given us five of their children to replace the four of our own so cruelly taken from us.'

No one could argue with *that* so all the men set about building a smallish bee-hive-shaped cocoon of rocks and mud. Over the walls, for added protection, mud was daubed to fill in the cracks and skins were donated as gifts to the moon child and placed in the dome. Even Akar Black Head gave his prized bearskin cloak as a present to the unseen Goddess. No one had ever heard of a moon child coming down to visit a Moon-talker and this could only mean their Ilgar was blessed with a powerful shaman's influence. So much for his unlucky birthdate, people thought. He was the luckiest in the whole clan and this luck would rub off on them as well. Perhaps he had even bought the Sun Children to their clan by his powerful magic!

The three Visitors joined in the activity of building and decorating the dome. Culvato, too, who had never shown much interest in the affairs of the clan before, was by their side, working just as hard. He seemed, thought Ilgar wryly, to have a bewildered look about his face. And why not! For an unbeliever, here he was ensnared by one Goddess and building a house for another! He wondered if he could trust his secret to Culvato, with whom he had grown up and shared many an hour of contemplative thought.

It was while the men of the clan were building the dome and the women were making it comfortable that Baba came up to Ilgar and touched him on the arm.

'Come to my hut tomorrow,' was all he said, with a genial smile.

But, as every Ilkari male knew, that simple summons was the shining light in their life. It meant that their story had been accepted by Baba and they could now have their Traveller's braid.

His mother, Kala, looked up from where she stooped at the opening of the dome, handing in some rabbit-skin slippers. She pushed her red hair away from her tired brown eyes and smiled faintly at him before turning back to her task.

Now Ilgar set off to collect S'shony from the protection of the boulders. Reading her new friend's mind she was already able to understand most of what had gone on and the story he had told, but she was still shy and fearful of his unknown clansmen. She wondered at the reception she would receive and hid her face and body in the kangaroo-skin cloak Ilgar had given her. Soon she heard a rustling noise and heard him call softly for her. But her sharp senses picked up the forms of others with him, so she cowered in the skins, hiding as much of her as she could.

For even though Ilgar had wanted to go alone, Akar Black Head had insisted on going with him—to keep an eye out for Nightstalkers, he said. llgar's second-cousin, Orange Horse, who was known throughout the land for his knowledge and skill with the wild brumbies he loved and tamed, and two boys, Oka and Joda, who had not yet had their stories, went along also out of curiosity.

The torch which Orange Horse held turned his thin sharp face into menacing shadows and caught his brilliant orange hair in an unholy glow so he looked like a Devil from the very depths of the sun. S'shony buried her head deeper into the skins.

'She doesn't look much like a Goddess to me!' the horse-tamer said doubtfully.

'Just a pile of skins and hair, ay cousin-brother! Perhaps she should be bathed in the glow of a moonbeam,' Akar Black Head joked. Yet his eyes were suspicious.

Ilgar knew that if the fierce-tempered warrior tried to kill the Nightstalker woman he would defend her and do the unthinkable—kill a member of his own clan. That was how much he loved this girl and it surprised him even now. A Moon-talker should not love any but the moon and the wisdom he wrote across the skies. It was a solitary yet rewarding existence. Most Moon-talkers only married when they felt they were too old to carry on and passed their skills to a member of their close family. But he knew nothing must happen to this girl. If anything did, it would be as if Father Moon had slipped from the sky never to return and there would be no reason to go on living.

'Who knows what a Goddess looks like, cous-cous.' He attempted light banter. 'Could you have told me, without a doubt, that they would be as black as Sister Sun's child, Fire, makes the wood of Sister Earth?'

'Who is to say that they *are* children of the sun?' Akar Black Head answered back.

'It is good to have unbelievers in our midst, to question all things and keep always the truth in our eyes, cous-cous. But remember, there is no storm without rain. If what we see and hear is true then it will be known to us.'

Akar Black Head just gave his famous grunt. He was a warrior: perhaps the last great warrior of the clan now his friend Yellow Eyes and the wild Grey Fur were dead. He would leave the philosophy to those who stayed at home.

But he could not resist one last dig, for it could not be said he was not a stubborn man. 'If she is a child of the moon why does she hide her face in fear at his glorious light—not that there is much around tonight?'

'That is so,' Ilgar replied, ever sharp off the mark. 'She hides her head in fear at the fact her father has disappeared from the sky.'

'Well, we should make a window in the top of her dome so she will be glad to see the face of her loving father smiling down at her,' Orange Horse suggested.

But Joda shook his honey-blond hair out of his hazel eyes and said, 'Who is the Moon-talker among us? He who knows best for this Goddess of his deity knows what are her desires.' The boy looked at the big warrior in indignation.

Akar Black Head gave him a friendly swipe. 'You, Joda? Can you tell us a story yet, little frog? We should call you Grey Mosquito for that is the only story you will ever tell. Killing the mosquitoes down by the river as you chase the young girls and only catch the stones kicked up by their running feet.'

But he was in a good humour, forgetting already whether the skins hid a Goddess or a sorceress.

Ilgar held her cool pale hand while he led her along. She used her senses to plot out a safe path and had no need of his guidance. But S'shony was grateful for his grip all the same. She still found it hard to follow the guttural, harsh accents of the Ilkari, so different from her own hissing tongue and not even the same as Willum's although similar. But she could read minds and she knew she must beware of the big hairy warrior striding in front, although she sensed the beginnings of friendship in the boy Joda and she 'heard' the auras of awe around the other two, while 'smelling' the love of Ilgar.

At last they got back to camp and she had to endure other pokes and pinches and prods and the ever-flickering close presence of her enemy, Fire. Her sensory system was in a whirl at so many new smells, sounds and thoughts. She almost fell over, so dizzy she became. But Ilgar and, surprisingly, the untrusting warrior grabbed her arms and steadied her. A loud clear voice called out to get back from her and leave her be and then she was pushed politely into a welcome black cocoon. She knew by her mind-sight that Ilgar had sat down in front of the heavy, skin curtains just as he had done those many times up on the mountain. Later, she hoped, he would come and join her in her new home.

But it was not to be this night because he was too excited about the morrow. He told her in whispers through the curtain, when at last they were alone, about what would occur. He told her also what she already knew: that she must pretend to be a child of the moon.

She felt happy for him and lay back in her new home that she could only think of as a cave, wrapping herself in these new skins that were a delight to her. Then she let her mind drift outwards as she used her senses to feel the other people around her. There were three she could not fathom for their thoughts were of things strange and dreadful to her. But of the others she was able to learn a little from their thoughts and dreams. There were children chuckling at children's jokes or contentedly feeding from their mothers' milk. There were people making unruffled love to each other. A few people were having a late-night feast and a soft singsong. She felt she was, once again, back in the caves of the Sun People. She felt again the smooth white skin of her stomach and the little person growing there.

Then she cast her mind out to the one they called Baba who was their Priest. He had a glorious, rich mind, as did many of these people. It gave her a thrill to touch it. She left in the recesses of his mind a thought that he would think was his own. She lay back exhausted, but she was relaxed now. She had started a plan she had only just conceived but which she knew could work. This seed of a thought could change the world. She could make it into a far better world, where everyone lived in harmony with their neighbours; where there was only one set of Gods and Goddesses—the best and most fruitful kind.

Others also lay awake thinking on this marvellous night of nights and these new times. For new times they were, when the children of the High Ones walked once more amongst the children of the earth.

Violet Lynx Foot thought about these new Gods and Goddesses; Akar Black Head thought about one Goddess in particular and Culvato thought of another. Kareen and Odi thought of their lover or brother Yellow Eyes, while Magpie wept silent tears for one she *had* loved deep down. Two mothers also wept a single tear and thought long of the sons they would never see again.

Sister Sun came over the hills in her red and orange afterbirth, having been born from the womb of her devastated sister once again. She strode across the bare red plains full of purple rocky outcrops and twisted patches of dead grey trees. Yet no one seemed to mind her this day.

Usually it was only the members of one's own clan who were present for their storytelling. But because of the importance of the story and, also, because of the Trade Fair there would be many people coming from the other camps. So work started early for the clan of Violet Lynx Foot of the Tribe Elk.

The women gathered firewood and water. And the oldest woman of each family rehearsed the tale passed down from mother to daughter in case they were called upon to give a special telling of it tonight. The men had slaughtered their best pig, goat, sheep or cow the night before and now their sons prepared the carcase. Their sisters started making wheaten or oat cakes or salads from their gardens where there was much chattering and chirruping.

The three Visitors had disappeared back to their insect and it was believed they, too, were preparing for the night's festivities. This was another great honour—that the children of the sun would join in a festival of Sister Earth.

The only two from the clan not doing anything this day were Ilgar, who had made his way to Baba's hut at daybreak, and Culvato. The thin, dark unbeliever was the only one the Moon-talker could trust not to pry into S'shony's identity. And he did it well, standing guard at the entrance with his sharp spear and even sharper tongue for those who lingered.

The house of Baba was as grand as it was mysterious. It was no wonder it was such a huge place, for on these walls and in the passageways of the Hall hung the braid of every Traveller who had died at home. Some had been killed in accident, most had died from Sister Sun and her daughter's embrace. Not a few had died in battle with the wild animals that frequented this place, attracted as they were to the dwindling river that was here. Others had been killed in battle with the Nightstalkers and a few of their braids were found by mourning relatives.

The first Traveller ever to decorate this wall did not have a braid at all. Instead he had worn a hat. But not an ordinary hat of animal skin that was often part of one's story. No! This was a hat that no one had ever seen the likes of and never would again once they walked from Baba's Hall. Once seen, the viewer was sworn to secrecy and must never mention the hat to any of the women or boys who had not had their story told. Even among the men it was seldom talked of, for this was a hat from the Old Time. So old it was beyond comprehension.

This was a hat of a strange, stiff, cloth-like substance, with one side turned up and held in place by a singular metal-jewel clip. The hat was a khaki colour and, in true reverence, it was kept in an even more uncommon complete glass jewel box to keep the damp and decay out. It was the first item ever shown to any who walked into the house of Baba.

This hat had belonged to the first Chieftain of the clan who had led his people out of the place of destruction to be here in this land at the beginning of the New Time. He had been a great leader, but not much was remembered about him as many Babas had come and gone since then and even the best story could become distorted in time. The rare metal clip, that was a curious brown colour, was in the shape of a rising sun to remind all his descendants to beware this High One, for it had been she who had killed most of his people. Three thousand years ago there had been a glare whiter than the sun as she walked on earth and a heat so great it melted people where they stood staring in awe at the rising Goddess. It was told, but this was not certain, that this is why the People of the Caves knew all the secrets of the mushroom fungi, for this was the shape the High One took.

But that was not really the story for Baba to tell. The story that had his listener in complete wonder was about the first one to bring his people to safety and why the male members of the clan Violet Lynx Foot always had to have a colour in their story name. For the first Chief's name had been Corporal Lesley Green and he had obviously been a brave Chief indeed.

This was the first and last time a Traveller would walk into the house alive. Next time Baba would bring in his braid and memorise his story. It was almost like looking upon a God and no one man would ever forget the experience.

Of course other clans from other Tribes had their own Baba and their own story with their own way of naming their men. But in every Baba's Hall there was an article from the first leader. It would be unique and unusual because it came from the Old Time and it would be that clan's special secret.

So, all that day Baba took the fascinated Moon-talker up and down the passageways telling braid stories to him. Each story he told had a significance to the youth. Later, he would remember the stories and figure out the moral that lay within. For now, he had only to listen enraptured to the Baba's gentle droning voice. Never had he heard such a richness of stories involving murder, gallantry, betrayal and love.

'And this,' the old Baba's grating voice whispered, 'is the hairpiece of your great-great-great-grandfather, known as Green Star. Do you see the colour? As red as is your own! It is spoken that he, too, was a Moon-talker, as was your father's grandfather, Ralgar Moonstreak. Green Star was a man of great mysteries. A wondrous and brave man was he, and many are the stories told of his fine deeds.'

Ilgar reverently touched the braid.

'How did he die, Baba?' he murmured, his eyes alight for a good story of stirring adventure. Surely such a one must have died a glorious death. Even perhaps like his mother's grandfather, Eric the Black Bat, who had slain *twenty* Nightstalkers single-handedly and saved the sleeping clan all by himself. He would have lived, too, had not one woman he spared stabbed him treacherously in the back before dying herself.

A sad smile passed over the old man's seamed and dried-out face. He noticed the admiration in the young man's voice. There was still too much blood lust among his people; even in the peaceful Moon-talker.

'He died of old age, young Moon-talker. Not everyone dies before coming in here. Sometimes a man can cut off his braid and hand it to me in a special ceremony. This means he wishes to settle down with his family and give up his travelling way.

He saw the look of confusion on Ilgar's face. Old age was not a well-known companion among the Ilkari.

'He stopped being Chief when your mother's ancestor, Morak, was sixteen. He who went on to become known as Grey Killer, being the only one on *all* the plains to slay one of the Devils called Elephant. For, you see, Ilgar, to die beside the fire of your grandchildren is not such a bad thing. Let us hope you, too, die beside a lingering fire with your children around you.'

The young man looked up and saw sadness and wisdom mingling in the old man's rheumy brown eyes. Baba was possibly the oldest man alive. He had been born at the time of Ilgar's great-grandfather, Eric the Black Bat, and had taken both his parents, his grandfathers, and many uncles and cousins through these corridors. His duties kept him indoors most of the time, away from the death rays and out of all the harm this land and its creatures could inflict. Even when young, a Baba would not roll in the dirt of the camp or mud of the riverside, naked and free, his skin turning brown, then almost mahogany, in the ever-lasting heat. From the age of five, the Baba's assistant would have his head shaved and be taken from his mother by the old Baba to be taught the sacred stories of the clan. When the old Baba died, the new Baba would choose another child to be his protege.

What had this world to offer since the rage of the High Ones had reduced it to ashes and the abode of Devils? Perhaps it was better to die a young brave death, red blood leaping to meet the red sand and a fierce war-cry springing from youthful lips. It would be the last sound the soul ever made before fading away to become a wind—an empty mournful wind—upon the desert.

'Life is yet still beautiful,' the old man murmured.

Ilgar looked at him, wondering if Baba could read his mind. He had heard people could do such a thing but he had a full enough time reading the sky. He remembered a saying his mother had once told him: 'I am so poor! How can they say a human being is the richest of the animals—I have not the solidness of a rock nor the beauty of a sunset over the Aegean sea.' When pressed as to what the Aegean sea was, he was told about a place of great magic and wonderment, surrounded on all sides by Gods and Goddesses, Monsters and Greater Mortals such as they would never see. It was a place from the Old Time still existing on the earth—a huge, purple, enchanted lake, where Sister Sun went to sleep every night and even *she* was offered brief respite in the bewitched waters.

He wondered what this life would be like if it ever became so beautiful. Perhaps it was the life we live when finally our spirit leaves us and it is properly sent home by the Baba. So we will dwell forever by the shores of the Aegean sea with the High Ones, Heroes and Heroines we have never met, Ilgar thought.

Thinking thus, he remembered he must soon go and see his mother for the second part of his ceremony this day. So he bade Baba goodbye and set off down the dusty track towards the river.

Kala sat by the bank on her own and he came to her in some homage. Today she was not just a mother. She was a wise woman who would become a part of him tonight, along with Baba. All three would weave the story that would be forever his.

'Ilgar,' she breathed.

She knew that after tonight he would have a new name. His colour name, given him by Baba, so he would be a proper man of the clan. But she had named him Ilgar. It was *her* name and she let the sound of it roll gently against her tongue. She—and maybe his beloved—would be the only ones to call him this after tonight and even then only when they were alone. She felt sad that she was losing her last son to the clan. But she was proud he was now a true member of the family.

'Mother-mata, it is with joy I see you sitting here.'

'It is with joy I see you standing,' she gave the customary reply. 'Come, sit with me. The time has come to tell you our family's woman's tale. I must comb the Devils out of your hair and wash away your boyhood so you are cleansed and empty as a newly made urn, ready to be filled with tonight's story which Baba shall give you. But our woman's tale is for you to hear as well and take whatever you see from it into your heart. You must never forget these words. It is the only time you will hear the truth behind them and these words are only for you.'

And so the second part of the ritual began. She washed his long, tangled, red hair gently in their river and then produced her special ivory comb. This comb was made from the tusk of the monster Grey Killer had defeated. It had been passed down the female line of the family and was yellow with age but no less precious because of that. She patiently began combing his flaming locks: a job that took some time, for his hair, that reached down his back, had rarely been combed, although it was always kept clean with mud, water and oils. It was only ever trimmed by Baba every seven years. This was the custom of the Ilkari men, until their Traveller's braids were at last plaited and then their hair was left alone. The women could comb and cut their hair whenever they wished, but most women let their hair grow wild and free like the men.

The story she told him was called Thin and the Black Man and it was a wondrous story indeed. It concerned a boy named Thin, who had a horrible, cruel father, from whom he had run away. Thin met up with a man so dark he was like a walking shadow, thus having no fear of the sun. The man had been accused of some crime and was running away. In the old old days, before the High Ones walked upon the earth, there were such things as prisons that were like the caves below them—cold, evil places. It was to this place the Black Man would have gone, so Thin often hid him from the wrath of others.

These two had many adventures, although it was mainly Thin's story. There were two warring clans, with a girl in love with a boy from the other clan. There were all sorts of Devils and magicians and even the weather itself took part in controlling their destinies. And all of this happened upon the biggest river in all the country. In fact, it was so big it took a whole year just to travel down it and it was ten times as wide as their own river (which everyone knew was the last of all the true rivers).

It was all right for Thin to be on all this water for he was a water boy, even though only a child, and had the luck and cunning of a male so blessed. With his clever hands he was able to fashion an object out of Sister Earth's gift of wood. An object called a raft that floated upon the sacred water. Imagine that! To float on water as easily as to walk on land.

It was a great and wonderful journey and story but the best part was how the two—Thin and the Black Man—changed their attitudes and thoughts for each other. In the beginning Thin thought just the same as other white people towards the Black Man, because he was as different to them as a Nightstalker was to an Ilkari. But in the end they both had love and respect for each other and parted as friends. The river also had a marvellous name that befitted such a gift from Sister Earth. It was called the Mississippi, truly a name of the High Ones.

By the time she had finished her woman's tale his dishevelled, knotted hair was shining, lustrous from brushing and, was free of all tangles. Her thin, brown, sun-spotted hand brushed away his burnished red-gold hair from his black-brown eyes and she stared into them.

He was her oldest child now. A brother had been struck down by Sister Sun and a sister gored by a herd of wild pigs that had invaded the family garden one afternoon. She had been glad her third child had become the clan's Moon-talker. It had meant he would be beside her until she died. But with all these great changes occurring, she sensed that her son would play an important part in this new order and that she could lose him too. Tears welled in her brown eyes that were so much like his own.

'Ilgar,' she breathed again.

'Water is a precious thing, mother-mata. Do not waste any on me,' he said, fingers brushing the tears away gently.

'Never forget who I am, wherever you go and whatever you do.'

'I shall not go anywhere,' he reassured her.

'I saw your eyes as I told of the journey down the biggest river. You were a leaf floating along beside the raft. A bird drifting with the currents,' she said quietly.

He looked at her then for a long moment.

'When I awake in the morning, joy shall be mine to walk upon the tears of the moon, each drop being a thought of you,' he said, just as quietly back.

And then they embraced each other. For the last time as mother and son.

When next they met it would be as man and woman.

The night was heralded by the sun's departure in a golden-red aura that covered the sky. On the horizon were some few wisps of clouds that shone golden orange in the purple-red haze. This also was a good sign for the Ilkari, so used to seeing empty, blue, dead skies. By that time the clan and their many guests were assembling.

That afternoon all the children of the clan had gathered at the riverbank and there had been much shouting, splashing and laughter. Then the girls combed out their long fine hair and all got into their best skins. There was Magpie in her rare and striking white kangaroo-skin robe and Joda in his deceased father's leopard-skin cloak. His constant companion, an arrogant, black cat with scornful, baleful, yellow eyes, whom many thought was his father's spirit, had also cleaned its lustrous coat for the occasion.

The musicians of the clan tuned up their instruments in anticipated pleasure at the night's dancing. Kareen, shy as she was bold sometimes, might be induced to play her harp and Culvato would be sure to play his people's lovely instrument that had been a gift from his mother—a guitar.

Soon the fires were burning and the animal-fat lanterns were smoking. The smell of cooked meat drifted everywhere as the feasting began. There was even the smell of fruit wine and honey mead as the clan's small supply of alcohol was dug up from corners of various tents for this auspicious occasion.

When the camp's little square was crowded, more fires were lit on the outskirts and more food cooked while more wine from other clans was passed around. Some musicians from other clans also came and joined in, so the music was wild and throbbing at full beat. When the Sun Children came back from the insect machine, the small male bought a drum of his own, a strange tall affair that made a different, sharper sound than the skin drums of the Ilkari.

It surprised the gathering that these beings enjoyed and played music, just as they did. It was also noticed that the four Sun Children every so often would light sticks of white material stuffed with pungent green, yellow or brown leaves. It gave off an enjoyable scent. They would put these in their mouths, drawing back so it flared and crackled on the end. And then it seemed as if their insides were on fire as smoke came from their mouth and nose. Was this some sort of High Ones' food, they wondered, for certainly no one had ever witnessed such a thing. Were their insides a mass of livid red coals? Was that why they were black all over their bodies and breathed smoke like the dragons of some of the women's tales? Those close to them moved away fearfully. But the Visitors danced with a liquid flowing motion and their faces were wreathed in huge smiles as white as the sun. Even the giant, who had left his stick and the insect behind tonight.

Then the storytelling began. First, the women of the clan were given their chance to tell their tales. Then Akar Black Head, being the last-surviving warrior of the clan, led off with a song concerning the exploits of those four recently killed. The women of the clan performed an erotic fertility song, moving seductively among the men and handing out the purple pebbles that were only found in the women's place further up the river.

But at last came the moment everyone waited for: when Baba and his assistant emerged from the Hall, carrying their striped white, blue and red staffs, and made their way over to Ilgar's mother's hut, where the red-haired youth and his remaining family had waited; a part, yet not a part, of the whole show.

An expectant hush fell upon the crowd. Here would be a story of some mystery for it hardly bore any reference to things of Sister Earth at all, except Ilgar had survived an attack by the Nightstalkers. Right here in this camp they harboured a strange child of the moon no one but the aloof Moon-talker had seen. All day people had surreptitiously glanced at him, wondering if she had cast some spell on him. Nothing untoward could be seen, but the Baba would know and he would let it be known in his story.

So the crowd went quiet and shuffled closer as Baba led Ilgar out and sat him in the honoured chair, known as Baba's chair, only ever used for this sort of festival, with his mother standing behind him. Very carefully, she began combing out his now untangled hair and anointing it with fragrant oils, while Baba began his story. Then, at last, she began braiding it. She chose to braid it the way of his long-dead father, with two narrow plaits falling down each side of his face and a thicker, more intricate braid down his back. Of course, no one braid could be the same as another and this was one of the women's special skills to make each of their males as cleverly different as possible. Part of the skill was also that Baba and the mother would finish their tasks at the same time.

And the story Baba told was this:

'The most mystical God of all is Father Moon, who sails lonely and sad through the sky. Every morning before Sister Sun wipes them away with arrogant feet, his bejewelled tears lie strewn upon the ground like glass as he weeps each night for his faithless wife. These are witness to his great melancholy and to his betrayal by Sister Sun and Sister Earth. But he is still a powerful God to uphold and any that wish to follow him must have a great inner strength. They must be willing to lead a sad and lonely life like the one they worship. They must be able to read the messages Father Moon gives to his children and which is his one gift to the children of the earth. No ordinary man can follow the illusive light of the moon. It is a dangerous gift, for one not suited will surely go mad, just as Father Moon did when he observed the love of Sister Sun for her own sister, Earth, and caught them in passionate embrace together. So he wept bitter acid tears of death and the face of Sister Earth was darkened in shame, as the sun hid from her behind thick black clouds of smoke, dust and rain.

'A child was to grow up with the light of the moon in his eyes and he was to become the most famous of this clan's Moon-talkers. More famous even than his distant ancestor, Green Star. Or his great-grand-father Ralgar Moonstreak who, although never having a story told about him, could read the sky most remarkably and that was story enough.

'Many was the time Ilgar went alone to the holy place on the rooftop of the world and every time he came down from there with a prophecy it was fulfilled: a birth, a bountiful crop, a victory over our enemies, a death. Father Moon had foreseen a pure and noble son—a moonbeam. Therefore, like a moonbeam, he was straight and true. The writings in the sky were never wrong for him.

'Also, this boy was blessed with a good nature. Everywhere he went he made friends and his merry laughter and happy smile were an inspiration to his family and clan. All Moon-talkers have been lone people, like their Father, and have kept away from affairs of the clan while they pursued their own mystic lifestyle. Many have been aloof and arrogant, knowing the power they had over the clan; even over the Chief and Baba. This boy however enjoyed the company of his cousins and cousin-brothers and often sought them out with a smile and a laugh. This boy who grew from youth to young man and, like his great-grandfather, had no story nor young girl to keep him warm and content. It was only his mind and most of his thoughts that he kept to himself and surely the clan would not begrudge him that, for it was his mind Father Moon had taken as his own. He filled it with plans and ideas for the future that greatly benefited the clan Violet Lynx Foot of the Tribe Elk.

'But there came a time when a great grey curtain of sadness fell over the clan. Even though the Moon-talker had seen this tragedy in the skies, there was not a thing he could do about it. One dark night, when Father Moon wept black tears at loss of his radiant though faithless wife and hid his head in shame, five brave members of the clan Violet Lynx Foot were caught out in the open on the red sands, far away from home. The mighty warriors Yellow Eyes and Grey Fur. The prophet Rabit-the-White. The child Ilki. And the Moon-talker, once known as Ilgar.

'From shadows, shadows were born. From the darkness of the pit below Demons came. They came that night from out of the night and caught our dear clansmen by surprise. Nine cruel soulless ones of the Tribe Nightstalker! Oh, they fought bravely, each one of our clansmen, although surprised and outnumbered. Even though one by one they died, so did they dispatch their enemy until at last the only one left alive was the Moon-talker, who had proven he was not just a mystic but a fine warrior as well.

'Wounded gravely though he was, he buried his fallen companions before Sister Sun got to them, then set off back to the roof of the world where he knew he could recuperate in safety.

'It was there that the strangest thing happened to him. The thing that was to change his whole life and make him different to any Ilkari ever born. For a visitation came to him while he lay sleeping. A marvellous woman, with hair and eyes as black as the night and skin as pale as the branches of dead trees bathed in the moon's light, had come down to him. She carried a fantastic stone sword of a rock never seen on earth before and a stupendous stone club, bejewelled with the glass that Strong Arm Kneels had already brought back from the moon those thousands of summers ago. She was a daughter of the moon, a true Goddess. From now on she would bring messages from her father to the Moon-talker. Powerful would be the wisdom of the Moon-talker and the magic of the clan Violet Lynx Foot would surpass all others.'

Now Baba paused. When he continued, the story took a turn that would shock and dismay most of the people gathered there.

'We must now go on a journey far from our homes. It will be long and dangerous, for the purpose of it is to gather an army to go into the ground below and destroy the evil that has so often destroyed us. For it is well-known that Sister Sun's tortuous embrace cannot penetrate there—just as she dare not enter *my* house. Thus, if we can live under the caves where the sun cannot get at us—just as I live in my house—and come out to plant our crops that are aided by Sister Sun, we shall have the best of both worlds. This is the wisdom of Father Moon and our guide shall be the moon Goddess.'

In her new cave S'shony was able to fully relax. She had sown the seed in her new companion's and the old Baba's mind, so it was *their* story and part of their culture. But her mind was reeling at the stories and images it had encountered on its travel through their incredible thoughts.

There were already murmurs amongst the other members of the clan.

'It is madness!' cried Cimarron Rose. 'The moon Goddess has put a spell on my cousin, the Moon-talker, and it has rubbed off on the Baba.'

'Everyone knows Father Moon can dispense lunacy as well as wisdom,' Dark Carmine called out and his brother, Orange, Horse loudly agreed with him.

'Who is to say this woman is a Goddess at all?' came Akar Black Head's ominous rumble from the back. 'Why cannot we see her with our own eyes and make our own decisions?'

'We should not leave our place by the water. It has been our home since the beginning,' the old Grey Wolf from the Yellow Plains quavered. He was the oldest man alive in the clan being some sixty summers and was regarded with great respect after Baba and the Chief. So much so that he had *two* colours in his name.

'Let Baba finish the story of Ilgar. We shall decide this in a clan meeting,' Violet Lynx Foot ordered abruptly. 'But tonight belongs to Ilgar, Baba, and mother-Kala.'

Never before had a story been interrupted by comments from the crowd. The telling of a story was a sacred thing and no more so than a man's first story as told by Baba. There were covert glances around the crowd as people gauged other's opinions in this matter and some of the guests moved slightly back so as not to get caught in the contretemps. There were so many unusual things happening to this clan now. High Ones dropping from the sky in weird insects; or sliding down the dark face of the moon like a teardrop bearing wonderful gifts of weaponry for one usually so peaceful.

What was an army, Violet Lynx Foot wondered. Obviously a word from Baba's past stories. This is just how the Old Time ended and the New Time began, with a series of different happenings. Words and things and ideas no one had ever thought of or seen before came to the minds and hands of the people. Gifts of the Devils, had they but known. Seeing this, and seeing how the people enjoyed them, the High Ones became angry and walked upon the earth. What had happened in the past could happen again. A saying from the Old Time was 'His story repeats itself'. Would this be the end of them now? So the only thing on Sister Earth would be the whispering wind moaning the song of some thousands dead?

The Baba went on: 'Yes, there will be some doubt. But only the bravest will go and great will be their adventure. The leader into this journey of the new life, and whose story it will ultimately be, will be Red Mond Star Light, once known as Ilgar.'

There was a suppressed cry from behind him as Kala let out a groan of pain. So the High Ones would even take this, her third child, from her. He had been born on an unlucky day but, in truth, it was she who had had all the bad luck. Her trembling fingers could scarcely do up the knot to finish the last braid. But her brown eyes, which she had inherited from the Keepers, did not give the merest hint of anguish when she gazed into her last son's proud eyes. It would have been unlucky indeed for her to have shown misery at her son's story. Besides, Baba had said this was only the beginning and the story would continue.

She had plaited his hair in the image of her husband, Red Crow.

Her fingers felt his hair one last time. Now he would go away—just like her husband, who went out looking for goats one day and disappeared out of life and into the spirit world with the other tormented spirits that had no burial place. Would he one day meet the son he had loved the best of all as they wandered the same world? She could not bear to think of it.

The next day, early in the morning, the clan of Violet Lynx Foot gathered for their most important meeting ever. So important it was and this issue was so astounding that whereas usually only the Chief made decisions, this time the whole clan must decide.

No one had ever gone beyond the crusty mountains on the far side of the Purple Plains that were known as the edge of the world. They remembered some of the Keepers' stories about giant animals and fire-breathing magicians that could turn from a bird into a huge red dog that ate up children before turning back into an old man. There were perils aplenty in the lands beyond the Purple Plains and the clan of Violet Lynx Foot had just suffered the loss of four young men. There had *never* been a time in all the Tribes' various his-stories when a clan had been without its Moon-talker who could predict the future, or comprehend a clan's problems by reading the book of the sky. Not only were the ones leaving in mortal danger but so were those who stayed behind.

Other leaders from other clans had also come to this important meeting and they put forth their opinions as well. Who, out of all three—earth, moon, sun—were the most revered by the Ilkari? Why, Father Moon, of course. And then Sister Earth, from whose loins they had sprung. Sister Sun and her evil kin were no friends of theirs and any way to escape her relentless grasping hands was welcomed most heartily.

So the arguments flew back and forth, just as the bird calls down by the river drifted between their words in whistling melodies. At last came the time for Red Mond Star Light to talk. He stood up amongst the men, a man among them now. His brown eyes swept over them all slowly and it was not the first time they noticed the power in the light that shone from those eyes. Power and magic that came from the Sister Earth herself.

He began his first speech as Red Mond Star Light:

'The moon and the stars travel across the sky in a long journey as does the sun every day. Yet they always return to the same place in time. Sometimes a star will appear where before there was nothing and sometimes a star will fall to earth. Baba knows best the story of when a High One visited us last, hundreds of summers ago, and caused the water of the world to rise up into the sky and the earth to crack and shake in fear. But the sky is still above us and life goes on. It is only because I am the Moon-talker that I know these things and am not afraid. The book of the sky is a complex book indeed and the stories within its pages will go on forever. The teller of these stories—Father Moon—*is* forever. And yet he fades away, only to come back again . . . another journey. I, too, shall fade away for a brief time only to come back again with treasures more precious than the purest moonbeam or the biggest moon stone. Would a bird forsake its feathers just because the other animals said it was not a bird? Should I forsake this gift from the sky because others don't believe in her? No, I shall go this day to the King of the Bats and to any adventures that will be mine.'

He looked around at the seated ragged clan, dressed in their skins and furs; with their bodies burnt black and often covered in Melanoma's kisses; with their wild eyes and untidy hair. These were his people and they had lived this way for three thousand years. But what if there was something better for them out in the unknown lands? What if he could find the Aegean sea of his mother's tale? Or the huge river Mississippi? He could lead his people into the beautiful lands of the High Ones and Greater Mortals.

These four black ones, whose physique was greater even than Yellow Eyes or Akar Black Head, were they really friends or enemies biding their time? Had they come from Sister Sun's womb or were they from other lands over the mountains at the edge of the world, just as his 'Goddess' was? These were things he wished to discover as well.

'These are new times and new rules apply. Therefore there will be no argument. I will go myself. I don't want to take away the lifeblood of the clan. So, if any of you want to come with me I shall only take four from among you and no more. Come! Who would desire to be the stars around the moon?'

There was a murmuring and mumbling in the seated crowd. Many felt sorry for Violet Lynx Foot who not only had to put up with Culvato's lack of respect for Ilkari laws but now his Moon-talker's blatant display of rule breaking.

Then Akar Black Head stood up. His thick and bushy black hair had been hard to comb into a braid so his oldest girl-cousin had finally just tied it into a pony tail that now was becoming a mat of wiry tangles. He was a very hairy man and had a thick, full, black beard, with some strands of white in it that were marks of the hard life he had led. Now he tugged at the beard while he stared back at Red Mond Star Light with very blue, very bleak eyes.

'I'll come and see this King of the Bats. He has caused much hardship to my family,' he growled. 'I also want to be there when we see this Goddess of yours at last. If she is anything other than what you say, she shall feel my axe. You understand that I do this only to save you from yourself. I am a warrior and not given to magic so I shall not be blinded by any spells she may have woven.'

The boy Joda stood up next, his hazel eyes bright with excitement and his honey-blond hair catching the sun in a golden glint. 'I wish to see what is over the mountains. It is the time for my story and what a fine story it will be!' His hands absently stroked his cat's thick black fur and perhaps he thought of his father, who had also been an adventurous, reckless type.

He remembered his mother telling part of her tale to him about a boy called Hawk and a fierce man from a Tribe called Pirate who was named Silver Jon Long and the times they had on something called an island, that was land in the middle of a river with so much water you could not see either shore. His mother had been a great storyteller before she died and there was not one girl left in his immediate family so the tale had died, too, in this clan. But, Joda thought, I can carry the story on by being as brave and cunning and adventurous as Hawk. He flashed a smile around at his clan and pretended not to see the dismay and horror on his auntie's face.

Kareen, the lover of Yellow Eyes, stood now. She was tall for a woman and big-boned as well so she made a striking figure. Her ancestors had come from the steppes of another colder inhospitable land and her face was both fierce and proud, with high cheekbones and grey slate eyes. 'I, too, shall go. There is nothing here to bind me anymore,' she said in her husky voice.

At this, there *were* protests. It was part of a woman's duty to keep the clan alive by bearing children. There were few enough women in the family anyway. Besides, it was for a woman to keep the much-needed vegetable patches alive and well. There were certain rituals only a woman could perform involving Sister Earth that would bring on the worst disaster if not completed properly.

Others said there was no reason she could not go. She was as good a warrior as Yellow Eyes and a better hunter than many of the men. As to a woman's sacred duties it was known that Sister Sun had kissed her womb and cooked any children that found their way there.

It was Kareen who solved the argument herself. She pointed at Red Mond Star Light.

'As the Moon-talker says himself these are new times with new rules. Red Mond is my true cousin. I am of blood kin more truly than the others. I shall go and look after him, to bring him safely back to his family.'

This was a strong argument to the clannish Ilkari who valued family even more than glass or metal jewellery. But if there was to be any more argument it was solved by the next set of events. For no sooner had she stopped talking then the four High Ones stood up as one and moved over to the side of Red Mond.

'I an' I ago wid you,' the woman leader said in her strange, broken, yet lilting language. 'You ago need us, bwoy! 'Im mountains fiesti place fe sure!' and the rest of her entourage nodded solemnly. There were mountains here where lay two of their brethren and sisthren. Buried beneath the rocks and soil of this inhospitable land. For they had been lost upon the face of this great continent about two months now, before the greatest good luck had delivered them to these people. The first humans they had found here.

So no one could argue against Kareen going if the two women High Ones were going—as well as the Goddess of the moon. Maybe they would need a mortal woman as well as men to attend to their every needs.

When Culvato, lurking near the dome's entrance, saw that the Visitors were going as well he called out, 'Of course, it goes without saying that I will go with you, cousin-brother. In case you had forgotten me.'

Neither he nor Red Mond failed to detect the slight smile that crossed the lips of the Visitors' leader's face.

Not for a moment did Culvato think this woman was from the sun. Of course in the beginning he had, along with everyone else. But like Akar Black Head, he did not really believe in any Goddesses or Gods . . . only spirits. And he had been close to this woman long and often enough to know she was no spirit. Her voice, tainted as it was by the speaking of another language, her mind full of a different people's ideas, the smell of her body and her perfumed hair, the warmth of her touch and the wicked look in her slanting black eyes told him this. Most of all, the way she leaned into him and listened with all her soul as he sang love songs to her out on the dunes at night, in the soft Gypsy language of his mother, told him she was a woman with a woman's needs.

'Len sos sonsi bela pani o' reblandani tere'la' was one of his mother's sayings. 'The river which makes a noise has either water or stones.' He knew what she meant by that now—ask nothing, gain nothing.

There was no joy for anyone else in the clan Violet Lynx Foot this day. Kala gathered her three remaining daughters around her and left on a woman's journey down to the all-soothing river. But even the coolness of the sacred waters and her Earth-Mother ceremonies would not ease the bitterness from her soul. A son born and a son dead, a daughter screaming in the mud as pigs tore her insides out, a husband gone forever. Now her other son would wander off through the dust of the Purple Plains—to become dust and a name in a legend. It seemed as though no man could survive in her family. She looked down at her three remaining girls and noticed the youngest was weeping for her mother's sadness. A wizened brown hand went out and swept back the red-gold hair.

'Hush,' she whispered, 'don't cry for your brother or me. He is gone and is no more. We must occupy ourselves with Sister Earth for she is our mother too and we must perform rites to enable the fertility of our clan and our food stocks to continue.'

So the four females painted their bodies and smothered their hair in the blue and green sacred clay of the river and performed ancient incantations passed down to only a few of the women of each clan, so precious and religious were they. This family would be a family of women from now on. They would become High Priestesses and guard the men against danger.

Others of the clan moped around the campsite all day. No one cried for Culvato. Many thought he was the one to cause this calamity in the first place. His spells had conjured up these other beings and now the clan members were being lured away. Anyone could see how he felt towards the black female Sun child. They hoped he would be smitten by a Devil and his shadow never darken their doorways again.

Only Durrilau was mourning. With sad eyes he watched his half-brother pack his few belongings in a goat-bladder bag. 'Paal, I would come with you!'

Culvato put down his bag and his black eyes gazed into Blue Berry's troubled blue ones for a long time, without the usual look of scorn they held for the rest of humankind. 'You know it cannot be. I've told you before, you are the Chief Blue Berry when Violet Lynx Foot dies. You will be a good Chief and lead these people well.'

'I am Durrilau, paal of Culvato,' the boy said simply.

'Always. But now is the time for me to go and set you free to fly alone. It was to happen some day. We both knew that. Only now it is happening sooner. The people will listen to you better if I am gone from here.'

'I have our mother's blood in me as well!' the boy cried. 'Do you think I would like to stay here? If it were not for my crippled leg I would be gone too.' He slammed a fist into his palm in frustration. 'You're leaving me! Forget me then!'

'Kek tatcho,' the Gypsy murmured. 'Java kevi.'

'You have no home! You said so yourself.'

'Home is the road, little Berry. The dust is my blood, footprints in the sand my bones. The wind in the trees is my song and every creature, big or small, my family. Gods? I have none. Women? I shall have a thousand. But forget you, little brother? I would sooner forget the Devils that wait behind my shoulder to remind me I am only human.' He leaned close to the despondent boy. 'Your kakkaratchi manushi. Cams tu lati?'

The boy nodded sadly; not even his love for the lovely Magpie could dim the pain at his brother leaving.

'Then it is a lover's position to stay beside the one they love. Especially as one day they must love the whole clan as equally as they do each other.'

'Are you going away because of love also, my brother?'

'It might be said that this is so. But I cannot really say. All I know is that you must never forget me, little Berry, as I will never forget you. Wherever I am on the road there will always be a room in my heart that is just for you and me. Remember, if anyone should ever ask about me—if anyone should mock me—you say with pride in your heart "Kaulo ratti adrey leste".'

'He has Gypsy blood in him,' Durrilau repeated softly and looked up into his brother's eyes. 'This room is in my heart also and the door will never be closed to you.'

'You must look after Violet Lynx Foot as well. *He* is your family now,' Culvato said, then stood up abruptly. Giving his brother a brief, tight hug, he moved swiftly away.

He was as upset at leaving his brother as Berry was at losing him. Strange that all his life he had dreamed of moving on from the restrictions here and, now he was moving, his heart ached for familiar things and for his brother.

He went out to the sand dunes and tuned his guitar in readiness for the journey. Besides, music washed his sadness away.

70

CHAPTER FIVE

Listening to the faint sounds of the music she thinks of the first time she saw this youth they call Culvato and how afraid he was. Then she thinks of the first time she saw the other, who was not afraid when he stooped through the door and was greeted by the others in their hard, guttural, murmuring language so difficult to follow.

He wore a vest of filthy skins and had long, tangled, crimson hair—redder in the shuddering light of the central fire. His brown eyes were as smoky as the room. Yet there was a clearness and a sharpness way back in them as they swept over the three of them (Cudjo refused to leave his precious plane after what had happened last time) that alerted her that here was either an ally or a most dangerous enemy.

He was young—perhaps as young as her. Indeed, there were few old people amongst this gathering, she noticed. He was slim and poised like a wild jaguar she had once seen in the Southern Jungle Land. She will never forget its beauty, power and total ruthlessness. He conversed with her and Surrey Anne and Port Rial each in turn and she wished she could have followed the muttered conversation better.

The mound of smelly skins, flung haphazardly over sticks, that these peoples called a home, stank with the press of fearful bodies. She saw Surrey Anne wrinkling her nose and wondering to what barbaric place they have come. Perhaps these people are the same as the Boat Men, who come across the sea in canoes to trade. Their skin is the same burnt brown, yet their babies are as white as whale bones. Never has she seen such pale people, except perhaps in the Northlands. Even Porky was never so fair.

Their hair is wild and ungroomed and their bodies near naked except for the stinking furs they wrap around themselves. Their village, such as it is, is filthy and unhygienic. They surely must be the most miserable people in all the world.

Port Rial tells her in a whisper that their weaponry is non-existent, being swords and spears mostly. And they are made of plastic or wood—with shards of glass sometimes as a bonus! They are no threats to their guns and grenades or Cudjo Accompong's rocket-launcher. She knows that he is telling her this to show her that the taking of treasure from these people will be a simple task. He is one of the pirate Race that come from the village of his own name: Port

71

Royal. Although what treasures there could be in the possession of these primitive people she cannot think.

Yet, for all the green and blue beauty on their Island of Springs, she knows their History is one of mayhem and massive destruction—with the technology to cause it constantly at their fingertips and forever stressing their minds at the thought of the next violent war. It was the only way those like herself and Cudjo Accompong know how to survive. Perhaps the treasures to be found here are in the very simplicity of life. Certainly these dirty, dying people seem more at ease with the new life this planet has wrapped itself in. The youth all the others admire for his ability to talk to the moon which she knows is, after all, just another star is a good example of these uncomplicated people.

His eyes are calm and a similar brown to her own instead of the curious pale colours of his companions. It was only once so often that the predominant black or brown was replaced by another colour on their Island. Porky's eyes had been blue and her frizzy hair blonde but she had been an exception. His gestures are gentle. He is the first of all these pale people to realise that she and her companions might not be Gods.

There is another who knows of this. The dark-haired one whose skin is darker than the others and who seems to be an outsider to the dealings with the group. He who now plays a melody on his guitar, as he has played for her on several occasions. He is the close companion to the red-hair and the first one she met. She endures the ribald jokes of Port Rial, the giggling fits of Surrey Anne and the scowls of the giant Cudjo Accompong, but she sees the love in this boy's wild black eyes. It is fitting he should be her lover. Port Rial has Surrey Anne and the giant his weapons now that Saint Catherine is murdered. But she has had no one after The Baptist. She will choose the when and where for their love. Memories are still too painful for love to bloom yet, but friendship is a fair companion.

The other Ilkari are too terrified of the power of the four, as High Ones, to form close relationships, despite Cudjo's feats of great strength, Port Rial's winning smile and infectious laugh and the beauty of Surrey Anne, who truly is a glorious example of womanhood. Her large, soft, long-lashed eyes and curvaceous mouth, her well-endowed breasts and well-rounded thighs and her very vitality that crackles and flickers like a fierce fire of passion are all there to drive men mad. She is an earthy woman who loved her female powers and of whom, in her country, they would truly say 'She rhygin!', a word that meant someone was everything, from extremely passionate regarding sex to spirited in their anger, lively in their personality. A cyclone in human form, in fact.

She herself is heavily muscled and is more at home with her own company than that of others. Her name is Nanny and, like her namesake of centuries ago, she is a powerful leader and a member of the mighty Maroon People. Like her namesake also, she is believed to have magical powers.

Her beauty pales beside Surrey Anne, who is like the parish she is named after: Saint Anne, soft and green with gentle rolling hills.

She is like the jungles of the Blue Mountain. And there is beauty even in a jungle—a wild untamed beauty that inflames men's hearts.

Cudjo reminds her ominously not to get too friendly with these people; to remember what happened with the other pale people whom she trusted too much. Perhaps because they were from the same land as the copper-skinned Boat Men with whom they traded.

Forget? How can she forget? Porky was wooed by one of the white men and then there was the treacherous fight when her lover The Baptist was killed and Porky brutally raped as well. It is why they are untrusting of anyone, but especially white people.

'You think me don' know this, nuh? Cho, bwoy, you mem'ry short feh long. Baptist 'im me brother wife brother an me irie-maan!'

'I-man dey pon worry-worry,' the giant rumbles placatingly and ambles away.

It was sad to lose The Baptist before they had even begun the trip. He had been a boasie tallowah man, proud and conscientious. Also, his strong religious beliefs had kept the predominantly Ras Tafarian crew members in check.

It does not matter now. This hot land has claimed the lives of Porky and The Syrian as well. Too recently for the horror and savagery to be completely forgotten. Other lands have claimed the youthful dancer Clarendon Jon and the user of obeah, Saint Catherine, whose magic might have won her Cudjo's heart but could not save her own life. The bones of her friends—and family—are strewn all over this wide world. They had not realised how big it really was. There are those on their Island home who would never believe the adventures they have had or the sights they have seen. They have been welcomed by the Island cultures dotted all over the sea, often being treated as Gods. They have hunted in the quiet dark jungles of the Southlands where the jaguar's screech is often the only sound. They have watched a mountain explode in stupefying violence and seen the blood of the earth drip down the shattered mountain sides. Even they, with all their technology, must still concede the incredible power of nature. They have seen black people and red people, copper, brown and yellow people. Now they have seen truly pale people with eyes like the sky or like the green jungles of their home and with hair all shades of red, yellow or brown. They had seen as many deities as a huge book would hold.

But no one would believe them at home. They did not even believe the aeroplane would fly to the Southlands. Well, she has proven it. She has flown her band to the Southlands and to the Northlands, the land of sickness and duppi's (and The Baptist's death). And she has taken them beyond on a grand adventure. But she has not found the Lion of Zion, nor the land that was the Ras Tafarian homeland, heard about in the songs of centuries.

Yes, the bones of her people are scattered all over the known world, so making the world a part of themselves. But the two most handsome things she has ever seen is a jaguar, shadowed with its own camouflage and the leaves of a jungle tree, poised to spring in proud arrogance—and the youth they all call a Moon-talker, as gentle as the creature was dangerous.

They travelled across the plains for three days and two nights, followed by the biggest throng of Ilkari ever to be seen. Everyone wanted to be a part of *this* story.

People gathered in large groups around each Tribe's best storyteller as new legends were made up about these Ilkari who had been elevated to the state of Greater Mortals. This was the first time it was chronicled that children from all three deities—Sister Earth, Sister Sun and Father Moon—would travel together in company. Majestic would be the magic of this reunion and they would defeat the dreaded enemy that came with the night's shadows—and any other Devils they came across. People wanted to touch the five chosen Ilkari so some luck would rub off on them.

The songs and stories were many and varied. It was more like a festival than the beginning of the unknown. There were some amongst them, though, that had no heart for music, either instrumental or oral. Violet Lynx Foot for one just trudged along each day, watching the craggy rocks stretching towards the members of his clan like greedy grasping fingers. At night he would light a lonely fire away from the rest of the clan and sit at it with just his thoughts. He was fond of all the members of the clan but his heart held a special place for Ilgar, now known as Red Mond Star Light, and, more so, for the boy he had reared as his own. Now, almost before he had ever really got to know them, it seemed, they were being taken away. He would miss them all.

'Cousin-uncle, you seem sad,' came the soft voice from the shadows and he looked up at the shadowy figure of the Moon-talker.

'A tear wept is precious water wasted. Sacred water from our soul must not be wasted. I am sad, yes, but I shall weep only when you are truly gone.'

'So many of our people go—never to return. But cousin-uncle, I promise you this. We *shall* return, bringing with us a better life for everyone.'

'Perhaps. Who can tell if a tiger or a lamb rustles the bushes?' the Chief said tiredly and his blue eyes looked away into the night. 'What did the moon really tell you, cousin-nephew? Some people believe truly in only one God—Father Moon and the words he says. I believe more in fate and good luck. It is good luck that will save you from the hooves of a stampeding cattle herd, not the moon. This is what I believe.'

'It is Father Moon who tells me if the cattle will stampede.'

Violet Lynx Foot gave a small smile as his pale amused eyes met the young man's own sombre brown gaze. 'There will come a day when you will meet people who have never seen the moon. Indeed, they hate it and all the stars around it. How will you read your book to them, Moon-talker? What good will your magic be then, to those who don't believe in it? If they have never seen the moon, has the moon ever seen them and, if he hasn't, how can he tell you stories about them? How can he warn you of coming dangers if he does not know these people?' Violet Lynx Foot asked, then burst out laughing at the look on Red Mond's face. 'What! Do you think me a heretic? No, I only question the greatness of those we worship. And it should be so, or else we become lax and submissive, tossed here and there like weeds in a river's current until we grow so many we cut off that current and the river dies. We all die before our time. We need some fish to dart about, forever questing . . . forever eating those weeds to keep our river we all need safe and alive.' He placed a hand on his nephew's shoulder. 'You are a fish as well—you, and all who go with you. Go with care and the love of your family-clan.'

He let go of the young man's shoulder and turned his head away but not before Red Mond saw a silver tear trickle like a fish down the scarred cheek of his young Chief.

The Moon-talker moved slowly and thoughtfully away from the fire to the one he and Culvato shared. So many tears being shed. So much sacred water being spilled. He looked across at his young comrade. Who would live and who would die on their expedition?

He sat down and listened to the tune Culvato played softly on his guitar. After a while Joda joined in on the flute and Kareen strummed her harp so it was a beautiful sound. He moved into the small dome that was being drawn by four of Orange Horse's beasts on a type of platform the High Ones had rigged up, using four of their insect's feet to make it move smoothly over the ground.

The music drifted about S'shony and the Moon-talker while they quietly talked about what was to come. Then Red Mond Star Light made gentle love to the girl he adored while all around them Ilkari sang or told stories about the two of them. That was how he spent his last night in the known land. As he slept afterwards, S'shony stared at him with her huge black eyes, feeling him and gently probing his mind, then she surreptitiously passed a message into his mind so he would know where to go on her journey.

The next day arrived as any other ordinary day. The multitude gathered silently while Baba blessed the five from his clan in a small ceremony.

He cut five locks from Violet Lynx Foot's yellow hair and placed a lock each into their soul bag that hung from each one's neck by a piece of leather. These small bags contained items known only to the wearer, collected in their travels or during their life. It was said the very heart of the person resided in this bag and to reveal the contents to any other would be to lose that person's essence. Upon death, the bag would be buried with its owner and thus all their secrets—and their soul—were safe.

But this was an important occasion so everyone saw what went into the bags of the chosen five. Besides, no one expected to see them alive again. They were about to step off the edge of the world into the lands of the Devils where only the Keepers could walk in safety.

As well as the small pieces of their Chief's hair, Baba also poured a small quantity of the purple sand into each bag and a tiny pebble that had been carefully chosen on the journey across the plain. A black pebble for the warrior Akar Black Head, a strong powerful colour and a protective colour, being as it was the same as the cloak of Father Moon. That was what he must be now, a strong protector. A yellow pebble for the woman Kareen, perhaps in memory of her lover Yellow Eyes or for the colour of her tawny wild hair, but probably because yellow was the comforter's colour and an earth colour. She would be to the men Earth Mother and comforter, as well, of course, a warrior. A white pebble for the boy Joda, who was pure and innocent and as yet had no story to be told. Also, because white was a magical colour it would protect him in the coming adventure. The Moon-talker's stone was a lustrous blue with flecks of mica in it that was like moonlight shining on water. It was a glorious gift indeed and needed no explanation as to what it meant.

For Culvato, even though he had no soul bag, he too was embraced by Baba. His pebble, that he placed carefully in one of his many pockets, was an iron red with streaks of black through it.

So, even Baba knew of his secret love. For the message in *this* stone was clear—red was the colour of love and the black here, as well as being strength and protection, represented the woman he loved. Still he should have known there could be no secrets kept from one who knew the secrets of centuries.

Culvato smiled back. 'Thank you, Old One. May this story you tell me come true. It would be a story worth keeping if it does.'

'This little pebble is only part of the story, strange wanderer. Soon you will be walking on a sea of pebbles and the stories told of Culvato will be innumerable,' Baba murmured, then stepped back and addressed them all.

'There is nothing more to be said than "Go in peace and return to the banks of our beloved sacred river soon." Doubtless you will see many amazing sights and come across many different conceptions about life. But keep the memory of your clan close to your hearts and your beliefs a warm bed against the cold of scornful rejection. Sister Earth gives you a bed at night and Sister Sun gives you daylight to travel in. Father Moon watches over you all the time.'

With a wave of their hands they set out into the unknown. Nine humans, one cat and some twenty horses from the orange-haired second-cousin of the Moon-talker.

The powerful figure of Akar Black Head went first, then Kareen, slinking like an alert muscled feline with her lion-like mane of hair; off to the side. The boy, Joda, and Culvato led the two foremost horses on the vehicle used to pull the moon Goddess along. Two of the Visitors led the string of horses with their equipment on their backs and the giant and his leader came behind, eyes darting everywhere.

The Moon-talker stood for a long time, silhouetted against the stark blue sky, looking down at his people. Red Mond Star Light turned and trudged after his small caravan. He was the chosen leader of this expedition and yet he really only understood Kareen, who was his cousin, and S'shony, with whom he was falling in love. Love, he had been told and had read in the sky many times, can cloud a man's emotion. He thought he knew Culvato but no one could say they really knew that wild youth.

His thoughts were interrupted by a heavy hand on his shoulder.

'The leader of our quest should not be swallowing the dust of his faithful followers,' Akar Black Head spoke, a glint in the back of his eyes that could have been humour or his usual anger.

'I was thinking out the route our Goddess told us of last night,' Red Mond Star Light replied.

'Yes. I saw you go into her cocoon but the sounds I heard were not those of religious conversation. So where does this moonbeam take us today, little cousin-brother?'

Red Mond Star Light sensed the suspicion still there. 'We must follow Sister Sun's course into her resting place until we come to a great river. Then we shall know when we arrive at our place of battle.' The Moon-talker smiled up at his clansman. He was optimistic and joyful, as were Kareen, who waved to him in friendly fashion as she prowled past, and Joda, who had a gentle smile on his face as he led his horse and stroked the glossy black fur of his constant companion.

Akar Black Head gave him a penetrating stare, then shrugged his powerful shoulders. 'Aah, well, I am only a warrior. I know nothing of these "gods",' he spat. 'A lot of use they were to us anyway, weren't they, when trouble really came our way. It was the High Ones who caused all the trouble in the beginning and now we have the company of *five* of them! What sort of trouble are they planning for us *now*? Akar Black Head shall watch out for it and stop it when it comes. I am a true child of the earth and must watch over you who live so high in the sky you might as well be a part of it.'

Then he stumped off back to Kareen. At least she was a warrior like himself.

The land they passed through was barren indeed. There were no trees to speak of. In fact, there was no vegetation at all. Only hard, sharp, orange, red or deep purple towers of rock that seemed scattered in some vast torment, granite fingers reaching up pleadingly to the merciless sun. It seemed as if some great calamity had befallen Sister Earth here for there was not a square bit of ground that was not cracked open in gaping jagged gaps. The rocks seemed torn from the very bowels of Sister Earth to spew upwards in tortured shapes. Not only had every drop of life-giving water been squeezed from this inhospitable place but also any resemblance of dirt was gone so the rocky ground was bare and burning hot. The only relief was from the ever-moving shadows of the rock pillars that reared upwards towards the bland blue land of Sister Sun. She was the true Goddess here.

The Goddess, who was only a human, shuffled along beside her giant companion, black eyes always on the alert.

She comes from a land as green and full of trees and waterways as this land is barren and dead. An Island called The Island of Springs, where the sound of water cascading down the mountains can be heard any day and the sight of great, sluggish, brown rivers is there for everyone. The waters carry the rich red soil down to the coastal plains, so there are fields of sugar-cane, or pineapples, or groves of bananas, mangoes, and many more types of fruit. All along the white, clear beaches, coconut palms sway like dancers welcoming visitors to their home. And all around the Island the blue-green sea breathes, its breath coming out as slow, rolling waves as the ocean's roar and crash is a gentle sound of peaceful sleeping.

Everywhere there is greenery: deep, dark green, rippling, pale green, lime green, lemon green, apple green. There is the verdant contours of the unmanageable jungle in the highest mountains and the vast yellow-green of the savannah and coastal plains. She is from the Cockpit County where the vegetation is a rich mixture of jungle and fruit trees.

Such fruit! Her people have never known hunger. There has always been an abundance of food from a vast array of vegetables to the many trees such as mango, paw paw, breadfruit, otaheite apple, the star apple, guava and sweetsops. Then, of course, the all-important ackee that was an ingredient in almost every Island dish.

Such trees. The national tree is the Mahoe, with a height of sixty feet and a flower that turns from yellow to red. The giant Ceiba whose trunk can be up to fifty feet around and was used by the original people for making canoes. Then there are the Guango or Rain Tree, the Spanish Elm, Casuarina, West Indian Cedar, Rosewood, Ebony, Red Bullet, Fiddlewood, Satinwood, and the very rare Mahogany: all wonderful names that brought clear and explicit memories into her head. Wonderful, whispering, moaning trees full of colour and elegant form. The flowering trees like the Indian Banyan, Tulip Tree, Annatto, Golden Shower, Jacaranda, Poinciana, Tamarind and Mountain Pride with their splashes of pink, white, yellow, purple and red.

Interspersed among the trees, climbing all over them, twisting around their branches or about their roots are many types of vines. The giant pea vine known as 'Cacoon', that grows beside the river banks and rests there like the alligators with pods over three feet long and a single plant covering an acre, is the biggest.

There are over five hundred species of ferns, so their pale, feathery fronds are seen everywhere, peeping from rocks or crevices or small hollows of the coldest mountains or bursting upwards in proud, arrogant array like the giant Tree Ferns of the John Crow Mountains. There are three hundred types of moss, so even the rocks are green and the many types of fungi add splashes of colour even to that strata of greenery.

Of course, the whole Island is not a jungle. On the limestone plateau there is even a type of desert where Cactus and Prickly Pear and Yucca abound. But even their desert is a paradise compared to this empty, sun-whipped terrain because they have two rainy seasons a year in their part of the world

The Island of Springs, that they left only a year ago, is constantly caressed by trade winds, setting its trees to sing in murmuring whispers and its flowers to nod in peaceful contemplation. Sometimes a 'Norther' might blow in, blustery and cold from the land mass up north of the Islands where the copper-skinned men came to trade in their giant canoes. This wind is the only one to mar the good weather but there is another wind to be wary of. It is one that blows in from the sea along the southern coast during the day and then out from the interior at night, bringing a big drop in temperature. Even though the wind in the daytime is called 'Doctor Wind', because it cools everyone down and freshens up a hottish day, it is the one at night that everyone calls 'the Undertaker' for it can bring colds and death-dealing pneumonia. Surrey Anne should know of this for her whole family were touched by the Undertaker's cold and icy breath, bringing to them all one last memory from the untameable wild Blue Mountain and the tangled jungles thereon, before death carried them away.

Port Rial complains about looking after the horses and leading the unknown woman's curious carriage. For mortal woman she must be, as none from the Island believe in outlandish deities from out of this world. He would rather be scouting around this country looking for treasures. It is a tradition for him. He comes from a long line of buccaneers whose sole purpose in life is to steal or to make a living as a smuggler of sugar, rum, ganja, fish or any of the other many commodities the Island has to offer.

She sees the one they call Culvato talking animatedly to Surrey Anne and—what is this? Is this a pang of jealousy she feels that she cannot be close to the youth with the enchanting black eyes? But there is a time for romance and now is not right as they march into unknown territory. She is the leader of her crew, the pilot that enticed them all away from their homeland. It is her responsibility to look after them.

The one she knows is the true leader has had a falling out with the large hairy man who stalks, alone with his thoughts, out in front with the tall woman. The Moon-talker's eyes are cloudy as though smoke is in front of his face—just like the first time she saw him. His incredible red hair (for she has never seen hair that colour) is neater in the plaits made by the woman, who must have been his mother. He looks more personable with his hair away from his face.

She wonders why she is so attracted to him. Had he some sort of obeah as they say Saint Catherine had? With her sensuous, mesmerising movements *and glittering black eyes and pink tongue flickering in and out of her mouth, she could bewitch any man with her sweet words and captivating laugh.*

He seems to wander aimlessly and yet there is a purpose in his walk. Every now and then he will go over to the carriage and appear to converse with the woman there. She wonders what sort of woman she can be who hates the sun so. Perhaps she is an albino like Porky. Although that young woman had not been a true albino but only an Islander with some of the white blood of her ancestors who had been on the Island before the Island's first great war and the overthrow of the imperialist rule those hundreds of years ago thrown back into her genes.

But what she wonders about most of all is when will he lead them out of this pitiless land, where not even a bird casts a shadow? Where there is not even an insect!

Back home there are perhaps a hundred types of butterflies alone—known on the Island as bats. The real bats—of which there are twenty varieties—are called rat-bats. She has some idea they are going to fight some giant type of rat-bat who has been killing the people. Well, they have their guns and grenades and the rocket-launcher. On the way they will find some petrol and then they will go home.

The silence here is as it must be like in death. Where, it is said, there is nothing but a great white emptiness, either blinding and terrible in its whiteness or gentle and soothing. And the last coherent thought one has is that you must endure this light for eternity, having no longer any eyes to close or head to turn away. Just a fierce bright light and no sound at all, if you were headed for Hell. That would surely drive anyone insane!

Surrey Anne teases Port Rial that there are some elegant rocks for his treasures. Not even this mean countryside, so different from her own civilised County, can sizzle away her sense of humour.

Cudjo Accompong, as usual, is silent and alert. His long wild dreadlocks hang right down his back to his knees and swing lazily around his scowling face. He has been named after two famous Maroon warriors—brothers—as well but he is more of a Ras Tafarian than a Maroon. Also Accompong means the Supreme Being in the Twi dialect. So it is a glorious name to go with a powerful man.

It is he now who lends his voice to the hot still air in a song from their Island by one of their most highly respected minstrels of old, Robert Nesta Marley.

Life is one big road with lots of signs
so when you riding thru the ruts
Don't complicate your mind.
Flee from hate, mischief and jealousy
Don't bury your thoughts
Put you vision to reality, yeah!

She looks up into the sun—this cursed sun that is their constant companion.

This sun these primitives worship with a reverence and fear not seen amongst any of the Nations she has come across. This sun they seem to think she and the others have come from to tread the earth as Supreme Beings. This hard orange ball that glows with the whiteness she fears after death. The sun that sails across blue skies imperiously—forever.

The same sun was observed by other eyes almost as dark as the Island woman's.

About thirty miles from where the small group struggled across the dry purple rocks a huge corroboree was coming to a close. Ten thousand Keepers of the Trees from all over the land had gathered for this special ceremony. Message sticks had gone out everywhere summoning the people to this place. There were members of the Lizard Totem, Kangaroo Totem, Emu, Cockatoo and Crow Totem and all the other Totems. Some were never seen or heard of, even by their own people, until such a time as this. Like members of the small remote Butterfly, Quokka and Bandicoot Totems, who had shown up and camped on the edge of this immense corroboree.

For the Keepers of the Trees these were the most important times of their existence. It was the time to gather and get the news from different parts of the Nation so they could see what parts needed healing. It was a time for alliances to be made or strengthened. Laws would be restrengthened also in secret meetings of the old people. Law breakers would be brought to justice and initiation and marriage ceremonies would be performed.

The only thing the Keepers kept from the white people's world was a collection of games and these were played in friendly rivalry, Totem against Totem. There was a game played with a possum-skin ball that proved most popular with its marking and kicking prowess. There were the more familiar games of skill with the spear or boomerang.

But, most of all, this corroboree was for their combined energies that kept the land pure and whole and safe from harm for another five years.

As usual there were songs and stories of the Creation of the earth and the creatures upon it, retold to the youngsters who had not heard them yet.

There was a reason why every animal was like it was, or bird, or flower, or contour of the land. The Creators were Julunggul; Ingaruko; Waugal, who lived in the waterways; Baiami; Darralulun, who now lived in the sky; Nurunderi, the huge powerful man who created the mighty river once known as the Murray and the lakes around its mouth and all the fish therein; Witana, who created the mountains in the southern part of this land once known as the Flinders; Nagacork, the gentle wanderer who loved and created all things then went up into the sky where the smoke from his fire was the great swathe of stars across the roof of the keeper's world. . . . And so the names went on. They had made every being from the earth and some of these beings had turned into parts of the earth. So the earth and the Keepers of the Trees were truly one and the same in spirit and soul.

What did it matter if these mountains and rivers, lakes and valleys, red dusty deserts and grassy plains held white man's names (if any were remembered now)? It was the white man's desire to establish some prestige that made him touch with a finger a million years of history, then claim it as his own. But there was no harm done. The Keepers of the Trees knew who the real rulers of this land were.

The Rainbow Serpent crept from waterhole to waterhole and the Wandjina kept each secret place, each birthing place sacred. The woman, Katunga, gave birth to children who then turned into egg-shaped stones. It was from these stones the Yalunga or spirit children were born, even today, so there would always be spirits in this magic land. Every Keeper of the Trees was born a spirit child. This was the one belief they could all agree on, even though every Totem had its own story of how it was created and, for some, its own Creator as well. There had been seven-hundred-odd different Tribes in the old days and thousands of language groups, so there were bound to be different stories. But nowadays they lived together in relative peace and harmony—their duty the well-being of the land.

The twins, Mungart and Weerluk, listened to the stories with avid interest and amusement. For part of the skill of a good storyteller was to make a story humorous and then leave the message to be chewed over by the listener as he lay thinking at night.

The story of Tjitty-tjitty and Kaarlmoot came from the tall timber country, Mungart and Weerluk's own territory. Each one thought he was the better hunter and this caused trouble. At last, the old men said for them to hunt in their own areas, which was quite all right, for the south-west Tribes lived in one of the richest places of this land as far as food went. But still Tjitty-tjitty brought back more food than Kaarlmoot, because he knew that hunting was not a contest but merely a means of survival. Also, which is correct, he offered thanks to the Korrndon Marma Man who was the south-west people's Creator—along with Waugal who made all the waterways in that fertile land.

At last, the jealous Kaarlmoot challenged Tjitty-tjitty to a fight to see who was the best warrior. A fight to the death! Kaarlmoot had first throw of the customary three spears but Tjitty-tjitty teased and tormented him so much that he became angry and missed every time. Then it was the turn of Tjitty-tjitty who pierced the breast of his one-time friend with his first spear.

Saddened by this he rushed to the side of his dying comrade and called upon his mabarn powers to heal him. He called out that his friend's greed and pursuit of glory was no reason for him to die. That he had learnt his lesson. However, even though Kaarlmoot was healed, the blood stains remained on his chest to remind others of what happened to foolish people who let arrogance and jealousy get in the way of good friendship. A new Totem of the Fan-Tail People was born that day, as well. Kaarlmoot, the Robin Redbreast.

Doubtless there were stories told about the wattlebird too, with warm roan coloured eyes and cheery song and the splash of chestnut to brighten up a dullish brown coat. But Mungart and Weerluk had their own wattlebird and her story was enough for them.

Dongkarak was very popular among the gathering, for she was kind of heart and good natured, as well as being as good looking as some of the women like Pirili, or the sun daughters of Bara, who were now stars. She had a way with children and was surrounded by them every day as she collected food or water with the other women of the Totem.

Kwila's three other brothers and their families had come to the corroboree as well. The four old men joined the other elders in the extremely sacred ceremonies and important discussions held away from the rest of the gathering. It was left to their sons to prepare their grandsons, or even great-grandsons, for the memorable initiation ceremonies they would be lucky enough to attend.

It was the job of the women and the younger single men, who had already passed their initiation, to gather the meat and seeds for each individual family. Even though there were many people here, everything went according to plan as if it was only a small camp. It was the only time the animals of the white man were allowed to be butchered and eaten so everyone enjoyed the taste of beef, pork, mutton, goat or even horse and camel.

Different Totems met and exchanged news and stories. Old friends were reunited. All across this vast land stretched intricate trade paths that connected the whole country. It was not unusual for, say, a Quokka man from the far-off place of huge white trees in the distant south-west of the land, to know a Pelican man from the balmy, palm-studded islands of the far north-east. So past companions on the trading trail caught up with each other for a laugh and a yarn.

Young men roamed in Totem groups seeking the attentions of young women who also wandered in groups, under the protective eye of an aunt or grandmother. Just like old Mother Emu and her covey of twittering chicks. But, occasionally, a young couple who fancied one another could creep off—even among this mass of humanity.

There was dancing and feasting every night and, during the day, those not involved in hunting or courtship joined in the games of sport or chance that were played everywhere; or gathered in groups for intellectual discussions on how the country was surviving. Women took the chance to teach the young girls women's business while young boys disappeared daily from the campfires in the company of an uncle or initiated older brother. And, of course, trading went on all over the campsite.

The family of Kwila had camped in a sandy hollow on the outer circles of the corroboree for they were only a small family of the Parrot Totem. In this Totem all the women were named after birds, the older men anything to do with water, the younger anything to do with the earth and their sons would be named after the sky and everything in it.

It was intricate and highly complex but was put in place to make sure there were no wrong marriages. At the end of the Old Time, there had been many Keepers who did not know who their family were or what Tribe they came from. The various Totems had devised ways of making sure this never happened again. The old women of each family were the custodians and were the only ones who could recite back to three generations each member's genealogy. So there could be no mistake of brother marrying sister or even cousin marrying cousin.

It was known amongst the other Totems of the south-west that the Parrot Totem and all its assorted families were strongly influenced by their women and the females had as much say in council as the oldest man in most things. Their initiation ceremony was different as well—but this was the case in most Totems. For the Parrot Totem the final acceptance from boyhood to manhood was when their ears were pierced as the old men sang the sacred parrot song and they had ear-rings of the red yellow and black beads inserted, so they could hear and understand the wisdom of the land. Then they had the right to speak in any council and the right to marry and so expand the family.

The family of Kwila was of the Kawar, or Purple-Crowned Lorikeet People, and numbered sixty-eight souls. They were not as small a family as the Heron People, who numbered only forty, or the Numbat Totem, only fifteen in all. But some of the other families ran into hundreds and came from Totems bearing over a thousand spirits. Like the Kangaroo Totem or even the proud and haughty Swan People.

The Kawar had been blessed with many sons from the five old grandfathers and they had had many sons, some of whom were away with their uncles now. Kwila, as leader by age of the five brothers, had no surviving sons. Two had been taken by Djanaks and, in the last attack, his beloved wife Yuwintj was taken as well. He only had his daughter left now and Djanaks had taken her husband five years before. Perhaps to compensate for such bad luck her only sons were twins which meant great blessing for the family.

So the whole family had protected them from birth and long had been the arguments between the uncles as to which of them would be favoured with teaching the two the law, the sacred songs and ceremonies of the family. Finally it had been Nolka, a powerful and cunning hunter, who had taken the boys out into their family land of the Kawar and up into the rocks where their secret paintings were. Everyone agreed he was the best of the uncles to teach the boys all they needed to know. Then their Uncles Kwoola, Billah and Kwila had been their guardians as well. So the twins grew up, not only fine hunters and wise in the ways of the Kawar but also as great storytellers and painters. For the brothers Kwoola and Billah were known throughout the south-west for these skills. As to dancing in the corroboree there was none better than Kwila, who leapt like the porpoise he was named after, so high it seemed at times he took flight. When it came time for their ear-piercing they too leapt and sprang from the red dust of strange lands. The whole Nation of all the Totems saw them and knew them, so the names of Weerluk and Mungart were known all over the land and they really were lucky—as was all their family.

Now, for the first time in several gatherings, another Kawar was to take his place among the newly made men. Yabini, the only surviving great-grandson of Mumboyet, the youngest of the grandfathers, had been away with his uncles being taught the final religious laws that would make him into a complete man.

Rain dances were performed to ensure that rain would fall in the places it still did and rituals were done to ensure plenty of game and food for the Keepers of the Trees. Incantations were murmured to keep the families safe from the various Devils that roamed the land, like the soulless ghosts they were. Not least amongst these, of course, were the Djanaks who would erupt from the earth like some stunted white monsters and take away babies or the unwary adult. The little evil white creatures seemed to hold a special hatred towards the Keepers of the Trees and this was reciprocated in full.

The People of the Caves were much feared by the wandering Keepers because there was not a single family in a single Totem who had not felt their sting in the dark of the night. Many had been the child, young girl or strong man who had been carried, screaming and shouting, back into the earth from whence the white shadows came.

But today was a happy day. Last week had been the most important rite of the corroboree when two thousand newly initiated youths had danced the dance of Manhood.

Every Totem had a different form of initiation: some had their ears pierced, others their noses, while still others were given intricate tattoos or sacred scars and still others had their front tooth knocked out. But every one of the boys was given some gift with the special colours woven in them—red for their earth and their blood spilled upon it, yellow from the Mother Sun who gave them life and fire to keep alive, and black for the colour of the people. Some, like Yabini, had ear-rings: others had bracelets, armbands, headbands of individual design, ankle chains, necklaces or even cleverly designed cloaks. When they all gathered for their dance of celebration the whole was a bright swathe of colour and the noise of their stamping feet and chanting voices was like the thunder of the greatest storm. The dust their pounding feet kicked up rose like a huge red cloud over the camp until a light breeze high up in the air gradually dispersed it. Just as the people would soon disperse and go their separate ways for yet another five years.

Dongkarak's beauty and good humour had bedazzled a member of the Platypus Totem from the south-east of the country. Her mother approved because the Platypus People had the same way of naming as the Kawar family, so was suited for betrothals.

The boy was named Twiuga, which in his language meant 'falling star', and he had become good friends with Yabini during the recent ceremonies together, for he, too, was a new man. Yabini in the south-west language meant 'stars' and the close similarity in each name made the two almost blood brothers.

The mother, Koobeaku, invited the mother and father of Twiuga to her camp when her daughter's intentions became known. Not only were the Parrot women more outspoken than others, they also could choose whom they wished as a husband.

With the boy's parents came his guardian uncle and his older sister. The father's name was Pemul, which meant earth, and he was a taciturn man, given to long silences. The fat, happy mother was called Muraong, the grand and wise emu. The uncle, who was not much older than the twins and had a great shock of curly hair and a small goatee beard he was proud of, was called Arakui, after a nut of a tree that grew in his homeland.

The sister's name was Gurrewe which meant white cockatoo but she was also known as Waratah, the pretty red flower that grew all over her country. She was pretty too, with her big shy eyes and coy smile, her long slender legs and lithe smooth body. Dongkarak, who was shorter and stockier but no less beautiful, had caught Twiuga like a fish in a trap, so this falling star fell from the sky to listen to a wattlebird sing, as Weerluk joked. Now the sister's deep dark eyes and crescent lips and swinging, pert hips and buttocks had stolen away Mungart.

The next day Weerluk pulled on his brother's long plaited locks playfully. 'Who would want to marry you, you ugly old snake? You can't even catch enough food for yourself but must come to my fire begging for food,' he laughed.

'Only because I spend my days thinking up easy dances simple enough for you to learn, you clumsy green frog.'

Then they had wrestled on the ground beside the waterhole where the women of the two families were. Weerluk let his twin win and toss him in the water beside their laughing sister who good naturedly scolded them for getting it dirty. He watched his brother unconsciously flex his muscles and saw Gurrewe hide her eyes behind long lashes and smile secretly.

He felt a pang that no more would they be as close as they were;

that another would come into their tight little world where, until now, there had been only themselves.

She *did* like the tall strong young man with the ochre-smeared locks, for he had decorated his hair in orange-coloured ochre for her pleasure. The scar across his forehead added interest to an already intriguing face with its alert dark eyes and wide, smiling mouth. He was a famous dancer, she knew, and last night he had shown his skill as a master storyteller, keeping everyone spellbound as he weaved a tale about the wildcat, the emu, the possum, the ringneck parrot and the magpie. It was a wonderful story full of love, jealousy and fighting. Of course, it also explained why each creature in the story appeared as they do nowadays. Whenever he took on the part of the grumpy wildcat, his shy and misused wife, the emu, the cheeky gigolo possum, the indignant parrots and the wise magpies, the character seemed to waver in the air in front of him for all to see. Such a storyteller he was!

Then her Uncle Arakui had repaid the hospitality by telling the tale of Yurumu, the wedge-tail eagle and his wife Narina and friend Kilpuruna. This had as a moral the warning of taking another man's wife. For this is just what happened. When Yurumu discovered this he tricked Kilpuruna into climbing a tree for sweet wild honey. Then the jealous Yurumu pushed him so he fell to the ground. Flattened by his fall he turned into the blanket lizard, forever in danger from the wedge-tail eagle whose wife he had seduced. Narina turned into a white cockatoo who flew from branch to branch, mournfully calling out for her lover.

'Just goes to show you cannot trust any women,' Weerluk the joker laughed.

'Only our mother, the sun,' piped in Yabini, anxious to show his knowledge of all things manly.

'Some say the sun is the cooking fires of a cruel woman who ate many brave warriors until Kudru and Muda killed her,' Twiuga joined in.

'They did not kill her. Only wounded her so badly she turned into a ball of fire and ran away, taking the light with her,' Arakui gently corrected.

'But it was the boomerang of the mighty lizard man Kudru who brought the light back so it travels across the sky,' Twiuga said, to show he *did* know the story.

'Others tell it differently,' Muraong replied, 'and say she is Wuriupranala, the sister of Purukupali, who was the first man in the world.'

'The sun is the sun,' Koobeaku murmured. 'It keeps away our enemies, the Djanaks, and its golden rain helps the plants to grow or kills them, depending on her mood.'

'It is true, though, that the lizard and gecko cannot be harmed by the people of the southern plains for it was they who made night and day.'

'The night is nearly made now,' Weerluk said, glancing at his smitten brother who sat with a dreamy smile on his face. 'And it is the time for all things of the night to come awake.'

Then he laughed and laughed at Mungart's embarrassment. Never had he seen his brother so much in love. He was like a parrot who had eaten too many sweet flowers and was stunned by the heavy, sweet nectar.

Pemul, who had not spoken all night, now coughed politely and wiped the sheep grease off his hands onto his possum-skin cloak. He stared, not unkindly, across at Mungart on the other side of the fire.

'A story I remember is true for it comes from our part of the country and it serves to remind us always to be on the alert for danger,' he began in his soft voice. 'Never let our fears or hurt make us forget there is danger for us everywhere. For this is what happened to the wonga pigeon when her mate went missing from camp. Well, she waited and waited but he did not return so she went in search of him. Now the wonga pigeon lives in thick woodland much like it seems your people do, so there is plenty of cover from their enemies. But in her grief the wonga pigeon forgot all but her missing husband, so she flew above the trees to see if she could see him. Just then she heard him call out in the forest below, and heart pounding with joy, she swooped to greet him. Too late! Their enemy the hawk had spun down out of the sun's glare and ripped her breast open. She escaped and hid amongst the flowers of the waratah and the hawk flew away. Yet again she heard her husband calling for her and, even though near death, she flew from waratah to waratah, resting on each flower to gather her strength. Every time she rested on a flower her blood stained the petals until, at last, she died. You know, the waratah flower used to be white but now they are mostly red, although, once in a while, you'll find a white flower. All red, from the blood of the poor lonely wonga pigeon who died alone without her husband.'

It was not as good as Mungart's tale of fiery passion and fierce fighting and Pemul was a softly spoken, shy man. But after the telling the whole camp was quiet. The older man looked up with sad eyes. 'This is the story of the wonga pigeon and the white waratah. But it is the story of Gurrewe too. It is why we call her Waratah.'

He would say no more, but gazed deep into the flickering fire. If Mungart wished to find out more about the story and its meaning he would have to ask Gurrewe, and if she told him then they would marry for the whole story was her secret one and only for her to give to a deserving man.

The sun had sunk into the eastern horizon, leaving behind a gentle peaceful aura as night came down. The night birds began their soundless flights across the vast camp as people settled down to sleep. The night animals came awake and there was much soft scurrying amongst the leaves of the trees and the sand upon the plain.

In the campsite of the Kawar People and their guests, the Platypus People, things fell naturally into order. The older women and the girls went to one side of the muted fire and the men to the other. They slept in their age groups tonight, for everyone sensed it might be a night for love. It was the woman's right in these two families to choose their own partner and tonight they were given free choice to do so by the older ones. Muraong and Koobeaku slept on the outskirts while the two girls slept nearer the fire. The older or married men in their turn also slept on the outer perimeter of the camp while Mungart and Twiuga slept near the fire and their women.

Some time during the night Mungart saw the shadowy form of his sister rise from the dust, as quiet as dust, and a soft whistle broke through the murmuring of the night. Then Twiuga crept forwards and, holding hands, they vanished into the gloom of the huge rock, whose shadow even in the day kept the white sunlight at bay. Mungart heard the suppressed giggles of his twin who slept a little way from him and wondered how many other dark eyes had observed the fledgling love affair.

Then Gurrewe also left her place and his heart soared as he watched her come towards him. But when he reached out a hand to touch her breast she gently pushed it away.

'Tonight let us just lie together. There are many things we must know about each other. There will be many other nights for us, my beautiful flower.'

'Mardingu,' he murmured in his language. 'I can wait for our love. We shall be happy together, I know, and just looking at you gives me great joy.'

So saying, he let his eyes run over her face, taking in her serene radiance, her strong nose and jaw line and wide mouth. Her large solemn eyes observed him just as closely. Suddenly she reached out a dainty finger and traced the line of his cruel jagged scar.

'Djanaks,' he whispered in explanation.

She sighed.

'That story my father told tonight for a reason. It was for me he told that story because I had told him already of my desire for you. After all,' she smiled, 'part of this corroboree is meeting partners. I had a man before but the Djanaks got him as well, one night. Now, for the last two years, I have been flying from flower to flower, staining them red in my sadness and forever hearing the calls of my lost husband. It is why they call me Waratah.'

His callused fingers reached out and brushed back her hair. 'There is sadness all over this land. But we are still alive. There can still be happiness if we search for it.'

She smiled then and she snuggled closer. They lay there feeling each other's body warmth heat them beneath their cloaks in the cold desert night air. They listened to the other breathe and smelt each other's body scents. Over in the darkness of the rock they heard Dongkarak give out a little cry of pleasure and they smiled at each other in the dark. The youngsters' abandoned passion seemed to bring the other two, more genteel in their love, closer. Just as did the wholeness of the life they led. The huge sky above them, the huge land all around them and stories of Creation everywhere. Their people had made this land, and the children of Mungart and Gurrewe's children would carry on the laws and traditions of this ancient culture in the same way.

Everything was right in their world.

But beneath the earth the sensitive ears of the People of the Caves had sensed the vibrations of the many dancing feet and their minds had probed outwards to feel the vast army of humanity above them. From their dank and twisting tunnels they had crept, gibbering in delight. For such a feast was not often to be had by the inhabitants of this part of the country. The land above offered few people as offerings and consequently many of those on their first sonaflite had to content themselves with the horrid flesh of a kangaroo or lost goat.

They were the poorest of the cave people but now luck had finally come their way. Now was their chance to taste sweet human meat and tear the skin off quivering bodies to make a proper pair of wings. What is more, their mind probes told them these ghosts were the despised ones called Keepers and great would be their delight in destroying more of the hated black people.

The leaders of these groups gathered all who were allowed to go into the Upside lands of the Devils. They snuffled and sniffed with ecstasy and pressed upon one another in their anxiety to dig upwards towards the softly vibrating ground. Their priests muttered incantations to keep the monsters from them and Beacons checked swords and clubs. The women chattered excitedly about this adventure for, except on their first sonaflite, most females were discouraged from going Upside. Those cave people who were just eighteen stones were awed into silence, yet honoured at this momentous raid for their wings. They did not use the chimneys and all the ceremony they contained because this was a unique occasion.

It was thought there were some ten thousand bodies up there, obviously gathered to worship that Devil of Devils—the bright eye in the sky. Soon they would be amongst them and the killing would begin.

And so they crept upwards, squirming their way slowly up through the loose sand of the desert. There were perhaps two thousand of them; white soft skin, hard black eyes and the scent of raw red meat in their nostrils.

Twiuga looked up with bright eyes at the face of Dongkarak as she bent over him. The light from the fading fire lit up her taunt small breasts and flat brown stomach. The stars shone down with the same peaceful light that was in her eyes. She murmured in contented joy as they made slow, satisfied love once more.

Over on the other side of the fire Arakui stirred and came awake. He sat up on his elbow and looked around the quiet camp. A movement at the side of his eye caused him to turn his head and he saw Pemul up on his feet, scanning the area. These were Platypus men, from the cold and towering mountains that edged their rambling way all down the east coast. It was a place of immense danger and sudden death. It was why there were so few Platypus People around. But the ones that were alive were so because they were hardy and always alert. Especially they believed and followed devoutly the sixth sense they had honed into a sharpness of survival.

The sixth sense both men felt now.

Twiuga also should have had this sixth sense, despite his young age. But he was, even now, closing his eyes in delighted pleasure as Dongkarak moved in the time-honoured love dance on top of him, tossing her head back to the distant stars so they, too, could share in this wonderful experience.

Neither saw the crumbling of the particles of sand as pale fingers pushed their way gently upwards to meet with the hated outside in a handshake of death.

Pemul glanced down at his brother, Arakui. In the distance a loud coo-ee was cut off in mid-call and in the other direction there was a confused babble of shouting.

Then the ground all about them erupted in a maelstrom of bodies and shrieking faces, hideous in their whiteness. One of the figures burst from the earth directly under the fire so the glowing embers scattered in the air like a new constellation, while the figure staggered blindly about clutching its eyes.

Pemul's spear finished it off and then he grabbed up his heavy wooden club and charged into the yelping melee, all quietness gone in his rage. His brother closed with several others while Weerluk kicked a woman Djanak in the stomach just as she was about to pounce on him. Koobeaku grabbed up a glowing firestick and, waving it in front of the little monsters' faces, screaming abuse as only a distressed mother can, she charged for the place where she knew her youngest child was.

She was too late! Dongkarak had been pulled off her lover by hungry hands and was being dragged, squealing, across the red dirt by her long curly hair and her arms. Already they were trying to tear her to pieces but her kicking legs kept them at bay. The boy Twiuga lay broken and bloody, a wicked stone knife having sliced his throat as his killer had risen silently beside him.

Mungart had sprung to his feet but his weapons were too far away. His love had blinded him to the constant trouble that slithered under this land. Besides, he had thought they would be safe here in this huge crowd of people. His strong hands flung away a bounding figure, breaking its neck and he grunted in pain as a stone knife slashed across his stomach. He could hear the cries of others of his family—his uncles, aunts and cousins. But the cry he heeded most was the cry of his sister and his mother's lamentations.

'Look out, ngooni. They are taking Dongkarak! Quick, to her side!' he yelled at Weerluk who, agile as a leaping kangaroo, sprang away from a swinging club and thrust his spear into his attacker's throat.

Yabini, dashing sleep from his eyes, sprang forwards, then stopped in shock at the sight of his mangled blood-brother. A figure, larger than most and almost certainly a Beacon, rose from the earth behind him and, as he turned, smashed his legs to a pulp with a single blow of his mighty club. As the boy fell, a javelin intended for his young back thudded into Arakui's powerful shoulder instead, sending him staggering.

Koobeaku was set upon by three female Djanaks and, at first, in her grief, she was unprepared for them. But then her rage and misery erupted into a violence and all four fell in a kicking, gouging, biting heap. They were joined by the mild Muraong maddened at the death of her son right at the beginning of his journey into manhood.

Weerluk ran towards the rock where his sister's screams were becoming frantic. Mungart was now in a quandary, He could not go to his sister's aid with no one to guard Gurrewe. Pemul was standing by his wounded brother's side, fighting with a fierceness only Platypus People could show, but he was heavily outnumbered. Mungart made his decision, much as it hurt him.

'Stay beside me! Keep watch for the Djanaks coming at my back,' he called to Gurrewe.

She fought like a Demon, possessed with abhorrence for these small, white, evil creatures with their cold, black, empty eyes.

He heard and felt with a twin's uncanny ability, the cry of anguish from his brother Weerluk as he watched his struggling sister disappear into the hot red earth. Her last smothered cry was for him to get her and her fear-glazed eyes beseeched him to save her, before her head disappeared beneath the earth.

Then another wave of enemy were upon them and Mungart had no time for anything but to fight for survival. He saw the warriors Pemul and Arakui covered in a seething mass of naked white bodies. He heard the woman of his desire call out a savage war-cry and the sound of snapping bones.

He felt the warm touch of her hand on his sweating, shaking shoulder, to remind him she was there as she always would be. He turned to face her for a moment. A few short moments ago it had been their knowledge of love—now it was knowing they could survive together in the midst of death that brought a faint smile to their faces.

'Mardong Yorga,' he breathed.

And then her head disappeared in a blur of blood and splintered bone as a huge club crashed into her face. He was covered in her spurting blood—a gruesome ochre indeed as her twitching body slid to the ground. Even as she did he could not touch her—not even in a last farewell—for eager hands beneath the ground dragged her downwards on her final cruel journey.

He could not speak.

He did not register the sudden disappearance of the Djanaks—it happened as quickly as they had come. A crowd of Koolbardi People from his own country and some Euro People from the forgotten middle of the land had bounded over to them from their own large fires when they had heard the commotion. A salvo of spears and boomerangs had decimated many of the attackers. The rest of the Djanaks, sensing that this part of the camp was too strong for them, had faded away.

He looked around at the carnage that remained. He heard moans and cries and people sobbing. But he still could not comprehend the full horror. He looked around for Gurrewe, the woman he had only known for two nights but had decided to know for the rest of his life. On the ground at his feet and all over his trembling, shocked body, her blood lay—the last waratah she would ever stain. But he still could not understand that she was gone. It was not possible. He would come out of this daze in a moment to awaken in her soft arms and her soft snoring. And it would only be a terrible dream.

'Mardong yorga,' he breathed again, but like the wonga pigeon's fretful call it went unanswered.

There was a keening in his ears that broke through his own personal pain. It emanated from his brother as he stumbled over to him.

'I couldn't reach her. I tried to grab hold of her. She was begging me to with her eyes. I touched her hand—and then she was gone,' Weerluk the joker cried. He would never laugh again, he promised bitterly.

The twins clung to each other, weak from wounds and grief. The Magpie and Euro men gathered around to stand guard over the small devastated camp of the Kawar People. Fires were built up to keep the Djanaks away. They also showed the extent of the damage done.

Arakui lay where he had fallen—still alive but in a bad way. Koobeaku was covered in bites and tears and was very weak—but also alive. Yabini groaned in mewing agony upon the ground, legs shattered beyond repair. But Twiuga lay dead beside him and the two girls had been taken underground. Only now, in the shockwaves of the aftermath, did they realise that quiet Pemul and gentle Muraong had gone the way of their daughter. Arakui was the last member of his family left alive. Others of the twins' family had been taken but no loss would hurt so much as that of their darling baby sister.

They looked around at this secret and magic place that now was tainted with death and evil. Never in living memory had they been attacked during the sacred ceremonies. There were those who wondered silently if the land was not turning against them. What had they done wrong that so many of their people should die right at the 'hallowed corroboree'? For some two hundred people were taken this horrible night. Some Totems were almost decimated. The larger clans had been able to defend themselves. It was the smaller Totems on the outskirts that were most badly hit, including the Quokka Totem who now numbered only nine and the Kawar who had lost some twenty people.

Book Two

Travelling

CHAPTER SIX

When the elders on the mountain heard the bad news they hurried down to see if their people were all right.

Kwila was inconsolable at the loss of his grand-daughter, Dongkarak. All the brothers were in mourning because the Kawar Totem had chosen an evil place to camp. The other Totems on either side were hardly touched. There would be an acrimonious meeting soon to decide who or what was to blame for this bad luck. But right now was the time to cry for the dead and comfort the living.

But there was no comfort for the twins. The blood of Gurrewe had soaked into the ground and her young life would only be a memory now, held deep in the heart of a sad-eyed youth. He who bore yet another wicked scar across his flat, strong chest also bore a scar across his heart. His brother Weerluk was fierce in his grief at losing their young sister in such a cruel and sordid way. He had restless nightmares not even his mother could soothe with soft song and relaxing herbs. He blamed himself for her death, thinking if only he had been faster he could have saved her.

After a week of daylight mourning and anxious nights when the whole camp was on guard, the old men of the family gathered under the ancient rock to have a meeting. Mungart, as a man, was allowed there too but his eyes were listless and sunken. The wound on his chest was healing— but slowly, despite the medicines the women had given him. There were those at the meeting who knew he had given up the gift of life and was now just waiting to die. This was partly why the meeting had been called. They were too few to allow one of their best men to let go of life.

But before they had really begun to speak their mind a wild figure burst into their circle. He was covered in intricate patterns of red, yellow and white ochre and his bushy hair was dusted with rare blue clay and a top-knot of red-tailed, black cockatoo feathers burnt in the unrelenting glare of the sun—a burnished hot red to match the heat in the youth's angry eyes.

'The Kawar's revenge shall be long and sweet,' Weerluk cried, and such was the change from the chuckling prankster who always had a smile for everyone, that the elders were shocked into silence. 'My brother and I have lost a bird. A bird who sang so sweet and whose feathers were of the most colourful hue.' He looked down at Mungart, whose eyes were still glazed in shock. 'My brother has also lost his heart,' he said softly. Then, speaking loudly again. 'The only way to find it is to kill as many Djanaks as we can. With every one we kill so shall we regain a part of ourselves. This my brother and I will swear to do until we must die.'

He reached down and yanked Mungart to his feet. His smouldering eyes flickered at his brother's dazed stupefied eyes. Then he slapped him viciously across the face.

'Wake up, brother-mine! It is time to use your sadness as a weapon. Never forget the woman you loved as I will never forget our sister. She came to me in a dream last night and told me what to do.' He slapped his brother again. 'They have eaten her now. Her skin flutters from some Djanak's shoulders and her hair decorates some Djanak's belt while her flesh has been devoured and her gnawed bones growing white in the underground world—just as has happened to your dear Gurrewe. We must kill every Djanak we meet without mercy so the very thought of the twins of Kawar will turn them cold in fear. Only that way can the women be whole in our minds again.'

'Then we must go into the lands of the unloved ones,' Mungart murmured, 'for that is where the Djanaks most love to be.'

There were utterings of discontent now. The lands of the unloved ones was rarely trodden by the Keepers of the Trees. They were just as fanatic as the Djanaks in their hatred of the dark people. Indeed, many said the unloved ones were the ghosts of the Djanaks, doomed to walk forever in the shape of men and feel men's pain and the burning sun they detested so upon their skins for all time. Besides, near the lands of the unloved ones lay the Silver City and not one Keeper had gone through those gates and returned.

'You cannot go,' Kwila ordered. 'You are the last of our young men. The best and also the luckiest. With you gone the Kawar will die and be no more.'

'There are better ways to free our land of this danger. Violence has never really been our way,' moderate Billah reasoned. 'We are the Keepers of the Trees . . . the peacemakers. Let the white man spill blood on this land. For we are but the caretakers of the spirits.'

But Nolka stood up and stared at his nephews with proud, dark-brown eyes—yet they were troubled as well.

'No brothers . . . uncles. Our nephews are men now and have seen their share of misery. Perhaps there *is* a way to destroy these monsters who have taken so many of us. Perhaps it is an omen that the twins of Kwila have both suffered a close loss. Like two parrots they will fly across the land and their shadows will be black upon the ground. Soft and silent will be their journey until a song of death is all the Djanaks will hear.'

98

Nolka was the greatest warrior the family had ever had and many were the songs and dances performed about him . . . many were the stories told all through the south-west. Besides, he had been the twins' guardian uncle and taught them all the laws of the Totem Kawar. He was believed to be a mabarn man as well, so there was not a lot of discussion after his speech. All those around the fire knew he spoke the truth. What else could a man do but go and look for payback from their traditional enemy for the murder of their loved ones?

The departure of Mungart and Weerluk was a hurried affair. It was not a joyous departure such as a man might make with his new wife or a trader might make on his travels. So there was no feasting or singing. The old men performed a very special ceremony for the two youths to make them strong for their journey. Certain rituals had to be observed and advice given in private. Then their mother passed over a bag of herbal medicine to Mungart that would be needed on their arduous trek. She embraced them silently, knowing she would probably never see them again.

Mungart, sensing her pain, briefly laid a hand on her shoulder while his troubled eyes stared into hers. 'This ochre I wore in my hair in honour of this ceremony I shall wear in memory of you, nangan. So you will always remember Mungart nyinak gulang yago. I will wear it until I see you again.'

Then Weerluk, his eyes still burning with his new-found, inner rage, grabbed his brother's arm and they both walked away; out of the camp, out of the Kawar families' lives—and into the folklore of this small Tribe's songs and stories.

They had only gone a short way when a coo-ee pulled them up. It was Arakui, still badly injured, who waited for them in a small grove of trees. The older man smiled faintly at them and came forward shyly. 'I, too, am on my way back home. I am the last of the Platypus Totem. So I give my brothers of the Kawar a gift from the Platypus. He, too, can go on your journey of revenge.'

He took from under his possum-skin cloak a heavy wooden club. It was shaped in a rough L shape, the smaller arm being honed to a vicious point. It had been made from a single root and was very hefty indeed.

'It is my brother, Pemul's,' he said simply, giving it to Weerluk. 'Go revenge him, my brothers,' he murmured and faded back into the trees.

For many days they walked across the plain and into the lands surrounding the unloved ones' territories. They met up with no one—neither unloved ones nor Djanaks. There were not even animals to be found and it took all their skill and bush-lore to find a decent meal a day. A few nuts and roots, some larvae, an occasional wild melon and—one glorious day—a rare wild orange tree where they rested under the shade of the dark-green leaves and gorged themselves on the sweet, yellow, juicy fruit and drank from the sweet cool water of the spring that nurtured this tree. It was one of the few times the brothers smiled as they rested there. But mostly they went hungry, except for the hatred that fed their souls.

Mungart's wound was healed now, just another scar on his battle-hardened body. A light had crept back into his eyes—a dull and smouldering light. A bleak black rage shone from his brother's hard face. They were not a pair to be trifled with. They were restless for war and, whenever they knew there was going to be a night with no moon, they would sleep all day and prowl around all night in search of Djanaks.

But not a soul did they see—neither spirit nor human. So their anger was unassuaged and grew and grew. Until one day, at last, they came upon some humans.

The scenery of burnt-out rocks and flat red dirt began to change as several lean, dry trees appeared, dotted on the landscape and the occasional scrubby patch of stunted yellow grass. A few times they even spotted kangaroos and killed one once for some much desired meat. Their sharp eyes picked out the tracks of other smaller animals or reptiles. They were approaching the hills that bordered the lands of the unloved ones but they had no fear. This is what they wanted, after all, for where the unloved ones dwelt, then so too did the Djanaks.

Perhaps it was their eagerness to do battle or their gnawing hunger that clouded their judgement that day. For, instead of following the trade route around a range of hills known to harbour evil spirits, they decided to cut right through the middle. After all, Weerluk told his reluctant brother, the spirits only came out at night and if they trod softly they would not wake them up. The more cautious Mungart would have preferred the time-worn track but was persuaded to go into the forbidden hills.

The hills were not huge, being only about five hundred feet high. They were covered in small trees that were extremely prickly. But there were birds everywhere and their songs brightened up a journey that so far had been repressive in its silence.

As the two of them moved further into the encircling arms of the hills, the shadows grew deep and black and menacing all around them. Even the mighty sun could not defeat the awesome shadows and, once more, a cold silence fell upon the land, broken only by the thin piping of some bird that echoed around the two wary travellers. The rocks were iron red and deep purple with slashes of white granite through them. Where the two brothers had found themselves, the hills were at their tallest. They towered above the twins, cutting out the sky. There was the amplified drip of water into a pool hidden somewhere among the rocks that sounded to Mungart like the deadly beat of some spirit's heart.

'Water! See how wise it was to come this way!' Weerluk said.

'Brother, are you a fool?' Mungart asked. 'This water is for the spirits of these hills. We should not even touch it, never mind drink it or take some with us.'

'I don't care about spirits. I am a dead man anyway, living only until the Djanaks kill me. From now on the laws of my ancestors do not mean a thing to me. I am already dead and walk with the ghosts of my ancestors.'

Mungart was shocked at this statement from his brother even though he himself had, only a short two or three weeks ago, willed himself to death. But now the desire for vengeance made him want to stay alive.

They made their way through the narrow gorges following the eerie sound of the constant dripping of the hidden water. Then they came out into a wide valley that was truly paradise. There were huge, pale ghost gums with their pale green leaves a pleasant contrast to their white trunks. Luscious green grass grew as high as a man. There was no sense of danger in this place, just a murmuring from amongst the verdant vegetation and a whispering from the trees. Up against the scarred red cliff face a waterhole of some width reflected the trees and rocks in its still, blue-green surface. Well . . . , not quite still, for every few seconds another drop of water would plop from where a spring oozed out of a rock, that thrust its moss-encrusted, slime-covered body out of the cliff face, some twelve feet above the pool.

Dotted amongst the slowly moving grass were purple and white flowers and by the waterhole's edge there were pink and white water lilies.

'Beautiful,' breathed Weerluk. And, for a moment, the anger was washed from his eyes. He had been the more poetic of the two and had always enjoyed the flashes of loveliness his country was constantly showing him. He knelt down and peered into the blue-green depths of the deep water. Such a deep and serene colour, it seemed to mesmerise him. Then he saw the orange plaits and troubled eyes of Mungart reflected over his bushy head.

'So is the body of the tiger snake a beautiful pattern. But that does not stop its poison from killing us,' Mungart muttered.

'You're an old woman! Why don't you go and dig up some roots as an old woman does and leave the planning to the man around here,' Weerluk sneered.

It was very rare for these two to fight but when they did argue they made sure each got his say in. Mungart gave a snort of displeasure and spun around.

'While you dream here like a young girl with no sense in her head, I will go in search of a kangaroo or emu since it is clear that, against *all* that you know is right, you intend staying here!'

'What evil spirits could live in a place like this?' Weerluk reasoned, but his brother had already departed, fuming, through the long grass.

Along the edge of the cliff where the spring-fed waterhole overflowed, the ghost gums gave way to giant lantana with their pungent leaves and brilliant, though odourless, flowers. Some of these were over one hundred feet high, having grown unchecked for some three thousand years. Dotted among them, Mungart was pleased to see, were groves of banana, paw-paw, guava or avocado trees. Now Mungart could see that all along the cliff face, water trickled like blood from the rocks. So the atmosphere was constantly humid and had formed a type of rainforest in the middle of this arid land. Some time, years ago, a wandering family not afraid of, or else unknowledgable about, the spirits who abounded here, had settled and sown a crop of exotic plants. Now the family were long dead or departed but the trees had remained as their testament and still bore fruit or sprouted new seedlings. The result was a wild turmoil of fruit-bearing trees that, because of the fear this place held, had not been harvested in many a year.

Mungart could not believe his luck. It was not often his people, coming from the cooler south-west lands, had a chance to taste the tropical fruit taken for granted by the Tribes up north. His worry left him—as did his anger at his brother—and he eagerly began searching around for fruit that was ripe, his black eyes bright with anticipation of the look on his brother's face when he returned.

He did not see or sense other black eyes that watched him with a bleak hatred.

The owner of these eyes came originally from a line of performers that had been in a circus before the High Ones had walked upon the earth. Afterwards the people not dead had dispersed. But the last to do so had set the animals free. His ancestors had roamed the land for three thousand years, a compact family group, sometimes as many as thirty, sometimes as few as six. He was the last one left now.

His female companion had fallen victim to a trap the villagers in the south had set some twelve years ago. He could not forget her but mankind had harassed and tormented him for so long now that all he could remember was the hate he held for these vicious beings. He was not to know that they feared him as much as he hated them and had even named him after a God. He had come to this valley to get away from them. But now it seemed they were even to follow him here. He quivered in rage.

Mungart, in the act of plucking down some bananas, caught a slight movement from the side of his eye. Kangaroo, he thought. Meat would go well with fruit and the brothers could enjoy a good feast. Maybe even a hungi which they had enjoyed with their northern countrymen when they had visited there once. He dropped to the ground, gathered up his spear in one movement and threw it with unerring accuracy towards the huge lantana where the movement had occurred.

He ran forwards towards the place, then stopped dead in his tracks, his face going yellow with fear. The hair on the back of his neck went stiff, while he went cold all over.

With a fearsome, squealing roar, a huge monster with flapping ears and a long snake where his nose should have been burst from the undergrowth, charging towards him—grey and craggy like one of the rocks come alive. Mungart's spear had grazed his leg but done little more than add another scar to his abused old body and anger him into a spine-tingling, killing, attack.

The giant old bull elephant, known upon the Purple Plains by the Ilkari with fear and reverence as Loki, bore down upon the Keeper of the Trees.

For a vital second Mungart froze as the monster—the evil spirit he had known all along to be here—came to collect him and take him away. Then reason cleared his numbed brain and he turned on his heel and leapt away, mere feet in front of the roaring, screaming, thundering nightmare and the long, gleaming white spear that hung out of his mouth, threatening to skewer him at any moment on its point.

Weerluk had been watching a stray shaft of sunlight bouncing patterns off the water on to the wall and forming a kind of rainbow (another uncommon sight these hot, dry days). He watched small insects slide in and out of the light and for the first time in ages was at peace with the world.

Then he sensed his twin's fear and confusion. He heard the distant roaring and heard the noise of the pursuit as saplings were snapped in half and bushes mangled. He took up Pemul's club and his two heaviest fighting boomerangs and turned to face the sound. So, his brother had been right and they had awoken the wrath of the hill spirits.

Mungart exploded from the long grass and the trees, eyes wild in terror and his body a shimmering layer of dripping sweat. Right behind came the apparition, not to be imagined even in Weerluk's worst nightmare. Still, he held his ground and hurled both his boomerangs with deadly force at the attacker of his brother. One—his best one made of a hardened mallee root—snapped in half on impact and drifted away over the wrinkled grey shoulder. The other glanced off the forehead and did absolutely nothing to halt the charge.

Weerluk's mouth dropped open. Then he snatched up Arakui's war club and crouched in readiness for battle. Djanaks or spirits of any kind. He would fight them all. Still, he would have preferred Djanaks to this horror.

But as Mungart sped past Weerluk he gave his brother a shove that sent him sprawling backwards into the water. Perhaps, Mungart's brain raced, the thing can't swim. In any case if we split up then one of us might survive and it is really me the monster wants.

However the shove put Mungart off balance and he stumbled to his knees. He rolled along the ground and almost got to his feet again, before stumbling onto his face. He heard his brother give a cry of despair and knew he was going to die in the next few seconds.

Maybe it was because where there had been one enemy there were suddenly two, or the diversion of Weerluk being thrown in the water and then the cry of pain as Weerluk foresaw his brother's death, but for a few precious seconds the monolith hesitated in his charge.

And then the better part of his face disappeared as there was another roar from over by some ghost gums. The elephant half reared up from the force of the blow. Then, already dead, it toppled over with a crash into the grass that, unperturbed by all this violence, still wavered softly in the breeze.

As Mungart rose shakily to his feet in the booming silence that followed the mayhem, three figures drifted from the shadows of the trees. Weerluk scrambled from the water and raced to his brother's side, steadying him. He clutched the war club of Arakui in his hand and tensed at these strangers' approach. Although someone who could destroy such a monster so easily would have little trouble getting rid of *them*.

They were not dressed in the skins of animals like the Ilkari or in the rags of the unloved ones. Nor did they resemble anyone from the Silver City who sometimes could be glimpsed as the gates of that strange place were opened briefly. The material, if material it was in which they were clad, almost shone luminously in the shadows of the cliffs—as it was said the cave mushrooms shone. One was a woman, the other two were men as Weerluk could tell by their beards. All had plaits but the huge man had the longest, going down past his hips. Everything except their suits was black: their hair, their beards, their eyes and their skin. Being so black they could only be spirits, he thought. The giant spirit held a round cylindrical-shaped type of stick, made from some sort of metal. Blue smoke drifted lazily out of it and there was an acrid smell about the instrument that neither he nor his brother had smelt before. The other male spirit was excited at the death of the monster and had even now run forward to examine it while the female spirit observed them both with calculating yet calm eyes.

The two strangers are afraid of them—she can tell. Just as she was afraid the first time she saw the pale men of the Northlands, the cruel sterile lands. But, she reminds herself, it was men of a different, browner hue in the greener, cleaner Southlands who had treacherously murdered the dancing Saint Catherine. No one is to be trusted she now believes—as does Cudjo most vehemently.

Cudjo Accompong asks the two if they are all right. They are twins, having the same finely featured faces with dark intelligent eyes and wide mouths made sullen by some recent sadness.

They move away in fear at the big man and he laughs out loud. 'Coo'pon I. Me still be God, nuh.' He laughs at Port Rial. 'Is lucky we got he power of Zion. Jah! One love, bredrin.'

'I-man be him God fe thieves,' Port Rial sings out.

She has never seen any Keepers of the Trees before, although on the journey she has listened to the stories the Ilkari tell of their neighbours. If what they say is true then these wandering nomads could tell them where some petrol is—as petrol there must be in this vast continent.

They are a slender though well-muscled people, as agile as some of the deer she has seen in other lands. They are more a deep brown than a true black. They wear kangaroo-skin cloaks and little else. On various parts of their body bright yellow, black and red ornaments shine with brilliant pride.

She holds out a hand but they shrink from her. They talk to each other in a gentle murmuring language and then the one with the bushy hair steps forward tentatively to touch the metal of the rocket-launcher but pulls it back quickly, obviously burnt by the heat that generates from it. Cudjo Accompong tries not to laugh.

There is more discussion between the two.

Then there is a cry of delight as Port Rial finds the one remaining tusk of the elephant is not destroyed. This is what he really wanted. Sometimes the thin, intense, young man wouldn't care who lived or died, just so long as he could get his treasure. He is a true buccaneer and, indeed, had to leave the Island of Springs for a while, because his activities were getting too prosperous and damaging certain officials of the Kingston government. Like most of his kind he lived by his wits and by his knowledge of how to get certain goods. A buccaneer had few friends and his closest companion was his sharp mind. Always ready for an opportunity to make easy money, most buccaneers were selfish and aloof.

God of the thieves indeed! she smiles to herself.

This whole meeting is a piece of luck, really. The four Visitors, sick of the hot red lands, had spied the hills some days ago. Where they came from, hills meant streams of gushing water and vegetation where fruit and bird life abounded. Their food supplies had been running low anyway and not even Surrey Anne's clever cooking with left-over food had been enough to sustain them.

An argument developed between Akar Black Head and the boy Joda when the warrior decided to kill one of the horses. Port Rial, too, expressed anger at the possible loss of a horse on which to carry his treasure. She had to use her diplomacy to avoid a violent incident, for the pirate, although good natured most of the time, has a fiery temper. She knows the cynical warrior has no belief in High Ones and would not hesitate to attack the slightly built pirate who has more cunning than brawn. She was grateful for the calm words of the red-headed one, Red Mond Star Light, and the woman Kareen also had some power over the sullen Akar Black Head. Such glorious names for a people so poor. But they are a proud people too, clinging with stubborn belief to their legends and way of life. She knows better, her land being on the earthly highway and so having access to other lands' technology. But this continent of the golden clouds and red sun and purple barren lands is so far away from the rest of *the world's affairs that they should be allowed their own beliefs and hopefully be left alone in their uneasy peace.*

But these two youths before her come from a people even older than the Ilkari Race. She can feel the power emanating from them, gracious yet unbreakable and purely magic—as far as her concept of magic goes. They are what Porky would have called obeah men but they were certainly not the Bongo men of the Convince cult with their crude ceremonies including necrophilia, blood sacrifice and violent trances. She has only to look into their eyes to know the magic they possess is from within—and is also tied with an invisible umbilical cord to the pulsating womb of the earth their ancestors have walked upon forever. With absolute certainty both they and the land are the same and they carry their land's aura with them; so even in this parched, inhospitable, stony desert there is life and an overbearing beauty.

'Which Totem are you from, brother? Do you come from the Islands out of the sea?' Mungart asked Cudjo Accompong shyly, for he realised these people were human. After all, his Race had lived with spirits always, so he could tell the difference between human and ghost. Their friends, the Ilkari, had some strange rituals indeed. But they were white and this curious trio were black and so one of the true people.

'They are human, Weerluk. Feel the warmth of their hands,' he said to his uneasy brother, and touched the woman's hand still held out in friendship.

'I have felt the warmth of their strange spear and like it not at all. I remember the stories told after the Dreamtime in the Old Time about how hundreds of our people died from invisible spears. The white men who came then were friendly and we welcomed them as brothers, just as you do now to these strange black people,' Weerluk muttered back and his eyes, as hard as pebbles, glowered at the female spirit—as he still thought her to be—with dislike and suspicion.

'They have killed the monster and saved my life which would have ended before our journey had even begun. I'll be their friend—spirits or not,' Mungart stubbornly argued.

Port Rial now came to their side and smilingly handed them some meat, dripping with blood. It was part of the liver of the elephant. 'Eat! Eat Rasta maan. De strength a de elephaant will be yours,' he grinned at Mungart.

'Come! We mus' a go and fetch de others. 'Im baas worry-worry now,' Nanny said. 'Unu take what we need fe meat, then I an' I leave.'

'Wha' aboot de fruit?' the pirate called.

'Red-headed baas, him might stay fe while, nuh?' Nanny said. 'So me can rest me weary feet. Coo'yah food, water, shade. No enemy no dey.'

'Raas! Him talk a moon and we carryin' de Goddess me never yet see!' Cudjo snorted. 'What sort of baas him is? Baas, me batti! Him bungo-rial, me seh!'

'Him country, bredrin. We only Visitors, me seh.'

'Well, me tell unu! Me wish I-man back home. Dis whole trip one huge mistake, girl.'

'We shall see—at de end of it!' she murmured.

'Seh yu du,' the giant grumbled and turned away to start walking back up the hill.

From the trees Port Rial had led a team of five horses and even now was carving out huge squares of meat from the side of the butchered animal with a wickedly gleaming machete he always wore strapped to his side. On one back pack he carefully loaded his tusk and several large squares of the softer skin.

'Do you see, Mungart? They wear the white man's clothes and use his tools and his animals. They are *not* our people and are not to be trusted,' Weerluk stormed.

'But the "elephaant" he nice,' Mungart mimicked and laughed as he chewed on his piece of the liver. Weerluk had thrown his to the dirt. Then Mungart gently punched his brother playfully on the shoulder—something he had not done in many a day. 'We will see, brother,' he said quietly. 'Come on, we can always leave if we don't like what we see. But we need to make new weapons. You only have the club of Arakui and it is best to be in company than naked on the plains with no weapon.'

'It is true that we want to kill Djanaks,' Weerluk conceded. 'Not be killed by them. We will go with these spirits. Perhaps they will give us one of their weapons!'

So they followed the three dark strangers at a discreet distance as they made their way up to the top of the hill. Port Rial, happy with his find, sang his favourite song, 'Babylon System'.

We refuse to be
what you wanted us to be
we are what we are
That's the way it's going to be.
You can't educate I
for no equal opportunity.
Talking about my freedom
People freedom and liberty.
Yeah, we've been trodding on
the winepress much too long . . .

Mungart looked towards Weerluk, smiling. They too had their songs and dances.

Another surprise met them at the strangers' camp. A small group of Ilkari with another of the black strangers—another female. When the two Keepers saw their Chief come forward they only had eyes for him.

His hair had been combed out and braided and his face looked older while his eyes also seemed older—wiser and full of troubled or deep thoughts. But they recognised him as being the one they had helped bury his comrades after the Djanaks had killed them; as the one their sister, now killed by the same Race, had fed kangaroo meat he, Weerluk, had just killed. Afterwards old Kwila had remarked that a tree had brushed that one's mother as she lay sleeping and he had the shadow of that branch in his soul. Their sister had remarked she would have liked to be a leaf on that branch to tickle his stomach as he lay sleeping and they had all enjoyed a good laugh.

Even Weerluk could not mistake the significance of this meeting and he relaxed at last.

They all four squatted down in the red dust—Red Mond Star Light, Nanny, Weerluk and Mungart—while Cudjo stood behind Nanny, as tall and impassive as one of the rock towers that broke the monotony of this place. Port Rial went over to Surrey Anne to give her the good news of the food they had found. The other Ilkari kept at a distance, respecting the Keepers' habit of staying away from all things white unless necessity prevailed. Besides, it was known amongst the clan of Violet Lynx Foot that their Moon-talker was often a guest of the Keepers.

In a mixture of the lilting creole of the Visitors, the Ilkari's accent and the Keepers' soft language, the story was told. Red Mond was impressed by the mighty power of the giant's weapon and was convinced now they *were* High Ones. It was well known that when they first walked on earth whole cities the size of the entire Ilkari Nation had been blown away with a breath. So he knew that if there were any evil spirits about, the High Ones would puff them away as casually as swatting a fly. He was also pleased to hear about the food and water waiting for them—and the shade.

Crossing the rocky, empty badlands had been an arduous journey for them all and now they knew why few people from other places found their way to the Ilkari lands. It was impossible to cross that country unless, like the Keepers of the Trees, you had the knowledge of the waterholes. But the one who suffered the most of all was his beloved S'shony, couped up all day in her stifling dome. Even though her eyes had been protected by the dark, her body had been affected by the heat. The skins and rocks had saved her agony a little but she had gone almost mad with the slow pain, and her body was covered in sores, some as big as Red Mond's hand. If it had not been Red Mond's kindness washing over her like cool cave pools she *would* have gone insane. It did not help that the drowsiness and unpleasantness of the beginnings of a pregnancy brought on visited her in this unhappy time. The only good thing had been the strengthening of her love for the red-headed youth who was as distressed as she at her pain.

But now he could bathe her in cold water and keep her in the shade until she was healed. He knew, from instinct and having read the sky, that the worst part of the heat was now over.

The time they spent at the waterhole was to be one of the most peaceful interludes of the whole journey and would be remembered long after they had left its shady sanctuary.

This was a time of recuperation and the forming of friendships for the long and unknown road ahead. Amongst the towering lantana and numerous fruit and gum trees, beside the silent blue-green waterhole, lovers came together and a bond was welded between the different peoples.

Surrey Anne and Port Rial are teasing each other again. They are young and life is new and alive for both of them. Nanny sees them, even now, slipping off into the lantana and, though later Surrey Anne will say with a giggle that they had gone off looking for fruit, she knows that a bashful Port Rial had gone to gather another thing. They, Porky and Clarendon Jon, were the children of the crew and she feels a special something for the two survivors. She is happy they are staying in this fertile valley for a while. It reminds her a little of back home on the Blue Mountain and she wants, very much, to think of home.

One night, after smoking some of Port Rial's sacred ganja and lying in a blissful dream by the waterhole, she is joined by Cudjo Accompong. For a moment she is tempted to drift into his powerful arms. Ever since his woman Saint Catherine died, she has sensed his loneliness. But, in time, she remembers she is a warrior and must be alert, for she is also the leader of their remaining party. She cannot allow love or lust to cloud her mind and bury her senses in vaporous thoughts. She cannot risk losing the rest of her companions. That is how their journey began, when Porky was raped and The Baptist was killed because someone fell in love with someone else and all caution was left to die in the hot sun.

But the black sombre eyes of the Traveller Culvato torment her with their longing. She, too, longs for romance again. But she must wait until the time is right.

The first night in this place of peace the Visitors brought out their drums and pipes. Joda, Culvato and Kareen found their instruments. They had a celebration for discovering this place in the midst of all the purple desolation. Only the two Keepers kept back from the firelight, watching everything cautiously. Akar Black Head also stood to one side and watched with distrustful eyes. But Kareen, putting aside her harp, danced past and, grabbing him laughingly, dragged him into the circle to dance with her.

Joda grinned inanely at everything. Port Rial had given him one of the High Ones' special sticks that made them breathe smoke. Now he too felt like a God. The colours were brighter and the sounds were clearer while every question he had ever asked suddenly became known and he walked above the trees with the cool white stars. Now he knew without a doubt that these marvellous black beings came from the sun. He glanced at Culvato, furiously strumming one of his people's fierce tunes, and knew he must tell him tomorrow. For they had discussed often whether these four were immortal or not.

The Gypsy Flamenco, the Jamaican Reggae and the gentle trilling of Joda's flute seemed strangely to gather together into an enjoyable tune that filtered through the skins and pleased Red Mond's and S'shony's ears. That day he had gone into the jungle paradise and found some native bushes whose leaves, sap and roots, his mother had taught him, were a tonic for the kisses of Melanoma. So he had mixed up a batch and spent the afternoon soothing her sore skin and jaded mind with gentle hands and soft Ilkari songs.

When he had gone out for some more cool water Culvato, leaning against the cocoon—which is what they all called it now—grinned at his concern.

'If every word this Goddess spoke turned into a star, cous-cous, then the whole sky would be alight,' he said, then whispered, with a cheeky look in his eye, 'If every moan she made was but a drop of water we would all be drowned by now.'

'She is sick and who are you—listening to the voice of a moon child's prophecies?' Red Mond said, trying to hide his embarrassment in indignation.

'I am your guardian, paal,' the thin dark youth smiled, then bursting into laughter, ambled away on one of his solitary journeys.

Now the two lovers lay side by side amongst the furs and skins given to her as gifts from his clan. His brown fingers caressed her white—almost luminous—body and they spoke of the things he had done that day. So S'shony became little more a part of his diverse world. That day, through a crack in the skin door, an incredible blue butterfly had wandered. She had been completely entranced by this fluttering vision of the world she could not see and spoke to him excitedly about it. From now on, her name for him would be this new word—Butterfly—and she would hold him to her as close as she did that memory. At first she had used him to gather an army that would destroy the King of the Bats. Now she knew she really cared for him and longed to share her life with this kind, courteous Ilkari.

But Red Mond wondered, and not for the first time since setting off across that awful dry wasteland, if he had done the right thing. This was all new to him—and the other Ilkari. They were going to where none of their Race had gone before.

Perhaps S'shony might have put his fears at rest if she could have looked into his worried mind, by gently soothing his thoughts with images of her own, as he soothed her body with his magic medicine. But her mind was in turmoil at the pain her body had gone through and the changes the pregnancy was effecting and it was all she could do to cast her smile at the man she loved while his eyes roamed inwards in some Moon-talker's dream.

They stayed by the waterhole for two weeks, as though sensing that this would be the last place of harmony for them before they continued their arduous journey. Besides, for the Ilkari, any watering place was sacred and this place seemed more so. Never had they seen so green a place, so they worshipped it with all their heart and soul. Almost every day Kareen's big rump could be seen swinging through the strands of grass on her way to some secret women's ceremony.

For the four Visitors it was as though they were home again on their wild, windswept Island, so many of the trees here were familiar. It was a welcome respite from the hot red deserts where they had landed. Port Rial, as usual, searched around for any treasures, sometimes with the restless Culvato who was the only one anxious to travel onwards.

But they found nothing, apart from some bones high up in a cave on top of the cliff and they agreed to tell no one about *those*. Also in the cave Port Rial found a collection of rose-coloured crystals hanging from the roof. His eager fingers plucked them from their sanctuary. In the way of treasure this land had yielded very little—in fact, nothing at all across the arid red deserts. But now he sensed they were moving into more fertile regions as he joyfully took the crystals. He would make the smaller ones into ear-rings and a necklace for his Surrey Anne and wouldn't she look fantastic, the blood-red, pink and purple rocks upon her naked black skin! Culvato looked on with troubled eyes and thought how dangerous it was to rob a dead person's grave. Trouble would be sure to follow, his Gypsy mind told him.

The only ones not happy about staying here were the twins, who made their camp apart from the rest, as custom decreed, and hunted their own food. They spent the time making new weapons and studying their rescuers. They, like Culvato, couldn't wait to leave. They would rather go on the hunt for Djanaks. Besides, who was to know if the great grey monster did not have companions hiding in the rocks and watching them with dark baleful eyes.

After a few shy attempts at conversation with the black ones, Mungart gave up and left them alone, deciding that whatever they were they could not speak the true language so must be some sort of white people. Why, they ate the white man's food and wore his clothes. It must be so.

After all, once the swans had been white-feathered until, crossing the red desert lands of the eaglehawk they had drunk water without permission. Attacked by the fierce Eaglehawk men they were left to die. But brother crow, often hated and despised by everyone including swans, had come on by and covered them with feathers of their own. This was a story Weerluk related as to their close proximity to people they were taught to avoid. Would they finish up like the swan? he asked.

Also, there was something curious about the Ilkari's cocoon on wheels.

Red Mond had told the two that it contained a star that had fallen to earth because he knew many of the Keepers' stories of creation gave stars human significance. It was Weerluk, suspicious as ever, who mentioned it to Mungart.

'I can smell something about that house that the Ilkari love so much. Some scent I have smelt before. Tell me, does it remind you of the caves?'

His brother crept over to the cocoon and squatted outside the doorway until Culvato came upon him and the Keeper, giving a guilty smile, slipped away.

The Gypsy followed his floating form with his black eyes, puzzled and worried. These were a fierce and unpredictable people and they had just suffered a gruesome loss. The land, it was said, shaped them and made them whole and the land was a cruel and evil place these days. His moon-talking friend could keep his head up in the clouds but Culvato would keep an eye on everyone and protect whatever his companion in life hid with such care in his cocoon.

'There is *something* there. I sense it,' Mungart reported back to his brother. 'I shall watch this miah most carefully.'

'While I watch the one whose miah it is.'

'He is our brother, 'Mungart said, shocked. 'We have shared meat with him and our own grandfather says a branch's shadow fell across his mother while she slept.'

'He is still a white man—with white man ways. Do not forget the history of our people,' Weerluk growled and turned his back, cutting off the conversation.

At last it was time to move on. They gathered up as much fruit as they could carry and the dried strips of elephant meat Surrey Anne had smoked over her fire.

Kareen went off on her own the last day there. She painted her naked body with yellow and red clay she carried in her gathering bag and rubbed rare blue clay into her hair. She gathered up jugs of icy water and poured them into the dirt, chanting ancient incantations all the while. From the mud thus formed she made timeless figures of Sister Earth, Sister Sun and Father Moon, handed down from Earth Mother to Earth Mother. She painted them also in the yellow and red powder she carried in her gathering bag. All the while she chanted softly as she had been taught by the sacred women, including her aunt, Red Mond's mother; chanting to protect her people, to praise the finding of life-giving rare water and to replenish the offerings they had taken from Sister Earth.

When she returned the rest were ready to go and the small caravan set out through the long, green, whispering grass of the valley towards other adventures.

The country they now passed over was more hilly, with stands of small twisted trees in the valleys and occasional pools of muddy, though drinkable, water. The soil was a rich red or black, and grass grew, juicy and greenish yellow. For the Ilkari this was a land of plenty and they were continually surprised by the enchantment of the next valley. They wondered if this country belonged to anyone and, if not, then they would bring the whole clan Violet Lynx Foot—if not the Tribe Elk—here when they returned from their journey. *Here* was grass for their animals, soil for their vegetables and shade and water in such plentiful supplies as they had never seen. How much better this land was than their own red-purple Home Ground with its forest of dead trees and its dying river, that soon would be no more than a trickle. Kareen's eyes became even brighter in her mahogany brown face and she became noticeably happier.

Red Mond watched the two brothers as their eyes roved over the ground, picking up signs he could *never* see. Several times he saw them huddled in worried conference but he did not push them. He knew if there was any danger they would come and tell him. Akar Black Head also noticed their concerns and he decided to spend more of his time watching out for enemies. Like Red Mond he had the greatest respect for the Keepers' skills.

They had been travelling through the gently undulating valleys for some two weeks, enjoying the peaceful feeling, the bitter scent of eucalypt and their honeyed flowers, the smell of the grass and the rich wonderful soil all these good things sprang from. While S'shony enjoyed the shaded trees that helped protect her skin, she was able to start manipulating Red Mond's mind again, putting an idea here, a thought there. Although there were times when one could almost forget the reason for their journey. It seemed impossible that the dreaded Nightstalkers could inhabit this place. Still, every night, when Father Moon had hidden himself in shame there was a guard posted, for old habits died hard. Almost every night the Moon-talker would go out by himself and search the wide and awesome sky for any sign. Often, unbeknownst to him, Akar Black Head or one of the Visitors would follow him covertly, just to make sure he was safe. If he died, then there was no one to talk to the stranger in the cocoon and no one to read the sky so their journey would fail.

These were the best readings Red Mond Star Light had ever had and he wondered if it was because he was in new country under fresh skies. He had a vision of an almighty lake from which huge cliffs and mountainous rocks rose. It was a sad place because it was the hiding place of Father Moon. There was a great yellow-brown river as big perhaps as the Mississippi told to him in his mother's tale and they must follow that wonderful river on their way to their final destination. Also, in the stars he saw massive hills, too big even to imagine, and a place that was colder than he could even begin to try and feel. His head swam at these improbable images the sky threw down at him.

S'shony's head also swam and felt light at the images she had to conjure up to imbed in Red Mond Star Light's mind. She was lucky to have gone on those long journeys with the Sun People so she knew the route approximately to the King of the Bats' cave, even though she was above ground now.

One night the Moon-talker appeared worried as he came back from looking at the huge expanse of blue-blackness, dotted all over with cold stars.

'That is the only God *I'll* ever worship! That and my axe!' Akar Black Head said, as he fell in beside the young man. 'They say a God is powerful and yet never can truly be seen. Well, that is the sky.'

'I thought you were your own God,' Red Mond Star Light teased lightly.

'As is every Ilkari. We are children of the earth.'

Red Mond—and Joda who had come along also to soak in the velvet-black peace of the night—was never sure whether the warrior was serious about his religious thoughts. Any thought in fact.

'We shall need some help from the High Ones. This I have read in the stars,' Red Mond muttered and glanced at Joda. But Joda had chosen to come on this mission so he had the right to know of any danger.

'A falling star touched the light of the red star tonight,' he murmured. 'That can only mean trouble in the future. A cloud shaped like a crow drifted across the dying light of the moon and that means betrayal in love . . . that will lead to death eventually. The night before I saw the sign of the crow also. This is the strongest message I can read,' he said sadly.

It was not as good as the heady omens he had seen the last few nights.

Akar Black Head, unbeliever that he was, laughed out loud. 'Ho! It is just as well our Little Mosquito has no thought of women.' He clapped a heavy hand on Joda's frail shoulder. 'Beware the passion of women for they will make you feel as big as the moon, yet their love is only the fluttering of bird wings. We don't need to read the sky to know *that*!'

'You have only to read the stars that are Kareen's eyes and the moonbeams that are her words, isn't it, cousin-brother? I could be a Moon-talker myself!' Joda cheekily returned.

For a moment the big man stared down at his little clansman as he chewed over whether he had just been insulted. Then he burst into raucous laughter again and stumped off towards the campfire where he sat with Kareen for a while every night.

Red Mond glanced down at the boy, the only one who could get away with being impudent to the warrior. He smiled slightly at Joda's latest sting. The boy's hazel eyes were dreamy, caught in the vice of the High Ones' magic, that dribbled from their noses and trickled from their mouths in slowly swirling blue wreaths.

'You are a favourite of the High Ones,' he stated.

'Yes. They enjoy my flute and I enjoy their friendship.'

'Be careful. They are children of Sister Sun and you are from the earth.'

Joda's hands ran seductively through the black fur of the cat that nestled in his arms. It had no name—just Cat—but it had been with the boy since it was a fluffy, playful kitten six years ago—just after his father, Brown Leopard, had died. Almost half his life. Its yellow eyes caught the glint of starlight as it stared at Red Mond imperiously.

'They are humans, such as us. I believe what Akar Black Head says. There are no Gods. I have seen them bleeding and sweating and—' Joda grinned suddenly, impishly. 'I have seen them make love. Just the same as any Ilkari.'

'I have yet to see them afraid,' the Moon-talker said solemnly. 'That—and their power—is sign enough for me. It would have taken *every* man of our clan, with the women distracting and confusing the animal, to bring down that elephant. They used just one man and what a mess *he* caused.'

'Well, as long as they share their magic I'll call them whatever they want to be called,' Joda smiled.

They arrived back at the camp, a hive of activity as the evening meal was prepared. But Red Mond didn't feel like eating. He made his way to S'shony's side and lay down in her dark world while her cool white hands ran over him. She could not understand the thoughts in her man's mind and the pregnancy was affecting her mind-reading so she was losing some of her power. It shied away from the light of the moon as she tried to probe that part of her lover's brain. He could not tell her of the message he had received. What if the message of tainted love was for *him*. It had been such a powerful message—so clear. He turned his dark-brown eyes to her equally dark, black ones, but all he could read in those weird eyes was affection.

She ran fingers through his red hair. 'Soon we'll be at the river. I sense it. Then our direction will be easier to follow,' she hissed in her sibilant voice. 'I can smell the two newcomers almost every day as they come around my cave on some story or the other. I can "smell" their suspicion and sense their hate, just like the hairy one I first met.'

He understood her fear and breathed in her ear. 'Don't worry. For me, you are a moonbeam that, like a sacred spring of silver magic water, came from below the ground,' he murmured. 'No harm will come to you,' he said softly, so she drifted asleep in his arms. But he remained wakeful for some time. The Keepers did not believe in the Ilkari Gods and Goddesses. They were not as afraid of the cocoon as others were. He would have to be careful.

Yet it was the Keepers who bought the next bit of news to the members of the caravan. The next day, as they were heading over a larger than usual hill, Mungart came up to Red Mond and indicated he should follow him.

On top of the hill there was a sandy depression and all over the sandy floor was a conglomerate of smudged tracks. Weerluk squatted in the middle of them, his eyes worried as his lips pursed in thought. He pointed down the hill at Port Rial's horses.

'Ngort. Yarraman. Many ngort. But they are not free.'

'Not free?' Red Mond said. He had difficulty with this strain of language from the multi-lingual Keepers and was not sure he had heard right.

'They are ridden by humans,' Mungart murmured beside him.

'Ilkari!' Red Mond said, his eyes lighting up in pleasant surprise.

The brothers looked at one another. They had no word for 'the unloved ones' that their new friend would understand. How could they explain that these horse riders might be enemy.

'They are bad people. We never come this way because of these people,' Mungart tried to explain.

'Then how can you say they are bad?' Red Mond reasoned.

'It is the law of our people never to have anything to do with white men—especially *these* white men,' Weerluk growled. 'You are all ghosts but these are the ghosts of ghosts who crawl out of the ground. If you don't listen to us then it is your own bad luck.'

'They were on horses today, watching us as we climbed the hill. This is what the tracks tell us,' the calmer Mungart said. 'Now we are near the top, they have gone. Is that the way of friendship?'

'Perhaps they are shy. If there was any great trouble coming I would have read about it in the stars,' Red Mond uttered. 'But all I saw was in the longer future, not today or even tomorrow. If this is their Home Ground then they can tell us where we must go towards our destination. Perhaps there are those who would join us. And we will need as many allies as we can get to go where we are going.'

Weerluk looked away over the rough and bumpy hills. They were now well into the forbidden country and had found nothing but peace and plenty of food and water. In a strictly forbidden place, he and his brother had even come unscathed from an encounter with a monster which the black ones had killed and even eaten a part of. There could be no danger amongst such powerful people.

'Then we go on, brother,' he said.

It was the end of the discussion and they set off on their long legs in their loping stride, further into the country their people feared. They were of the Kawar family, of the Parrot Totem, the grandsons of Kwila the Shark—mighty warriors, famous dancers and they had no fear.

CHAPTER SEVEN

It was not long before the mysterious riders made themselves known. The first warning was a nervous squeal from Port Rial's horses and a milling around as they scented their brethren. Then Kareen's sharp ears heard a thundering off in the hills to the right of them. Quickly she called to the others and they gathered in a loose group, weapons ready. The Visitors realised trouble might be coming and unslung their unusual spears, preparing themselves. The two Keepers came loping in from their far posts.

Suddenly, over the rise appeared many horsemen—some ninety in number. They reined in about fifty paces from the caravan, in a great flurry of dust and flying pebbles from prancing, excited horses. Then a great silence descended onto the valley.

At last, one man nudged his pony forward. He wore a cap made from a sheep's head with small horns attached and around his dark throat he wore a necklace of yellowed sheep's teeth. His face was wizened and darkened by the sun but his black eyes glittered with a bright intelligence and his teeth shone white in a smile.

'It is true then! There are Ilkari living beyond the desert. We thought we were the last of the lost Tribes,' he said. His voice was strangely accented, but understandable.

He leapt from his horse and, after a wave of his hand, the others followed suit. Giving their reins to every fifth man, they gathered around the caravan in a noisy, jolly crowd, smiling and touching and pressing against the strangers from across the desert. Curiosity was alight in their eyes, especially at the sight of the four Visitors. Their hands reached out to touch their faces or coiling strands of hair or their strange silvery clothes. Surrey Anne, remembering another incident, was much afraid and clung close to Port Rial, whose usually pleasant face was hard with anger as he glared at the men, with fierce eyes. His hands moved on his weapon but Nanny called out, 'Them bredrin fi me friends! Dreadie nah get feisty, yaah.'

Cudjo Accompong fingered his giant stick ominously and stepped back from the noisy, excited throng of small men like the huge proud elephant he had recently killed.

Red Mond Star Light did not notice the apprehension of the High Ones. He was happy and amazed to meet people of his own Race in these foreign hills of great beauty. People that Baba did not even know existed. What a story this would be. Kareen and Joda also relaxed at the similarity of the men to their own wild clan.

In truth these people were darker than the average Ilkari—more like the Gypsy Culvato, whom some embraced as one recognised. Their curly hair and glittering eyes were all black with only a few blond or red heads and blue or green eyes among them. Whereas the Ilkari men from the Purple Plains wore wild animal skins to do with their story, these men had draped over their shoulders skins only the very young or the women would wear back home—the skins of domesticated animals.

And there were other slight differences as well, Akar Black Head noticed with a soldier's vision. None of them wore the Ilkari's Traveller's braids; indeed, their hair was cut short, being shoulder length at the longest. None of them carried weapons that he could see and this relaxed him. But what worried him most was that some had their front teeth filed to points, in the manner of the Nightstalkers. Many had some sort of tattoos on their face and arms.

Joda, on the other hand, had his eyes wide open in surprise and delight. That he should be a part of *this*! The discoverer of new neighbours. The stories he would tell his young friends at the river bank back home! He remembered one campfire story of two High Ones who walked upon the earth many years ago. Nearly as famous as the greatest of the High Ones, Strong Arm Kneels, who went and visited the moon. But the story had been so outlandish that it could not be true. Now he could step into the story as well and become like Mark Pole and Christos Column.

'Welcome to my family. Mi casa tu casa,' the leader in the sheep's-head hat cried, grasping Red Mond by the arm. 'You have come a long way?' he questioned. He pointed at the cocoon on the carriage. 'What unheard of gifts do you bring from afar?'

'A Goddess whom we follow towards a great adventure,' Akar Black Head called out, somewhat derisively.

'She is a child of Father Moon and I am the clan's Moon-talker. We must go to do battle with the Nightstalkers,' Red Mond explained.

The man and those around him stared at the youth blankly. Then a sad smile creased the wrinkled countenance of their leader.

'Brother. We are all from Sister Earth—it is easy to tell. But just as there is good rich red earth and good rich black earth there is the earth of our gardens and the earth of our deserts. We come from all this soil yet we are as different as that soil. The moon to us is just the moon.

'Come. We shall escort you back to our village and then we shall talk more of this Goddess of the moon. Old stories tell us she was a beautiful huntress. And so she is, creeping from cloud to cloud and spearing us with her light.'

It was Red Mond's turn to be confused now but he chose not to say anything until he was completely sure of their beliefs. But . . . Father Moon a woman? Even a brave and mighty huntress. It was hard to conceive. Still, he thought, they at least believed in Sister Earth.

The three women were very aware that these little men washed their dark eyes over their bodies with a hungry gaze. In the Ilkari clans of the desert the men and women shared everything and Kareen was worried that there were no women among these riders. Did that mean there were no women at all? She had heard of groups of young Ilkari men who gathered together into a sort of cult.

Surrey Anne remembered another group of dark-skinned males where there had been no women and she heard the last despairing cries of Saint Catherine as they tore her lithe, graceful body to pieces. She shivered at her memory.

But they seemed polite as they murmured in their lilting language and flashed her shy, white smiles. They were a happy, relaxed group on their small shaggy ponies—although they tended to smell a bit too much of sheep or goat.

The journey to the village was not long. It was up on the very top of one of the taller hills. In the Ilkari clans the only stone building was the Baba's house. But here *every* house was made of grey mud brick or knobbly red rocks. They resembled grey termite nests having no roof or wall as such but rose as a mound from the ground. They had no windows and the door was a circular shape covered by the usual goat or sheep skin.

When they arrived Kareen's fears were seen to be unfounded because women and children poured from the mounds and into the square that was the centre of the village. They were the same as the men, small, swarthy and predominantly dark featured.

On the way up the hillside, the caravan had seen row upon row of luscious vines with twisted grey trunks growing in what appeared to be an orderly fashion. There had been bunches of yellow, green or purple fruits growing on these vines. Now they saw that many of the women— especially the young girls—wore the leaves and tendrils of the vines in their thick black hair.

The boisterous crowd gathered about them and, once more, they were subjected to touching of the face, body and clothes. They were fascinated by the jewellery Red Mond wore in memory of his fallen cousin-brothers and the great sword and club he carried. They almost tore the silver clothes from the Visitors' bodies in their frenzy to see if they were real and there would have been a fight were it not for Nanny's calming voice above the din.

Akar Black Head and Kareen closed around Joda, worried by the clamorous crowd.

'Don't you notice, Kareen,' the big man murmured, worriedly stroking his beard, 'there are no pets.'

'This is a curious thing but not one to be worried about,' Kareen murmured back. Then: 'So why am I uneasy?'

'It is a strange land and these are different people—but the Moon-talker would not lead us into danger. They are Ilkari, the same as us, it is easy to see,' Akar Black Head said. 'Besides,' he grinned, 'we have nothing to fear. We walk in the shadow of the Gods.' He smiled down at Joda who clung protectively to Cat, made nervous by this noisy throng after weeks of relative quiet.

Another who was nervous of this village was Culvato, whose fierce eyes were not warmed by the smiles of the small dark people 'The tiger purrs before he leaps' was one of his mother's many sayings. He had liked it out in the wilds with his own thoughts for company. Still, he wondered if any of his people were here in this wild, happy crowd. These people who gathered around him certainly looked a lot like him and one or two words of the raucous language sounded like that of his mother's tongue.

He looked around, then nudged Red Mond who walked beside him, keeping inquisitive faces from prying into the jolting caravan. 'The Keepers have left us.'

And so they had. Somewhere on the journey to the Hill People's village the two brothers had melted away as silent and unobtrusive as only they could be.

'They are wary of our kind, cous-cous. It was only because they knew me that they came with us—and even then they kept their distance. But, see, we have our army now!' He waved his arm around the square.

'I don't trust these keepers of sheep and growers of vines,' Culvato growled, but Red Mond turned his warm brown eyes upon him and laughed softly. 'You trust no one but yourself and Durrilau. I wonder if you would be happy even with your own kind. That is why I brought you along.' The Moon-talker smiled and wrapped an arm around Culvato's slender shoulders. 'But, see, the sun is shining and the only people I have ever feared are those who hate the sun.'

By now they were in the middle of the square and surrounded by dark, animated faces and studied by bright black eyes. Then a man wearing a ram's-head hat, with marvellous curving horns, stepped forward. 'Mi familia,' he called out, 'stand back and give our guests room. There will be time to meet them later. This *is* a gift of the Gods that they should arrive here during this week of festival.'

The crowd moved back and fell to a muttering quietness. The leader then turned to Red Mond Star Light. 'My name is Don Sebastion. My house is yours. We shall break bread together upon my table and drink the sacred wine.'

'You shall be a part of our story, as is the dust that drifts from our feet,' Red Mond replied.

They were led into a house larger than the others. All down the centre of this huge hall were ornate columns carved from stone—exquisitely decorated with stone figures and flowers. There was a huge wooden table right down the middle of the room and it was to this that all the people moved. The guests were placed in the middle next to Don Sebastion and his son Miguel (who had first met them in his sheep's-head hat). The others spread out on either side or sat along the sides. There were perhaps two hundred people here and they all fitted into this one room.

Never had Red Mond seen such a large clan. In the clan Violet Lynx Foot there were perhaps forty and that was a big clan compared to others. Had not Don Sebastion called all these people 'his family'? The Moon-talker looked hard at his host.

He was, like all the rest, small and wiry, with a beard growing grey only on his chin, like the goats they seemed to have so many of. Just like his shaggy hair that was as curly as Culvato's. But now the young man saw there were many wrinkles upon his face, and his hands were hard and callused. There were several scars on his face and arms that showed life in these pleasant green hills could be dangerous. But his smile was as warm as the sun outside and his shrewd black eyes were alight with *bonhomie*.

He told the Ilkari a little of his village's history. There were several 'families' in these hills. They all spoke the same basic language which was handed down from generations ago. But each family worshipped a different deity and that was as far as their religion went. The people in *this* village believed in Diana, a famous huntress who now took the shape of the moon. They worshipped the Goat-God Pan, who was the main God of the hills and woodlands. Then, because they were mainly farmers here, they worshipped Bacchus, the God of fertility. He was this family's special deity. It was Bacchus who had taught them how to grow the vines and make the sacred wine. Also he made sure their crops grew well and gave them plenty. He was a wild, youthful, exuberant God and his ceremonies were enthusiastic and merry affairs that usually lasted a week or two with eating, dancing, singing and, of course, drinking. They were in the middle of one such ceremony now, Don Sebastion explained.

Other villages worshipped water spirits, or men with the heads of bulls or the bodies of horses or goats or other monsters of creation. Some worshipped trees or lakes while still others worshipped stars. Some of these the Ilkari had heard of in their mothers' tales and this made the bond between the two groups even closer. All these deities came from the same place that Red Mond recognised as the Aegean sea his mother had told him of. They came from a time so long ago that humans had hardly begun to walk on the earth and the desert Ilkari were amazed to be in the company of a Race so old.

Their stories were magnificent.

'Aaaah, stories,' called Akar Black Head. 'Our people also worship stories. Let us swap them in the old Ilkari way.'

'What of the worries you had before?' whispered Kareen, as she looked around the crowded room with sharp grey eyes.

'I see nothing to worry about here. Here is a feast and here are stories,' the big man grinned, happy with simple pleasures. 'You heard yourself the Chief say they were having a ceremony.'

'A ceremony for Gods—of which you don't believe,' Joda grinned from beside him.

'I could rather believe this goat-footed God who sings up women on his pipes than the moon child our sage and fine leader has hidden in his heart.' Akar Black Head smiled back and glanced down the table at the red-headed young man in earnest conversation with the old Don Sebastion and his son.

Culvato and the Visitors watched as the tables became full of haunches of goat and sheep and platters of corn, potatoes, turnips and other wonderful food.

Sometimes on the Island of Springs they have seen such feasts—although the food there is mostly fruit.

She looks around this great hall. There are no doors out. Only the one and that is far away. No windows, just a hole in the roof for the smoke to get out. Cudjo Accompong sits beside her and glowers. He is remembering other times when they came into villages of stone huts and been welcomed so they had danced and smoked the life-giving weed with strangers—only to be betrayed and see their comrades slain before their very eyes.

Surrey Anne, beside him, also enjoys the music and tells herself this is a new land with new people. The only danger she has seen here has come from animals: the roaring raging beast that tore The Syrian to bits and the snake that quietly took away Porky's young vibrant life. They had flown over this vast continent like a lost and lonely bird and tried to put all their past sadnesses behind them. But every time they ventured out to find supplies of the illusive petrol they know must be here, this bird had laid eggs of death and in the two months they have been here the elegant, graceful Syrian and sweet-natured, giggling Porky remain broken fragments of memories. They hold their own counsel and keep their guns within reach.

In the cocoon, that had been lifted into the hall by eager hands and now sat behind Red Mond, the cave girl was terrified. Her mind was reeling from the many emotions that ran through it. These minds of these people were even more complex than the other Ilkari she was just starting to understand.

Hatred, jealousy, love, curiosity, joy—and a nagging sense of awe, even fear, permeated her brain. Now she had set up a shield to protect herself and cowered under her skins at the terror of these amazing images. She had not seen Red Mond since she first sensed the thunder of the horses' hooves as the Hill People came to take her lover and his friends to the village. She had no way of warning them if they were in danger because her condition had totally exhausted her powers. She now knew her mind was clearer and sharper than any of the others and that it was child's play to manipulate their thoughts for her own causes. It was a gift well worth having and she was sad none of these people who lived Upside would ever have the gift the People of the Caves took for granted.

Joda's dreamy hazel eyes took in everything and he laughed along with his friend, Port Rial. He had never seen so many attractive girls dressed only in the leaves of vines, fluttering over their golden skin. Yes, their skin was golden and their movements lithe while their dark eyes were alluring. It seemed to the boy that they had eyes only for him and he basked in the High Ones' shadows.

Port Rial rolled some of his magic green weed into a smoke and the three of them—Joda, Port Rial and Surrey Anne—shared it so he floated with them up into the sky and he saw the flames of Sister Sun in every girl's eyes.

He suddenly remembered his cat, who snuggled up, warm and close against his skin, under his calf-skin coat. With his knife he cut off some of the rich red meat and, opening up his coat, gently fed her.

As the cat's dark face peered out to find the source of the scent she desired, there was a momentary lull in the conversation from the immediate vicinity as those who saw the sleek black head and round yellow eyes paused to stare in fascination and . . . something else. Then, up the other end of the hall three young men sprang up and, producing guitars from somewhere in the shadows, they began a wild pulsating tune.

Culvato could not believe his ears. For here was a flamenco—just as his mother had taught him. The music flowed into him and his blood ran hot and he also leapt to his feet. When he dragged out his guitar there were cries of: 'La Guittaro!' and 'Bravo! Bravo! Come play with us.'

There followed then a fantastic guitar duel, with the notes mingling with the frantically dancing girls, the swirling smoke and boisterous laughter.

'Joda! Bring out your flute and let us show these strangers how the clansmen of Violet Lynx Foot play!' Culvato called.

So, from another part of his coat the boy brought out his beloved flute and soon its sweet notes were joining with the wild tangled rhythm of the guitars. This endeared him even more to the gyrating throng and the girls danced around him covering him with leaves from their sweating bodies.

Voices among them began calling out. 'Here is a young God! He has come to visit with us. Surely now our crops will be fruitful.'

With the meat and vegetables from the garden were also copious jugs of warm red wine and cool pale wine. At home there was one in the clan who was known for his magic with fermented fruits but his potion was nothing compared to this wine of the Hill People. For Joda, who also was smoking the Visitors' enthralling cigarettes, the wine made him climb higher than he had ever been before. Just as the green weed made him see things much more clearly, so the red drink of the Hill People made him speak words that he had not realised he even knew. He smiled at the near naked girls. They were right. He was a God and this was his story.

Akar Black Head quaffed jug after jug and, after each jug, his stories became wilder—much to the delight of those listening. Kareen forgot about her slight misgivings and began dancing with the women. She could appreciate that this was a celebration of Sister Earth so she joined in, and the girls draped her body in vine leaves. Culvato laughed with mad abandon and played passionately upon his guitar.

Only Red Mond and the four Visitors did not drink the intoxicating brew. Red Mond because it clouded his judgement as a Moon-talker, and, besides, he was having an interesting and intellectual discussion with Don Sebastion about their respective Gods. The Visitors did not drink because back on their Island were rum shops where men went to meet and they all knew what violence and stupidity happened there sometimes.

Now the smoke from the fires became denser and the dancing more frenzied. Couples united on the floor and made frantic love to the beat of drum and guitar, and others fell into trances as the ceremony overtook them. People threw off their clothes and bathed themselves with flowing jugs of wine so the heady aroma of the grape and the bodies filled the room.

Nanny was reminded of the religious cults back home. Especially the Zion Revivalists with their ritual dancing and collective possession of spirits. Surrey Anne was reminded of the more sinister Convince cult and was a little afraid again of these crazy antics that bought back memories of obeah, belief in amoral spirit power, necromancy and violent trance behaviour.

Joda was playing his flute when a young girl about his age brushed her naked body up against his. '?Me permite este baile,' she murmured.

He didn't understand her but in his dreamy mind it seemed her voice was entirely enchanting—like the trickle of sacred water from a hillside spring. He allowed himself to be led out into the middle of the dance floor. Two or three other women and girls joined him and pressed themselves up to his body. He felt their cool hands run over his skin and stroke his cat who clung close to him, digging its claws into his skin in fright. But he did not feel a thing. Only the hands that lulled him into a wondrous dream. He twirled round and round, his flute, it appeared, stuck to his lips. The young girls entwined vines through his honey-blond hair and around his body, laughing all the while.

'Pruebe uno de estos,' one called, shoving a jug of red wine into his hands. 'La bola!' she cried in explanation.

He drank and he thought it was the sweetest thing he had drunk all that exciting night. Then the first girl drifted up to him and whispered seductively, '?Donde nos encontramus.'

So saying she pressed her hot moist mound between his legs and pushed her naked, sweet-smelling body close to his. In the eyes of the boy she was the only one existing in the huge noisy crowd. This boy whose only friend was a black cat and whose only adventures had been beside his clan's dying river.

Now he would make another friend tonight and his story would begin. He turned drugged eyes to her rapturous face and bent to kiss her.

Then his long hair was caught from behind by one of the girls. Another sliced a knife across his throat.

Culvato, fingers numb from his playing, saw what had happened through the haze of grey smoke and froze.

Port Rial also saw what had happened and pushed Surrey Anne to one side as he rose up shouting. But his voice was drowned in the roar that followed.

'And so his flesh shall be the corn; his blood the sacred red wine. Long life to our God Bacchus. Long life to our God Pan.'

For a moment Joda stood there, while blood spurted out of his neck. Uncomprehending eyes stared at the girl and then he fell. He did not feel one girl grab his terrified cat and lift it high for all to see the creature only a God could have. He did not see another wave his precious flute aloft and he did not see the line of dancers move forwards to dip their fingers in his pooling blood.

Culvato leapt for the safety of his companions. 'They have killed Joda!' he screamed.

Akar Black Head stopped in the middle of his story and spun around looking for Kareen. But she was over on the other side of the room. She, too, had just understood what had happened and an anguished cry was on her lips. The big man brought the clay jug he had been drinking out of down upon the head of the man who had just been enjoying his story, crushing it and shattering the jug. Then he leapt over the table and charged through the crowded room to the lover of his best friend. His big fists snapped at least two necks along the way.

There was consternation and confusion now as the small dark people gathered themselves from this attack.

Didn't these outlandish people understand? They had brought them the soul of their God to be sacrificed so that the crops would grow. These people should be happy with them.

Kareen raked a girl's face with her nails, ripping an eye out. A girl she had, only moments before, been sharing a drink and a dance with.

The music died in a spluttering cacophony of sound and the dancers and lustful lovers came out of their trances, bewildered. At the death of the God every month there was always an added fervour to their antics. Not this sudden violence.

'To arms! To arms, amigos!' Don Sebastion cried before Red Mond's mighty sword pierced his side.

'Stay together!' Nanny cried and Cudjo rose to his full height, raising his awesome weapon. Port Rial and Surrey Anne had grabbed their slimmer weapons while Nanny pulled out a round egg-like object. She tossed it into the milling throng while the others fired simultaneously.

Such a noise had never been heard in those hills for three thousand years. Such carnage had never been visited upon the village. Instead of a harvest of fruit and grain, Joda's death brought a harvest of mutilated bodies.

Men, women and children were tossed into the air, or else danced a crazy jig as invisible swords smashed into them. The laughter turned into screams of terror and there was a mad scramble for the door.

Another blast from Cudjo's weapon and another bloody mess of bodies. Some made it outside and ran shrieking for the darkness; others lay whimpering on the floor until a raking fire from Surrey Anne and Port Rial finished them off. A small crowd huddled in the corner and stared with horror-filled eyes at the shattered remains of their family.

Cudjo Accompong slammed a third missile into his hot, smoking pipe and raised it to cover the cowering pitiful crowd. Amongst them were two of the girls who had sacrificed Joda.

'Me bredrin. Is enough killin', nuh,' Nanny murmured beside him.

'Look dereso dey bwoy. Me alias Rasta man, yaah. Them all should die,' Cudjo hissed.

'Them children a Babylon dey about, Ras. Me seh them sins take them away!' she reasoned.

He began to lower his weapon, then raised it quickly once more and fired straight at the two girls. At such close range they, and two score or more around them, disappeared.

'Me sins tak 'em deh, quicker,' Cudjo said. His bleak black eyes stared at her a moment and she saw the ghost of Saint Catherine's revenge shining back in the unfathomable depths. Then he strode outside.

'Me dey pon hurry. Quick-quick, yaah!' Nanny called to the stunned Ilkari.

They could not grasp the image of such destruction. Out of nearly two hundred people who had laughed, shouted, eaten, drunk and danced in that room, only about thirty had escaped with their lives. Some of those would be horribly maimed as well.

They themselves had only killed about five. Even Akar Black Head could now no longer doubt the power of these four strangers. But now there would always be a barrier of fear between them. Twice they had seen what these beings could do. They could barely comprehend such power and they could not understand such violence.

It was a subdued group that rode out of the village moments later.

Red Mond and Kareen had gathered up Joda's body, for he must be buried in the bosom of Sister Earth. Port Rial collected another string of horses. He would not spend time looking for treasure though. He had lost a dear and much-loved friend and no amount of treasure could bring him back.

They rode. Oh, how hard they rode away from that place of death. Every now and then the Ilkari would glance in the direction of the sour and silent Cudjo Accompong, then look away hurriedly at the grimness they saw in his face. There was no time for talking. They were grieving over their young clansman's death and the explosion of carnage it caused.

In her cocoon, S'shony was in a state of near paralysis that the mass of deaths had given her mind when they died almost instantaneously. She couldn't talk as she was bounced along in the darkness. Every time she reached out to touch a mind she was repulsed by horror or hatred. All she could do was clutch her skins tightly and moan in the pain all the shattered mind waves had given to her. One mind she couldn't find—the young one who had such vivid colourful dreams and who played the flute so well on still desert nights, and who loved an animal called Cat.

Once or twice Cat had come into her refuge on its aloof journeys and she had marvelled at its elegance. She had been able to smell the boy on her dark thick fur. It had been a friend and a link to the outside world.

At length they pulled up in a shallow grove amongst the valleys of the hills. There was a soft pink sand upon the ground and feathery, blue-leafed trees all around. They stared at one another in the blue twilight.

'We must bury Joda,' Kareen said at last.

'What are we going to do with these dealers in death? We thought we had a bee and now find we have a poisonous wasp,' Akar Black Head growled with his customary bluntness. 'Did you read of this in your precious stars? The murder of women and babies!' he shouted at Red Mond Star Light.

'Show the Moon-talker some respect,' Kareen gently admonished.

'We walk with dead feet. Already our bones rot upon foreign lands. I would like to know more about this journey and why the Moon-talker did not see this in his stars! What else doesn't the moon tell us?' the big man argued angrily.

'The Moon-talker weeps also, Akar. Joda was a member of his clan as well,' Culvato murmured from the darkness. 'Let him have his sadness in peace and leave the moon floating in the sky where it has always been.'

The warrior, Akar Black Head, drew out his sword and glared at the alert bunch of Visitors, who were not sure of the reactions their actions would bring. He drove the blade deep into the earth, feeling impotent and small, weak and insignificant. He, the strongest warrior of their clan! He could never fight against the shattering magic these people had—and he was one who didn't believe in magic. He strode off into the shadows of the trees to be alone.

Kareen began shaking as the shock overcame her and she moved over to stare at the face of Joda, his brown skin yellow in death. Culvato moved over to comfort her. Her strange, almond-shaped eyes, appearing almost like the Children of the Moon's were supposed to, looked up at him with their clear sharp gaze.

'That music you were playing, just before Joda died. How did you know the tunes they played? You played well, I know that. Better than I have ever heard you,' she queried in her soft voice while her grey eyes were hard and bright upon his face.

'It was the music of my mother,' he said just as softly back.

'Then you do not deny that these murderers were of your Race?' Her voice was still soft but now a coldness crept in and her eyes narrowed even more.

'They knew my mother's music and a few of her words. But they were not of *my* Race. *I* am a Gypsy,' Culvato said proudly.

'You are as dark as they. Everyone knows you have no clan—no love for anyone.'

'You are wrong,' he said simply and his eyes dared her to continue the argument.

All of this was conducted in fierce whispers and the two had concentrated all their energies upon each other.

They did not hear the soft footsteps until Nanny's thin hard form stepped in between them. 'Coo'yah, no fight no dey. Kass kass with them Baldies a Babylon. We brethrin an' sisthren, nuh?

Kareen recoiled in fear at the black hand. She had seen that same hand lazily toss a harmless egg into the midst of people, only to watch it burst into an insane orgy of destruction. She was one who *did* believe in Gods and Goddesses and she was fearful of the casual whims of this High One.

'Relax! Me nah hurt I, girl!' Nanny breathed, her angry face softening. Culvato stared at her with hard black eyes, then turned his back and stalked over to his horse.

'Cho. Dese quashie men? Don't them see we save deh worthless hide?' called Port Rial. 'Dem monkey-rial me seh,' he added in disgust.

But she was sad their friendship with these simple wild folk had ended with the loss of innocence. She had wished rather that they had never seen the gifts progressive society had bestowed upon the Islanders. Even those who thought of them as humans would be in awe of them now.

'Have fe bury yuh dead now, girl,' she said quietly and pointed with her lips towards the slumped figure of the boy on the horse.

She seemed to pass on the meaning to the Earth Mother because Kareen moved forwards protectively to Joda's side. She knew he had often watched her as she walked ahead of the caravan and she had had a quiet joke or two about it with Akar Black Head as they shared a feed and a fire and a few words at night. He had been too young to die.

'This is our clan's business. We shall bury the soul of Joda in the Ilkari way.'

Over by the horses they heard an anguished cry and, as they both turned around, they saw Culvato raise his guitar above his head shaking it at the imperious pinpricks far above.

'I shall not play your bewitching music again,' he cried to the uncaring moon.

Red Mond Star Light had gone to comfort S'shony and saw none of this confrontation. But he was past caring now and both he and the cave girl clung to each other tightly in the safety of their little home, gathering depleted strength from each other, although neither was in a condition to really comfort anyone. Once again he had seen cruel death touch his clan with cold white fingers as it flew past on soundless wings. Joda was the same age as Ilki had been. Red Mond Star Light had led the group that had included Ilki, his true cousin, to their deaths. Now he had led Joda to *his* death.

He clung to the girl he loved—and yet did not really know—and she saw his sadness and confusion. She loved him for his gentle nature and the peaceful blue aura that shone around him. She felt upset at his pain, yet was too weak herself right now to do more than hug him. Their different pain joined into one throbbing beat.

Later on he slid into her warm body and she closed around him, pulling him into her mind and soul. He touched her long, plaited black braids and ran his fingers over her cool white body, tracing the veins that crisscrossed her skin. Her strong callused hands fingered his Traveller's braids and ran pale hands over his burnt skin and jagged scars. It was impossible that two such enemies should ever be close but here they were.

The next morning, before the sun had risen above the hills; when her pink light that was the blood of her shameful birth washed palely across the sky, they buried Joda.

From her gathering bag Kareen took ochre of red, white, blue, black and yellow and solemnly painted death designs on Akar Black Head and Red Mond Star Light, then on herself. Culvato was not a true clansman, but he came and stood at the grave-side of his friend and comrade along with the silent Visitors.

Kareen took charge of the simple ceremony. It could not be as complex as it usually was, for few of the needed participants were there. But there were enough Ilkari present to make a decent funeral.

Red Mond cut off a long honey-blond lock of the boy's hair. He would plait it into the hair bangle he had made of Ilki's hair and so keep the boy beside him on their journey. Then they gathered wood from underneath the trees and built a huge funeral pyre and rested the frail thin form upon it. As the flames began to lick around his body, Kareen led them in a death dance, shuffling around the fire and calling out a warrior's chant to send Joda on his way.

Halfway through, as Red Mond rounded the fiercely burning wood in a semi-trance, his eyes caught a movement amongst the trees and he glimpsed the two Keepers sitting there, as still as blackened tree stumps. Their eyes were in shadow but he could sense they were sympathetic. He was reminded of the other time they had met and sacred tears fell from his eyes while his feet stumbled. Then he righted himself and continued with the ceremony.

They fed the fire with sweet-smelling wood until Joda's body was mere ashes and the sun was peering hungrily over the tops of the trees. They dug a deep hole and poured all but a pinch of his ashes into it. A thimbleful was placed in Red Mond's soul bag. He would add it to the other ashes of his clan when they returned one day. Akar Black Head and the giant Cudjo Accompong then moved some boulders, only they could, on to the grave. The other three of Violet Lynx Foot's clan made a fence of rocks around the grave to keep the spirit from wandering. The twin brothers came forward and splashed red ochre over the rocks. Mungart touched Red Mond on the hand briefly for a moment. But Weerluk, aloof and cold, only glared at the new grave for a moment or two then strode away, ignoring everyone. He sensed the tension in the camp and, besides, he was angry at the white man for not heeding his warning. If he had Keeper blood in him he should have had more sense, Weerluk thought bitterly.

The trees that grew in this grove were strange to the Ilkari. They were tall and bushy with dark brown—almost red—branches and blue-grey leaves covered with a white powder. Among the leaves were bunches of flowers, weird, yellow, fluffy balls, the same yellow as Joda's hair. They rustled and whispered to themselves and kept the song of Joda amongst their shadows and leaves. It was Red Mond who said that, forever more, these trees would be known as 'The Trees of Joda'.

And so they did become known.

As the attitudes of the small meandering party had subtly changed so too did the country around them. The hills that had rambled over the land began to flatten out and the great patches of broken red or grey rocks began to disappear. The clumps of white-stemmed trees with their pale green leaves became less frequent.

The weather also changed. The puffy clouds that had followed them overhead when they were in the hill country did not appear as often and the sky remained a pale relentless blue. Not as hot as the cracked Purple Plains the Ilkari called home, but hot enough to warrant a rest at midday as they had once been accustomed to.

As they passed through the hills away from Joda's burial place so too did the living essence of that boy pass slowly from their collective memories. But not altogether, of course. Sometimes something small and insignificant would remind someone of the boy's cheerful presence.

It might be the fact that at tea someone would idly toss a piece of meat over their shoulder before remembering Cat was no longer there to gather it up. And he was especially missed on nights when the music of Kareen's harp and the High Ones' drums drifted around the fires without the benefit of his ethereal flute.

Port Rial missed him most of all. The thin rangy Islander had enjoyed sharing his endless supply of marihuana with his new friend, watching him take the sacred smoke to his bosom and float with the pirate in his land of dreams. Now, at night, he would glumly roll a thin cigarette and share it with Surrey Anne. Or else walk out into the night and smoke it by himself, staring up at the stars. One night Nanny came upon him, sent there by a worried Surrey Anne, who had watched Clarendon Jon Cannu fall into the same quiet mood and finally be mauled by the huge shaggy bear when he was not agile and alert.

'Coo'pon, dreadie! He face too long 'im fall a ground.'

'Is not I face me worry! Me ain't no God. I-maan ony Rasta man from Island long gone. Yuh see dese people feared us now,' Port Rial said glumly. 'Yuh carn get no coconut from him persimmon tree.'

'Wisdom fi you deh?'

'Is 'ow I-an'-I get back to plane when dis all ovah is de word a wisdom Rasta seeks.'

'Like de prophet Mohammed mus' we go a mountain. Me tell yuh no lie, dread. Coo'pon your love a life, your woman. She treasure trove fe you, nuh, natty?' She smiled.

'Aaah, yuh raas.' Port Rial smiled and punched her lightly on the shoulder.

She smiled back, her teeth gleaming in the dark. She had brought another of her wandering flock back to the fold. Her flock that was slowly dwindling. They all missed their Island home and their people and the comforting sameness of language, customs and skin. Soon . . . soon, she promised herself, they would fly away and never venture from their Island of Springs again.

Akar Black Head had taken to following the four Visitors, secretly watching them. He wanted to learn all about their awesome power, so if they ever turned it against his clan he might know of a way to stop them. So for many nights he trailed along unseen beside Surrey Anne, as she searched for roots and herbs, or shadowed Port Rial on his lonely walks during the day. His eyes kept track of Cudjo Accompong and Nanny.

Now he pondered what the two had been talking about. Had the young man been casting a spell upon Joda and what had happened been the result? For there was no doubt now in the warrior's mind that these people were magic. But he held a great dislike for Gods and Goddesses, knowing full well it was the High Ones who had caused this world's sadness in the first place.

He would watch and wait and learn. When the time was right he would steal away their magic as so many of the women's tales had mortals do to High Ones. Then he truly would be the most powerful Ilkari there ever had been.

For one whole turn of the moon they meandered their way through the hostile hills, always alert and on the look out for trouble. But, at last, one day they crawled out from the last of the gently rolling contours. In front of them, as far as the eye could see, there stretched a plain of tall, whispering, wavering grass, unbroken by any sign of tree or hill.

It was immense, this plain, and ranged in colour from yellow through to brown—but all with some shade of green within. After the closeness of the hills the feeling of open space was breathtaking. They felt overawed by the wide swathe of land they must now cross (and, for the Ilkari, by the sight of so much tall grass which their water-starved lands had *never* seen). They camped that night close to the shadowy arm of a lone hump of high ground that dawdled out into the plain.

On that last night before they set off across the vast savannah there was, for the first time in a while, real peace in the camp. They all sensed that by moving from the hills they were leaving a cruel and malevolent place behind; a place where they had encountered sudden death for the first time on this journey. And who could tell what adventures lay ahead?

Culvato, as usual, stood guard by S'shony's hut. A full moon climbed high in the sky to show a new phase had entered *his* journey as well. Unimpaired by mountain or tree the sky seemed to go on forever, just like the plain before them. The whole land was bathed in a soft blue light and there was not a sound—not a bird nor an insect to break the incredible silence

He saw Nanny come slowly towards him, the hazy light picking out her fine, high cheek bones and almond eyes.

'De night is cold, you say?' she murmured. 'Is a night for man him woman be one an' one.'

He could not follow all her words but her hand on his shoulder was gesture enough. Even so, he pulled back slightly from her touch.

'Me no Goddess, bwoy! Me only is woman with she woman mind and flesh. I-an'-I go a strange lands, nuh? Shall we a go together?' she breathed.

'I must look after my cousin-brother's secret. It's what I came for—to be forever by his side until we both must die,' he said and pushed her hand away, leniently.

'Look dereso, bwoy! 'Im in de bed fe woman. Make him bed fi you, sweet one. Me know yuh feelin' loving-love,' she murmured again.

She swayed seductively in the moonlight—the bright moonlight that could tell the truth to some and lies to others. The youth, who had only ever loved his crippled half-brother and had little time for other people and *no* time for their beliefs, was caught up in her amorous play. She ran long black fingers over his arms and over his chest. Gently she traced the sharp outlines of his face. Then she smiled at him with her mouth and eyes and his soul melted.

She has been worried ever since the night of Joda's murder. She has seen the hatred and confusion in his face and this upsets her more than the fearful looks she gets from the rest. He has moved away from her in his solitary way, perhaps also in disgust, as he sensed she was no better than their worst enemy, where before she had been a Goddess. This is what she senses and it makes her sad.

Often she tells herself she cannot afford the luxury of sexual relations. She has temporarily been taken up by the mighty strangeness of this huge, beautiful, yet terrifying land. For a while she believed these folk's conception of her Godliness. But, after Joda's death, she realised that they can all die and, oh!, she has been without a man for so long.

She is attracted to this dark, fiery-eyed youth and she knows he likes her. What if they both die soon from some unknown danger lurking in the wavering sea of grass? Her body has become heated as she thinks of him and her decisions are becoming blurred when his face appears in her mind every day. She has decided she will taste this dark sweet fruit. It will not become an infatuation. No, rather it will be like one of the frenzied dances of the Pocomania religion, when men and women couple in a wild desire and release of pressure to become whole and at peace with themselves again.

She leads him away from his guard place and out into the plain. They are the first to enter this awesome sea of grass and this too makes her feel powerful. Her head is in a spin and she seems to go into a semi-trance. Her feeling is shared by the Gypsy Culvato for he shakes beside her in anticipation of what he has only ever dreamed of.

As they leave she hears a soft muttered comment from Surrey Anne, who misses nothing, and a low laugh from Port Rial.

She does not see Cudjo Accompong as he kneels beside his beloved weapons, cleaning them in preparation for any surprises tomorrow might bring. But she senses his dour glance and dark disapproval.

But now she is a bird—a free-falling star drifting through timeless space. She clutches him with hungry hands and begins divesting him of the dirty animal skins these barbarians wear. At first she is gentle, sensing his strangeness to these affairs, but then the need catches hold of her and she goes into a frenzy of kissing, scratching, biting. He, too, casts aside his inhibitions—and his ever-present sharp spear—as they fall to the ground, a black body and brown, to become part of the tall grass's shadows . . . a part of the earth. And there they dance a love dance such as neither has ever danced before.

In the farthermost part of the camp the twins smiled as they heard her cry of pure passion. They could remember other nights with other women. But that was all over for them now. They wondered what this new country would bring them.

The next day rose wild and red so the whole plain was bathed in a pink glow from the cloudless sky. The ten humans stood by the side of the hill and looked out at the vast emptiness. An emptiness however that was full of life as the tall stalks of the grass rustled gently in the breeze that, even now, blew across the open spaces. Where it touched the tops of the grass, a moving shadow was formed and thus the Ilkari could actually see the passage of the wind. It was a sight they had never seen before except occasionally when a dust Devil had been made spiralling up into the sky as it raced across the Purple Plains. This was much more spectacular though.

'So where is this river the Goddess of the moon talks so much about in her sleep at night?' Akar Black Head wanted to know and spat on the last rock the hills had to offer before they became this mass of grass. 'I am glad we have seen the last of *that!*' he scowled. 'Now let us see this true enemy we must fight. Enemy we know!'

'We are in strange lands, cousin-brother, and so we will find strange enemies,' Culvato murmured from beside him.

'And strange friends,' the warrior quickly replied as Kareen suppressed a laugh. His dark-blue eyes bore into the youth so Culvato turned a shy, blushing head away.

'You can lead us into this wonderful new world then, Akar, since you are so anxious to leave the last one.' Red Mond half-smiled.

He was glad the caravan was settling in together again: like mud in a river after a stampede has gone through. Even though some of the mud moves to a different place it is still the same old river bottom. That was something his father had told him before he disappeared. Nothing would ever make him forget Joda, just as he could never forget his cousin Ilki. He fingered once more his hair bracelet made from the red locks and honey-blond locks of his two young clansmen and stared into the middle distance with dreaming eyes.

'Come, my cousin,' came the soft voice of Kareen and she took him by the hand to lead him into the forest of grass.

It was a curious world they went into now. The grass was as thick as Cudjo Accompong's legs and taller by a head or two than the tallest horse amongst Port Rial's entourage. It could be brushed aside or sliced with swords. Sometimes a meandering path could be found, made by some creature. But none was seen and the only sound heard was the rush of wind through the grass. Because it was so constant, one's ears became used to it and it blended in with the environment.

The only living things they encountered were a myriad of insects. There was the high-pitched clicking of crickets or cicadas and the hum of bees, wasps, dragonflies or other hovering insects all day long. Butterflies were everywhere—of such colours and such a size as they had never seen before.

It seemed that living a life of seclusion amongst these mighty grass stalks had caused the insects to evolve into larger species than their more normal kinfolk. Indeed, such was the size of the grass that the ten humans felt like insects as well. The Ilkari were reminded, every one, of stories about giants and they felt themselves to be in some weird world of the giants. The four Visitors felt that there was something desperately wrong with this land. The only one not affected by this curious shrinking feeling was the girl S'shony who was closeted in her cocoon. It was with no little relief that Red Mond Star Light would join her each night. At least he had the comfort of four walls and a confined reality to keep him sane. Some of the others were beginning to get run down by the enormity of it all.

The ants were the veritable lords of this land and their cities were everywhere, as were their roads and roving armies. Some of these ants were some three feet long and their nests a good acre in width.

After some confrontations with these monsters—in one of which a fearless Akar Black Head was stung on the arm repelling an attack on the camp—the savagery of the Visitors' weaponry was proven once again as they decimated a small horde of the giant, red, vicious-looking insects, with their heartless black eyes and cruel pincers.

It was after this attack on the camp that Akar Black Head became more friendly towards the Visitors. It was Surrey Anne's herbal medicine and kind administration that stopped the burning wound becoming anything worse than an ugly jagged white line running down his arm. While he was recovering and the caravan rested a few days, Port Rial struck up a type of conversation with him, just as he had done with Joda.

It was no good trying to interest the big man in the sacred weed for he refused to touch it. But he enjoyed a good story, so Port Rial engaged him in stories about his Island home and the other places they had seen and what had happened to members of his party: Saint Catherine, The Baptist, The Syrian, Porky and Clarendon Jon Cannu. The language was hard to follow but Port Rial was a great mimic and adept at sign language as this was how he had managed business affairs throughout the known world. Of course, although Port Rial was telling the truth for the most part to Akar Black Head, these stories were of great mystery and excitement to the warrior.

Akar Black Head enjoyed being close to all that unknown power and his alert eyes followed everything the Visitors did.

CHAPTER EIGHT

Then came the day when they lit upon the beginning of the river promised in S'shony's vision and all of Kareen's dreams and wishes became true.

This river that flowed before them now was huge and blue and unbelievable. Just like everything else on this plain it was larger than life. Or so thought the Ilkari who had never flown over the incredible width and wonder of the mighty Amazon in the jungles of the little people as had the Visitors.

Here, at last, were real trees again, where they clung with gnarled roots to the sandy banks of this massive waterway. The other side was a mass of hazy blue shapes on the horizon, distorted by distance. This was the Father of all waterways, Kareen decided. From his waters came all the other rivers known to Humankind. This was a river that would—and could—never die. She was glad when Red Mond Star Light decided to camp here a short while.

For Red Mond came the memory of his mother's story about the Mississippi and he marvelled that her tale should mingle with his own story.

That there were fish in this river was soon proven by the two Keepers of the Trees. Their quick spears soon captured a dozen fat silver gifts of the water. Fish was a rare food supply among the Ilkari, except for the inevitable cat-fish. Only Akar Black Head in his wide travels had eaten fresh sweet fish so big one could feed a whole family. So the meal that night was long and pleasurable.

For the first time in days the Visitors brought forth their musical instruments and Kareen found her harp. Everyone danced and sang the night away. The tall grass had stopped about half a mile from the river and the ground now was clothed in a soft blue-grey, sweet-smelling type of grass that, at its highest point, was only knee high. There was a sense of achievement in their mission. If this great water existed as told from the moon Goddess's prophecy then, so too, must all the rest of it be true. Soon they would be at war with their hated enemy.

That first evening all ten of them bathed together in the cool blue waters of the river. Kareen performed a special ceremony blessing this river so huge it could be given no name.

For two moons of every twelve on the Purple Plains of the Ilkari it rained in their hot shimmering Tribal lands. *Then* the plains were alive with flowers and the river ran full and flowing to the end of the known world. That was the birth of Sister Earth and the river was her umbilical cord, so the stories of the Ilkari told. But the other ten moons were the revenge of Sister Sun. The grass dried up and the river became sickly brown and green. A few bad times it had dwindled to a few sparse waterholes and once it had dried up altogether, causing much distress and death. For without the birth of Sister Earth there was no point in living.

The giant Cudjo Accompong kept close to the edge of the water, weapon as always in his hand and a scowl upon his face. But the woman with Culvato was happy and smiling as she rarely did. Red Mond Star Light admired again these Visitors' ebony nakedness, so perfect were their bodies as opposed to the burnt, scarred, melanoma-kissed bodies of the Ilkari and the slim, scarred bodies of the Keepers.

That evening a wedge of ducks noisily skimmed upon the water to settle down for the night with raucous quacks and calls. In the trees other birds sang and whistled and the sounds were enjoyed by all whose ears had been assailed for so long by nothing but the moaning wind through the grass and the chirruping of giant insects. The sunset was especially fantastic that night as it was reflected in the great waters of the river and this seemed to be another good omen.

Red Mond was watching the dying embers of Sister Sun's blaze and listening to the throaty croaking of the many frogs who nestled in the oozy black mud. This was a whole new sound to him; an orchestra of high chut-chut-chuts down to deep burping and other sounds in between. The croaking, whirring chorus seemed to be Sister Earth's way of saying goodbye to Sister Sun. Perhaps she was crying out for her brother-in-law, Father Moon. Anyway, the frogs' song came from the heart of the earth and, with the cries of wild ducks as they flew back home, the song settled upon the earth with the song of the wind, bringing a sense of peace with it.

Red Mond was joined by Culvato. These two had not seen so much of one another while they were crossing the grassy plains and it was pleasant for two old friends to sit together in this setting.

After a while Culvato spoke. 'So, paal, what new adventures does tomorrow bring?'

'I have been unable to read the stars for so long. I think I will read them tonight.'

'This land is a sad land, do you not think so? Sometimes at night the song of the grass was a lonely and mournful tune. It seemed as if we were the first humans in a long while to cross this plain,' Culvato whispered. For it seemed the sort of place where a whisper was appropriate.

'We were as alone as the most far-flung star,' Red Mond agreed.

'Yet even that star has the light of the sun to comfort it and make it into what it is—a light in the sky,' Culvato argued.

'I feel at peace now. That much the stars tell me.' Red Mond half-smiled, refusing to be drawn into one of Culvato's philosophical arguments.

'I, too, am at peace and have found my home at last.' Culvato smiled. 'As your home is in the cocoon with your Goddess, my home is in my heart.' He grinned at the Moon-talker, who wondered just how much this unbeliever with the wandering feet and mind knew. But he could trust this friend as he could no other—not even his true cousin, Kareen.

Culvato placed a hand on his comrade's shoulder and the two of them watched as the last of Sister Sun's crimson skirts went rustling over the horizon.

'It was said, in the old times, that the song of the frogs began to die,' Culvato began. 'Where before there had been joyous tune there was nothing. People began to wonder why the frogs were disappearing. But they did not wonder enough for it was Sister Earth's cry for help and her cry was only heard by Sister Sun who kissed her with treacherous lips. It is well to remember that the earth is a complex place and that every little thing makes a whole.'

His eyes, that had lost much of their fire of late, gazed out into the huge still waters of the river.

'It is good to hear the song of the frogs again. Perhaps this time we will listen to what they have to say.'

The next morning the two Keepers of the Trees set off early because Weerluk's sharp eyes had spotted signs for kangaroo. They were sick of depending on the white man's food. It hadn't been too bad, though—possibly because it had been cooked by the black woman with the name not much different from names of their own language: Surriyan.

They had kept their thoughts to themselves on what had happened at the village in the hills when the white boy was killed. After all, that was white man's business. They had been killing each other forever and when they were tired of that they had turned on the Keepers of the Trees and had killed them as well.

They could sense the result of this destruction on these desolate pages of the landscape they had just passed, where not a single tree stood to hold the spirit of an ancestor close to the earth. It was a forgotten land—an unhappy land for the Keepers of the Trees and they were glad to get out of it.

The caravan moved leisurely along the river bank now, savouring the calm and enjoying the view of and sights upon this huge river. The Keepers' spears caught many fish and game while their boomerangs brought down many wild fowl. They became the main hunters of the group now. Twice, Akar Black Head and Culvato surprised herds of the wild pigs rooting among the rich black mud of the flats, so those days the Ilkari and the Visitors dined well on pork.

Red Mond was interested to note that the giant Cudjo Accompong would only eat food he had himself caught and prepared. He would not eat the occasional shell fish they found, nor would he eat any fish that by nature lived on the bottom of the river amongst the mud. I am learning a new thing every day, he thought.

The Visitors sat down one evening and all four began repairing a net they had with them. They had many strange and wonderful gifts brought from the sun. This was one of them, made of fine clear line that, despite its delicate look, was almost impossible to break.

She hums an Island song along with the others:

Dready got a job to do
And he's got to fulfill that mission.
To see his hurt is their
Great ambition
But we will survive
In this world of competition
Cause no matter what they do
Natty keep on coming thru
And no matter what they say
Natty de deh every day.

They could almost be home again on the swampy banks of the Black River. Thinking this, she instantly glances around for sign of alligators, but there are none. Beside her Surrey Anne talks eagerly of the dishes she can make up when they catch their hoard of fish. Port Rial teases her, mentioning his favourite dishes. He was born on the coast and grew up practically in the ocean, although this wide blue water is different from the choppy blue-green Carribean sea that laps against his front door. Even Cudjo is happy and content to leave his weapons alone for once. He too must be reminded of the Black River, for he has lived far up it in the quiet places the true Ras Tafarians liked to frequent—as did the descendants of the Maroons.

'Me t'ink yuh ahready catch yuh fish, Nanny. Tell I 'ow does 'im taste?' The giant suddenly gently teases and a rare smile crosses his sombre face.

As their journey progresses so too does the deterioration of their air suits. Cudjo alone has managed to make his last but the others have taken to wearing skins like their hosts. Now his sausage-sized fingers feel the yellowish-red, wild-dog jacket Culvato has given her and she so admires.

'A present fe she Queen. Queen from sun she go a earth. Cho! What famblys fi you think of us now,' Cudjo laughed, much amused.

'Is nuttin' wrong with be in love, natty,' she says, embarrassed by the big man's teasing and the others' suppressed laughter. 'Me say you try it some time, nuh!'

'I-man did an' see what him get me? Nuttin' but consternation and trouble-trouble, sisthren, seh deh,' the giant said, his smile disappearing.

Before the pleasant mood can be broken by bad memories, Port Rial bursts into a pirate song of famous buccaneers and the damage they gleefully did so long ago.

They travelled the river for perhaps a week, going ever onwards towards the setting sun as Red Mond informed them the stars had told him to do. Sometimes the tall grass came right down to the river's edge, but mostly it kept well back as though afraid of the murmuring river. There were signs everywhere of animal life, if none of human, and in the distance small herds could be seen. There were antelope of several kind and zebra, vast herds of wild horses and, of course, kangaroo in their hundreds. There was also a sign of the occasional bear and, once, Akar Black Head smelt the strong odour of a lion on the air—but no sign of it was seen.

One day, when the sky was gradually gathering up scurrying fluffy clouds in its huge blue hands; when the nights were getting colder while the days were becoming shorter, Kareen and Surrey Anne sauntered out to search for medicinal plants. By rights, an Earth Mother should have been wary of a child of the sun but these two women were both the healers of their two different groups and they had formed a warm alliance.

Bees buzzed busily amongst the flowers that still grew on the wild herbs and their fragrant scents blessed the air. For a while there were only the sounds of their snipping off the leaves or flowers and their heavy breathing as they exerted themselves.

'The river looks inviting. We should go for a swim later,' Kareen said. 'It is a good feeling to have water all around you instead of sunlight,' she added, before remembering that being a Sun child probably the opposite would apply to her charcoal companion.

'I-an'-I a go make cake fe Port Rial birthdate. Is why me gatherin' 'erbs now,' Surrey Anne explained, unconsciously fingering her brilliant purple necklace—his gift to her on *her* birthdate.

'A birthday? For the skinny one?' Kareen said surprised. 'Then we must make him something special,' she said decisively. She pointed in the direction of a clump of tall straggly reeds that bent weary heads towards the slowly swirling currents of the river. 'There could be some duck eggs in there. That would be a pleasant taste for him.'

They ambled over to the reeds. When they arrived they surprised a small deer who sprang past them on agile feet. It so startled Surrey Anne

141

that she fell over and the look on her face sent the taller, older woman into fits of giggling mirth.

They waded through the shallows and—sure enough—nestled in amongst the reeds in a wide curved nest were some twelve, large, white eggs. Kareen smiled as she chose six small gifts from Sister Earth to one of her nieces; this Sun child who still worshipped her partner's birthday.

She turned her smiling face to make some mild joke about this—about High Ones living forever so what was the point of a birthday—when a rustling in the reeds behind her stayed her thoughts. As she rose from where she bent over the nest a throaty cough caused her instantly to freeze, while her grey eyes dilated in fear.

The cough turned into an angry scream as a large male leopard—beautiful in its dappled coat, terrifying with its sharp claws and glistening teeth—deprived of the small deer he had been stalking, leapt upon the two women.

The creature's scream was echoed by Surrey Anne. Kareen had no time to do anything, for the leopard had chosen her as his victim. Now its warm, soft, stinking body pressed down on her as teeth and claws sought to still her squirming.

Surrey Anne dragged her gun from off her shoulder and with shaking hands aimed it at the roaring cat not three feet away as she relived the horror of The Syrian's death. But when she pulled the trigger nothing happened! She pulled it again but there was only a harmless click.

Another leopard, smaller than the first, came streaking across the grass towards its fat, sweet-smelling meal. The stench of fear in the air only served to make this female more excited at the thrill of the kill.

Kareen, fighting for her life with only her fists and feet, kicking and punching the rank, heaving sides of the bigger leopard, had a split second's image of Surrey Anne's raw terror before she was bowled over by the creature. Kareen had another second to reflect that these were just ordinary people, after all, who had no magic powers over all the creations of Sister Earth. Her whole world fell apart and such was this revelation to the Earth Mother's soul that she almost gave up there and then. But a searing rake of the vicious claws across her breast and shoulder jerked her into the moment.

Using her great strength she rolled out from under the leopard, gushing blood. She clung with dear life to the neck so the teeth and claws could not reach her. At the same time she tried to exert pressure on the neck to break it. The graceful animal was an accomplished killing machine and his muscles were too sinewy for her to grasp. Besides she was weak from loss of blood.

He tossed and twisted and then, at last, managed to hurl her off and sink his teeth into her other shoulder. She gasped with the pain of it all while his powerful jaws worried her body, shaking her like a puppy with a cloth doll—like the doll she had had as a child not so long ago. She felt herself slipping into unconsciousness and into the cruel embrace of sudden death that would be so sweet for her, if it would mean the pain would go away . . . The most horrifying sound now was the contented rumble of the leopard's purring as it tore away at her still-living flesh.

A spear, sharp and bright, flashed briefly in the sun before burying itself deep into the leopard's head, entering through its ear. It fell across Kareen, instantly dead.

The female had been temporarily stopped from her murderous course by Surrey Anne's swinging gun. But then it had fastened its teeth into the coat Kareen had given her—the lion's coat which her lover Yellow Eyes had made for her from his story. It started to drag her away into the tall grass and she felt herself fainting from fear. Knowing that at any moment the saliva-flecked teeth would rip into her flesh and the cruel green eyes, alight with primitive rage, would gloat over her pathetic death throes, turning her into a quivering mess, she lost all control of her body—and almost her mind.

Then there was a fierce cry and someone was beside her. Through her tears of fright and pain she glimpsed burnished red hair afire in the sun's rays. A heavy club smashed into those green eyes and when the leopard let go of her and crouched to face this new enemy, another figure approached from the other side and brown hands jabbed a sword into her mottled splotchy side and she sank with a strangled growl down to the grass to die.

Culvato and Red Mond Star Light stood, chests heaving together as one. Then they turned distressed eyes upon one another just as an anguished cry escaped from Akar Black Head as he arrived too late.

'Kareen! My Kareen!' he cried.

Over by the fallen male leopard the big form of the Ilkari warrior knelt down tentatively.

'Is she dead?' Red Mond asked in a shocked whisper.

'She breathes,' Culvato whispered back.

'We must get her back to camp at once and stop her bleeding. The High One? Can she be hurt?' Red Mond said and moved to the side of the shocked, dazed Surrey Anne.

Now Nanny and Mungart came running. The five carefully picked up the wounded Kareen and did their best to staunch the freely flowing blood. Nanny wrapped a comforting arm around her countrywoman's shoulders and led her stumbling away, murmuring to her in their sing-song language.

As the four men carried Kareen into the camp, Mungart's coo-ee was answered by his brother, who came running from the long grass. He had been out hunting but even he had heard the terrified screams and had set off at a lope, leaving the fat kangaroos to live another day.

Red Mond was beside himself with grief. 'Come back, cousin-mine!

Don't leave me alone in this strange cruel land where beauty is only a disguise for unspeakable evil,' he lamented.

Weerluk skidded to a halt beside them, his dark eyes concerned. In a few bursts of musical language his brother explained what had happened. Then Weerluk turned and ran towards the river.

Culvato gently prised Red Mond away from the quietly moaning form. Her tawny hair was clotted with blood and her left breast was ripped to ruination. The white bones of both her shoulders lay bare where the beast had gnawed away at her. Her usually calm grey eyes had dilated from shock and pain and she recognised no one.

Akar Black Head knelt beside her once more and carefully took off her tattered skin coat. His eyes looked up at Culvato's, so devoid of their cynicism and anger that it was another shock to the Gypsy. 'She will die. We have no knowledge of medicine and, besides, the wound is too deep and severe,' he said softly.

'Nooooo!' came Red Mond's scream. 'This was not what I read in the stars!'

'Read in the stars!' snorted Akar Black Head, and his violence, never far from the surface, returned. 'There is *nothing* to read in the stars. Do you see what happens when you follow these "High Ones"? Kareen would never have let herself become so relaxed if she did not think she had the power of a Goddess to get her out of trouble. Where is the sword she always wears? Hanging on a tree by her camp, because she has the love of a High One to protect her. See what that love has brought her!' he shouted.

But before his anger could spill over, Weerluk arrived panting from the river. In his hands he carried fine white clay and this he pressed rapidly into the cruel wounds, thus staunching the blood flow. He ignored the others gathered there as he spoke to Mungart, who nodded and silently left. Then he turned dark eyes to Red Mond's distressed brown ones.

'Brother, we have medicine here. A cure as old as the land. We will comfort your cousin and she will not die.'

His voice was calm and soft as he stared into the distraught face. Of the two brothers he had been the most wary and the most unfriendly, keeping much to himself.

He had seen that, although they were all different and often argued among themselves, they were all united in their respect and love for this red-headed one. He had wondered which Keeper of the Trees had been his ancestor and what his Totem would be. He knew this white one, who was not really white, had the magic and the beliefs Weerluk's people possessed.

He had also noticed and watched the gentleness of the big, tawny-haired woman who had a name not dissimilar to one of their own women's names—Kareen. She loved the land as much as did the women

144

of his family. He had slipped out after her at times and studied her ceremonies.

This was why he forgot about all those crowded around him and bent over the woman, quiet now the clay, cool and soothing, had eased her suffering.

That very morning Mungart had killed a fat emu and even now he had been cooking it on their fire in preparation for tonight.

Now he came back with several furs taken recently from the many possums that lived in the trees along the river and a small container of emu oil that bubbled softly and sent its pungent odour to the air. Also he had some of the sacred red clay, which his people called wilgi, hot from the fire.

Carefully, on the great wound of her shoulder, Weerluk placed some possum furs and then he bound it up with other furs. The wound on her breast and other shoulder was just as succinctly washed clean while Mungart mixed the warm red clay with the emu oil. This putty Mungart applied to the wounds and then another possum skin was wrapped around them.

'We must keep this warm at all times. But we cannot stay here,' Weerluk said to Red Mond.

His brother looked up from where he mixed more emu oil with wilgi and said something Red Mond could not follow. They seemed to have an argument for a moment before an unhappy Mungart capitulated, shaking his head.

'We must take you to the Silver City. There you will find medicine more powerful than ours perhaps. There, at least, you will be with your people.'

'What is this place?' Red Mond wished to know.

'It is a huge camp beside the banks of a huge river—bigger than this one.'

'What do you mean "my people"?'

'They are white, like you.'

'So were the people in the hills.'

'We told you of their dangers, brother. You would not listen.' Weerluk's dark sombre eyes never left his own and Red Mond had to agree the Keeper was right.

She watches Culvato come towards them where they gather around the stricken Surrey Anne. The coat Kareen had given her has saved her life, Port Rial cries out joyfully. But he is the only one happy. Cudjo Accompong is grey with rage as he berates the young girl for failing to check her weapon. An empty gun is useless! How can they expect to survive this trip if they don't take care of their weapons! They are the most powerful people on this Island, don't they see! Only because they have the weaponry to destroy a whole culture if need be. But what use is that power if you walk around with no bullets in your gun! To be killed by a leopard—a wild animal. What stupidity! Has she forgotten already the fate that befell Clarendon Jon in the Northlands and Porky and The Syrian here?

'*But him country beautiful yah, Ras! No danger dey about,*' *Surrey Anne wept.*

'*You see him danger!*' *Cudjo cried.*

'*Enough! Leave she alone. Her already face him one leopard t'day, maan!*' *Port Rial butted in suddenly.* '*She friend dyin' deh.*'

It is unusual for the little pirate to face up to a confrontation. His whole mode of life is based on one of stealthy attack and quick withdrawal. Still, the greatest treasure he possesses now is the laughter and smiles of Surrey Anne. He will fight to the death to protect them.

'*Jackal growl at him lion,*' *Cudjo says wonderingly, as he moves into battle stance.*

'*Jackal him steal de lion meal many a time b'fore, me seh,*' *Port Rial says bravely, not stepping out of the giant's shadow.*

It is her way to let arguments come out before she assumes control. It is good to argue and get everything out in the open, especially when she had such diverse and fiery people on the crew. But now she must intervene. She has never had to stand in for Port Rial, who has only ever been interested in his treasure, his sacred smoke, his singing and dancing and, of course, Surrey Anne after Clarendon Jon Cannu was killed.

'*She bungo-girl fe havin' him gun empty. But she alive,*' *she says.* '*We in Babylon an' the temptations of he be everywhere. We mus' keep each other's company an' stand backaback.*'

She is worried over Cudjo Accompong's remark—made in anger it is true—about how they are the most powerful people on this Island. It is true, but has the charade of playing a God finally turned into reality for the giant Ras Tafarian? He is not noted for his love of white men—or indeed of anyone not truly of his faith. Is he becoming carried away with the fearsome hold he has on these ignorant people of different Races? That is how the Muslims rose in power on their own Island and is one of the reasons they left, to escape the strict laws being enforced on parts of their home.

'*Every hill has only one tiger,*' *she murmurs in warning to the giant.*

'*One love, sisthren.*' *He smiles back. But it is a haughty smile.*

She is glad to see Culvato come across towards them. Cudjo shrugs and grins.

'*Wha' magic me woman Saint Catherine leave she Captain? So you a go bewitch de bwoy. Will you take him from him home a fi you beloved Island? Or will she Captain leave him gaspin' like him fish dey pon shore?*'

Port Rial laughs out loud and even Surrey Anne manages a watery smile. So she has diffused the argument at the price of her dignity.

And what will you do, strong and independent Nanny, warrior of the Maroon? When the war is over and it is time to pick up your dead (if dead there be) and go home to the quiet green trees and glades of your Maroon community? Will you pluck him like a flower only to watch him dry up and die, or will you carry on home alone and just die a little yourself as you did when The Baptist was murdered?

It was a sombre group that left in the cold light of early morning. There were those among them who could not understand the fickleness of these High Ones who could destroy a whole village of men, women and children at a whim because of the death of one youth, yet could stand back and not use their magic when the most peaceful and kindest among them was mauled by one of her own creatures.

Before they left, Culvato and Akar Black Head skinned the two cats—and it was not lost to them that these were the same Devils who took away Joda's father. It was their intention to make them into a wonderful blanket as a gift for when she recovered: Kareen, beloved member of their clan, friend and Earth Mother to them all.

For a week they wended their way along the river. Every evening Weerluk would add some clean putty to the smaller of Kareen's wounds and the two Keepers would sit beside her all night, keeping the emu oil and ochre mixture warm. As soon as Surrey Anne got over her shock, she, too, would sit up with them, putting mixtures of her own concoction onto the larger wound. Sometimes she even rested her rose-crystal necklace on the wound, believing in the healing propensities of that rock. But there was really very little any of them could do for the awful gash that had laid open the shoulder.

She never regained consciousness.

One day, as Mungart, Culvato and Port Rial were out ahead of the main group, foraging for food, they came to a great bend in the river. They had come to a huge forest in the last two days where mighty trees threw dark cloaks of shadow around them and kept the light both from Sister Sun and the tormented Father Moon away. All they had seen was a leafy canopy over their heads and the thick, gnarled, twisting trunks of trees some thousands of years old. They were reminded of the grassy plain and the fears they had had there. Now it seemed as if the grass had turned to trees and they, once again, were dwarfed by nature.

So it was not without a little fear that the Ilkari trod these paths, made soft and silent by countless fallen leaves. They were not used to the presence of trees in such number or of great height. The only sound they had heard for two days was the clear, bell-like calls of hidden birds that seemed to echo in this quiet place (Port Rial would have said like church bells) and the murmuring of the river as it ran on beside them.

Mungart, with Port Rial and Culvato just behind him, had been following the tracks of a kangaroo that led down to the water's edge. Here, right beside the river, with their very roots dipping into the water, stood a grove of about five trees, the likes of which neither young man of such diverse cultures had ever seen before. Not even Mungart who should have known every tree upon the land.

Their massive trunks were roughly barked and brown or grey, yet when they became narrower branches they were smooth and green. But it was their shape that was most surprising. For as their branches became thinner then so did they hang down in great cascades like bright green hair. The bigger the tree the more spectacular this looked. Their green heads soared some two hundred feet up into the air and their green hair fell like a waterfall to float out in long strands in the water. Each of the three young men paused, all thought of hunting gone, as they savoured this marvel of Nature.

The trees breathed softly back at them—a mellow lowing sound as a small breeze pushed through the myriad of narrow, deep-green leaves.

Then Mungart's sharp ears heard another sound and he raised a warning hand to the other two. Mindful of what had happened the last time everyone had relaxed in the presence of great beauty, they crept forward after Mungart—ready for anything.

They heard the sound as well—the tinkling of carefree women's laughter. They crept up to the trunks of the trees, each of which was some eight feet across.

In the cool, green-brown water twelve naked females cavorted as they laughed and played.

Never had any, including those with experience of Nightstalkers, seen a person so white and yet out in the sun. For their skin was as pale as a waterlily's petal or a soft summer cloud or the bones of a desert-dried animal or the purest, best, white ochre. Their hair also seemed white, so blonde was it. Except for one whose hair was a deep, dark, auburn red.

'They are women from the Silver City,' Mungart whispered. 'We must not scare them and be careful for there will be a guard about.'

But Culvato understood only a little of what he said and Port Rial none at all. Indeed, it was the Visitor who stepped boldly out into this idyllic scene. For what dangers *could* there be in such a setting with the trees, and women bathing in the water and caressing the river's sand with lightly dancing feet. And if there was danger, then he would meet it with his gun held now with alert fingers.

It was not the women who first saw the gangling, black figure in his outlandish uniform of a rapidly fading, silver jump suit and bedraggled furs.

The youth who had been sent to guard the women had settled himself between two great roots of a tree and had snuggled into the soft bed of fallen leaves for a snooze. It was not allowed for men to observe the naked flesh of a female, unless she were his wife. Especially *these* females, who were precious to the well-being of their city. Besides, there was never any danger at the House of Willows, these particular women's most sacred place.

So when he heard the dry snap of a twig he thought it just a branch cracking in the heat of midday. But when he heard the murmured voice he could scarce believe his ears. No Outsider ever came this close to the city unless it were to rob the gardens in quick and furtive raid. Slowly he raised his tousled head above the twisting root, then his sleep-bleary eyes opened wide in fright as he saw the Demon not thirty feet from him. Carefully he raised his bow and silently notched an arrow to his string. He was hidden by shadow and a curtain of leaves and obscured by the root so the Demon had not seen him yet. He drew back and aimed, difficult though it was, lying on his back and his target almost unseen by the waving strands of tree branch. But he was a soldier and greatly skilled in the defence of his King's domain.

His fingers began to let go of the taut string.

Port Rial was still grinning at the bevy of females relaxed in their own little world, as yet unaware of their guests, when something whistled past his ear. He turned startled eyes upon Culvato who, even now, leapt forward with a fierce cry, dragging his sword from his scabbard by his side.

Culvato's spear had slammed into the young guard's shoulder and buried its wicked point in his white flesh. He fell back with a gasp of pain, letting his bow and arrows fall uselessly to the ground. Now he watched in horror as this other dark Demon leapt from the shadows it had been born of and charged towards him—murder in its eye.

A cry from the red-headed woman stopped the Gypsy in his tracks, for it was a heart-rending cry of real anguish. He noticed this boy was of the age of Joda and also had curly red hair like the woman's. He turned to face the auburn-haired beauty and lowered his sword.

'We mean no harm, sister-cousin. But we have lost our brother to strangers before.'

'You speak our language,' she replied.

'Are they Outsiders?' a blonde girl called querulously.

'They are Demons. The sons of Phineas come to burn us in their fire,' cried another in great fear, then gave a little shriek with all the rest as Mungart stepped from the trees. The red-headed woman looked first from Mungart to the others, then back again.

'But this is strange,' murmured their self-appointed leader. 'What kind of Keepers are you?'

'We are not Keepers, sister-cousin. I am Culvato from the Ilkari and this is the High One—a child from Sister Sun—they call Port Rial.'

At the mention of his name the Visitor gave a dazzling smile at the girls. He was still amazed at their translucent whiteness. He had not yet seen a Nightstalker and on his Island there were no white people. The people he traded with mostly tended to be olive or various shades of brown. Then he shook himself out of his reverie and went quickly over to the stricken guard and knelt beside him. He smiled reassuringly at the boy and told him this might hurt. But the boy only cringed away in terror at the Demon's language he could not understand. Port Rial grasped the sturdy haft in both hands. Before the lad could protest he gave a mighty twist and push, forcing the wicked barb through the skin and pushing the whole spear after it, trailing blood. To stop the gush of blood that followed, Mungart clamped a wad of possum fur over the wound and Culvato took his spear to wash the blood off in the water. But Jarebb (for Jarebb was his name) heeded none of this, as with a fearsome shriek he had fainted.

Meanwhile the other women had gathered at the water's edge in a frightened bunch, their little world shattered and all their peace flown on hasty wings. Differing shades of blue eyes gazed at these three, unusual, dark men in fear, awe, curiosity . . . or even boldness.

Then the red-haired woman lowered her eyes and said demurely, 'It is the law that no man may see us unclothed. No man may come to the House of Willows unless he is a guard and even then he must stay hidden.'

'Your laws are your laws,' Culvato said brusquely. 'I have no laws and this one is a God who makes the laws while this one is a Keeper of the Trees upon whose land we all walk. So talk to me no more of laws. But get dressed by all means. And hurry if we are to save my clanswoman!'

Their clothing was singularly colourless, being of a silver-grey cloth that, when wrapped around them, showed no more of the women than their hands, feet and eyes. They wore no shoes and now Culvato noticed their feet were hardened and cracked from the rough terrain; that both their feet and hands were burnt black by the sun, a strong contrast to their bodies' ivory skin. They resembled the feet and hands of the Ilkari and Keepers and indicated that the same hard life was led by these white, curiously dressed women. He relaxed a little at this familiarity.

Their eyes bore into his own.

'What will you have us do now?' said one, whose eyes were the deepest royal blue, with flecks of green and yellow.

'Our clan sister has been hurt and we would go with you to your city where, it has been told, you can heal her. That is your home—is it not?'

'It *is* our home. And our home only. Strangers are not welcome there,' said another woman. A wisp of red hair, that had escaped the clothing, showed she was the leader. Her eyes stared hard at Port Rial, who was no longer smiling but staring back at the women in some puzzlement.

'We are not welcome anywhere yet we still travel on,' Culvato said almost to himself. Then he looked up at the swarm of blue eyes buzzing around his face.

'You will follow the Keeper,' he said. 'We will follow behind with the boy. And don't forget the one with me is a God with the magic of a God. Be warned, I have seen him and his three companions destroy a whole village.'

He could not fathom what effect this had on the women, being able only to see their eyes. But they all set off in single file after Mungart, with never a word of protest. He and the Visitor supported the wounded boy. Port Rial tried to tell him something—something about the children of Babylon. It seemed to do with the way the women were dressed in cocoons, almost as though they were afraid of the sun, and it appeared to upset Port Rial not a little. This made Culvato even more alert, for this man—God or Human—had seen more than *he* ever would. A shiver ran momentarily up Culvato's spine. They were seeing so many unusual and new things lately that these could be some sort of Nightstalker (perhaps even the ghosts of Nightstalkers) and they had wandered into their Hell. We shall see what we will see, he thought.

When they arrived back at camp the first to see them was Weerluk, who knelt beside Kareen. They had been warned a few moments earlier by his brother's coo-ee. Even Nanny and Cudjo Accompong had sensed the uneasiness in that call, and as the twelve women were ushered into the clearing, the same look of worry was cast over the faces of the other Visitors as that of their compatriot, who held onto the boy, Jarebb, as though he were the worst type of vermin.

'Muslims. Is all we need, sisthren. Them dey pon fanatical!' Cudjo snarled.

'The banana he ripe but tarantula he hidden,' Nanny warned.

'Muslim alias. Him uprisin' in Kingston killed much-much people. I-an'-I lost part we soul deh!' the giant reminded her.

And how could she forget? The burning houses, the screaming children, the blood-drenched bundles of rags that were once humans as the Muslim element of the Island had turned the paradise into a slaughterhouse when they tried to wrest control from the Baptist Government and the Ras Tafarians. She had lost her three brothers, her father and one sister as the Maroons rose up once more to fight for their beloved Cockpit County. She only had her mother left—a wreck, old before her time at the calamity that had befallen her family—and a baby sister scarcely into her teens to look after her.

'Cause no trouble, Cudjo, nuh. Wait a see what way she cradle rock.'

The women crowded into the clearing and there was a brief pause while each group stared at the other. Then one pointed at Akar Black Head's blue eyes and Kareen and Red Mond's hair and there was a muttering among them. Then the one with the bluest eyes pushed forwards and knelt beside Kareen.

Red Mond moved forward also. 'My name is Red Mond Star Light and this is my cousin Kareen. Can you save her?' he asked plainly.

'I am Shimona,' said the red-haired woman and she pointed to the one beside Kareen. 'This is Ruth, our healer. Let her look at our sister.'

'For sister she is!' cried one. 'As he is our brother, Shimona. Look at his hair.'

'See the big one's eyes? As blue as our own.'

As Ruth bent forward to carefully peel away the possum-fur bandage, Weerluk's hand grasped hers roughly and his hard black eyes scowled up at Red Mond. 'She is from the Silver City,' he told the Ilkari. 'If this woman dies then so shall she. I swear on my father's grave.'

Weerluk got up in his abrupt manner and stalked off, Mungart following behind him. Weerluk had just spent several nights beside this white woman, the longest and closest he had spent with any white person, and he had developed a special affinity with her.

'We will wait for you beside the gates of the Silver City until she is well, ngooni. Don't forget, you are going into a world you have never dreamed of. A world we know of only in the stories of the Old Time—that came after the Dreamtime and all its creating,' Mungart called over his shoulder.

Then the forest swallowed him up, and his brother.

'You must come with us, Red Mond Star Light. To our home where we have doctors and medicine to fix even this cruel wound. The Keepers' medicine is good too and has saved her arm but now she needs proper help,' Shimona said. *Her* deep blue eyes had flecks of colour that were almost as grey as Kareen's own. They stared over Red Mond's shoulder in wonder at the gathered Visitors.

The other women huddled together fearfully, looking at the angry scowl of Cudjo Accompong and the hard face of Nanny. Even Surrey Anne had a bleak look upon her round face.

But Red Mond had no choice. Besides, he felt a great calming effect when he looked into these women's eyes. He felt as though he was engulfed in a great barrel of sacred water—water all around him and all his problems gone. And he had had so many problems of late.

The woman Shimona moved up close to Red Mond Star Light and he could smell a faint flower-like scent from her body. It was the first time he had ever smelt perfume and it pleased as well as surprised him. She put long, delicate, yet callused fingers against his mahogany brown cheek and the gentle feather-like touch shocked him to the spine, with a wave of utter relaxation. Now it truly was as though he were in another world, spinning crazily through space, with only her husky soft voice to keep him in control.

'I can sense that you fear us, brother. But we are sisters of your blood. We are the daughters of Abraham and no harm can befall you at our hands. There is much for you to learn and much for us to see.' Shimona embraced the young man and her cool lips kissed him on each cheek. 'Long have we missed the children of Ishmael. Now you have come back home.'

Not all of this Red Mond could follow but he felt safe and comfortable in this woman's company. Momentarily he forgot about his Nightstal-ker woman.

But she did not forget him. Her mind, awakening from the sluggish sleep her pregnancy induced, had leapt out at the presence of so many strangers and she had caressed their minds. Such an aura of placidity and calm she had never felt before. So, not knowing, her mind had stumbled and she had almost been swamped by their collective minds before she pulled herself back and set up a shield. She probed her lover's mind and found it full of thoughts of the leader of the calm ones. She also sensed these new minds setting up shields as she came into them and this worried her a lot. So there *were* others in this world who had the gift of her people. Perhaps they were another form of her people. If this was so, they were all doomed. Yet it was confusing because she sensed a genuine mood of sympathy for the damaged Kareen and she knew they would heal her. But, after that? She could not tell. For the first time she had come up against minds that were as powerful as her own. And she had no strength to warn her lover.

Four of the women moved forward gracefully and carefully picked up the litter they had made for Kareen. One peeled off one of her voluminous silver robes and covered Kareen's body with soft, gauze-like, silver material. Already it seemed that they had taken control of the situation and taken charge of the company.

'Come. You shall follow us into Canaan,' Shimona said. 'You must meet with the council of Prophets.'

The procession moved off slowly through the trees. At the back Culvato and Nanny carried the wounded boy. Then came Kareen, lulled by the swinging of her litter, while the women who carried her sang softly. Port Rial led his string of horses and the rest of the caravan clustered around S'shony's wagon home. The other women seemed to float in front of them all. Now and then they would stop to pick a leaf or flower from a particular tree: Ruth for her medicines, Red Mond guessed, but the others merely for decoration on their hair or clothes. Akar Black Head had a vision of naked dancing girls with leaves wrapped in their hair before Joda was sliced open like one of the fruits on their table and was sullenly wary.

So they moved through the forest.

It was an ethereal and dark place, opening out now and again into bright sunlit meadows, often covered in colourful flowers that were like pools of sunlight caught forever by the dark twisted branches of the trees. It was a truly awesome place for the Ilkari, who were not used to the closeness of the mighty trees.

Every now and then on their brief journey Red Mond noticed one or other of the women touch the gnarled huge girth of a tree and whisper a welcome to it in passing. This pleased him as well for he knew the ways of Earth Mothers back home and they were the same.

But if the Ilkari thought the forest was awesome it was nothing to what they felt when, abruptly, they came to the end of it and they faced the Silver City for the first time. Even the Visitors were impressed.

Her eyes squint in the sudden harsh sunlight as they burst from the forest into ordered fields. But it is not so much the sunlight in the sky as the sunlight on the ground that make her eyes squint so. She hears Surrey Anne's gasp and Port Rial's soft call of surprise and sees even huge Cudjo falter in his steps. And they all, at least . . ., have seen the city of Kingston with its tall buildings and multitude of tin-roofed humpies catching the sun in a white glare.

She glances beside her at Culvato and he has blanched, not being able to conjure up this image in his wildest dreams—or nightmares. She hears him mutter, 'The sun has come to earth again, to kiss her a second, last time,' and she hears Akar Black Head shout, 'It is a trick. These are true children of the sun and we shall be burnt forever. Who would follow the path of a Moon-talker, as erratic and useless as it is?' And this time she knows there is no cynicism there but pure terror.

And why not, she thinks? These people have never seen any building larger than their priest's crumbling two-storey mansion and are used to a conglomerate of skin-covered tents. They were impressed by the Hill People's collection of hovels and would be flabbergasted at the sight of Kingston. But this place! The walls alone are five times the size of the Baba's house and the buildings behind them seem to tower up, reaching the very sun. They are all made of some sort of silver material, it appears. Thus the name everyone has given it. They are all awed into silence at the majesty of it all.

But it was not only the size of the buildings that caused consternation among the gathered few. After all, they had seen giant ants, giant butterflies, giant grass, huge rivers and enormous trees. Why not big buildings as well? No, it was that every tower seemed to reflect a part of the sun so the horizon shimmered in a white-golden artificial sunset. The whole city glowed with a throbbing light and seemed to be alive. Then, behind the city and stretching to the true horizon was an endless expanse of water and this too glittered silver-white under the azure open sky.

'We go no further,' Akar Black Head cried and stopped.

Where the trees ended the grass fields, full of livestock, and the gardens began. The mighty river had been trained and harnessed into many smaller streams and these meandered through a virtual paradise aided by water wheels, canals and flood gates so the ground was always well watered. There were many figures upon the open plain. Some stopped their gardening to come towards the procession.

'We go on,' said Red Mond. 'We know this place was called Silver City and now we know what that means.'

'Would you have your friend die, brother?' the healer Ruth said. 'You have no need of fear. You have the same eyes as us, after all,' and she touched Akar Black Head softly on the arm.

But he shrugged her off violently. 'You are no sister of mine. They are all dead. Three of them by Melanoma, your *true* sister,' he snarled at her, so she pulled away from him and lowered her frightened eyes. 'Lead on, then, but I warn you. I only go to cure Kareen. The Keepers were right to leave us—once again. And *this* time I am ready for any little tricks.' He hefted his mighty double-bladed axe so its steel blades gave a pale, pathetic imitation of the Silver City's glow.

Cudjo had sensed the anger in Akar Black Head and he threw a glance over his shoulder at Nanny.

'Look dereso, Nanny! Could dis be deh Mecca fe him murderin' Muslim? Are we lambs a go walk in den fe bear,' he queried.

But already the caravan was proceeding cautiously towards the massive silver gates set in the wall that looked like the most impregnable mountain to the desert-reared Ilkari. It was bigger even than the rooftop of the world, to say nothing of the buildings that were rearing and craning their silver bodies behind it.

And such a garden had never been seen before by any of them, including those from the fertile Island of Springs. There were neat rows of vegetables of all description, stretching forever it seemed, and small groves of apple, orange, apricot, peach, fig, pears, plums and other delectable fruits dotted across this paradise, breaking the monotony of the endless fields. Small quiet streams, weaned from the main river, ran between the rows, watering them permanently. Everywhere was lush and green and productive. On the horizon crops of corn or wheat or barley waved.

The majority of the occupants of this fertile plain were female and now they gathered around the travellers, whispering, nudging and casting enquiring glances at the women with this band. But no words were spoken out loud. The few men (who appeared to be guards of some sort, dressed in hard plates of leather and carrying the curious weapon of the boy or the more usual sword or spear) called out to them to come back to their gardens. The guards themselves moved towards the huge gates. But by the time they had arrived so had the caravan.

Shimona stepped forward. 'You must open the gate, Israel. We have a sick woman here.'

'These are strange Keepers to come into the city of Canaan willingly. Keepers with red hair and blue eyes. Could they be the children of the uncircumcised?' asked Israel, a man almost as big as Cudjo Accompong, with a great curling blond beard.

'They are the children of Ishmael, the outcast,' Ruth agreed. 'But the woman is hurt. Let us pass,' she ordered.

'Not without a heavy heart,' the big man growled. 'But this is a decision to be made by the King. We are certain he would meet with this black woman and our hearts are gladdened by this. As for the others we shall see.'

From his side he took a great, curved, iridescent instrument (that Port Rial recognised instantly as a conch shell) and blew two long eerie blasts upon it. Then, with scarcely a murmur, the huge gates swung inwards and the travellers had their first glimpse of the Silver City—known to the inhabitants as Canaan or Little Jerusalem.

Book Three

The Silver City

CHAPTER NINE

The journey across the vast gardens had been long enough for a crowd to have gathered to meet the strangers. For when the gates opened some ten thousand of the city's forty thousand inhabitants stood in expectant silence to observe the return of the children of Ishmael.

They had only ever seen the odd band of Keepers wending their solitary way through the gardens; or the occasional gang of marauding Outsiders that came to steal the fruits of their labour. Once—a memorable time—an army of Hill People had come across the Dead Sea (as the plain of tall grass was known) and laid siege to their city for two months before being driven off by the Heroes of Little Jerusalem.

This is the sight that faces her. This mighty crowd—all of them dressed in the same silver clothes. The women in their voluminous robes and veils, the men in hard shiny armour that looks like some type of plastic or aluminium. She looks at Port Rial and already his sharp mind has grasped the wealth this could mean, for the buildings are made of the same material. A whole city made of aluminium! Bauxite is the principal ore used for making aluminium, and on their Island is the biggest deposit of bauxite in the known world. This is what they have travelled all over the world for and suffered the sadness of losing five of their companions. Perhaps, now, they have found the city of the Lion of the Desert, after all. They could fly in the bauxite needed for this aluminium city's expansion by the plane load. A few years later they would be the richest people on the Island.

She turns her attention to the people now—her soon-to-be trading partners, she thinks. The men, in their shiny shoulder pads and breast plates and smooth grey helmets, seem bigger than they really are. Every one of them is of a pale complexion and what little hair can be seen is blond or red while their eyes are uniformly blue—as blue as the Carribean sea back home. Unlike the women, the men wear shoes of some sort and have gloves upon their hands and, of course, they don't wear any veils. It seems this differentiation of clothing styles takes place early in life for even the children are dressed thus: boots for the boys, veils for the girls. The very sameness of the whole crowd that stares back silently at them is unnerving.

Then a man steps forward from the silent silver wall of humanity. His finely groomed beard is soft and silky yellow—as yellow as the skin of a ripe banana. His lips are a brilliant red against his white skin. A lean face full of great sorrow and great wisdom.

Something curious happens to her. All thoughts of immense wealth now fade from her mind and she has only thoughts of him, this interesting man in front of her. As his eyes meet hers it seems they are alone together and nothing else matters.

Red Mond pushed his way forward. 'We have come because we have a wounded woman. She is our Earth Mother . . . and my cousin. I am Red Mond Star Light of the clan Violet Lynx Foot of the Tribe Elk from the Ilkari Nation.'

Even uttering the full regalia of introductions, his little speech still came out inadequate. In all his fine tooth necklaces, ear-rings and best skins, Red Mond would look nothing more than an awkward boy in front of this man, who was dressed in a blue flowing cloak as well as the armoured plating—which put him apart from the rest of the silver men. With him were two men in blue dresses who seemed intent on drawing something on small square pieces of leather which they held most carefully.

'I am King Solomon the twenty-third—King of Kings amongst the people of Canaan,' the cloaked man's voice boomed out. 'Greetings and blessings be upon you and welcome to our homes. We shall break bread together, Red Mond Star Light.'

There was a mighty cheering from the crowd then, frightening after such solid silence. But Red Mond noticed this King of Kings had no eyes for him. Instead he had an intense look for Nanny who returned it. It was as though they had met somewhere before, which Red Mond knew, was impossible. The King's blue eyes burnt into hers with a sombre fire.

Cudjo noticed this. 'Coo pon fine maan fi you. Him lookin' chunky at I! What yuh wild little maan seh aboot that, nuh?' he grinned.

Culvato also saw the King's look and fire clashed with fire as he glared at this man. But now wasn't the time to fight. They had to heal Kareen.

As the King welcomed them the crowd surged forward and the travellers were separated by the milling throng. Women lifted Kareen carefully off her litter and carried her through the crowd. But when the Ilkari tried to follow them, they were gently but firmly barred from doing so by a line of guards.

Before any argument could start Shimona grasped Red Mond by the arm. 'We are taking her to the women's quarters, where no man may go. Do not fear, our brother. You will see your cousin soon.'

'We must stay by her side! She is from our clan!' Culvato shouted above the din. But Red Mond put an arm on his shoulder.

'She is safe, Culvato. I sense it. She will be made well by these good women.'

Culvato glanced at him in surprise for a moment. Did he not care what became of his cousin? Had he forgotten the last time they went into a village? He looked over his shoulder and saw another surprise: Akar Black Head, their warrior, staring into space. Did he not adore Kareen? Now it seemed he did not care for her at all. He saw the King of Kings, Solomon the twenty-third, escorting Nanny away from the crowd while Cudjo, Port Rial and Surrey Anne followed laughing behind. Had the whole world gone mad?

They moved down a wide, white boulevard with the noisy but orderly crowd pressing around them and people gathering on balconies above them as they went past, to shout and cheer and throw flowers at the travellers. The few that were not blond and blue-eyed seemed to be a type of outcast. They were pushed without ceremony to the outside of the crowd although one, a wild-looking, black-haired girl who wore no veil and was in a red dress, grabbed hold of Culvato and gave him a penetrating stare before being cast aside by one of the armoured soldiers.

The crowd also pressed around the wagon that carried S'shony, with an exuberance that threatened to topple it over. She was pushed from side to side in the darkened cocoon and her mind went out to touch her lover and feel safe. But she could not find him! All around her, other minds probed and prodded at her own so she became giddy and disorientated. She had to withdraw back to herself and set up shields against these probes. Yet she had to be careful not to let on that she had a similar skill to these people, so her shields had to give a certain amount of herself away. What to give the inquisitive minds snuffling and pawing into her private world was the trick. She sensed these minds were too advanced for her and she was afraid for her lover. Already the woman she knew as Shimona had planted thoughts in his head too deeply rooted to budge with thoughts of her own. This woman Shimona gently controlled his footsteps as they went further and further into this ant's nest of a city.

Cudjo Accompong strode through the crowd that, like other crowds before, gaped in awe at his giant size. But for the first time in his life he felt dwarfed not by people but by the immense constructions all around him. They were really the most amazing shapes he had ever seen. The sprawling mass of Kingston was nothing to this: huge, sleek, grey towers erupted towards the sky, windowless and frightening. There were buildings that rolled, twisting and turning in intricate shapes some special architectual brain had dreamed up. Amidst this incredible, yet sane, chaos were large perfect spheres of a mainly white colour.

A great calmness began permeating his consciousness and, for the first time since coming to this land, he felt safe and secure. He looked down at Port Rial and smiled. 'I-an'-I a go have de easy life for now on, me seh!'

The wiry little pirate's eyes lit up as he grinned up at his huge companion. 'With all dese women an' sea him down by he bay me feel me in Kingston again.'

The city was not only full of awesome shapes. They passed areas of great open spaces where many of the trees these people called willows grew in graceful beauty. Everything seemed planned to bring the greatest pleasure to the eyes via shape, shadow, light and symmetry. These open spaces were covered in different-coloured paving stones as well, and the whites, blues, reds and browns were pleasing to gaze at and thus were soothing to the soul.

The use of water shocked Red Mond by its sheer wastefulness. Tinkling waterfalls fell over rounded colourful stones or great gushing geysers that turned into molten silver in the sky or large, flat, quiet, blue pools—as blue as the eyes of the multitude. Then there were the water sculptures of horses, humans, birds . . . almost anything made out of cunning fountains. Their yellow-brown river they loved so at home seemed like a mud hole now.

Surrey Anne smiled at the beautiful, perfect figures of the grey-clad men. Their beards were finely groomed and their serene eyes full of warmth. There was not an angry face or a weapon to be seen, apart from the guards, and from the tight-pressed multitude of bodies there wafted a fragrance as sweet as the wild trees of her Island home.

Nanny held the hand of the King of Kings and a thrill went through her, as she had never felt before. She had had her share of lovers throughout her turbulent life but this was something altogether new. She had the most curious sensation that they were already abed and it thrilled her to think of them both naked before the city's population.

'My Bathsheba,' he murmured and his lips were so red and his hand so white when he removed his glove that she could almost make up a song about him. 'Indeed, the prophecies have come true. Elias, Elias Raphael,' he incanted, then cast his eyes up towards a group of men in deep-blue cloaks, who clustered at the top of a wide sweeping set of magnificent stairs that led to the biggest building of them all. 'Jegar!' he cried and placed his hand in hers.

At this an enormous cry went up, for by now more than half the population of the city had gathered around. Unveiled women on the outskirts of the crowd, by moving their tongues rapidly up and down, gave vent to an ululating chorus, whilst veiled women trilled and men whistled and roared.

'The prophecy has come true,' they cried. 'Our Queen has returned. From the vineyards of her home she has come and her mother has not deserted us.'

Everywhere—all around him—Culvato heard the cries and cheers and ear-splitting shrieks. He looked up at Nanny but it was not the woman he knew up there. Her almond eyes were closed to slits of pleasure as she acknowledged the calls with a faint smile over her wide mouth. Where was the woman from the hot, red deserts who made love like the desert winds; where was the woman who moved as gracefully as the tall slender grasses out on the treeless plain, where they had first made love, and sang to him a song as gentle as the breeze through the green tops of the grass? He looked around him at the crowd that must have tripled the entire Ilkari Nation—yet he felt so alone and so afraid. His hand stole into the pocket where his red-streaked, black pebble nestled and his fingers curled around it like he would have liked them to curl around his woman and drag her out of her dream.

The men in the royal-blue coats came down to join the King of Kings. The one in front was the tallest of them all and also the whitest. His skin was as pale as the mushrooms found sometimes under rotting logs, thought Culvato; the mushrooms his mother had taught him were poisonous unless cooked a special way. His eyes were as blue as his cloak, as blue as Akar Black Head's. But they were emotionless eyes—the eyes of a cruel, or, at least, uncaring man.

'So our Queen must come from the hordes of the uncircumcised? From the harlots of the Philistines and the whores of Syria doth our Queen come,' this man breathed in a whispering hiss. 'Sprinkle our King with myrrh, bathe him in the water gathered from a rose's sweet petals. Rejoice in our King's rejoicing, oh children of Canaan. Our Queen has come from the vineyards of Magadela and the fruits of her loins are full.'

As the tall man made this speech the others also descended from the top of the stairs.

'Thus spake Jothaim for us all,' called another of the blue-clad men. This one had some red in his blond locks but his most obvious feature was a missing right hand.

As Culvato glanced around he could begin to pick out individuals so they were not frighteningly similar. He wished he could get close to Red Mond but the crowd had pushed them apart. Now the blue-robed men, whom Culvato heard being called the Prophets, gathered around his friend, greeting him. Most with smiles, some with handshakes or touches, a few with disdainful scowls, Jothaim one of them. All had another look just behind their *bonhomie* that was like a snake's, cold and dangerous. Yet Red Mond was like a singing bird in a bush, completely unaware of the rustling trouble creeping up on him.

'Truly, he is the son of Esau—'

'Nay, he cometh from the land of the Ishmaelites.'

'Those with him are not the children of Phineas. Surely they are not from another Tribe?'

'They are the brothers and sister of Bathsheba, hence are Kings and a Princess in their own right.'

163

'Do you carry with you false Gods? There is but one Ark of the Covenant. What do you carry in this covered wagon?' Jothaim said sternly to Red Mond.

'There are many questions we would ask of *you*,' cried Culvato, 'before we answer any of yours! Such as why do our friends the Keepers of the Trees dislike and avoid this place?'

He shoved his way through the now silent crowd and stood beside his paal, glaring at the group of white men. Akar Black Head also made his way to the head of the stairs, but his eyes were confused and his footsteps sluggish.

'We are Ilkari, from the purple desert, under the shadow of the roof of the world. Beside the sacred river are our lands, the lands of the clan Violet Lynx Foot. Our cousin and clan member and Earth Mother is hurt. You will fix her and we will be on our way,' Culvato ordered sharply.

'Yes,' Akar Black Head suddenly said, as though coming from a dream. 'My woman needs your help. Then we will leave on our journey.'

'We know what your journey is.' A young man with long hair plaited in hundreds of thin plaits smiled. 'Your Moon-talker, Red Mond Star Light, has already told us of it.'

'Come, come, my untamed friend. There is no cause for anger here,' the King of Kings said softly. 'We are all, in a way, from the same family. Even the ones you call the Keepers and we know as the children of Phineas who was cast out of his father's house just as Ham was from the house of Noah,' he murmured. 'It is so for it is written just as is the prophecy that a woman comely and black—as black as the tents of Kedar—shall come forth and be my wife.'

'I know nothing of these people you talk of. Or these prophecies! What are prophecies? Some sort of spell?' Culvato snapped, his eyes ablaze at the white glove upon Nanny's ebony shoulder.

He wondered why he was doing all the fighting alone. Why did not Akar Black Head use some of his famous cynicism against these people? Why did the High Ones stand there and let their leader be taken away? Why did not Red Mond Star Light tell everyone they would wait for Kareen outside the city walls where he was sure *he* would feel safer at least?

'Prophecies are words of truth.' The King of Kings threw wide his immaculate hands. 'Lo! before you, you see the truth. For twenty-three hundred years has the King Solomon waited. Now our true lineage may be forged with Bathsheba, Queen of Sheba. Long have our people waited and now our heritage will be fulfilled. Our people will be strong and true again and you have nothing to fear from our hospitality. The city is yours. I, the King, hath spoken.'

'But let us see what is in the box these people carry so carefully with them?' Jothaim said again. His eyes became sly. 'Perhaps it is a gift for our King of Kings brought across the Syrian desert from the strange and exotic lands of Bathsheba, just as three eastern Kings brought gifts to Yahweh's son in Bethlehem.'

Before anyone could move forward Culvato leapt to the cocoon, his body taut and his face hard, his knobbly hand upon the hilt of his sword and his spear ready at his side. 'I will kill anyone who touches the skins of this tent. That is *my* prophecy!' he swore angrily.

'Jothaim. They are our guests—as are the Babylonians and the Tribes of wandering Arabs. Let them keep their Gods. We know there is but one true God and he is the Lord our God, Yahweh,' said the youth with the plaited hair.

'Arainias, God is perfect.'

'Grace of the Lord, Jothaim.'

So saying the thirteen men departed sedately, followed by King Solomon the twenty-third and Nanny. The crowd below the steps began to disperse, still discussing events excitedly. The caravan was left alone in the middle of the square.

Surreptitiously a dark-haired girl crept out of the dispersing crowd and approached Culvato. 'Brother, I will see you, paal,' she whispered in Romany. 'My name is Jaala and I must tell you about this city. Do as did our fathers and sleep outside. You must not go into their buildings, especially the white eggs you see around the city.'

Hearing the familiar words of his mother's tongue, spoken so easily, shocked Culvato into silence. He glanced at the girl and recognised her as the one in the crowd who had earlier tried to approach him.

'Tonight,' she whispered.

Before he could answer her she had slid away at the approach of the other women.

A Gypsy *here*! In the midst of this place he felt most uncomfortable in was one of his own people. The meeting he had dreamed about thousands of times had finally occurred.

Now the grey-clad women they had first captured came to them.

The one called Shimona took charge of their welfare. They made it understood in their courteous yet firm way that Surrey Anne must now leave the men's company and go to the women's quarters. Port Rial was not too happy about this, until Cudjo Accompong reminded him that it was sometimes good to have a change of fruit. 'A taste fe she guava only make pineapple sweetah,' he said. The Ras Tafarian was happy, for several times he had heard the name Yahweh mentioned and it seemed to be their God. Just as his was the great Jah, a similar sounding name and God.

There were many rules in this Silver City, they were to find. Ways of greetings only used by men and words only used by women. Some words were to have a different meaning if a male or female were to use them: Eden, for example. In male conversation it meant an expression of delight, whereas in female terms it meant someone was enchanting.

Jaala was Eden—in both senses of the word.

She did not come the first night, nor the second or third.

In fact it was a week before her tiny brown hand quietly shook Culvato awake and the waning moonlight shone in the whites of her wild eyes.

She came in the dark of night as he lay huddled into his skins on the steps of the curious building the men had been assigned to. Akar Black Head had protested, saying they must stay together but Red Mond remembered that back at home Culvato had always preferred sleeping in the open. Besides, no one would get past Culvato if he slept outside this dome-shaped hall that was so different from the smoky skin tent, smelling of animal fat, humans and earth that was Red Mond's usual place of abode. Culvato did not say he slept outside because he no longer trusted his former compatriots.

She greeted him in the language his mother had taught him was the most pure of the Gypsy tongue and this was another surprise for him. 'Damen devla saschipo ando mure cocala,' she breathed.

She nestled down beside him then. Her body was so warm it burnt him and she smelt of savage places. Her movements were quick and constant, as though she were perpetually on the lookout for danger. She looked up to where the yellow moon half hid behind a huge scowling tower, then turned black eyes onto him so he became captivated by their sable grace.

'I could feel you were of our people. That is why I came to warn you. You must *never* tell the gorgios you are a Gypsy because there is a story that it was a Gypsy that hammered the nails into the Lord, their God, helping him to die. Those that believe this story hate and despise our people.'

'Are there more of our people here?' Culvato asked.

'My sisters, Phenice and Tamara, and my brother known as Gilead.'

'These are not the names of our people,' Culvato mused. 'As neither is yours—Jaala.'

'If you live in this city for long you will learn many disturbing things. People disappear every day. But so, too, do memories. My two sisters were once known as Juva and Sinerella while my darling brother was called Sastra. But you will learn that every name of a person means something in this city. Hence Phenice and Tamara both mean "from the palm tree" and Gilead means "rocky ground".'

'And Jaala?' he probed gently, but she stood up, ready to move away.

'My two sisters have the names of strangers—but they have passed themselves off as strangers and Phenice is married to a gorgio even now. Yes, they are the Children of Lilith and, as such, are mostly safe from the evil ways of this city.' She moved off into the darkness of the quiet alley. 'I am a Daughter of Delilah—you can tell by the red dress I wear.' A sob tore suddenly from her throat. 'But my brother Sastra is an unclean man.'

Her voice, as her footsteps, faded away. 'You have much to learn about our beautiful city. Beware the one called Jothaim for he is the most dangerous man of all. Already he senses you are a menace to him. Beware also of the serpent of the stone.'

That night Culvato could not sleep. It had been a dream of his to finally meet up with his own people. Now that he had, they appeared to be in some sort of trouble. All because of some long ago story about yet another God, Culvato sneered. Gods certainly were a lot of bother, it seemed to him. The good thing was all this thinking took his thoughts from another supposedly High One—Nanny.

None of them had much time to see their womenfolk—except for Red Mond Star Light. But S'shony was fully occupied these days as the worrying possibilities slowly grew to reality. These people who had also developed their mind power over the centuries were ten times more powerful than *her* people. The People of the Caves used their power to 'see' and 'smell' in the dark, dangerous tunnels, rather like a type of sonar. They could slightly manipulate thoughts of other people. But they were still predominantly the thoughts of the other person. They could also see into another person's mind. But *these* people could completely take over and control a person's thought patterns. Indeed, it seemed as if they could substitute another person's mind altogether. The frightening aspects of this gift became only too obvious when she tried to read her lover's mind, as he caressed her on that first night in the cocoon. It was like walking around a huge empty cavern that had once known human occupation. It was as though he had become a shell and the inside of him was a stranger.

She began using her full power to probe into the minds of her companions, still putting up shields to keep her own mind safe. As long as they all remained in the same room it was easy for her to juggle their mind waves. But she had to be extremely careful and always on the lookout for alien thoughts. These people also had the ability to latch on to a person's thought or idea and use that to get back into that person's mind. It was, to her, all very scary. But to her companions, who had not the slightest idea of the war being waged in their minds, nothing seemed untoward.

Port Rial and Cudjo Accompang, who had such wonderful foreign thoughts of things S'shony could barely imagine even in her most colourful dreams, were confused yet at peace. It was obvious to the cave girl that they were already lost to this swirling blue mist of calm that swept around them. Akar, with his angry thoughts, was fighting this strangeness, but he was not clever enough to understand what was happening or strong enough to resist. Soon he, too, would become a mind slave to these people. Her lover also, she was sad to see, was a puppet twitching in the hands of the harmonious Shimona.

The one they called the Gypsy; the one who had often talked to her in soft tones as he guarded her doorway, was the one unaffected by any of the events happening silently around him. And she could not work out why. He was upset by his woman's betrayal (and she longed to tell him it was not betrayal but it was too dangerous to give him a thought these people could latch onto) and unhappy at Red Mond's supposed turnabout. He hated this city. The probing fingers of the minds that swirled all around him could not touch him and she sensed the worry and annoyance of those minds. Just to be safe she set up a mind shield for him. But it was a weak one because she needed all her energy to keep her own mind safe and, of course, that of her growing baby.

If only she could talk to him she would have an ally. But he stayed out of the building and kept to himself. She could understand his loneliness in this city full of smiling sinister strangers.

The men could go anywhere in the city except the King's Palace and the women's quarters. Akar Black Head, Red Mond Star Light and even Culvato were astonished at the size of the river upon whose shore this city stood. They could not see the other shore and some of those they spoke to suggested there *was* no other shore—just a tossing blue-grey-green plain owned by the wild wind horses from the sky.

Culvato soon realised there were different sorts of people in the city. Of the women there were four types: one small group—thirteen in all—dressed like the Prophets because they were the wives of the Prophets. They were called the Edra, the Women of Power. A larger group were the grey-robed women known as the Shama, obedient women. The Children of Lilith wore no veils and their clothing was yellow, orange, purple—any colour other than blue, grey or red. Their hair was often any shade of black or brown as well as the usual blonde or auburn and their eyes could be black, green or brown as well as blue or grey.

The Daughters of Delilah stayed hidden, so were not often seen. They were the darker people, with swarthy skin and long tangled manes of blue-black hair. Every one of them wore a red dress and, like every woman, their hands and feet were bare.

All the women, except the Daughters of Delilah, took it in turn to work in the garden outside the city gates every day.

In the classes of men there was the King of Kings and his Prophets of course, then a huge army of blue- or grey-clad blond or red-headed men. These men were occupied in different trades.

Most of the traders were known as Mordecai's Children and were the male version of the Children of Lilith. Indeed, all their wives came from that same group and they all lived in a certain segment of the city, near the centre.

But there was a class of man that eventually even disturbed Red Mond, caught up as he was in a peaceful, dream-like trance of Shimona's making. At first these men didn't affect them if they were seen, because bare feet and rags were common among the Ilkari and the city streets of the Visitors' Island home. Besides, there were not many to be seen and as the five were often in the company of their new friends these men would keep well away. But, if ever any of them were alone, then these men would creep up and meekly or warily touch them and gabble at them in an unintelligible tongue.

They were unkempt and dirty, and cringed like kicked dogs. The filthy rags they wore scarcely covered their naked bodies which were covered in welts and bruises. They were the only men the five ever saw who wore no shoes or gloves. Even the fishermen had a type of rough leather glove they used to protect their hands. But it was their eyes that disturbed Red Mond the most for they were deep, dead pools of madness, whirlpools of insanity. Yet, right at the very centre of this whirlpool, there was just a glimmer—a tiny spark—of common sense. A knowledge that they themselves knew they had once been ordinary men. That tiny spark burnt out at the shocked and disgusted people around them and saw the looks of distaste and horror. Thus did the man become even more insane as he tried to tell the world he was not an animal.

Culvato was saddened by these people more than disgusted. The Ilkari had their share and more of cripples and madness in their clans as Sister Sun ate away at a man's brain and the radiation that was everywhere ate into their bodies, but they were always loved and cared for as fallen stars or tears of the moon. His own brother, he reminded himself, was one such fallen star.

One day, as he walked along with the mighty, broad-shouldered soldier named Israel, whom he had befriended, a skinny pathetic man, trying to get out of the way of the man's great strides, slipped and fell against him.

Israel, who was usually full of hearty good cheer, gave a roar of rage and, picking the poor beggar up by one frail arm, hurled him into the wall, where he lay broken and bleeding and moaning. Culvato ran forward to see if the man was all right, ready to remonstrate with Israel if he were not, but the giant soldier grabbed him moderately, his composure once more calm.

'You cannot touch him, brother of Esau. From the very pits of Sodom and Gomorrah have they crawled, abominations in the eyes of the Lord. They must suffer for their sins against the Lord our God and then they can become lambs again before the very seat of Yahweh,' the huge man explained. 'You must never let one touch you for they are the unclean ones.'

Unclean! So one of these pitiful people was the brother of Jaala and was his *true* brother, a person of Gypsy blood. Culvato's eyes went even blacker with hatred and he had to turn away lest the amiable giant saw and realised his feelings. The poor broken creature before him stared up at him and he allowed a faint smile of compassion to cross his lips.

Port Rial had given up his quest for treasure in this city of treasures. The wiry Ras Tafarian pirate had been pleasantly surprised to find himself so near to the ocean once again and spent all his time with the sailors and fishermen and their small wooden boats.

The fishermen were allowed by Royal Decree to have bare hands, although most wore the leather gloves they fancied, for it was the law of Yahweh that they were a special breed of men. It was said that Yahweh's son was a fisher of men's souls and when he came back to his children he would come by way of the ocean, walking across the water. It was said that many of his close followers were ordinary fishermen also. So, because in a way these fishermen also walked across the water in their wooden boats and knew the ways of the water, they were looked upon as almost divine. They were delighted when they found that the brother of their King's consort was also an experienced man of the sea. He made two particular friends amongst this hearty band—the broad-shouldered, gap-toothed youth, Ithnan, and the small, quiet, red-headed man called Siddon. Their names, as usual, had something to do with themselves or their personality. Ithnan meant 'the strong sailor' and Siddon simply meant 'fisherman'. He began staying out with them longer, as they went on lonely journeys to the fishing grounds deep beneath the sea. Many were the stories he astounded them with, in this private, though tumultuous world, as they were tossed upon the waves. He also became friendly with Ithnan's young sister, Meras.

As for Surrey Anne, she spent her days with her new companions, gardening and learning things of the soil. She also spent a great deal of time caring for Kareen who, due to the administrations of the gentle Shama, was gradually recovering. Every day one or another of the blue-gowned wives of the Prophets would come and sit beside the Ilkari woman, softly singing songs and lovingly caressing her brow.

On the surface everyone appeared happy.

But Akar Black Head stumped about the city, seeing none of its beauty and suspicious of all things. The only trees here were ones carefully cultivated and as captive as the animals that resided in great yards outside the city. There were no pets—no cats or dogs or such—and he remembered all too clearly the other village where no pets had been seen. He sorely missed Kareen, and his new friend had changed subtly and spent all his time on the huge water in the company of these people from the sun, whom the warrior could *never* trust—no matter how often they smiled at him. So the big hairy man became closer than he ever had to the former outcast of the clan who, at least, did not like this city as the others appeared to.

'I am sick of this city and all its friendly people,' he confided to

170

Culvato one day. 'Where are all the campfires and the stories that go with the campfires? Where are the wrestling and games and arguments?'

'I long for the desert and the winds of the desert that sing a truer song than these,' Culvato answered.

'I tried to go out the gates to see if our comrades, the Keepers, were there, as they said they would be,' the big man mused. 'But Gabriel would not let me pass.'

Culvato cast sharp eyes at him. 'What do you mean?'

'Once within the walls we cannot leave of our own free will. We must wait and leave together or not at all.' He grasped his axe in his huge hand. 'Well, we shall see,' he growled. 'When Kareen is better it will take more than this band of men who are as women to stop Akar Black Head, killer of the black bear and slayer of more than a score of Nightstalkers.' His anger subsided briefly and he looked away. 'I like not these children of the sun. They are true children and have the deceit of their mother. Why else would they build these mountains to catch her light and yet hide out the light of the moon?' He ran his fingers along the hard, hot, pink pavement they sat upon. 'Why else would they hide Sister Earth beneath their city of silver light?'

His eyes glowered into Culvato's. 'Something is happening to me. Inside. My thoughts are not my own. At night I dream of a cold, dark, damp place. A place where there is no light at all.'

'Under the earth? In the land of the Nightstalkers?' Culvato asked softly. 'Akar, that is the place of death.'

Akar Black Head let out his old familiar rumble of laughter. 'Even death, our old friend, will find it hard to take *me* by his boney hand,' he shouted with glee and clapped Culvato on the arm. 'We must stick together, you and I. The High Ones are with their brethren, to use their word. Red Mond wanders everywhere in a dream, like the fool he is. If *I* was the leader I would have brought us all through safely. We have not even arrived at the home of our greatest enemy and already the expedition has lost its way. Why we follow the words of an unseen Goddess I'll never know. She has led us into nothing but trouble.' He looked away again and a shadow seemed to cross his eyes, making them darker.

'Sometimes, though, it is good here. The women are the prettiest I have ever seen. Especially the one called Sydel. A glorious name, Sydel,' he muttered. He looked closely at Culvato then. 'Have you a certain woman that you see, cous-cous? Do you desire the warmth of a particular woman by your side tonight?' he questioned softly.

Something told Culvato to say nothing about Jaala. His big countryman's eyes were strange. There was a mystery here he could not understand. Abruptly Akar Black Head rose from his seat and walked away, leaving Culvato to wonder at the words he had spoken and the meaning behind the words.

CHAPTER TEN

The days dragged into weeks and still there was no sign of Red Mond Star Light wishing to pursue his Quest. In fact, the city seemed to have swallowed him up—body, mind and all. The most interesting thing he learnt was the work of the four Scribes: Obadiah, servant of God; Beniah, son of the Lord; Zachariah, God has remembered; and Adriel, from the Lord's Kingdom. These were all men of a great age with pure white hair and beards and the light of wisdom in their serene blue eyes. They were even older than Baba and—dare he say it?—far more knowledgeable than his clan's revered historian. He met them one day, on his wanderings, in their house they called a Synagogue. It was a huge, windowless, grey building ten times the size of Baba's puny Hall. Such was the amount of knowledge they had stored.

It was the Scribes who taught Red Mond the true meanings of day and night, weeks and years, and introduced him to the item called calendars that kept these days and nights prisoners for all time, never to be forgotten but always available for scrutiny by the Scribes. He learnt more of the ordered life that the occupants of the Silver City enjoyed. He learnt that the moon and sun and stars had always been here and made up the days and nights of the calendars; that Yahweh had made them, as he had every thing that walked, flew, swam or crawled upon the earth, including Mankind. And how did he know this was all true and everything he had believed in up to now was lies?

Because it was written.

This was the most amazing discovery he had ever made. It far outclassed the finding and love of S'shony and the arrival of the High Ones he now knew were just humans. Ethiopians, in fact. For it was written: 'Can the Ethiopian change his skin, or the leopard his spots? then may ye also do good, that are accustomed to do evil.' And it was also written about a great beast with the body of a leopard, feet of a bear and the mouth of a lion, all animals of which were familiar to him and those of his clan. Now he knew he was *meant* to be here—it was all written down before he was born. He had come to do great things and to battle the beast of his own ignorance! All around the walls of the massive building were layer upon layer of what the Scribes called Epistles.

And, in every one of these Epistles were the thoughts of men taken from their minds and kept forever upon the glorious white pages.

He knew this because the Scribes gave him a test once to prove the magic of these magnificent Epistles. He told one of the old Scribes something only the youth, of everyone in the city, could know. This was the name of his mother Kala and of their clan Chief Violet Lynx Foot and their physical attributes. Upon the page, the old man made a series of unintelligible scrawls and yet, when the other Scribes saw these scrawls, they were each able to say exactly what Red Mond had said.

The illiterate Ilkari gazed into the amused blue eyes of the four and realised their true magic and power. Every thought of man was in those Epistles and every deed ever done was thus recorded. It made the Hall of Baba look ridiculous in comparison. But when Red Mond looked at the pages that passed secret and unknown things from Scribe to Scribe, all he could see was a lot of curious marks that made no sense at all. He began spending days in the Synagogue, for he wanted to understand these masses of Epistles that surrounded him. Often, the answers he sought were already in the Epistles and they would be taken down and shown to him. It became his catch-cry. It is true for it is written.

The more time he spent away, the more time Culvato spent guarding the doorway of the building where S'shony lay. At first, one or another of the Prophets or their wives would come bearing food or wine for their unseen guest. But Culvato was quietly adamant. No one would gain access except the Moon-talker. Even though he seemed to have forgotten his Goddess, Culvato had made a promise and he would not break it. He would stay guard until his bones turned to ash.

And it seemed that these powerful men and women believed him. A curious look would come into their eyes as they stood and stared at the wagon, carrying the cocoon, and the wiry, dark, fierce guard. An uneasy look came into their eyes as they came and went on silent feet.

As the days turned into weeks, it was too late for S'shony to engage the only one she knew was not affected by this city's vibes in conversation and so warn him. Now she sensed a mighty force beaming in on her, trying to get into her mind. If she spoke to the Gypsy youth it might open a chink in her armour and, like a great flood, the thousands in this city would pour through, stealing her mind with their own.

Culvato had to find out about the dangers that abounded in this city another way.

It was a restless murky night, when a storm had passed over the sky, that Gilead came to see him. There was still the faint whisper of the receding rain and it was this that hid from Culvato's sharp ears his visitor's stealthy footsteps until he was by Culvato's side, a darker shade of the night.

'Ando bersch dui chiro, ye ven, ta nilei. O felhegos del o breschino, te purdel o barbal,' he spoke hoarsely in the old language. But somehow Culvato knew he was not talking about seasons, rain or clouds.

A scarred, burnt, black hand, with the middle and index finger missing, rested on Culvato's shoulder. He turned over in his bed upon the steps and looked into intense, alert, black eyes much like his own. Even in this sombre gloom they seemed to shine with a passionate glow.

'Yes,' the voice continued, 'it is as Ambról says. You are a true Gypsy as still am I and my beloved sister. As was our father and mother before us. Deyvil has crossed your palm with silver, my paal.'

'Sastra,' Culvato whispered back.

'You remembered my name. I am Gilead only to those balos who so named me. But I *am* a rocky, dry place and there is no relief for those who hunt me on my land,' he laughed bitterly, then squatted down beside his fellow Gypsy.

'It has been many days, brother, that you have lived with us in our fair city,' he smiled cynically. 'We have watched you and your kindness towards Simeon was not forgotten.'

'Who was Simeon?'

'The one Israel threw into the wall, with as much feeling as if Simeon was, indeed, only a hyena as his name implies and not a man that Israel's leaders have half destroyed,' he spat angrily. 'But, fear not. The hyena also feasts upon the lion's flesh.' Grim eyes pierced Culvato's own and the youth remembered now he had not seen the jovial giant for some time.

'Why should one man do that to another? We love our fallen stars where we come from,' Culvato pondered.

'Fallen stars?' Sastra murmured, a faint smile of unknown description upon his face. Then he roused himself from his reverie. 'What is the name of the Tribe you shelter with, brother? Do they not kill other men?'

'Only Nightstalkers,' Culvato replied.

There was a long moment's silence from Sastra and his brow furrowed in thought.

'Nightstalkers,' he mused at last. '*There* is a name I have not heard of in years. We have much to learn about this country, do we not? That there is a Tribe left that will only kill for necessity and not for fun or experiments of their twisted minds.' His eyes went dark with hatred. 'That does not kill because they say we are from a despised Race.'

'Life is precious, brother,' Culvato murmured gently. 'Everyone knows that. Thoughts are only ornaments for our own vanity and pride—as often are the Gods we worship and the women we admire. There is enough death amongst the people where I come from to bring more death from our own hands.'

Sastra nodded sagely. 'Ambról was right when she saw you in the crowd. She knew you were of untainted mind.' He smiled genuinely for the first time. 'It is good. This prophecy they have all awaited for so long has brought a prophecy for me as well. With your help we can escape this city of madness.'

Then Sastra told Culvato the story of this city and much that was muddied in the rivers of his mind became clear and fast flowing.

The city had always appeared as a haven upon the horizon to the wandering groups and families of those unfortunate enough to be born somewhere else when the world ended. The Gypsies were a free people and a Race steeped in their own beliefs or languages, centuries older than any of those formed in the New Time. Some, his grandfather Petul for instance, had said it was the curse of the Gypsies to have no home because Duvel had come from heaven to tell the Gypsies of the coming disaster and they had not taken time to tell the rest of the people, so preventing the disaster. Therefore, the old man said, they must roam bitchadey pawdel, a lost and rootless Race. But the Silver City seemed a sanctuary for a family who had lost many of its members in abrupt, cruel death out on the plains of whispering grass or up in the evil, black hills where murder was a common occurrence and a person could disappear as easily and unexpectedly as a sneeze.

Except on extremely special occasions, like the arrival of Red Mond and his band, entry to the city was strictly limited to one Sunday each month. So for two weeks the family camped beneath the shadow of the wall. They were all much loved by the motley crowd of homeless people.

Then came the great day when the gates were opened two hours after sunrise. They would stay open until an hour before sunset and then they would be closed another month.

But a Gypsy is only strong if they are with their family. If his father Boshomengro had only known what awaited them within the walls of the city, he would have taken his chances out in the desert.

First, Boshomengro's two green-eyed daughters, Juva and Sinerella, were taken from the family's bosom, yelling and screaming. They had been the first-born and much loved by the younger children. The darker members of the confused family were sent down a pink-pebbled pathway with others of similar hue.

Boshomengro's heart went cold as he thought of this dangerous place he had brought his family to. Already the city had claimed his two oldest daughters . . . And who could tell what would happen to the rest of them? He had seen the mind power of these people when a man, trying to escape through the gates, had clutched at his head, as if in pain, and collapsed weeping to the ground. Several of the soldiers had carried him away. He was to tell his son not many years later of his feelings that day and thus save his son's life. For Sastra was prepared for any of the tricks they might try to play on the remainder of the family.

At the end of the aisle where the people were led, everyone mourning the separation of a close relative as families had disintegrated, a surprise awaited them. Cool pools of clear water to bathe in and food and wine. Blue-clad women were there to serve them and later to lead them up other pathways to their final home. Even the most suspicious of them relaxed in this calming atmosphere.

They were subtly separated: old people, young people, males and females and Keepers of the Trees. Finally, the Gypsies were led through meandering narrow streets until they came, at last, to a great compound surrounded by a high silver wall all covered in luscious ivy. Indeed, it was a type of city within a city for behind the walls were numerous small houses. Over the gateway to this little city a black triangle was etched in between two white crosses.

Imagine their joy when they discovered within the compound others of their Race. Not a great many, perhaps fifty or so—but Gypsies all the same.

Here was to be their home for many a year. They were left alone for the main part to live their Gypsy life. Some of the women worked in the garden with the other women. But there was no need because every morning a pile of food would be left outside the compound gates. At last the wandering Gypsy Tribes had found a true place of sanctuary. And, because they were all together, here was a chance to learn the language, songs and stories of their scattered Race.

They had a Kral who dispensed justice, organised marriages and settled disputes. Every now and then a member of the compound would leave and, thus, it was the Kral's wish that they could go forth a proud Gypsy, to spread the net of their culture across the land. Often messages came back to those left in the compound. Messages only the teller could know—and whispered to close members of the family in Gypsy by the blue-gowned women.

When Sastra was twelve he learnt the horrible truth about this city. It was the beginning of his war against the city and his hatred for those who ruled it.

He had a friend named Rockstone, whose sister was called Ivy, for not everyone in the compound was Gypsy. No one knew why these other people were there but they were treated with courtesy for they lived the same life as the Romany—even if they were gorgio—and they, too, would disappear from time to time. Rockstone and Ivy were treated with more respect than the others for they were twins, identical in every way except their sex, and carried all the mystique of those born that way.

It was Ivy who alerted the other two to the mind games that went on outside the compound. These twins were not only special because they were identical in looks. Rockstone and Ivy also had the power to read minds and transport thoughts from one to the other. As they grew older they were able to blanket the thoughts of another person and thus allow their own thoughts to take over that person's mind.

Being only children, the walls of the compound meant nothing to them and their adventurous feet travelled throughout the city. They even crept into the hallowed walls of the Palace and spied on the King of Kings in his lonesome reveries. Soon the three of them knew most parts of the city and had become the closest of friends.

By knowing all the parts of the city they discovered things best left unknown. As die we all must some day, sometimes it is better to die in ignorance. He saw his two sisters, Sinerella and Juva, now called Phenice and Tamara and both married to or courting prosperous Mordecai's Children. But a warning by looking into their dulled calm eyes and complacent faces told him to stay strangers to them.

They saw the hidden cruelty of these grey-clad, blond, blue-eyed people who wished to control everyone's mind and were brutal to those who resisted—or those who were darker hued.

But the first real insight he got into the pure malevolence of these people was when he and his two friends chanced upon an exodus.

As only once a month people were allowed into the city, so once every six months people were allowed out. But not the way the Kral had thought. This abomination of a departure was called an exodus. The people taking part in this exile were thin and naked. They were shoved and pushed and spat upon by the normally cheerful and undemonstrative occupants of the city; pummelled with fists and taunts, while rocks and rotten fruit were hurled at them ferociously, often bringing them bloodily to the ground. The twins tried gingerly to probe their minds and recoiled in shock at the sadness and madness whirling there. They were poured forth through the Gate of Shame, that had a huge yellow star painted on it. This gate led out, not into the bountiful gardens but into the raw, dry desert lands. They stumbled forth, naked and lost, and their tearful howls rent the soul. Any who still had sense left enough to try and escape were driven back with torches of flame from the soldiers who followed behind.

He saw a girl named Grasni, whom he was particularly fond of, limp out the gate, her skinny naked body covered in welts and her sparkling eyes now empty as the desert into which they stared with forlorn gaze.

So this was how his people went forth to throw a net of their culture across the land. He turned anguished eyes to his two subdued companions.

Thus, it was Sastra who alerted his people to this great calamity and much was the keening that night as everyone remembered a member of their family who had walked so proudly from the compound.

When next the soldiers came to escort someone to their freedom there was a revolt. But it was short-lived and only the twins and Sastra were able to escape. He watched in horror as his mother and father were herded with the rest to their doom in the white eggs. He saw his sister and other young girls separated from their parents and hauled, crying, away.

He bade them a silent farewell then brushed the tears from his eyes. He promised that he would never cry again and promised vengeance on this uncaring city. It was the transformation of Sastra the iron into Gilead of the rocky place. It was a name to worry and confuse the Prophets for many years.

In the beginning, the twins would go down to the bathing pools where the people first arrived and by diligently testing the arrivals' minds they would themselves control the owners instead of the Prophets' wives who came to stare into their souls. They could not do this to everyone, for their gifts were not as great as the polished skill of the blue-robed, blue-eyed women, but they saved one or two and their army of friends slowly grew and spread throughout the city, as sailors mainly, because they were the only ones to have time to themselves out on the wide blue ocean, away from the perpetually probing minds. But there were also merchants, soldiers and even women of the Shama. Even—their greatest coup—when one of the Prophets' wives died, the one who took her place was one whose mind had been touched by the twins' gentle thought patterns.

This form of subterfuge lasted for some ten years. The twins would claim people with their minds and Sastra would claim unsuspecting victims with his knife.

During one of these nefarious exploits he learnt what had become of the Gypsy womenfolk. As he crept back to one of their hide-outs one night he heard raucous laughter coming from a street down the way. They were Mordecai's Children, and they were drunkenly pursuing four women dressed in red who hurried up the road ahead of them. Sastra recognized, with a sharp pang, his sister Ambról, now grown into an attractive seventeen-year-old. Her brown legs carried her fast over the pink stones. But the other three were not so agile and were caught. Their red dresses were unceremoniously torn from them and Sastra saw that burnt across their backs were crudely etched crosses. The women were buried beneath a squirming, milling, laughing crowd.

Then a swift merchant caught up with Ambról. He cried out in delight when he saw her hard, angry face. 'It *is* her! The Gypsy whore. Now here is some fun at last. Yours is a wild mind, untamed and unsubdued.'

He caught hold of her and spun her around as he laughed in glee—then gurgled as a knife sliced open his throat. Then the city swallowed brother and sister up. It had been ten long years since last they had touched and they hugged each other long and hard and wept tears of happiness.

She told him she was a Daughter of Delilah and had the cross branded on her back to prove it. She was any man's lubbeny and could not refuse them her mitchi wherever whenever. It was the fate meted out to any dark-skinned girl who came into the city. Occasionally Children of Lilith and, very rarely, Shama also suffered the same fate. She had been a Daughter of Delilah for ten years now and nothing shocked or hurt her anymore. But they did not own her mind, she smiled savagely, and any who wanted her had to fight her.

Many had had her though.

They deemed it best that they should stay alone, meeting on only the darkest, safest nights. But they never left each other's minds and with the other free minds they strove to escape this city. They bided their time until their numbers had grown. *Then* they could take over the city and change it for the better. Those who wished to go could at last do so—but never again would the Gate of Shame be used.

However, one day, down at the quiet gardens where the arrivals bathed, a trap was set.

One of the Children of Lilith, named Madeline, was placed in the garden as a supposed new arrival. But her thoughts had been tampered with and a trigger was set to catch hold of Ivy's deft probing of Madeline's mind and hold her own mind captive there. It was highly elaborate and had been devised by Jessamine, the wife of Jothaim. Ivy could not escape and as the wives of the Prophets tuned into the Child of Lilith's mind there was a channel of thought leading directly to Ivy's head.

They had her then and, after a fierce battle of wills, were able, at last, to control her. They brought her, pale and subdued, to the steps of the Palace. With all the wives of the Prophets focusing their attention on the mind of the young woman, it was easy to break into the ineffectual defences that Rockstone had set up and soon he too stood upon the pink steps of the Palace.

The Prophet Jothaim had devised a cruel revenge. But first he wanted to capture the last member of the rebel group—and a despised Gypsy at that. So he led the assault on Rockstone's crumbling thoughts. But, with one last effort, the gifted natural telepath came to Sastra as he lay in a restless sleep. He told him to go at once and never to frequent any of the places they both had known or else he surely would be caught. Even now Rockstone's brain was being murdered and soon everything he ever was and all he ever knew would be the property of others.

By this effort Rockstone was able to save his friend but was himself ruined. They sent him to the pulsating white sphere and when he came out he was known as Simeon.

As to his sister Ivy, a particularly evil jest was played. Every one of the wives of the Prophets left in her empty head just one thought each—a type of gift of the damned. At any given moment she would turn into a rooster crowing out loud, or a pig grunting as she snuffled amongst the rubbish, or a monkey cavorting about the highest rooftops, or a snake hissing and sliding on her belly down the street. She had an unenviable choice of thirteen creatures she could become and she provided great fun for the residents of the city as she stumbled, crawled or hopped from place to place, uttering the noises of the creature she had so briefly transformed into. Of course, a certain strain of intelligence remained in her head so she could look at herself and ponder on her foolishness at fighting the power of the Edna and how degraded a spectacle she looked to everyone now. Her eyes rolled in her head and her mouth drooled and she had lost the control of her bodily functions, but there were still those who sought her out as a special kind of Daughter of Delilah, for sickness rages in every society. She had become a plaything of the city. She was not even given the dignity of a name.

Many others of the twins' friends were caught in the whirlpool of drowning minds that occurred in the Pogrom after the capture of the twins.

The one wife of the Prophet, whose mind Ivy had once touched, used her own power to keep it a secret from everyone else. The gift this Prophet's wife gave to Ivy was that of a dove. So, for a short period of every horror-filled day, the young woman could sit quietly on the edge of a roof structure and coo peacefully, giving her some respite from the nightmare her brain had now become.

Sastra's story ended and there was a long pause while the sky to the east became smudged with the pink lips of the sun, as she kissed the day good morning.

Now Sastra laid a hand on his brother Gypsy's shoulder. His words were as earnest as his eyes were dark with threats. 'You see now the place where you have come. You must help me to leave with the aid of your friends. None of you are ordinary visitors to this city so you are treated with some kindness—but mark this well! That kindness can change as quickly as the direction of the wind. While you still have some control we must hatch our plan. Your friend the Kálo is palor with my companions Ithnan and Siddon.'

Sastra had organised that the two sailors became friendly with Port Rial as soon as he learnt of the pirate's interest in the ocean. These two and Ithnan's sister were the first three Rockstone had saved. Many a lonely hour on the murmuring waters hiding the fishing grounds had been spent in planning the downfall of their enemy.

Sastra leant close to Culvato. 'I will tell you why they hate the Gypsy and the Keeper people so much, these white, blond, blue-eyed monsters. It is not our colour or the old story told of the carpenter that they hate. The secret of why our minds are untouched is because we don't believe in anything. If you have no real God then they have no strong thought patterns, no essence of the soul you are, to creep into your mind and steal away your brain. The one you call Akar Black Head is like this and they fear him. But he is not strong enough to resist them and soon he will be their slave. You, as a Gypsy, have only the Gypsy way—a way so alien to them they cannot control your mind.' His eyes were sombre with bitterness. 'Although with every death of a Gypsy mind they know a little more about us, the same with the children of Phineas. It is why they are distrustful of you all, especially Jothaim. The only one they completely control is the one you call Red Mond.'

'And Nanny? What of the black woman in the Palace?' Culvato asked anxiously.

'She has been wooed by the King's own magic of sweet talk and jewellery. As with her friends she has an alien mind. But Jothaim would not dare do anything to the people of Sheba. They are the safest of you all.'

He got up then and stretched, as he looked warily around but there was no one on the empty streets.

'I am only a human, not a monster as these humans have become. They say they are God's children as it is written in the Miduveleskoe, the Godly book. Romani also believe in this God but in our own way. How can they say they are God's children when they are the spawn of Bengui.' He leant close to Culvato again, as if fearing even the walls of this cruel place had ears. 'Beware the one they call Zoheletha—or even the ones called Evadne and Sarah. They think, the men, that they rule this city but it is the women who have the final say. Women as evil as Sister Sun herself. Your friend Akar Black Head is right. This is the city of the sun. These women are as close to a Goddess as you will see and are more powerful than even their King of Kings.'

He rubbed a hand across his dark brow. 'Soon—one day soon—she will capture me, for I am growing tired and her mind is the only one that can find mine, or yours. And don't think they aren't trying to find yours. We must leave before either of these things happen or she will destroy you all as her people have destroyed all of ours.'

Culvato was still too upset for this to sink in. He could almost hear now the lost souls of Romani chavo and Romani chi crying out to him. That his mother's people, his people—and most probably relations—should come to this.

'Chal devlehi, paal,' Sastra murmured gently, realising his feelings.

'Chal devlehi. Coliko we shall meet again,' Culvato answered in a broken voice.

Then he was left alone with the rising sun peeping down over the buildings and the first of the buildings started to glow silver in her light. For he felt truly alone now—in all the land. It seemed almost half his Race had been wiped out within these walls.

An unaccustomed tear crept from his eye before he swept it savagely away with a sunburnt hand. There were plans to be made and no time to waste if he were to save his clansmen and woman, his companions, his people . . . and the woman he loved.

Quite soon after the meeting with Sastra the day arrived that Kareen was pronounced healed as best she could be. She still had horrendous scars across her chest and shoulders but a miracle had seemingly been performed by the Shama and the Prophets' wives and she was quite healthy. This should have been a time of great rejoicing and a gathering up of possessions and leaving this place, onwards towards their quest.

But there was no packing up and leaving. Her recovery only made the others more relaxed in the company of the citizens of the city. This was especially so in the case of Akar Black Head, who smiled a rare true smile when he saw his beloved.

The two of them spent some time alone, when the tawny-haired Kareen came out of the women's quarters, but Culvato observed them from afar. He could see that Kareen had become more like Shimona during her stay among the women. The blue fire had left her grey eyes that were no longer proud and fierce but dulled by the uniform calm of the city. He knew then that the wives of the Prophets had crept into her spirit and was taking it away. She, too, was a puppet in their hands and now they used her to break into Akar Black Head's mind, for this was one thing he believed in, the love of Kareen. She would win over the hulking, untrusting warrior, who had become her friend. All too soon he also would lie under the spell of this city.

Cudjo Accompong often left his weapon in the building the men stayed in—an unheard of thing before. Surrey Anne spent all her time dreamily in the gardens, working and chatting away to the Shama women. Nanny wore silk gowns and slept in a satin-sheeted bed with her King and had no time for her former comrades. Only Port Rial seemed to keep some of his cunning integrity. But that was because he was out on the ocean all day or with Meras, his new love.

Culvato knew the pirate was safe with Sastra's friends but *he* was still here, all alone except for a child of the moon he could not see.

The greatest change was to Red Mond Star Light. He had forsaken all the bone and skin ornaments he had worn with such pride, even the hair bracelet of his cousin Ilki and clansman Joda. They now resided in the cocoon with his abandoned woman. How he could forsake the deaths of his two young clansmen so easily was hard enough to comprehend, but when Culvato saw Red Mond had put away his soul bag he knew the Moon-talker was lost. Now he wore a blue gown like his new friends the Scribes and spent all his time with them. He did not even talk to Father Moon anymore nor go and visit his moon woman, whom Culvato could tell was getting more and more depressed. He was the only one around to hear her tears at night. Why, Red Mond even wore the white gloves of the menfolk of Canaan and it seemed to the Gypsy that his best friend had become like the moon itself, floating through velvet skies, far out of reach of earthly affairs—or else alone and pale in the blue gaze of this silver city. There would come a time when they would be friends again, he knew, but now the Moon-talker was lost to Culvato. The others of the caravan also floated around him, black as the night or like the stars far away and beyond help.

Culvato had never cared for rules and now he flaunted them even more. He wore his desert clothes with pride and he wandered the city wherever his feet would take him. He often slipped past the guards and went into the women's quarters or the forbidden zones. Soon his journeys caused some ire among the Prophets and they asked Red Mond to speak to him.

'You must follow these people's laws, cousin-brother. It is the way, and the way is written in the Epistle.'

'This Epistle to you is nothing. You can't understand the lines drawn there! What of your book in the sky?' Culvato growled, staring with distaste at the white-gloved hand on his shoulder. 'What of our quest?'

'Soon. Soon we shall travel onwards,' Red Mond said in his new calm voice. 'But there is much to learn here that can only help our people at home.'

'You have become one of them. This city will be your grave. What will become of your moon child then?' Culvato asked brusquely.

A sad look passed over Red Mond's brown eyes. 'She does not know me. We have lived together these many months now and she does not understand that this world is a huge and wonderful place.'

'You do not need books to tell you that!' Culvato scorned. 'What of the stories of our clan and Tribe?' He reached out and touched the elaborate pattern Kala had woven into his Traveller's braids. At least he had not got rid of them yet.

'This is only hair and they are only stories,' Red Mond said smilingly. Then he brightened up considerably. 'I have learnt so much, cous-cous. It is all in the fabulous Epistles. It is written, for instance, that the women shall be the gardeners and bearers of fruit. They are special and much revered. That is why you must wear gloves and boots for it is forbidden for a man to touch the earth, which is the women's sole domain, with any part of his skin,' he said earnestly.

'The soil is the blood and bones, skin and soul of Sister Earth and we are her children,' Culvato said, annoyed at this weak thing that had once been their wise Moon-talker and his friend.

A look came into Red Mond's eyes then. A look of cunning that frightened Culvato because it was not his boon companion sitting here looking at him but one of the Prophets.

'Do you really believe that, Culvato?' Red Mond Star Light purred.

'*You* believe in it!' Culvato said sharply, 'or, at least, once you did. Now you believe in these Epistles you can't even understand. How can you know that the words which these Scribes write and speak are, indeed, the truth?'

'What is the truth?' said the Moon-talker with the Prophet's eyes. But the Gypsy was already moving away.

'Just do me one thing, Culvato. Keep out of the women's quarter. It is the one rule this city will enforce, even on you, a revered guest and my friend. Many times now the Prophets have discussed this with me and soon their patience will be at an end,' Red Mond called.

'What use have I for their laws!' Culvato called back and, stooping, he picked up a pile of rich red soil from out of the rose garden they had sat around. His eyes challenged Red Mond as he let it trickle through his fingers.

'See if their duvel will strike me down, paal! Aunsos me dicas vriardao de jorpoy ne sirlo braco.' He spoke the Gypsy words defiantly. But inside he was hurt. Their quest for adventure had ended and they would finish their days in this towering, tormented city. For him, also, his quest was over. There *were* no more Gypsies. They had been murdered by this city. He was sad his friend had fallen under a spell but there was nothing he could do for him now. Soon, as the plan went, he, Sastra, Ambról and some of the sailors would sail away. For even those considered Divine in the Silver City now saw that man and woman had become too greedy. Their belief in complete power had destroyed any good that power had. The sailors knew it was time to go so, once more, Culvato would roam free. He would live with Ambról and they would start up their own Tribe. All that had happened before would be mere tracings in the flames of their campfires.

So he continued to flaunt authority. He ate often and in public the only fruit forbidden to be eaten by man. He was fond of the fresh crisp apples so he always carried a few around in his pockets. He had bare feet and hands and walked wherever he chose to.

Jaala, whom he knew as Ambról, warned him to keep a low profile and not bring attention to himself. It was dangerous. And not to use so many Gypsy words. If they learnt he was a Gypsy they would destroy him immediately.

They were lovers now, this youth who had once loved only the wide empty places of his adopted home and this girl who had known too much lust and very little love amongst the men, and sometimes women, of the Silver City. He began to forget about the woman who languished in her new Queendom, was fed the best of the luscious food from the gardens and bathed in goat's milk or cool water scented by the petals of roses.

Sastra also warned him, when he crept out of his hidden places to talk and formulate plans. Ithnan and Siddon had carefully asked questions of Port Rial and he would come with them because Meras was going.

But Akar Black Head was lost.

He spent all his time with Kareen and a peacefulness had softened him. In fact, they had even been given a house in the streets of the merchants. With his blue eyes and her grey eyes and golden-yellow hair they qualified as Mordecai's or Lilith's Children. Even though he wore no gloves and still had his Traveller's braid and the bear-teeth necklace and bear-head hat, given to him with pride by his last remaining aunt during his storytelling, Culvato could tell the big man was lost, by his dull eyes and placid smile on a face that had only ever shown scorn, anger, or a mighty fighting spirit.

He was not even planning to take with him a strange woman he had never seen and only rarely heard her speak. Then it had been a soft sibilant whisper that sounded like the hissing of the wind through the beautiful she-oak trees that grew down by the river of his home. But she had known of his half-formed plan before he told her. Indeed, when he came to her one dark night and she realised he knew the truth about this city, she told him her secret and that she was protecting his mind as best as she could. To prove it she released her hold on him for just a split second and he felt the enormous pressure as other minds jostled and probed all around him.

He really *was* afraid then, his face blanching to a dull yellow. Here was something in all his life he could not comprehend. And not being able to understand, yet knowing it was happening, terrified him with its very unknowing. He felt her mind wrap his up again in a warm blanket of love and friendship and became eternally grateful to this stranger who had so protected him.

'I try to keep control of Red Mond Star Light too,' she told him sadly. 'But he never comes here anymore and I must be close to those I protect now, for I am not as strong as these others. I have lost the one called Akar Black Head as well.'

'You must get me out of here when you go,' she begged. 'Soon they will control my mind and then they must destroy me as they destroy any with their skill but not of their beliefs.'

Her fear was so genuine he could almost smell it through the skins and rocks covering her home. He sensed that if ever they did control her mind they would drag her out of her cocoon and then she would not be the wonderful butterfly to emerge in her own time but a helpless larva, a toy to be squashed as by boys' idle fingers in a cruel game. He remembered the story of Ivy and shuddered at its cruelty. Of course he would take this moon child who had used her powers to protect him!

'Fear not, sister. You shall come with me and Port Rial at least. Soon we will be free to lead you on your quest. You shall have a new army beside you.'

So he made love to Ambról at night and by day he would wander around the city. He tried to follow everyone's advice about not breaking the rules but it was his very nature to question. What harm was there, after all, in playing his guitar again? But every time he played a tune he would horrify and terrify the passers-by with his 'music of the Devil'. The only music allowed in the Silver City was the playing of harps. And even then only by a few special women. All other music was banned, as was dancing. Hence, because it was banned, Culvato would sit in the middle of the busiest boulevard and play merrily away, incurring the wrath of the frustrated Prophets and even of his former companion, Red Mond Star Light.

Once he even swam in the pool that only the women were allowed to bathe in, earning a visit and the wrath of the King of Kings. 'Water is only water,' he scowled at this thief, who had stolen an ebony jewel from him.

He refused to look at Nanny, who looked down on him disapprovingly. She was bedecked in foreign finery and her face was painted in scented colours. Her fingernails were long and tapered and painted purple and her small fine feet were bare except for an elaborate number of gold chains going from her ringed toes to her ankles. So, even the Queen is as other women, Culvato thought wryly. Then his smile faded as the Prophets began to question and harangue him.

'The women's water is sacred water. You have violated it and now they must begin the long purification ceremonies to another unsullied pool. This will waste time with the harvests and put strains on the wives of the Prophets whose job the ceremonies are,' King Solomon said, upset for the first time since Culvato had known him.

'You must obey the laws or there will be no order,' Red Mond said from beside the King. 'This will be the last time you break these laws. The Pharisees have spoken,' he said.

Culvato glared with black hatred into the eyes of Jothaim and the other Prophets gathered around.

'These Pharisees are nothing to do with *me*! Why can't we go now Kareen is better?'

'She needs a while to recover. Her wounds were great and, besides, it is only you who wish to go,' came Red Mond's annoyingly calm monotone.

'Then why can't *I* go?'

'We came together and we will leave together. When the time to leave is right,' Red Mond murmured. He placed a gloved hand on Culvato's shoulder. 'My brother, why can't you be happy here?'

Culvato glanced sharply into Jothaim's eyes. There was an uneasy look there, away back in the cold blue. 'Ask your new friend, the Prophet,' he sneered.

'There can be no arguments in the temple of Yahweh. For he is and will always be the wisest of the wise, Creator of all things and blessed among the highest,' intoned the Prophet called Joash.

'Thus shall he govern all men and the paths they tread,' added Hiram, then bowed to the other. 'Joash, loved by God.'

'Hiram, God is exalted,' Joash murmured, bowing as well.

There was too much ceremony and politeness here for Culvato, especially as he knew what sort of people these Prophets and their wives *really* were. He stormed out of the Palace, ignoring Red Mond's calls to come back. He made his way down to the wharf where he found Port Rial in the drunken company of Ithnan and Siddon, with his golden-eyed Meras. He spent an enjoyable night singing illicit songs to them in the Gypsy tongue.

Three days later and despite the words spoken in the temple and the warnings given, Culvato was once again back in the women's quarters.

He sat amongst the feathery leaves of a giant weeping willow, hidden from the eyes of the world and, of course, the women he loved to observe in their place of no men. Some of their comments and motions would have shocked those pious ones who were their husbands and Culvato enjoyed their uninhibited humour. It was why he came so often to this forbidden place. Especially the compound right in the middle, where the twelve women he had first met resided in a most beautiful garden. In some of the jokes told he wondered if perhaps the teller did not know that he was a hidden listener. Occasional glances from sly eyes were perhaps also proof that he was not as concealed as he thought he was.

Suddenly, several of the Prophets' wives led by Jessamine, the wife of Jothaim, came into the twelve's garden. There were, of course, other Shama women visiting, as they did every day. But it was rare for the Prophets' wives to come in here. They brought with them an uneasy tension and up in the willow tree Culvato could sense their arrogant, probing minds.

One by one his twelve friends were singled forth with the Prophets' wives' eyes until they stood in a nervous, wondering huddle, Ruth and Shimona out in the front.

Then, through the gates came three women Culvato had never seen before but he knew without a doubt that it was the feared Zoheletha with her assistants, Sarah and Evadne. They were taller than the other women, the tallest one in a pure black gown, the other two in transparent white. The one he assumed was Zoheletha had hair that was totally colourless, it was so fine and white, although her face told him she was only young. The other two had thick black hair. They all three had the most startling blue eyes. It seemed to the astonished youth that their eyes were all pupil with no whites at all. They were worrying eyes and they now seemed fixed upon the unfortunate twelve singled out to face their light.

'What have we done, oh mother of the serpent from the stone?' cried Bethesda.

'Have we displeased you in some way, our mother?' Shimona murmured as calmly as she could. But her voice shook as did her hands clasped tightly before her.

'But you know what you have done, my children. Surely you did not expect to escape punishment from Zoheletha, the Highest of the High,' said the black-robed, white-haired woman. And her voice was a lulling, lilting tune that seemed to seep deep into the listener's brain.

There was a shouted command then, from somewhere beyond the wall, and the gate opened to reveal several soldiers. Culvato recognised the boy Jarebb whom he, Mungart and Port Rial had surprised so long ago it could almost have been in a dream he'd had.

Men! Here in the women's quarters? In this special place in all the city, the garden of the twelve special Shama? The tremors of shock could be felt as a fluttering in the breeze. Women turned their faces away at this invasion of their private world and eyes were lowered in bewilderment and confusion.

'Tell me, is it true what Jarebb says about what took place the day the strangers came?' questioned Jessamine.

'You must answer before God. Remember you are the Chosen Ones—and the Children of God. He will know if you lie!' ordered Danette, the wife of Janan, another powerful Prophet.

'What is it that Jarebb, the lively son, has told you, our mother, that you should come to the garden of women yourself?' asked Ruth the healer quietly. She alone of all of them looked squarely into the frightening, all-engulfing eyes of the three powerful women.

'You stood naked before the eyes of strangers. Yea, even one of the sons of Phineas, who are as nothing in the eyes of the Lord. Worse, one who crept like a snake into the Garden of Eden. Yea, even though you knew this, you stood naked before them as Eve did to Adam in the days of innocence. Yet not one of these men was to Eve as was Adam,' Jessamine cried.

'It is true, great mother,' Jarebb cried out also. 'The men they laughed and their eyes shone with lust and sin. They gazed upon the hills and valleys of our sacred women and their thoughts were vile as they ploughed furrows across their white flesh. Invaded, the women of the House of Willows stood and made no attempt to hide what only the Lord may see. For are they not the twelve virgins from the House of Willows?'

'Yes . . . and, so being, they are the very soul of the Shama. To allow this to happen is unforgivable. It is written that no man may gaze upon the naked body of a chosen virgin, for it is through a virgin that the Lord our God will walk again. You have betrayed your city and your law and—if not for Jarebb's honesty—you may have spawned a Demon,' Zoheletha intoned, her eyes even darker than before. 'A Demon to destroy us all.'

'Take them away to the place of stones,' Danette then said to the soldiers and, with much weeping and begging for understanding, the twelve were dragged stumbling and sobbing away.

The other women followed silently in a stunned, serious mass behind the Prophets' wives and the Highest of the High.

By following the devious, concealed paths that he now knew so well

Culvato was able to keep track of the procession of females. Everything had happened so fast that he scarce had time to regulate his thoughts. He only knew there was trouble coming for those he considered his friends.

They came to a part of the city that he had never seen before but its ominous feeling, that permeated through the very bricks of the buildings, warned him to be careful. Then he saw the huge gate with the yellow star painted upon it and he knew he had arrived at the Gate of Shame.

All the women gathered around the little group of twelve. The fact that not a word, not a sound was heard, except for the sobbing of the twelve, made the scene even more frightening to the youth hidden up on the roof of one of the buildings. From somewhere a bell began to toll and from out of every doorway and alley men appeared, just as silent. They formed a passage between them that led from the women to the Gate of Shame, which now was slowly winched open to reveal the harsh red desert outside.

The wind that blew in from the desert touched Culvato's nostrils and he almost salivated at the scents that free wind brought after so long being locked up in this grey, sterile place. It would be easy to creep from roof to roof and leap down at the last building, making the short dash to freedom.

But he had promised too many people he would look after them. There was Port Rial and the sailors, his Gypsy brother and lover . . . and the strange woman in the cocoon who had saved his life. His escape would have to wait.

Then, down in the middle of the crowd, Jessamine stepped forward and roughly tore Shimona's grey gown from her trembling body so it crumpled around her thin pale legs. The women on all sides crowded around her naked body, hiding it from the view of the men.

'Little Princess, you have the task of choosing five more of you who will pass through the Hall of Justice,' Jessamine purred.

'What of the other six?' Shimona whispered, fear filling her normally tranquil eyes.

'They shall go to the spheres,' Danette answered her smugly.

'Then there is no choice. We are all to die because strangers from a strange land wandered into our House. Such is the hand of God,' Ruth said and stepped forward. Her eyes were clear now and her mouth set firm. 'I will walk with my sister through the Halls of *Justice*,' she sneered at the last word and her eyes boldly stared at the Prophets' wives.

Shimona's low voice falteringly chose four more: Bethesda, Naomi, Zillah and Carmela. As each name was breathed the woman was roughly grabbed by Prophets' wives and her gown torn from her so they stood naked and shaking in fear and sobbing in a pitiful group. Only Shimona and Ruth stood proud and quiet, staring with calm eyes into the wall of blue around them as they accepted their fate.

'Now, Shimona, name the one who will cast the first stone from among your sisters,' Danette ordered.

'I would have Jarebb the accuser cast the first stone,' Shimona said in a voice loud and clear at last. Her eyes sought out the youth.

'That is not the law. The first—' Danette began.

But Jarebb had taken up the silent challenge thrown down by Shimona's cool gaze. He stepped forward from amongst the soldiers, picked up a chunk of rock and moved up close to the red-headed woman. But it was not her he hit. It was the healer, Ruth, who had helped save Kareen's life, who crumpled to the ground with a low moan as the rock smashed into her face.

Then the brutality began.

The six women were shoved forward by the other women into the passage between the men. A great roar set up amongst the jostling crowd. Fingers pointed, lewd remarks were made and raucous laughter echoed above the roar. And stones, sticks and rotten fruit rained down upon the stricken women while any man close enough kicked, punched or jabbed their comely, soft, white bodies as they ran for the gate.

Run? After a few paces they could scarcely crawl as that cruel torrent of abuse and pain swept over them. One by one they fell into the filthy mud underfoot, where their inert bodies were pummelled into raw, bloody heaps. Even half dead they crawled on broken bellies or limped on shattered legs towards the dubious freedom of the open Gate of Shame. First the beautiful Bethesda and frail, dark-eyed Zillah fell, then Carmela, whose ruined hands would no longer strum her adored harp, and finally Naomi. She was blinded by a bloody wound across her head, so she kept staggering into the unfriendly jeering crowd where her body was prodded and pinched. Some wits in the crowd would spin her around so she stumbled back the wrong way, her small hands stretched helplessly in front of her. The crowd enjoyed the joke and enjoyed feasting on her helplessness so they let her live longer. But, at last, she too fell in a heap to the muddy bloody ground, where immaculate boots and gloved hands kicked and tore her to pieces. Like the other three she soon became an unrecognisable heap of meat and bones.

Only Shimona, supporting a dazed Ruth, made it to the Gate of Shame. Her red hair was redder with spilt blood and her cheek was split wide open, revealing broken teeth. Her left eye had been gouged out by a well-aimed stone and her entire body was blue and yellow and red and covered in stinking fruit. But she had made it to the safety of the desert.

As soon as she touched the safety of the outside earth no hand could be raised against her. For it was written that any who survived the walk through the Hall of Justice had been chosen by the Lord to be forgiven and to go forth and redeem their sins in the outside world of the Devil.

So a great silence fell over the crowd and there was an eerie stillness as they watched Shimona swaying and quivering just outside the huge gate. She had borne the brunt of the attack. Ruth lay in her arms almost untouched, except for the jagged cut across her forehead that Jarebb had caused. Shimona looked down at her unconscious friend for a long moment, then her one good eye surveyed the empty red desert all around her, with the heat waves drifting like flames across the harsh, hot, orange surface.

A curious smile drifted across her battered face and she bent to kiss Ruth with her destroyed mouth.

Then, with one deft movement she snapped the healer's slender neck and stepped back into the shadow of the Gate. Her smile still lifted her lips and shone from her blue eye.

There was a moment of shocked silence and then a single voice called out, 'Murderess! The Devil is inside her. He was waiting for her.'

Stones of all shapes and sizes fell upon her, hurled with vehemence by the scandalised men. She stood there smiling, refusing to fall until a huge brick smashed into the side of her head and shattered her skull and Shimona was dead before she hit the ground.

CHAPTER ELEVEN

Something in Culvato's strained mind snapped as he watched the women he had admired for many weeks torn down by the bloodthirsty crowd. Vengeance glowed from within so his eyes shone with a bright anger and with each death a little of him died as well. He knew he must kill tonight or never rest again.

Now they dragged the remaining six women, protesting their innocence still and gibbering now in real terror, through the streets until they arrived at one of the smooth white spheres. The laughing crowd of men, many still spattered with fresh blood, followed behind.

At the sphere Zoheletha stood before it a moment until a door appeared from nowhere, it seemed to the amazed Gypsy. Inside, all Culvato could see were smooth white walls. He could see nothing to cause the fear these women displayed or of the danger Jaala had warned him about. One by one the struggling women were lifted and tossed screaming into the silent, white-walled space. Once in there they appeared dazed and confused. They stumbled about clutching their heads and shielding their eyes. If any made a weak attempt to escape they were stopped, it appeared, by an invisible wall of energy. One, Clemence, Culvato thought, just sat and stared out at the mocking crowd with lost eyes, already dull with acceptance of her fate.

They seemed to stare right into Culvato's soul for an instant before the sphere wall materialised and there was, once more, only an innocent glowing white sphere, the like of which were all over the city.

It was time for Culvato to leave and gather what forces he could. He sensed with the coming of Zoheletha and her helpers there would be a Pogrom, just as there had been before when all his people in the city were killed.

The first person he found was Red Mond, sitting beside a small fountain whose tinkling music dripped into the silence of this peaceful place. But his eyes were dazed and a frown furrowed his brown brow. The second Shimona died, her control of his mind obviously died too, leaving it empty and huge in its loneliness. As yet no one had filled the void with thoughts so, for the first time in many weeks, his mind was his own again.

He gave a weak smile at Culvato. 'Cous-cous, I have had the strangest dream,' he murmured.

'The time for dreaming is over,' his friend said abruptly. 'Come with me and I will show you the truth.'

He grabbed Red Mond by an unresisting arm and led him over the rooftops to the site of the white sphere. It was hard going, for Red Mond had become soft in his new life as a Scribe and the gown he wore impeded his movements. But at length they arrived and lay hidden from the noisy laughing crowd of men.

'What is so truthful about a crowd?' Red Mond wished to know.

'Be quiet and you will see!' Culvato snapped.

Then the invisible door opened again and the six women fell, crawled or crept to freedom. If freedom it was! For these were not the same six women Culvato had watched from afar. They screamed at unseen Demons and flailed the air wildly at invisible ghosts and saliva trickled from their open mouths so they resembled a sextet of simpletons. But it was their eyes, their empty hollow eyes, just like the beggars of unclean men that once had so disturbed Red Mond Star Light that disturbed him now.

'I know these women,' he began uncertainly.

Two of the women, Vida, beloved, and Abigail, source of joy, began fighting each other, scratching and gouging in the dirt on the street in a fight to the death. The men gathered around in a much amused mass of laughing humanity.

Somehow Culvato realised it was no coincidence. These two women had been the best of friends and inseparable everywhere they went.

'Do you see Clemence?' Culvato hissed savagely into his ear. 'Do you even remember her?' He shook his stunned comrade's shoulder viciously. 'We must go and go *now*! Any who don't follow us may stay in this cruel city. But you and I and your woman—the one I have guarded with my life and the one you have forgotten—must go now!!'

'Yes,' muttered Red Mond from afar, 'this is not the land of our people. I would go home to our Tribe Elk and cook meat on the fire of our clan Chief Violet Lynx Foot.'

Culvato put his hand into his pocket and withdrew the Moon-talker's soul bag he had collected from S'shony many days ago. 'Do you remember this, brother?' he asked. 'Here is the lock of our clan Chief, your uncle's, hair. Here is the stone Baba gave you as here is mine.' He drew out his own pebble, polished with much handling. 'But mine never left me, paal.'

'We *are* brothers, you and I,' Red Mond breathed. 'I thought I learnt a lot but I forgot more.'

'Stay beside your woman. She is the only one who can save you. I must go after the others,' Culvato ordered. 'Remember, don't leave her side or you will die.' He shook his head sadly and added softly, 'I have seen too much death on this day.'

Then he led Red Mond Star Light away from the scenes of madness being played out below them.

Back in the building, that had been the men's home, only the giant Cudjo Accompong rested. Unbeknownst to him, S'shony's protective probes kept the thought control from harming his mind whenever he came here. All he knew was that whenever he was in this room he could dream of his Island home, so he slept here as often as he could.

He sprang up, alert and ready, when the two crashed through the door. 'What 'appenin', maan? Look fe fire?' he cried.

'Stay here!' Culvato cried, in control now. 'We are leaving as soon as we can.'

'Nanny? She woman, yah?'

'Whoever comes comes! We have no time to explain what is going on. But *don't leave this room*. The power that can save you is with the woman in the cocoon!'

Confusion came over the craggy face of the huge man. He cast doubtful eyes at Red Mond.

'We have been tricked. All but Culvato,' the Moon-talker said quietly.

As soon as he entered the room he was filled with a warm glow of familiar memories as a joyous S'shony was able to flood his mind and set up as effective a mind shield as she could.

Cudjo Accompong believed in this youth and the other was a friend of Nanny's. He picked up his fearsome weapon that had spent so long alone in this room.

'Me get feisty a children fe Babylon. You a go fe others, bwoy, and I-an'-I wait 'ere fe you return.'

Culvato needed no second bidding. He left as fast as he had arrived and, following the secret paths that the unclean ones trod, he made his way to where he knew Port Rial would be. On the way he came across Surrey Anne, tears rolling down her plump cheeks. Like Red Mond Star Light her mind had been set free at the deaths of these peaceful women who had been her friends. Unlike Red Mond she had been set free in an atmosphere of confusion and bloodshed. Unseen by Culvato, she had been present at the stoning of Shimona and the others. Her eyes were full of abhorrence and she kept away from the smiling, blue-eyed people, who had become such monsters.

Culvato spared a moment to comfort her and pointed her in the direction of Cudjo Accompong and Red Mond. Then he set off at a lope towards the docks.

When he got to the fishermen's shacks that clustered beside the ocean like the swooping, shrieking gulls, Port Rial, Ithnan, Siddon, Meras, Jaala and Gilead were waiting for him with some others he did not know. When a crime of this enormity became disclosed the whole city learnt of it in no time at all. It was not often the feared Zoheletha and her assistants came down from their tower to dispense justice. So he was a hunted man now and could not hope to escape the power of the Highest of the High. By finding Culvato she would find the others and then the last element of resistance in this city would be ended. It was said it had been Culvato's act of swimming in the women's pool that had finally sealed the fate of the twelve Virgins—the most sacred and protected of all the Shama.

Their words greatly distressed Culvato.

'We must go at once, my love. Ithnan has the boat ready. You are here so now we can leave,' Ambról cried, waking him out of his reverie.

'I have given my word that I would return for the others. We could not bring the cocoon, for the horses are stabled across town. The spell has broken and they are in as much danger as ourselves.' He grasped his lover by her slim shoulders and said softly, 'A Gypsy's word is their honour and what are we if we are not Gypsies.'

'There is danger,' Sastra said firmly, then touched Culvato on the shoulder briefly. 'But we will wait just a little longer.'

Ithnan stepped forward, saying solemnly, 'Beware. The powers that our friend Rockstone gave us are not as strong as our enemies'. But you must hurry! When the shadow of the mast reaches the shore then we shall sail, with or without you.' He looked at Meras. 'I have my own family to think of now.'

Once more Culvato left on his hurried journey. This time, though, the other two Gypsies came with him to show him even quicker ways to get back to S'shony and the others. The three slipped through the darkening afternoon as the sun slid towards the sea and the great waters turned silver in her honour.

They had not gone far when they heard a host of cheerful voices and ducked into an alley to watch as a contented crowd ambled past. Suddenly Culvato's eyes lit up with a fierce light and his body stiffened like a dog, who senses a dangerous wild animal hidden in the grass.

'Wait here,' he hissed and ducked out of his place of concealment before Ambról could restrain him.

There before him staggered the person he hated most at this moment. A drunken Jarebb in the arms of his equally drunken companions, Darkon and the giant Elon.

He did not give him a second's thought of mercy.

'Jarebb. My lovely Jarebb, oh lively son,' he breathed.

When the boy turned bleary eyes to him, Culvato dug his knife into his ribs up to the hilt even as the boy's eyes widened in terror at the naked look of hatred on the face of one he regarded as a Demon.

'Dance with my little churi, mi kálo hinjiri.'

He did not hear Sastra's cry of 'Noooooo, paal! We are nashkado.' Nor could he hope to hear Ambról's whispered 'Merel' before Elon's mighty fist knocked him senseless. He did not see Sastra leap forward to try and pick up his limp form and escape from the charging soldiers. But Darkon had recovered his wits and sprang upon the small dark Gypsy with a gleeful cry of recognition.

'Tis Gilead! Oh, happy day this is when Yahweh looks down upon me, Darkon, to capture the scourge of our city.'

Others came to assist him and a crowd formed around the fighting pair as more hands reached for the elusive figure so many had heard of, yet so few had ever seen. It was not a long struggle before Sastra was held by triumphant hands. The great frame of Elon beamed down on him.

'Dear Gilead, how kindly will Zoheletha treat us now we have caught the thorn that grows amongst the lilies. Do you remember the screams of your harlot friend, the animal woman? They will be as the sound of sweet birds singing compared to your cries for mercy.' Idly, he nudged the unconscious Culvato with his sandal. 'Here is one who also must suffer. All know the penalty for murder and he has broken enough laws.' Benign blue eyes gazed wonderingly into Sastra's hot black stare. 'But here is the famous Gilead whose name is written in the Great Book as an enemy of many years. Caught by drunken soldiers off duty.' He gave a rumbling laugh. 'Gilead the unclean.'

'I am Sastra, the son of Lothario also known as Boshomengro and the woman Pacuaro. I am Rom andrees and live Romaneskoenaes,' the Gypsy bellowed, before breaking away from hands that had become lax in the sure knowledge that—for him—there would be no escape. He leapt upon the still twitching body of Jarebb and pulled Culvato's knife from the boy's chest only to thrust it into his own.

'I die by my own hand—a free man!' he cried, before sinking to the ground.

In the silence that followed, Ambról gave herself away by her muffled sobbing. Eager hands dragged her from her hiding place.

'She is a Daughter of Delilah!!'

'Sydel! Sydel!'

'She is certain to be a slut of these two.'

There were cries all around her and hands pawed at her body. But her wildness had dissipated as she watched her brother's death. She slumped on the ground beside her dead brother and unconscious lover. Hands ripped at her dress but Elon shouted, 'Don't you know who this is? It is Jaala, sister of Gilead the unclean. There is no time for that now. Take her to the place of stones.'

Ambról and Culvato were hoisted above the crowd and, heads and limbs lolling, they were carried forth to whence Culvato had left only that morning

As the triumphant, rumbling crowd went on its way it passed the quarters of the Children of Lilith and Mordecai's Children, several of whom came out to stare curiously at the advancing horde. This was indeed a day of excitement, for rumour had already got around about the destruction of the twelve virgins. Some of the colourful merchants or their wives had seen the remnants of the six once-sacred women scrabbling in the gutter and they got their revenge for the jealousies they had harboured, with a sly kick or punch to the defenceless Shama. But here was something new again and they came to stare and join in the growing crowd.

Among the crowd of gaily dressed merchants were the two sisters of Sastra and Ambról but the daughters of the palm tree stared with scorn—and yet surprise—at the roughly handled red-dressed woman. It was not often a Daughter of Delilah was sent to the place of stones.

Also in the group of people who gathered at the gates to the merchants' quarters were Akar Black Head and Kareen, for Kareen had not been feeling well all morning (in fact, the instance Shimona's head had been split open) and they had decided to visit their old friends. Now, to their surprise, one of their clansmen was being carried forth to who knew what fate.

Akar Black Head went to leap into the throng and grab Culvato. 'Stop! Let go of our cousin-brother!' he cried, but his voice was lost in the multitude. As he laid his hand upon his sword, the wiser, calmer Kareen stayed his emotion with a touch.

'Where do they take him?' cried the big warrior.

'To the place of stones. To the Gate of Shame. The desert will devour more souls of the unclean,' a green-eyed Child of Lilith sneered in savage glee.

'We must find Red Mond at once,' Kareen whispered in her lover's ear and she dragged a reluctant Akar Black Head away. They headed off towards the building he remembered as the home of the other men and their cocoon. Hand in hand they ran and the warmth that passed through their fingers reminded them who they were and where they had come from. When they arrived they were greeted by an anxious Cudjo Accompong and Red Mond and a tearful Surrey Anne who told them as best she could of the ritual murders she had witnessed. Red Mond told of the spheres.

'Now they will do the same to Culvato,' a shocked Kareen gasped.

'I will kill them first,' growled Akar Black Head. For the first time in weeks he placed upon his head the frightening bear's head and hefted his double-bladed axe. He was ready for war again.

'Then we will all die. These are a powerful people,' Red Mond Star Light whispered, distressed and confused. 'If I see the King and get Nanny to see as we have seen, there is some chance we can save Culvato,' he mused. Then, without another word, he strode out the door. 'It is important you stay here until I return,' he called as he left.

Even as he arrived, the Royal Entourage was about to depart for the Gate of Shame for it was, coincidentally, that special day all the city's undesirables feared—a day of exodus through the gate. And *no one* would miss an exodus.

Red Mond Star Light looked at Nanny and he had a clear image of when he had first seen her across the smoky confines of Violet Lynx Foot's tent, with her proud dark eyes and flaring nostrils and wide smile. She was now so different from the fierce predator and proud leader he had known. Now she was docile, dressed in fine silk gowns, with scented oils in her hair and paint upon her hands and face. Ornaments of gold, silver and precious pearls bedecked her feet and neck and her gold-painted eyelashes hid placid eyes that held thoughts only for pleasing her master. A complacent smile drifted across her face as another's thoughts drifted across her captive mind.

The Prophets stood protectively around her—she was just like them, thought the young man, whose own eyes had been brutally torn awake. He looked down at his own silk-clothed feet and white gloves and pale-blue gown. Who was he to criticise? The moment they had walked through the gates of the Silver City they had been captured like bees in a honey jar. They would have drowned in the sweet facade. All but one who now would surely die—his cousin-brother, a member of his clan and his paal.

For a moment he felt like ripping the offending clothes from him but he sensed he must pretend continued compliance if he was to rescue any of them at all.

'Laws have been broken this day,' Solomon the twenty-third said, 'but because the law-breaker is of my Queen's company, I have prayed to the Lord to save his soul.' His blue eyes bored into Red Mond. But Red Mond stared right back, no longer awed by all his riches and might.

'But he has danced with the Devil and the Devil's spawn!' cried Jothaim. 'His companions have been Gilead and Jaala, the Gypsy scum who killed our Lord's only son and refused hospitality to His mother, the Virgin Mary.'

'Like a staff of comfort he came amongst us, only to turn into a snake before our eyes,' Johanan said.

'I will forgive him his sins. He is henceforth absolved of any sin. But he and his mistress may not live amongst us. He shall follow the other tainted souls through the Gate of Shame,' the King said.

'Let it be written that Solomon the Wise was like a lamb before the Lord, yea, even as a child, innocent and forgiving to the wolves that gathered around him,' chanted Elihu, the Highest of the Prophets.

'Thus saith the Lord; I will make the multitude of Egypt to cease, by the hand of Nebuchadnezzar, king of Babylon . . . And I will scatter the Egyptians among the nations, and disperse them among the countries; and they shall know that I am the Lord,' chanted one of the Prophets.

'God is peace, Absalom,' came one's intonation and 'Girvan, the Lord's grace,' came Absalom's reply.

Red Mond was sick of all this pious ceremony. He saw through it all now and knew it only to be words. The true thoughts and actions of these men were as hidden as their minds.

A pale-blue gloved hand rested on his arm with the lightness of a butterfly. 'I know he is of your Tribe. But it is the way of our city to expel without compassion all murderers and rapists. If he was of our kind he would be dealt with by the Highest of the High, Zoheletha, who is even wiser than I,' the King said kindly.

'All murderers must suffer as did Cain. For it is written that he slew his own brother, Abel, and hid his face from the Lord, saying any who found him would slay him,' Tobias quoted.

'Yea, so it is, Tobias, God's goodness. And the Lord sayeth whosoever slayeth Cain, vengeance shall be taken on him sevenfold. And the Lord set a mark upon Cain, lest any finding him should kill him,' cried another Prophet.

'So it is that men today walk forever with murder in their hearts, the mark of Cain,' Jothaim murmured and his eyes bore deeply into Red Mond Star Light's soul. But his woman had cast a blanket over his mind that would last awhile yet and it deceived the Prophet. 'But all this Esau knows, reading as he does the Book of Truth with the help of our beloved Scribes.'

'Therefore shall no man grow gardens nor shall they even till the soil as Abel did. They shall be the protector of sheep and the fishers of men,' Nanny suddenly said from beside the King and her voice and phrasing were so different from her lilting language that Red Mond knew she was, indeed, a different woman.

'We are not an evil people, Esau. You have lived with us for a quarter of a year now and you have seen no cruelty. To show our good faith we ask you to come and bid your friend farewell. You will see that we do him no harm,' Jothaim purred, his eyes biting deep into the young Ilkari.

Red Mond had a flutter of distrust but he felt he had to have one last try to rescue Nanny. If he stayed close to her he might have a chance to bring her close to S'shony, then his woman's magic might break this cursed spell put upon them all. He knew that the only hope they had lay in the powers of the woman he had neglected for so long.

They set off. A regal procession: the Prophets and their wives, the King of Kings, Elia Melchoir Solomon the twenty-third, and his Queen Bathsheba and her many handmaidens. Behind, lost in thought, followed Red Mond Star Light. Every once in a while a Prophet or one of their wives would steal a glance back at his pondering figure.

It was not long before they arrived at two big aluminium gates that, even in the dying purple light of the sun, shone cold and silver and foreboding. Outside several soldiers guarded the entrance while from within came the anguished cries of the damned.

'I would ask to see my brother alone, with the Queen who was his closest friend. It was *he* who guarded her across the wastelands to her destination here and many was the time he saved her life,' Red Mond said.

'This wish is granted. Remember the privilege I am giving you. Only because he is of the uncircumcised—a son of Ishmael, as are you—am I granting this one wish,' Solomon the twenty-third said.

Red Mond and Nanny were motioned through the gates and they set off down damp stone passageways where the light of day would never be seen. The only light came from fluttering flames of torches stuck every so often into the walls, so everything was bathed in a wavering, flickering red glow. People were cramped everywhere, mostly bruised and naked and many with some form of birth defect. Some had no or extra limbs; there staggered a pair of Siamese twins joined at the head, here were several dwarves and quite a few had cerebral palsy or suffered from mongolism. A young woman had a horribly disfigured face while a boy, perfectly formed, had skin membranes over his eyes; another had been born with no ears or nose but just had little holes from which the mucous continually trickled. Those apparently not damaged in body stared out at the world with pools of crazed madness or dull resignation.

The air was rent by shrieking, wailing, sobbing or groaning. It sounded and looked like the Hell the Scribes had told him about in their Epistles, Red Mond thought. He would have liked to hide his eyes, cover up his ears, but he had to find Culvato amongst all this misery. When he glanced at Nanny none of this world seemed to touch her. She was totally impervious to it all.

'Paal!' a soft voice called and in the far corner of one of the dim rooms he just made out a dark face.

'Culvato! Why have they brought you to this place?' he cried.

But the Gypsy's eyes were looking beyond him in a cold silent stare. 'Why did you bring *her* here? Has she come to gloat like Delilah upon the slow death of Samson. That is one story I have heard from your Book of Truth,' he snarled.

'Culvato me love!'

Red Mond turned abruptly and caught the glimmer of horror in Nanny's eyes. It had worked! Bringing her down into this pit of insanity, to see her old lover, had broken the spell!

But then her eyes went dull again. 'This is no place for a Queen. If any of these people are my subjects then the crime they have committed is a crime indeed.'

'I killed one who killed your friends Ruth and Shimona—who were women just as you are!' Culvato retorted then turned, ignoring her. 'See here, gul eray,' he said softly to the Moon-talker. 'They think I am a fallen star.'

Now Red Mond saw in the Gypsy's arms a small baby, scarce a

month old. Its face was in peaceful repose and a smile tried to form on its tiny lips. But it had no arms or legs at all.

'They have mistaken me for my brother, Durrilau,' he laughed quietly. 'Every star shall fall to earth and Sister Earth shall cover it with her clothing. Unloved by Sister Sun they fall and become one of the children of the earth,' Culvato breathed, his eyes burning into Red Mond Star Light. 'Have you forgotten that story, my paal? It is one of our very own.'

He smiled down into the little peaceful face.

'They think they can punish me by sending me out into the desert. They could not destroy my mind though.' His smile faded. 'They have done their best with Ambról but I pray to all my mother's spirits that they were not good enough.'

In the shadows Red Mond then saw a slumped form and heard a high mewing noise as of a kitten in pain. So this was the woman the men called Jaala and laughed as they spat her name; who had stolen away his clansman's heart.

'They come for us soon and then I will be free, either in life or death, it does not matter now. I will die out in the open, away from these cursed walls,' Culvato said. Then he leant close to Red Mond. 'It is your turn to escape now,' he whispered.

Red Mond Star Light stared at him. He could hear the clattering of the barred gates as they were opened, and the squawks, screams or pleas for leniency from the tormented, as the boots and spear points of the soldiers moved them on.

'Goodbye,' Culvato said abruptly, then stalked away from them, scooping up his woman under one arm so she leaned into him, uncomprehending in her great grief at Sastra's death, her wild eyes vacant as her world crumbled about her.

Such a small word to end their travels together.

But when he looked up to say something Culvato was gone. Soldiers stood before him now, led by the mighty Elon.

'You must come with us,' the golden giant said. 'The King of Kings awaits the return of his Queen. Worry no more for the Gypsy Culvato and his whore. They go back to the land of the Moabites and Ammonites from whence they came. May God curse their name, the Gypsy dogs! I laid my hand many times on him in friendship—and on her once or twice in pleasure. But I did not know he was Gypsy filth!'

Red Mond Star Light could say nothing. To do so would have betrayed the fact that his mind was his own again. But he felt like the man, Peter, in one of the Epistles he was learning to read. 'Three times before the cock crows you will deny me,' his friend Jesus had told him and he did. Thus did Red Mond deny his beloved clansman.

As he was led out the door he heard the first ear-splitting roar as the foremost of the exodus touched the street of blood and mud and the first stone was thrown. A silent tear crept out of his eye before he rubbed it away furtively. He could not even cry for his friend without giving himself away.

Back with her King, Nanny turned and glowered at Red Mond, before turning to Solomon. 'An enlightenment of my troublesome people's ways, my Lord. I shall see the rest of my subjects do not molest your laws again. If they do they will face the severest penalties,' she said.

They started to move off before Solomon said, 'Wait! I will have Red Mond see one more thing on this precious night. A thing of great beauty.' Red Mond did not like the smirk that crossed Jothaim's face.

They set off down a different path and it was as if every member of the city had gone to the Gate of Shame, for the streets they passed were empty and lonely. As they moved away from the muffled roars it became eerie, even ghostly in its awful hush.

At once, coming from the narrow dark streets, they were out in a square. The smooth white sphere was awash in a creamy, silvery, pale, throbbing light. Red Mond remembered the place from this morning. The hairs on the back of his neck began to prickle and he nervously fingered his soul bag that hung alone around his neck. Then every hair on his head and arms stood up in fright as he watched three women *fly* towards him.

They floated some five feet off the ground in front of him as his legs went weak. They stared down at him with eyes that were just black holes devouring him. Then the one in black spoke to him in a numbing gentle voice, that turned his reason to ice.

'Such a sweet child. Did you think you could ever deceive me into not knowing your plans,' she whispered and shook her head sadly. 'Why, child, I know everything about you.' She swooped lower until she was only a few inches from his paralysed face. 'I have, for so long, been wanting to play with you. Life is so dull with only simple souls to study. But you, my little Moon-talker, you can tell me of so many new and exciting things.' A smile lit up her terrifyingly bland, pale face. It was the face of an evil wax doll, with no emotion on its countenance whatsoever. 'Why, you could take me to the stars.'

Now he could feel her clawing into his mind. He watched as the sphere opened up before his eyes. Against his will, his feet moved sluggishly towards that opening. His eyes, rolled back in fear, took one last glimpse at the composed, calm face of Nanny.

'I forgive you,' he whispered to her.

Every thought in his mind was being erased, devoured by the woman. New horrifying images were put in their place. It was devastatingly frightening and he began to shake and whimper like a little, cold, lost puppy.

'Perhaps you would like to say farewell to the moon you love so much. Soon we will fly up there, my new lover,' Zoheletha sang.

He gave an anguished cry as his reluctant feet dragged him into that dreadful white void.

Back at the building S'shony shuddered as she suddenly lost control of Red Mond's mind. She echoed the anguished cry of her lover and it reverberated around the room, chilling to the core all those without.

Kareen leapt to the doorway of skins, her usually clear calm eyes wild with fright. 'What is it, my moon Goddess?'

'Quick! There is no time to lose. Take me now to the white sphere in the middle of the city!' S'shony replied.

Kareen did not question how a woman in a cocoon, who had never left this room for months, should know of the sphere. There were more important things to worry about now.

Akar Black Head and Cudjo between them became horses and dragged the wagon through the streets, following the two women as fast as they could. Through empty streets their feet thundered as they charged across the city.

Inside his own cocoon the Moon-talker looked around slowly. A white light throbbed all around him and he could not tell if it was in the sphere or inside his head. Then the images came.

His mother being caressed lovingly by Demons from his worst nightmares. One had the face of the moon and another the shape of an elephant. Its trunk crept up between his mother's legs and she moaned in ecstasy. Nightstalkers invaded every space. But these were Nightstalkers from Hell, with extra arms and heads and filed, sharp, bloody teeth. Friends and companions were distorted and tortured, swaying in the awful white light. There was Yellow Eyes, except now he had no eyes for they hung dripping blood from his face and he was mercilessly pursued by a Demon cat that breathed flames and had glowing coals for eyes. There were his sisters and dear kind Magpie being sodomised by monsters with the heads of bulls and snakes for tails. Violet Lynx Foot disappeared limb at a time, then reappeared in a horrendous waltz with some apparition. Grey Fur was eaten alive by a slimy toad-like creature covered in fur. So it went on. Everywhere he looked, people he knew and loved were raped or tortured in a hideous manner.

And now his mother's head exploded, even as she stretched out hands towards him for help, and a glistening green body of some unspeakable Devil slithered from the jagged, bloody hole of her neck.

'I am your true brother,' the abomination seemed to shriek.

He clutched his head in agony and shook it but it was no use.

Outside, the motley cortege invaded the cold tranquillity of the courtyard. There, before their startled eyes, hovered the three women with the Royal Entourage, the Prophets and the King's guards, gathered like carrion birds to feast off the torment of one man's soul.

All four who could see this incredible sight were confused. But the one who could see only the murky shadows of her home saw more than any of them and she was *terrified*. The perverted Priestess, the woman no one could win against in a battle of the wills, was a hair's breadth away from getting into S'shony's own mind. She had to retreat from Red Mond Star Light's mind and set up a shield to protect herself.

Leaving him at the mercy of this evil woman, his mind was pulled out of his head and he experienced a great emptiness. Then he seemed to soar to the stars and into the very belly of Father Moon himself. He really did go mad then.

Zoheletha was able to turn her attention on the others now. 'Ahh, all my pretties together,' she smiled. 'Such fun we shall have on this night of all nights.'

'Let go of my cousin, you bitch!' cried Kareen and it was so unlike the affable Earth Mother it galvanised the others into action. The two men let go of the wagon and came forward at a crouch, Cudjo Accompong loading his weapon. Surrey Anne flung her heavy body into the huddle of Prophets and their wives.

'Away from me, you white duppis!' she shouted.

As Akar Black Head raised his great axe, his mind suddenly spun and the weapon was hauled from his grasp and hovered menacingly in the air above him. Akar Black Head fell to his knees and it appeared his own axe would slice off his head as he sprawled there. The giant Ras Tafarian could only gape, his weapon forgotten.

'You would dare try and attack *me*, Zoheletha, mother of this city and serpent of the stone,' came the high-pitched tones, whistling in anger now, of the floating Priestess.

Then S'shony let her whole mind pour into the head of the one she knew hated her people with *all* his spirit. She cried out in his mind, 'Save Red Mond! Kill the black-gowned woman. She is a Nightstalker', even as she felt the first cold probes coming into her vulnerable unprotected brain.

He leapt up, yelling in pain and fear but also rage. All this simple man could understand was his own great strength and his hatred for the Nightstalkers. He let everything come with him in the bravest charge of his life as he, too, seemed to fly through the air. He grabbed the woman around her slender neck with his two outsized hands and, with one spasmodic squeeze, he snapped it. She was, after all, only a frail woman. Only her mind was strong and, with no life, there can be no mind.

As soon as she died her spell was broken. Akar Black Head's axe fell crashing to the ground and the sphere shattered into smithereens. It was as though a storm of white rain occurred over the square, for a brief while, and from out of the storm crawled a pale, shaken Red Mond.

Now Cudjo Accompong leapt to join the fray with his small countrywoman. Akar Black Head swept up his axe and decapitated the giant

Elon with a single stroke. The Highest of the High Ones' two assistants still had some of their power left and the Prophets still had some collective powers but they were confused.

'Someone is keeping us from using our powers,' Jothaim called out as he watched Elihu disappear into the darkness, hurled over Cudjo's enormous shoulder. 'How can we call down the wrath of the Lord upon these Philistines?'

Cudjo Accompong came to Nanny's side. He had seen too many people under the influence of Pocomania or obeah to question the dazed look in her eyes. He merely slapped her hard across the face, awakening her to the sounds and sights of reality. He pushed her back to stand beside Surrey Anne.

'Oh Jerusalem, hear our lament!' wailed Solomon the Twenty-third, before a punch from Kareen knocked him senseless.

But the Ilkari and their Island companions were still heavily out-numbered. The fighting was fierce in that quiet square. Akar Black Head suffered yet another slash to his already highly scarred chest and a soldier stabbed Cudjo Accompong in the shoulder, getting his neck snapped in return. Surrey Anne received a cut hand. Then, just as things looked lost, there burst from the shadows, with the rattle of a machine-gun heard for the first time within this city, Port Rial and the friends of the Gypsies.

With the savage swathe of death that issued from Port Rial's gun, several Prophets and soldiers died—as did the assistant Sarah who was flung through the air by a stream of bullets. The rest milled about in confusion or fear at this new weapon.

Ithnan and Siddon and a few other husky sailors became the horses for S'shony's wagon, with Akar Black Head and Port Rial coming behind as a rearguard action; the hulking Cudjo prowled in front. Red Mond was supported by the women who followed behind the wagon with a growing number of refugees. Most of the latter were women from the Keepers of the Trees who had become Daughters of Delilah or a few who had their minds saved by Rockstone before he became Simeon and who had escaped the purging of the city at his capture.

Port Rial and the others had waited for the Gypsies' return and had then debated whether to sail without them. But Gilead was the hero to them all and Jaala the comforter and protector of the Daughters of Delilah. It was Ithnan who said, 'It is better to all die together than let them torture one of our best leaders and a man who has been our champion.' So they had come to the white sphere, knowing the cruel ways of the city and knowing the Prophets would settle for nothing less than to destroy Gilead's brain as they had Simeon's.

Imagine their joy when they realised the hated Zoheletha and her assistant Sarah lay dead, as well as a number of Prophets and their wives, while the rest cowered like normal human beings—no longer the haughty, all powerful Pharisees and Edra they had been.

Everyone clattered down the paved roads towards the Gates they had first come through. The buildings were black and empty, no longer seeming elegant in their shapes, but sinister. The trees whispered their farewells in the moonlight. At the gates it was a small task to overthrow Gabriel the Gatekeeper and the few soldiers there. Then they hoisted the gates open and the glorious sight of the garden shone in their vision like a warm and comforting campfire, the best story that they had ever heard told.

A number of people had been camped nearby, waiting to go in when the Gates opened on the fourth Sunday. Among them were the twins, Mungart and Weerluk, who listened with sombre faces and shadowed eyes to the story Red Mond falteringly told. With the death of Zoheletha her hold on him had, of course, dissipated, but he could never forget the horrors she had conjured up nor the brief alarming moment of pure madness he had experienced. The telling of their story went on into the long black hours of the night and into the early hours of the next day.

For two weeks they scouted all around the walls of the city. They even ventured out into the harsh desert for a while, before being driven back by the heat. But not a sign of Culvato, Jaala or any of the crowd of unfortunates could they find. The desert winds Culvato loved so had swept every trace of them away.

They left the walls of the Silver City behind and moved back into the forest to continue their journey. It was a great relief for them to be amongst the verdant darkness of the forest. Once again a fire would be made every night and the pungent smoke of the burning wood drifted around the company, enclosing them in a world they could understand. The leafy songs of the trees reconciled them.

They did not talk much of what had happened in the Silver City. Most were ashamed of how their minds had been violated, as if they had been caught naked and vulnerable, exposed to the eyes of the world. Sometimes they could not meet each other's eyes as they gradually let their bruised minds heal. As quickly as they could, they discarded all thoughts and clothes of the Silver City and tried to pretend all that had happened had been a cruel nightmare.

But the loss of Culvato was keenly felt. The empty place by the fire and—especially—from where he had skulked beside the cocoon, as the perpetual guard of the moon Goddess, was obvious to all. When Kareen began tentatively to play the harp again at night the notes of his guitar were sorely missed.

As her mind becomes her own again she knows without a doubt that she misses him. She thinks often of the first time she saw him as she ascended from the aeroplane into that dry, hot desert so different from the Island she called home. He had been the only one unafraid—bold even—of that great crowd. It is not enough to say that everyone lost their mind to the city's ways. It is her fault they stayed so long, as the city embraced her as the Queen. Strutting in all the power she was given she forgot her people, her new friends—and the man she had really loved. She had watched him go to his death while her eyes were devoid of any emotion. With those same eyes she has stood and watched as Red Mond Star Light was sent to his death. Only the love of his woman was stronger and had saved them all.

She remembers the words of a song Surrey Anne and Port Rial sang together as they struggled out of the Silver City that terrible night.

Babylon system is the vampire
sucking the children day by day,
Port Rial sang, and
Building church and University
deceiving the people continually
Me say them graduating thieves
And murderers, look out now
sucking the blood of the sufferers,
Surrey Anne had added, casting a glance in her Captain's direction.

It is true. She has worshipped a false God—and one who was white, at that—and done nothing to prevent the certain death of her friend.

The tall trees and small, sunlit meadows cannot ease her sorrow. She walks alone and her heart grows harder. She is through with love and all its fickle emotions. Now she will remain a warrior, as her Maroon ancestry demanded, and become the leader of her charges.

It was the cynical Akar Black Head who took charge of guarding the cocoon entrance now. He had a vague knowledge that, in some way, the unseen Goddess had saved their lives. Besides, it was all he could do to repay Culvato. He had had his doubts about the city as well and if he had joined forces with the Gypsy Culvato might be with them today.

S'shony needed the time in the great forest, surrounded as she was by nothing but trees and birds with their peaceful singing . . . and her few friends. She had never taxed her mind power so much as she had in the last three months and especially the last few days. It had not done her developing baby any good either.

But all her precautions had been to no avail in the saving of Culvato and she was much saddened by the empty space in her mind. The colour she had associated him with was a livid orange and now it seemed the fire had flickered out.

After two weeks of living like royalty in the forest on the results of raids into the massive garden, it was decided they must move on and fulfil the prophecy of S'shony. One prearranged night Port Rial went back to the city to meet with Ithnan and Siddon, who were getting him some horses. Doubtless he saw Meras again as well, but that was his adventure and he told no one of it. He did say there was a great deal of restlessness in the city. There had been fighting and some looting. People whose minds had always been controlled now found they were free to do as they liked. Some did not like this new freedom and there was the stirring of rebellion on the placid pink streets and in the quiet squares.

But on this night they raided the gardens one last time and set off through fields of waving corn, glad to be away from the Silver City and everything it stood for.

Skirting the edge of the desert was a sweep of thin, scraggly trees and bushes that crowded into a series of hills and valleys. It was rough going but at least here was shade and small pools of water and consequently game was to be found too. For two weeks they travelled through this country and the old ways of the caravan began slowly to merge.

It was Weerluk who learnt of the stranger that followed them from afar. When he went out hunting he came across small signs of their hidden partner: a broken twig here, a crushed plant there, an overturned stone or displaced branch. He waited another week until he was absolutely certain and then he laid a trap, with his twin. He would get whoever it was to follow him, as they seemed to do when he was alone, then he would get Mungart to sneak around behind and so capture the intruder. It would be easy for these bush-trained Keepers, who often played such games as children.

Weerluk led the stranger far out into the hills, pretending he did not know he was being watched, as he found the tracks of emus and he followed those precious birds to a she-oak glade, where his quick spears killed two tender birds as they fed on the nuts of those trees. The oil from their bodies would come in handy, he thought, and, besides, the sweet meat of emu was his favourite.

Now there was just the great panorama of silent bush, his brother and whoever followed. It was time to finish this charade.

Some white cockatoos took off screaming from a tree way over to his left so he headed towards the right, to the cool shade of a steep ravine. His eyes were always alert for enemies, human or animal, in this unknown land.

Once in the ravine, he contrived to disappear amongst the scraggly grass and purple rocks that lay jumbled at the bottom, prised from the split hills that rose above and around him. It was as though he had never existed at all and the follower was confused just long enough for him to glimpse a shape of blue, before whoever it was realised it was a trap and disappeared too. Weerluk gave the call of his family, the purple-crowned lorrikeet, and it was answered over towards the entrance to the ravine.

The trap was set and it was no time before the two, crawling stealthily through the friendly bush that embraced them with loving fingers, hiding them, surrounded the cowering figure and pounced upon it with eager brown hands.

She was a woman from the city! Her blue eyes gazed terrified into the two pairs of dark eyes that studied her as they held her tightly.

'It is one of the white women!' Mungart grinned, remembering the women at the river.

'Remember what these yorgas did to our ngoonies and tjuks,' Weerluk hissed, more practical. 'Let us be wary as if she were a dugite.' And his eyes were as merciless as that snake's.

'We will take this white woman to meet her Queen!' Mungart giggled. Over the days since his own personal disaster he had recovered his sense of humour and he found the idea of Nanny as a Queen a good joke. For his people had no class or stratus of society, except perhaps that earned by respect.

'Why are you following us?' Weerluk growled.

But she could not understand him and only shook with fear while she hid her face in the folds of her gown. Even when the more friendly brother clapped a hand on her shoulder and grinned down at her.

'Would you fly through the air for us so my brother can spear you like a wild duck?' Mungart laughed.

He had not experienced the horror of the Silver City, so, for many of the tales told by the awed survivors of that time, he could see a humorous side. Besides he knew women could fly. How else could they reach the outermost limits of the sky and become the stars that looked down on them? The stars that told a story of someone brave or beautiful, cunning or clever, greedy or foolish, who ended up guiding the Keepers' paths with their light and their lives with the moral that each one held.

The story of the women who made up the seven sisters, for instance, could be told many different times over. Some said they were the Emu sisters, the Makara, who were escaping from the cruel Dingo men who wanted them as wives and who lit a fire to burn off their wings. But the sisters, in stepping over the fire, stretched their legs so much that they became the fastest beings on this land. They ran to the end of the earth and up into the sky but the Dingo men still followed and became another set of stars strangely resembling an upturned saucepan like the Ilkari used for cooking. But still they could not catch the fleet sisters who made it over the western horizon first every night, thus gaining a brief rest from their eternal pursuers.

But there was one story they *did* believe and that was the one of how these people had some sort of control over other people's minds. They had seen the female Keepers of the Trees come out the Gate with Red Mond and the others. They had seen how they were affected and had listened to their tales. So they looked on her as an evil spirit woman and were careful of her.

'Don't look into her eyes, brother,' Weerluk warned.

'We will take her to our red brother and leave her fate in his hands, as her countrymen left his fate in the hands of these women,' Mungart said, serious at last.

The two of them set off through the silent bush and said not another word nor spared a glance in the stumbling woman's direction. Weerluk kept a firm grip on her clothes so she could not run away, although it seemed she was, in some strange way, glad of the company—as if this huge wide countryside caused her fear. Why then had she hidden from them for two weeks, following them, if she had nothing to hide? Her calmness and resignation of her fate only made the twins more nervous and they began to wonder if they should not kill her right away. In their stories there were many beings who were not as they appeared. A rock could be an evil man, killing someone at a touch; a balga bush could be pregnant women full of magic. Hills and trees and swamps could hide spirits. The brothers looked at each other, remembering. What about Meetagong who took human shape to lure victims away?

They were glad to come into camp.

But a heavy silence met their arrival as all of the occupants froze as one, to stare at the blue-gowned and veiled figure—one of a Race they hoped never to see again. The scars on their minds were still too fresh.

'Kill this evil Demon,' cried Akar Black Head and sprang forward, swinging his axe dangerously in his hands.

'Peace, Akar. At least, let us hear what she has to say,' murmured his more serene partner, placing a hand on his heaving shoulder.

'She woman put Keepahs in trance, me seh. Any moment she friends come fe take I-an'-I back a city!' cried Surrey Anne.

'There *is* no more city,' the Prophet's wife whispered. 'Only the wind through the willow trees echoes the weeping from our hearts.'

They gathered around her cautiously and this time their silence was one of incredulity. The huge city with the teeming populace and mighty, towering, silver buildings was no more? The image was hard to visualise.

'I know you,' Nanny said quietly. 'You are Laelia, the wife of Joash.'

'Laelia, devoted to the Lord,' the woman repeated.

'There is no Lord here,' Akar Black Head growled. 'Look around you and you will see there is no Culvato either.'

And he did not know how much he hurt Nanny with those brutal words. A spasm of pain erupted in her belly and shivered up her spine.

His hard blue eyes—that they could now say were as blue as the wind-swept back of the ocean they had all seen—speared into the equally blue eyes of the woman.

'Why do you lie about this city? It is a trick to capture us again,' the big warrior sneered.

'Wait, cous-cous, and we will listen to her tale,' muttered Red Mond Star Light.

They all went back to the fire—for there can be no story without a fire—keeping a sharp eye on their unwelcome guest. They settled down around the smoky rim, then, hesitant and heartbroken, Laelia told of the ending of her world. Her soft voice, usually so self assured, cracked with the strain of misery and her eyes were confused. She was not as good a storyteller as the Ilkari women, for all her stories were in books and the written words. There was no body language to give the tale personality. But, still, it was a terrifying enough story.

It was not a long one.

In the old days before Armageddon, as was written in the Book of Revelations, there were those among the people who used ten per cent of their brain power to develop the world God had made for Man. After the war at the end of the world, it was the duty of every man with any goodness in him to develop what intellect he had and, thus, be close to God. Therefore, as century took over century the men had only one object in life and that was to reach God through their minds. In doing so they eventually far out-passed the brain power used by the cleverest men in the world of old. They began to discover that the impossible was indeed possible and the imponderable was only so because that part of the brain had never been explored.

Soon such things as creating buildings with the mere twist of a thought; of flying through the air; of controlling other people's possessions, both animate or inanimate; of talking without speech and seeing things no one could imagine. These all became a thing of regularity. So regular as to be normal. And the Prophets' wives were among the most advanced in these skills, second only to the incredible power of the Highest of the High.

But the wives of the Prophets' lives were lonely and sterile. They had, for example, no need for sex and all the passion that act might entail, for the thrill of taking over a wild mind, full of alien thoughts, was much more exciting. They could never get old as age was only in the mind and they could turn their thought patterns around to become young again. They had no fear of death, as any illness could be cured by previously untouched regions of the brain. They had no need for the physical reproduction of children since their incredible energy took up all their time and they could create whatever they wanted—angels, fairies, mermaids, centaurs or the most perfect child—all using their amazing minds. In the old world, it was said, Man had created a machine called a com-pewtah. But the Highest of the High had originally been created by God and this made her special and a thousand times better than even the best com-pewtah. She walked on the right-hand side of God and was even more powerful than the King of Kings. Twenty-three times had a baby girl been chosen from among the Shama and had her mind filled with the mind of the previous Highest of the High, as was the ritual. Each time had the knowledge been gained from one hundred years and the special training of that particular mind.

So the woman Zoheletha had twenty-three hundred years of knowledge within her. Through the energy spheres around the city she could control her energy—and thus her city—by harnessing her incredible powers within the humming domes.

Most men had some knowledge of this power, but only the Prophets were allowed to use it.

Thus it was written. Any imperfections of the mind or body were taken to mean that person could not see the Light of the Lord through their own darkness. They would be sent to the desert through the Gate of Shame. Also it was written that the dark ones, the children of Phineas the Egyptian, were the slaves of Canaan, for the crimes of their descendant Ham. Therefore the women became the Daughters of Delilah and the men mind fodder for the city. Any of the Gypsy Race who wandered into the city were children of the very Devil herself and the worst kind of sinners. There was no way they could live in this world of the pure so they must die and crawl on their bellies, like the snakes they were, through the Gate of Shame, after their mind had been stolen and purified and left in the city.

So had they lived for three thousand years in peace and security—the purest Race, the Twelve chosen Tribes with their blond hair and blue eyes and perfect, clear minds, building a stairway to God and his heaven on High.

They glowed like angels and flew like angels and some knew the answer to everything their world had pondered upon. Truly, they were in Heaven on Earth and the gardens flowed around them like the first garden their Lord God Yahweh had made. It was why no man could touch the earth, for it was from the earth the apple tree had erupted with its fruit of red fire and its branches like snakes, black and twisting. It was why all men were forbidden to enter the gardens, for it was there that woman had tempted him and he had fallen under her spell. The first man had bitten into the juicy white flesh that was the brain of Yahweh and thus had tasted just a little of His knowledge that had made him hungry for more. In this hungry scramble for knowledge Mankind had almost destroyed himself.

Now strangers that were neither the children of Phineas the Egyptian nor Mordecai, nor Lilith, nor Delilah, nor any of the Tribes of the Devil's desert had come. The children of Ishmael the wanderer, Ishmael the banished, had returned to the shadows of their walls. Yet they had brought a gift, Bathsheba, the true Queen of Solomon the Wise, as was predicted in the Book of God in the Song of Solomon and so it was that, after twenty-three centuries, their wish was fulfilled and they really were the blessed ones.

But with the wish a curse had come as well. This curse that was hidden in the words of the Song. For did it not say:

Who is she that looketh forth as the morning,
Fair as the moon,
Clear as the sun,
And terrible as an army with banners?

And this army with banners had indeed come. It was the only thing any of the exalted could not see. Not seeing with their pure and blessed minds meant it was a sign of God and so was unavoidable.

At the death of Zoheletha there had begun the splitting of the intricate system that held the city together. With the further deaths of Jothaim and several others of the Prophets there had begun the rapid decay of the purity that held the Twelve Tribes together. Ithnan and Siddon's revolt had been the trumpet blast that brought the walls tumbling down. No one knew the amount of damage that would be done or the rapidity of the revolution.

It was like the cities of Sodom and Gomorrah. It was like the last days of Babylon. The Book of God was full of the vengeance of the Lord but this was the greatest vengeance of them all. It was remembered—too late—that the Babylonians had built the Tower of Babel as a stairway to Heaven and the Lord had destroyed that too, with devastating results.

Here were only humans, after all, with faults of slothfulness, lust, pride, envy, greed, avarice and wrath.

They had burnt the Synagogue and all the Epistles and Books of God. They had murdered the four Scribes, the woman Laelia wept softly. Men, hungry for the feel of a forbidden woman, had stormed the women's quarters and Tribe had turned on Tribe, as the city collapsed around them. From out of the dungeons and from out of the darkest streets the unclean had risen. The Daughters of Delilah had come seeking revenge against the men who had for so long abused them. They came with knives to castrate and cut the throats of bewildered men who pleaded for the mercy they would never receive.

What distressed her most of all was that she knew she had been part of the downfall of her beloved city and her King of Kings, for he too now wandered lost and alone in a frighteningly strange forest—just an ordinary man. He must defile himself by going into the forbidden gardens and picking fruit or berries, as did other meandering men from their city.

Yes, she had brought about the destruction of her life and world because she had been the one to help the red-headed stranger's mysterious woman against Zoheletha's power. She was the Prophet's wife who had been saved by the sage Rockstone and his incredible mind. For years she had moved up the allotted path her mind made for her, until she was a Prophet's wife. For years she had awaited word of her escape, keeping her deadly secret safe with her.

So, at the end, she had caused the hated white sphere to explode because of her memory of Rockstone, who had become the grovelling, drooling Simeon. It had been she who gave the gift of the dove to his sister Ivy, when all the wives had bestowed their cruel presents upon her.

'Why should we believe you?' Akar Black Head growled after she finished her story and only the wood popped and cracked in the awful silence. And the bear's head atop his own looked particularly fierce in the firelight to this gentle woman. 'To me you are still a woman from the city—one of those evil ones who would have killed us all. You stood by and let them take away our clansman Culvato,' he snarled.

But again Kareen placed a hand upon his knee and her grey eyes shone with faint amusement.

'Since when did you regard Culvato as anything more than a cheeky upstart with no respect for clan or Sister Earth?' she murmured. Then her eyes became serious and she lifted back her leopard-skin cloak to reveal her ruined breast and torn shoulder that were still faintly scarred. She pointed at Laelia. 'This woman saved my life. At home I would have died long ago and, even with the magic of the Keepers and Surrey Anne, I would never have been the same. You know that, all of you. When I was in the women's quarters it was this woman here and her companions who sang to me. Her songs healed the tendons and skin of my body.'

Now Red Mond Star Light spoke from across the spluttering fire, from where his jet-brown eyes had studied the woman Laelia as she haltingly told her tale.

'This woman called Laelia has spoken true. She caused me to escape from the Demon's egg and the clutches of that she-Demon of the Sun. So, also, have I seen the women of this city kissing trees and touching stones in a special way and running water through their fingers. Just as do our own Earth Mothers. Again, Kareen speaks true when she says these women saved her. Where there is hatred there must also be love, for the two walk hand in hand and are shadows of each other. One might say one is the other, depending on who you are. We have seen many strange things on our journeys and we will see many more but there have been none so strange as the happenings of the Silver City. I must seek the help of one who was not affected by these things. I must talk with the Goddess of the moon.'

'Coo'yah us. We gettin' him chance fe opinion, maan?' Nanny spoke up. 'Me rahtid this woman welcome coo'pon no Culvato dey 'bout.'

'This he land. Him make business him own,' Cudjo Accompong surprised everyone by rumbling beside her. 'You nah talk. No opinion no dey fe she!'

'Yes. You boasie Queen a go Bathsheba so fine fi you fancy clothes. Livin' wid a white maan!' Port Rial joined in.

'De Black bredrin an' sisthren fi you city. You heard what 'appen to them, nuh? Woman she wish she dead while him men walkin' dead, girl,' Surrey Anne growled. 'Zombies and voodoo, dereso. Cho! You she Queen

fe obeah, me say. But Saint Catherine she nevah turn against her people!'
She, who rarely lost her temper, spat viciously.

She puts her head in her arms so none can see the pain there. They are right, of course. If she had only been able to see the tricks and the traps opening up before her she would have warned Red Mond Star Light and kept them safe from the city. She, with all her worldly wisdom and intelligence, could surely see what the genteel, blue-gowned women were doing! Could she not see what was happening to her and her friends? As soon as the women arrived in the camp, as soon as they saw the great silver-grey domes of the city they were doomed—and yet she could still have saved them. She comes from a country and a people who are steeped in technology and also tradition. She is a Maroon, a warrior woman from a free Race of fierce people. Yet she was as easily taken as a dozing dragonfly might be taken by a frog.

She rises abruptly from the fireside to walk off alone. Now she knows what loneliness really means. This is a lonely land despite being a land of awesome beauty and massive stillness as the very mountains seem to breathe slow and deep.

The others looked around the fire at each other and everyone, except the Keepers, ignored the blue-gowned woman. *They* had never seen one of the Silver City people to really study before. Mungart played gently with her fine, gossamer-like clothing and marvelled at her pale skin—yet hard, brown hands and feet—until Weerluk gruffly reminded him to have nothing to do with white people and their ways.

'She is as blue as the flower back home. The one that looks like pools of evening sky upon the ground,' Mungart breathed, fascinated. 'Her skin is as white as the light of the sun.'

'And the light of the sun plays tricks on men's eyes. The light of the sun that drives a man to madness so he walks in circles and sees the blue, blue water everywhere,' snapped Weerluk, ending the conversation.

Laelia, devoted to the Lord, crouched between them, her eyes downcast in fear. For all her life she had been taught to fear and despise those she now sought refuge with.

She had discovered also that the further she moved from her once prosperous city, the more her power was diminished. So for the first time in her life she knew the feeling of helplessness and terror. She hid her face behind her veil, sensing the hatred all around her.

Then she felt a female mind touch her own briefly with the warmth and comfort of mother's milk. The mysterious woman was welcoming her as a sister! A faint smile lifted her mouth a fraction—the first hint of a smile she had given in a month. She raised relieved eyes and sent a wave of thanks flowing towards the tent while she watched Esau come smiling from the doorway. Why could none of those who knew everything in the world not see the genuine warmth and heartfelt passion in these people's embraces and arguments and love of life?

S'shony, in her dark world, had felt the unrest when Laelia first arrived and had sent out mind probes to see what harm had befallen them now. Imagine her dismay when she realised she was dealing with a superior mind from the hated city. She quickly withdrew and set up a barrier around her own mind. But when Red Mond Star Light came seeking her advice and told her Laelia's story, she searched the newcomer's mind again and found it to be true. Here was the woman who had rescued her lover from a horrendous death, so she could not refuse her anything. Compassion and forgiveness were two more new words she had learnt from being in Red Mond's company.

Laelia, devoted to the Lord, was welcomed into this hybrid band by the mysterious woman. S'shony showed Laelia her world, that was as different from the Prophet's wife as could be. It terrified her, this new place of no sunlight, no love. She was supposed to know everything that had ever existed yet right under her feet was a whole vast world. That was something to ponder on as well.

A dark, damp and dangerous place for a violent people as pale as she, but with black eyes and hair and black, cruel minds. But she was interested that this woman was soon to have a baby—an unusual emotion for her to share.

Laelia's other friends were Kareen and Surrey Anne and it is them who give her the name of 'the Blue Woman' because of the remarkable colour of her clear eyes, as well as the robes she wears all the time. Often she would join these two, shy and silent at first, in their forays into the bush for food or medicine. This wild, tangled landscape was so different from her own cultured gardens that she really was of little use. But the other two were kind and patient with her.

Of the men, she was most frightened by the scowling, hairy man who protected her true friend with a heavy axe and cold blue eyes. The other men ignored her—except an enthralled Mungart and a quiet Red Mond, who would shyly converse with her a few moments before hurrying away.

The woman who had been her Queen kept very much to herself. A great sadness burdened her soul and the others left her alone.

The old ways of the old days before the Silver City gradually crept back, like favourite dogs around a cooking fire, so there was laughter and jokes, friendly chiacking and conversations, music and songs and the smoking of Port Rial's weed. But there was always something missing— the same thing that was missing in Nanny's black, almond-shaped eyes.

Book Four

Meetings

CHAPTER TWELVE

After the bush-covered hills, they had made their way to the sparsely covered sand dunes near the huge river that had no other shore.

Now they moved away from it but could still hear the faint roar of the incredible ocean. The country alternated between sparse, hardy bushes set upon a sandy plain to clumps of tall, straggly trees. Game and water became scarce although this was no desert. But they were used to hardship and the clever hands of Kareen and Surrey Anne found sustenance where there appeared to be none. Now was the time when the Keepers of the Trees came into their own. By following ancient paths, even they had only heard of, and by following the signs of bird and creature, they always came back from a hunt with food for all and every night they camped by some form of fresh water.

They saw no humans although there was plenty of signs such as abandoned campfires and deserted camps, which indicated that this desolate place was occupied. Those who knew what to look for saw, for the first time since their departure from the Purple Plains, the signs of conflict with Nightstalkers. This sharpened their senses to the dangers of this new place.

The season the Canaanites called winter was upon them now and sometimes, from the blue-purple ocean, cold sleety rain would come dripping from the mouth of the hungry winds, like saliva from a wild dog's mouth. The days were bleak and grey, while the nights echoed to the lonely boom of the ocean, and a mist caused by the spray from the huge waves spread over the evening fire's flames. They huddled into their skins and wondered at the emptiness of the land that seemed to have swallowed up every living soul and left only as ghosts the pitiful remains of their camps.

One night, while the rest snuggled into their rags and Red Mond Star Light kept solitary vigil over the faded orange embers of his fire, there appeared a figure, almost as if by magic.

A tall gaunt figure with a wrinkled, wizened face, alive with a million creases which this Ilkari, not used to old age, found frightening. His eyes were deepset, being far back in his skeletal head. Long wild masses of white hair fell to his knees. There had been some attempt to control it with various bone combs but this only made him appear wilder than ever. It flowed around his body like the mist from which he had materialised. He was clothed in a long, ragged blue cloak that swirled around his ragged blue trousers and clung tenaciously to his thin shoulders.

'Peace, brother. Fear not the might of an old man whose strength lies only in dreams now,' he croaked out a greeting.

As he came closer to the fire the youth was able to see the oldest man in the world. His hair was as white as the sands of the river beside the Moon-talker's home and his flesh seemed eaten from him. A great, knobbled, gnarled, wooden staff was gripped by one stringy hand.

'I have travelled far across these lands and would seek a little warmth from your fire. You are, I see, not the same as others of this land. For instance you have women with you, who are not slaves.' He began to fold his long frame down upon the stony ground and a smile cracked his craggy face, awful in its age. The old man's eyes, still hidden in the shadows of his face, glanced in his direction and the youth sensed a bright light studying him as intently as he himself studied this newcomer.

'My name is Red Mond Star Light of the clan Violet Lynx Foot,' the Moon-talker said. 'Who do I share my fire with, cousin-uncle?'

'I am Prince Michael of the Ants. You have come across the plain of grass from new lands as yet untrodden by my path.'

'How do you know this?' Red Mond said, curious yet wary of witchcraft.

'I am Prince Michael of the Ants,' the old man repeated. 'I read it in the tracks upon the sand,' he said simply.

The youth, who read the paths of the stars, could understand that answer and he relaxed.

'Tell me then, cousin-uncle, of the people from this land. What do the tracks tell of them?'

'There are no people. Only animals—and Demons. Has not the wind told you this?

The land of faery,
Where nobody gets old and godly and grave
Where nobody gets old and crafty and wise
Where nobody gets old and bitter of tongue

'That is truly an enchanting song,' said Red Mond.

'They are the words of a famous man who lived many years ago. But are not words great, for they remind us of who we once were in the poems of those long since dead.' And he quoted with obvious love, softly and melodiously:

Land of Heart's Desire,
Where beauty has no ebb, decay no flood,
But joy is wisdom, time an endless song.

He sank back down into himself again and smiled a cracked smile with broken yellow teeth. 'William Butler Yeats. The Land of Heart's Desire. That is where you are now,' he chuckled.

'We are on a journey, Prince Michael of the Ants, and our feet have taken us through many curious lands. Tell me why the people of this land of heart's desire should not desire to see us?'

'They have been taught to hate people and hate truly is a powerful emotion for it eats at reason until men are insane and only hatred keeps them alive.'

His hidden eyes stared into the Moon-talker's. Although Red Mond Star Light had welcomed strangers into his camp before and had brought only disaster, this old man with his beautiful words had about him only an aura of peace.

The old man lay down where he sat. Red Mond sat up the rest of the night, watching him. At last the Moon-talker was able to converse with the panorama above him that was like the scattered coals of Father Moon's fire. So the two, father and son, shone like moonbeams in the dark velvety night and he became strong again and pure. All the lies that had wrapped around him in the Silver City were washed away by the pale light of the dying moon. *Here* was his book and he read it well.

There were the signs of forbidden love and yet also a great and vibrating love and there was a sign that power could destroy trust, but he could not fully understand that sign. Falling stars indicated a change of direction and new meetings with evil people—who could only be Nightstalkers—and he determined to warn the others to be on the alert. A slow-moving star or new, strange moon drifted across the sky, one he had never seen before, and he wondered at the message it brought with its ethereal restless light. It too seemed to be on a journey as he was and it looked to be heading towards the sun that, even now, peeped slyly over the horizon, prying into the Moon-talker's world.

The first to see their new companion was Akar Black Head.

'Who is this? Another God our Moon-talker has found?' he growled at the ragged pile of bones. 'Could it be old Father Moon himself?'

'He is just an old man who sings songs,' Red Mond murmured.

One deep and penetrating eye opened suddenly and peered up at the big hairy man and said in a slightly different voice to the one he had used last night:

I made my song a coat
Covered with embroideries
Out of old mythologies
From heel to throat;
But the fools caught it,
Wore it in the world's eyes
As though they'd wrought it.

Song, let them take it,
For there's more enterprise
In walking naked.

'He is mad,' the big man whispered in awe.

For, to the Ilkari, a mad person was the best sort of luck. A mad man or woman lived in their own world and often saw things that others did not—rather like the witches and sorcerers in stories told about the old times.

'Semel insanivimus omnes,' Prince Michael said, sitting up from his pile of filthy blue rags. 'That is my motto and my heart. The words pump life into me so I keep walking and talking. Semel insanivimus omnes: We have all once been mad.'

Now in the morning light Red Mond could see the colour of the old man's eyes under his jutting brow. They were a piercing blue—the blue of the rare new metal the swordsmiths from Ilkari clans used for some of their best weapons; as blue as the flames used to forge these weapons. These eyes were weapons too, the Moon-talker realised. And behind the blue swam something dangerous, like the shadow of a shark that he had once seen Ithnan catch and which had so terrified him with its impersonal black eyes and huge teeth. They were the same sort of eyes that had so disturbed him when he first moved into the Silver City—the eyes of an unclean man.

At that moment Laelia awoke from where she had slept beside Kareen.

No one had seen anything but worry, sadness and fear in her eyes ever since she had first joined them. But it was nothing as compared to the look she gave the tall gaunt man beside the fire. And *his* eyes, when he saw the familiar blue robes, went hard and he leapt up and strode over to a cringing Laelia, crying out:

Lo, all our pomp of yesterday
Is one with Nineveh and Tyre

'And it is written,' he loudly preached to her. 'Thus spake Yahweh to Jonah who was angered by the repentant being forgiven: "And should I not spare Nineveh, that great city, wherein are more than six score thousand persons that cannot discern between their right hand from their left hand; and also much cattle?"'

He glared down at Laelia with such hatred that Red Mond wondered if, once again, his kindness and good nature would bring death to the caravan.

'Oh, daughter,' the old man said sadly, 'could you not see that Yahweh is as El and they are only one? From the land of Canaan they said Eden flowed verdant and luscious where the four rivers met and El was our master. Can a man become a God? Does a God belong to any single man or woman? Aaaah,' he sighed, 'who can tell what games the Gods will play?'

Then he threw back his head and sent forth a dreadful cackling laugh that chilled the listeners' very bones.

The beauty of Israel is slain upon thy high places:
How are the mighty fallen!
Tell it not in Gath
Publish it not in the streets of Askelon;
Lest the daughters of the philistines rejoice,
Lest the daughters of the uncircumcised triumph.

His lamentation awoke the others so they crowded around him, staring at this weird apparition that had come among them in the night. Laelia cowered at its feet and Surrey Anne moved over protectively to her new friend. Black eyes glared up at the face of Prince Michael of the Ants. She stood, her hands on her hips, immovable.

'Get from she, you Bongo man,' she hissed, putting a comforting arm around the white woman's shaking shoulders. 'She name Laelia she sisthren fi me,' she added vehemently.

A softness came into his crazy blue eyes and he stepped back, staring at her smooth, round, black face and long-lashed, inky eyes. He stared at her for such a long while that she became embarrassed and shyly ducked her head.

A lovely lady, garmented in light
From her own beauty,

the old man breathed, then turned and strode away from the group, his wild hair streaming out behind him.

At the clearing, he spun about and raised his staff. 'To the legions of the lost ones, to the cohorts of the damned,' he cried out in quotation, before disappearing as quickly as he had arrived.

Then all but the two Keepers and Laelia gathered around Red Mond, asking who this man was. How had he come to be with them? Would he bring them harm? What if he was a spy for the unseen inhabitants of this desolate country, gone now to lead them against the caravan? Cudjo Accompong wanted to know most stridently why Laelia had been afraid of him, since they obviously both came from the Silver City, but the young woman got up, shook herself free of Surrey Anne's hand, and walked away by herself.

'He is an old man and where we come from any lucky to be kissed by old age are loved and welcomed by our clans for their wisdom and knowledge,' Red Mond said.

'We love our maas too, nuh. But lion grow old him teeth rot. Him nah so-so wise. Sometimes him quashie,' Nanny replied.

223

'Then he is harmless and has been touched by Sister Sun, yet lives. Such luck we have needed for a long time,' Kareen answered.

'We have lost two and gained two,' Akar Black Head grinned. 'Now we have Father Moon come down to earth to see how his daughter is. How does he find her, cous-cous?' He grinned across at Red Mond while an impish look winked in his eye. 'Is that why he shouts such foolishness? Because he has seen the licentious relationship his beloved son has with his daughter?' and the big man laughed and laughed. His laughter was infectious and even the steel-eyed giant gave a faint lifting of the lips. Then Kareen rested a hand on Akar Black Head's broad shoulder, while a warm light shone in her eyes.

'You mustn't tease my cousin,' she admonished leniently. 'He will be your cousin by marriage as soon as we get home.' She smiled at Red Mond.

'And my father-in-law will be this moon man,' the warrior guffawed with simple mirth. 'We know he is a fallen star.'

There was a brief flash of remembrance in Red Mond's mind and a voice whispered as soft as the dreams of the wind: 'See here, gul eray. They think I am a fallen star.'

He saw again that dark, damp, screaming room, full of shadow upon shadow and weeping and mutilated minds and stumbling, destroyed, bewildered bodies all around him. He had almost led his friends to these cruel depths. Indeed, he had lost his truest friend in that wicked place. Any who had come from there—and this old man had certainly come from there by the look in his alarming eyes—could never be turned away by conscientious society.

He had done that once too often already and even now, out in this empty wasteland, Culvato might be stumbling about, cold, hungry, lost and alone. Would his sharp black eyes shatter into shards of insanity like the eyes of the old man? He could not bear to think of it.

'He shall stay. He does us no harm and the words of his songs are soothing to hear. They will be new stories from these lands to keep us warm at our fires,' he said softly but firmly.

'What of the Blue Woman?' Nanny asked. 'Him faastie fe she.'

'She, too, came as a stranger and we have welcomed her. Even your Surrey Anne,' Kareen said.

'Perhaps her story will be in one of the songs he sings,' Akar Black Head grunted.

The two Keepers kept their own counsel. They also, like the Ilkari, had respect for old age—although a little fear of madness. For it was madness that had destroyed their world in the Old Times and it was from madness the new world was born. Madness, they believed, was a white man's disease and so they were disconcerted when it raised its head amongst the nomadic Totems of the Keepers. But they, too, had love and kindness for any the Ilkari called fallen stars and they in their own language called kart warrah or winyarn.

So began the unusual relationship with the gaunt old man. Some days he wouldn't be seen at all, appearing like a white and blue wraith at night and disappearing in the morning. He slept where he last sat down and ate very little. Surrey Anne discovered if she left a plate of food at the edge of camp, the food would be eaten by the morning. Often his cracked voice could be heard shouting at the sun or distant mountain ranges. And the words he shouted were glorious songs.

His hatred and persecution of Laelia went unanswered and unexplained. She stayed out of his way as often as she could and kept in the company of Surrey Anne. The crazy old man had taken a liking to the Islander girl and often brought her a bouquet of flowers from his rambling walks. This the pirate Port Rial found most amusing and told her she had found the best treasure of all the land in the old man. But when the two from the Silver City were pressed together in the confines of the camp, Laelia would pretend not to hear his rasping, cruel words. She would hide her face in her veils and duck her head, pretending neither the words nor the man who spoke them was there.

Only once a tear crept from her eye—and only Surrey Anne saw it—when the gravelly voice creaked:

The toad beneath the harrow knows
Exactly where each tooth point goes;
The butterfly upon the road
Preaches contentment to that toad.

Before the dark little woman could rouse her temper to defend her friend she—and, again, only she—saw him bite down on the words and the look he gave the blue-cowled figure before him was something akin to idolatry. He whispered:

We look before and after,
And pine for what is not;
Our sincerest laughter
With some pain is fraught;
Our sweetest songs are those that tell of saddest thought.

Surrey Anne, who knew about devotion as much as she knew about cooking, wondered at the strangeness of that look, in eyes that had only held vile, flaming hatred for the shy white woman.

The two Keepers took him into their hearts and made a special place for him there. Theirs was a nation of mimics and being able to simulate the strange customs of the white man had been the skill of their best comics. So they came to enjoy the old man's erratic characteristics, even though they did not understand a word he said.

When Prince Michael came up to Mungart and said:

An' for all 'is dirty 'ide
'E was white, clear white inside
When 'e went to tend the wounded under fire,

Mungart laughed and laughed until tears rolled down his cheeks and even Weerluk raised a dour smile. From then on the orange, dreadlocked head of Mungart was never far from him and the youth's loud hoots of laughter could be heard all over the camp.

The two Keepers gave him the name 'bidit warda kadak' which simply meant ant man of importance. Not even the fierce kirlirl, or bull-ant, would bite him and he would never wittingly hurt an ant, no matter how small. The two brothers treated this as a sign of respect for the land and all the land's ways. For even the ant had its place in the stories of Creation. Some ants were even heroes in some Tribes' stories and were, as with everything else, Totems of other families. The fact that this ancient man loved the ants so much only showed he also loved the land from whence the Keepers had come.

The only person who did not know Prince Michael was S'shony, who had reached out with her mind cautiously, to feel him when he had first arrived, and was repelled by the swirling rages of madness she had felt there. It tumbled right down into her belly—even to the tiny heart of her unborn child nestling in her body, so her whole womb went icy with terror. She could not let her child have this influence going into its developing mind, so she cut the old man out immediately. She tried to find out about him by secretly probing the others' minds. More specifically her friend called Laelia, to whom she had given the colour of turquoise—a nice peaceful colour that was neither blue nor green but a constantly changing medium between the two. But it seemed that no one knew anything about him, except for the songs he sang that she could not understand. Laelia knew something about him but S'shony sensed she was blocking it from her tentative mind probes.

There was something very much wrong with this old man but she could not work out what, for his insanity was a good disguise. She huddled into her skins and rags and felt a cold wind drift over her.

There came a day—a cold and grey and windy day—when the meandering troupe could no longer stand the lulling boom of the distant waves from over the sparsely treed sand dunes. They decided to, once again, visit the side of the huge river that had no other shore.

For the four from the Island of Springs the ocean was no great phenomenon, but to the Ilkari it was a most fantastic thing. For a while they had been so awed by this huge expanse of water they had been afraid to go near it. But for some time Kareen had been devising a ceremony that would be fitting for such an occasion.

The two Keepers had seen the ocean many times in both her calm or tempestuous moods. They believed their spirits would one day travel across the waters to Kuranup, a place where there was no pain or tribulation. But, as usual, they respected the beliefs of the Ilkari people, for it takes all kinds of power to hold a Kingdom together and beliefs are more enduring than the human body or mind.

Laelia was the most frightened of going too close to the wide and wild, blue-green expanse, because of *her* belief that it was a man's place and a stairway for the Son of God to walk upon down to earth and so be the salvation of them all. Her place was the gardens she missed so. But her new friend Surrey Anne—whose last name meant 'whom God has favoured'—relished the idea of swimming in the salty, frothy waves again, and this helped lessen Laelia's fears.

Their lunatic singer of songs had gone off on one of his vacillating walks but they knew he would find them again. He seemed to have some uncanny knowledge as to their whereabouts.

As they trudged over the sand dunes, Sister Sun broke free from the coils of black cloud that were flung around her neck, like the muscly arms of some lover. The whole wide ocean turned molten silver and, close to shore, was a clear pale green. The waves sang to them a melody of tranquil, booming joy. Seagulls and other seabirds swooped and swirled upon the choppy empty plain of water and the large, curved white beach. The scene made every one of them feel momentarily alone and minuscule in the face of Nature's might. Then, they too were swooping like the seagulls, whooping like the waves, as they charged down the coarse-grained side of the hills.

They tethered the horses that led the wagon with S'shony, close to the water's edge, and then discarded their clothes and leapt into the magic water. Even though the first bite of the swirling blue currents was cold they laughed and splashed, ducked each other, wrestled among the waves in the sheer joy of living. Even Nanny leapt among the waves, sending her laughter to join the shrieks of the disturbed seabirds, and Cudjo Accompong put aside his thunderstick weapon and strode into the waters like a huge black elephant, his teeth bared in a very rare dazzling white smile.

Red Mond Star Light collected a container of water and carried it into the cocoon so S'shony could enjoy the ocean. He also brought a collection of shells for them to examine. The whole beach was covered with them and some were prettier than the best glass or plastic jewellery found upon the Purple Plains.

He smiled as she tasted the salty water and enjoyed the cool wet kiss of the ocean. Of course there were pools and lakes and even rivers in her cold, dark, underground world. But the water was colourless and devoid of life or movement. Never had she heard of such water as was outside except when it poured roaring into tunnel towns, leaving them empty of life. What frightened her, though, was how there was an unending open space so that the water and sky met as one. She, who was used to cramped, confined spaces, had difficulty in grasping this image.

'Of all the sights I have seen so far, this is the greatest,' Red Mond murmured. 'I wish you could see it too.'

'Port Rial tells me Father Moon's travels have something to do with the water's travels too. They have a road called tides that they travel upon and this road also tells us when a year is up—just as Father Moon in his journey across the sky tells us. So the ocean is an old companion of Father Moon's.'

'And how would a child of the sun, as you know him to be, know so much about our Father Moon?' she teased, for she could see he was relaxed and happy and the terrors of the Silver City were behind him.

'You sound more like Akar Black Head than a Goddess of the moon. I had to pretend I knew all these wise things that you, coming from the moon as you do, had already told me,' he smiled.

'Have I told you today that I love you, Ilgar my butterfly?' she whispered.

While a mild wind blew amongst the sand dunes, whistling as it threw sand in the air, and the ocean soothed them with its roar and crash, crash and roar of perpetual waves, they ran hands over each other just like the waves ran up the smooth white beach—as white as her marvellous body. His fingers lingered over her gently breathing, swelling belly and he was content with life.

There was a soft call from the doorway and he left her with a final caress and smile.

Outside Kareen squatted, letting the shadows of the clouds run over her naked golden body. The faint scars across her stomach, breast and shoulder were still visible. 'I go now to perform my ceremony, cousin.'

Over by the water's edge the four Visitors, with Akar Black Head, cavorted amongst the waves like black porpoises and a hairy whale, creatures he knew lived in these waters from stories told by the fishermen, Ithnan and Siddon. Laelia dipped her feet into the very edge of the ocean—and it took a lot of courage to do even that. She was the only one who would not remove her clothes. Mungart found this highly amusing and he chuckled as he idly fingered her fine gown, with dark fingers, until he was led off by his brother who sensed the white woman's consternation. Now they walked, arms over shoulders, down the beach on a fishing excursion, spears in hand, and joking with each other.

Kareen rested a warm hand on Red Mond's sunburnt arm. She was darker than him, being a golden honeycomb colour all over while he, with his dark-red hair, tended to be a yellow brown. But it was obvious in the shape of the nose, the tilt of the chin, the look in the eyes that they were cousins and, just for a while, they shared that closeness. He thought of another cousin, in a time long ago now, with red hair and blue eyes, whom he had led to his death before a story could be given him. He looked down at the hair bracelet upon his arm.

'We have had a few adventures, cousin-sister,' he said, remembering. 'What do you think the future holds?'

'More adventures. Some of us will die.' Kareen shrugged. 'But you can surely tell that from the moon.'

'In the Epistles of the Silver City I learnt that the moon was just a piece of dirt and rock. Also that Yahweh made it along with the sun and earth,' he whispered.

'At times the clouds roll in across the sky, purple and black—yet there is no rain. Do not always believe what you see, cousin,' Kareen said quietly. 'We have all seen strange things and met with strange people. But if you have faith in what *you* believe—and you only—then you will pass through this life in peace.' For a moment her eyes went dark and serious. 'How else do you explain a Goddess of the moon amongst us?'

She stared deeply into her cousin's eyes then smiled as she stood up to go. 'I must go and dance for the Earth Mother now. I have thought this dance out long and carefully and now is the time to do it,' Kareen said.

She swayed off along the white sand, her large golden body a part of the earth it appeared to Red Mond Star Light, who watched her go, with worried eyes. So even graceful, gentle Kareen had her suspicions about S'shony. Was that influenced by Akar Black Head or did she know something? Would even kind-hearted Kareen set her warrior side free when she saw who this 'Goddess' was?

He looked over at the shiny, water-flecked bodies of the playing Visitors. Everyone, including the unbeliever Akar Black Head, treated them as High Ones. They had incredible powers—that was true enough!—but they were almost certainly human. But only almost! This was a most confusing and bewildering time upon earth, he thought.

Surrey Anne came out of the water and called out to him to go and join the rest but he shook his head and smiled and went back into the cocoon to discuss his thoughts with S'shony. Surrey Anne dragged on her ragged silver pants that were all she had left of the suit in which she had walked out of the plane. She let the sun warm her back as she set about preparing a meal for them and hummed one of their Island tunes.

They say de blood runs
And it runs through our lineage
And our hearts, Heart of hearts divine
John seh dem comin' with de truth
From an ancient time.
Brotherly love, sisterly love
I feel dis mornin'

I feel dis mornin'
Brotherly love, sisterly love
I feel dis mornin'

Her man came out and lit up one of his smokes then idly wandered about the camp, dragging the scent of the sea and the sweet smell of ganja back into his lungs. Totally relaxed, he absently fingered Red Mond Star Light's mighty club that had belonged to The Creeper. It was truly a fierce weapon, the pirate thought. One of the best clubs of its kind he had ever seen and, if not for the knowledge of his superior firepower, he would have been awed by its brutal shape.

His sleepy eyes looked up as a movement caught his attention but it was only Prince Michael of the Ants. He languidly raised a hand in greeting. Then froze as other figures crowded around the man.

There were perhaps a hundred of them and so quick and quiet were they that they had already spilled onto the beach and had them surrounded before he could even raise a yell.

In the cocoon, S'shony's mind was suddenly assailed by a multitude of minds, all cruel and insane, so that she gasped in pain and laid a warning hand on Red Mond's arm—he who lay so blissfully unaware of the perilous situation outside.

With their three best warriors naked and in the water and another three away fishing or performing a sacred ceremony it would perhaps have been wiser to be polite and subservient. But Port Rial was neither at the best of times and especially when he saw three strange white men, ogling his woman, slobbering and giggling.

For men they were every one, or boys. And every one of them had something unusual about him. There were many dwarves. But others had hands growing from their shoulders, or skin membranes where their eyes should have been. There was a pair joined at the hips and several had no legs. Many had something wrong with their minds and could be distinguished by their obese bodies or mongoloid eyes or mumbled talk. There was one child with the softest blond hair and bluest eyes of whom it appeared there was nothing wrong at all, because he had the face of an angel. But if one looked closely into his eyes one would see there was absolutely no emotion there at all.

Those who could be were armed with vicious spikes of wood or jagged swords or great clumps of wood hewn roughly into the shape of clubs. One or two had steel javelins and all had hard, violent, burning eyes. They were not the vacant eyes of the mad, but were alive with evil.

Many of them had a form of tattoo upon their body in green, blue or black design. Mostly upon their face or arms but also occasionally on their torso or legs.

'Me knew you cheatin' lyin' old man. I-man see Babylon before me face, but you nah kill Rasta so easy.'

So crying, Port Rial sprang towards the three at Surrey Anne's side. Then there was a crack and he stumbled in mid-stride, as a rock from a slingshot slammed into his waving dreadlocks.

Then a huge hand casually slapped the side of his head again and he went sailing ungracefully through the air to thump into the soft inviting sand, unconscious.

The man who had done this was as tall as Cudjo Accompong, with a long thick beard just as black. His head was shaven and was covered in bumps and scars across its shiny burnt dome. The boy who had fired the slingshot stood beside him. He only came up to just above the giant's knee but his twisted shoulders were broad and powerful for one so young: he was only about sixteen years old. But he had the eyes of one much older. Cold and green they stared out at the unloved world.

Now the giant strode forward in a single stride and picked up the fallen club. His voice was a rumble from deep within his massive chest as he hoisted it aloft for all to see: 'I know this type of club. It is the club of our old foe, 'The Creeper'. This sword too is 'The Secret-maker's Whisperer'. How does it come to be in this black stranger's possession?'

He bent down and with one hand he effortlessly picked up a terrified Surrey Anne. His merciless eyes were as green as the boy's and he looked her over as a cat will look over a mouse before playfully clubbing it to death.

'And this strange Keeper woman,' he looked across at Laelia. 'How is it you walk in the shadow of the enemy?' He casually tossed the Islander woman away to whimper at the feet of the two dwarves and a man of vacant mind who had first surprised her. They began gurgling with laughter and roughly caressing her body.

Their hands groped her warm body while they mewed, 'Woman! Woman!' and her thoughts went back to another time in another land when men had torn at her friend Saint Catherine and ripped her vibrant, vital body apart with animal hands. She was in a state of shock at how casually her man had been disposed of.

Other hard-eyed men moved towards Laelia, who was numb with fear.

In the water the other three eyed each other and made a silent decision to attack as soon as the men reached the shaking, quaking Laelia who had fallen sobbing to her knees, too afraid of the sudden presence of violence to use her calming powers.

'Aah, well, the crazed one was right. There is an enemy of the people here. One of the Gatekeepers who turned us out.' He hefted the huge club in one ham-like hand, as though it were a feather. 'They all must die—' he stated with finality. 'Except the women, of course. Keep them alive a little longer.'

'No,' cried the old man in one of his rare moments of lucidity. 'I brought you here in good faith to meet my new family.'

At these words the giant stared around at Prince Michael of the Ants and, in words softer than he had used thus far, murmured, 'These are not your family, old man. See how they use their power even now to confuse your mind. Surely you know the danger of this enemy after what they have done to you in our Silver City? They didn't steal my mind for they thought that the Night Bats would steal my body, so I can see these people to be what they really are. And all enemies must die.'

He raised the club just as Port Rial gained consciousness. The first thing the pirate heard was Surrey Anne's anguished cry and the first thing his blurred gaze saw was the sun winking off the glass chips of the club about to descend and snuff his life out like a taper on a candle flame.

Even as the club began its gruesome descent and the three in the water began their clumsy race towards shore, a spear thudded into the club and wrenched it from surprised hands. Three more spears smashed into unprotected chests and a steel boomerang slammed into a head reducing it to crushed bone, while blood and a last dying moan trickled from the mouth.

Outlined against the grey sky some thirty black angry men stood, spears and boomerangs ready in every hand.

When Mungart and Weerluk had gone fishing they had come to a cove where a whole Tribe of Bailer-shell People were feasting off the huge harvest of oysters that grew there. They had been greatly interested in the two brothers' tale and, against all tradition, decided to invite the white people (and amazing black spirits) back to their camp for a corroboree. The Bailer-shell men decided to go and see for themselves these curious people and escort them back to where the women stayed, preparing the camp for the feast that night.

But as the band approached they had sensed the tension in the air so had fallen silent, slithering on their bellies up the slopes of the dunes, where their black eyes observed this white man's argument. Except it wasn't white but two of the black people who were getting rough treatment from the white men. Hand signals fluttered along the ridge and, at that moment when Port Rial faced certain death, Mungart led the attack with the first thrown spear and the others followed suit. But only enough blood was shed to show who had the upper hand. That was the Keeper way; to kill only to gain control or punish a wrongdoer.

Now the two Tribes faced one another and the anger crackled in the air. There were three times as many white people, but only a third were armed while every one of the silent, grim Keepers of the Trees was armed and ready to fight.

Then the cracked voice of Prince Michael spoke out as he puffed himself up and strutted to the forefront.

So 'ere's to you, Fuzzy-Wuzzy at your 'ome in the Soudan.
You're a pore benighted 'eathan but a first-class fighting man

he called out, pointing to Mungart on top of the hill, then, like a ragged old crow with torn and flapping blue wings, he turned to the giant and walked up to him, shaking his finger while he quoted in another voice altogether: 'We've all had a jolly good lesson and it serves us jolly well right.'

The giant's face remained blank as this lunacy washed over him but, as usual, Mungart was captured by the mimicry. The hard lines and angry look in his eyes melted away and he began quietly to shake with laughter. The surprised—even peeved—look in his brother's face made the other Keepers see the humour of the situation so they began to chuckle as well. A slow smile broke out upon the giant's face as he also grasped the joke.

'It serves us jolly well right,' he softly repeated, then looked at his gathered men. 'And so it does. Lay down your weapons. There is no enemy here.'

He himself carefully laid his sword down on the ground. The deformed little boy beside him laid down his lethal slingshot. The Keepers up on the dunes now squatted down or otherwise relaxed. But they would not come down the slope and their weapons were ever handy to finger or toe grip.

Nanny, Akar Black Head and Cudjo Accompong came out of the water. Nanny rushed straight to Surrey Anne, disregarding her nakedness and the men's hard stares. Akar Black Head, who had not long ago called her a Devil woman, now put an arm around the shaking shoulders of Laelia, muttering in his hoarse voice words of comfort. He looked at the tattooed figures and remembered with vivid clarity the men in the hills, who had also been tattooed and womanless when first they met. He wished he was closer to his axe that lay further up the beach. Cudjo Accompong dragged on his tattered silver trousers and coat and stood by his rocket-launcher, dark eyes smouldering at the shaven-headed giant. The two huge men stared at each other and the tension still shimmered in the salty, windy air.

'So . . . perhaps you too have been hurled from that abomination they call Little Jerusalem,' the green-eyed man muttered. 'For you are the hated colour of black and are as tall as I. Do you have one of these though?' He tore open his filthy skin jacket to reveal a purple stain splashed all over one side of his chest. On the other side was a green and blue and red monster curling around his side, so it looked for all the world like a huge snake drinking from a purple puddle. 'This birthmark was all they needed to toss me out when I was seven years old, after my mother concealed it for that long. She did not last long. Females never do in our new world. But I grew up to become Leef. That is *my* name and I carry it with pride.' Now his face became bitter as he glanced at the blue-clad woman. 'My mother was a Shama. I never dreamed I would see the likes of you again.' Here he gave a harsh laugh. 'It was you and your people that killed my mother, not the wild dogs that tore her to pieces. She only wanted to love her son and for that she died!'

'Leave she alone, you raas!' cried out Surrey Anne and she pushed roughly through the men to stand beside Laelia. 'She me ilie sisthren, irie an' me rahtid alias, maan!' Her angry eyes glared at the men who had dared touch her. 'Leave she be in peace, yaah!' she grated between clenched teeth, hands on hips in a classical Island pose for fighting.

Up on the dunes the Keepers of the Trees watched with alert eyes. All they could understand was that the big black man and the short black woman were angry with the big white man. Some toes and fingers crept warily towards lain-down boomerangs or spears.

Then from out of the cocoon Red Mond Star Light emerged. Beside the huge Leef, he appeared frail and insignificant but the light that flashed in his dark eyes told the man that here was one just like himself.

'Who are *you* to come and terrorise our women? You, who watched your mother die?' the Moon-talker cried out, while his deep red hair blew in braids around his face, just like the snake upon his opponent's chest. He looked upon the birthmark and remembered that Durillau, Culvato's beloved brother, had one similar. For an instant his superstitious mind thought this was some sign of Culvato's. He looked closer at the giant.

'We have no mother, this is true,' said Leef, strangely gentle again in his wildly fluctuating moods. 'All we have are our bodies and it was our bodies that put us here!'

'We are the Outsiders,' the boy by Leef's side said and his voice was soft and melodious coming from his malformed body, 'and we care for no one just as no one cares for us.'

We are the wastage of war. We are the broken men
Made old by our pain though young in the count of our days.
Gone is the pride of our strength; vanished, and never again
Shall we know the joy of the race, the feel of the bays.
Ours was the courage of youth. Ay, and before us there lay
The path to the shining heights, glorious, blazoned with gold.
It has led to the shadow of death, and we wither away
Grasping the prize of our labour, a handful of mould
came Prince Michael's voice.

'We are the wasted men, but not the broken men, old friend. Broken in body and mind—but never in spirit. Oh yes!' growled Leef. 'For they took our minds for their own enjoyment and took our bodies for their pleasure and cast us out upon the deceitful desert without our souls!'

We have done with Hope and Honor, we are lost to Love and Truth,
We are dropping down the ladder rung by rung;
And the measure of our torment is the measure of our Youth.
God help us, for we knew the worst too young!

Prince Michael rambled on.

'There is no God!' shouted Leef. 'If there is a God then he is a cruel and evil God and I will fight him one day for the pain he has caused us!' Then he whispered, 'And, here, the old man, who was one of the first to go through that well-remembered Gate, legend has it . . . . his only crime was to sing songs. The songs he sings to us now to keep our fires and our hearts warm.' He looked long and deep into the Moon-talker's dark eyes.

Red Mond gazed around at the other silent, sullen figures. 'Why don't these others talk? Are you their leader?' he asked.

'They do not talk because they have nothing to say. As for leaders, I hold them together only because I have lived longer than most. Not only was I blessed with a birthmark, I was blessed with abnormal strength and a great height. Many of the Night Bats have felt my wrath. It is why I know this club, for 'The Creeper' and I are old adversaries.'

'Well, 'The Creeper', if it was he who owned this club, is dead. I watched him as he died,' Red Mond said.

'You killed 'The Creeper'?' Leef murmured and a look of respect flitted across his eyes while the boy peered at him dubiously.

'You can see none of us are normal,' the boy then said. 'That is why some don't talk because they can't. It is the reason they walked the Gate of Shame.'

The God or Goddess of life had certainly been unkind to him. Each of his hands had five instead of four fingers, the extra finger being joined by a flap of skin to the little finger. His right foot had no toes at all but was just a lump of hard, scarred flesh. Upon his back, perched there like a malevolent gnome, twisting his broad shoulders out of proportion was a large hump. His hair, though, was soft and flaxen, curling around his unlined, smooth, pink face and his green eyes shone out with an intelligence that belied his years.

'We welcome death as an old friend. Some of us laugh as the Night Bats carry us away,' said the boy and he wrapped an arm around the giant's leg. The man laid a massive hand gently on the boy's curly head. They looked at each other a moment, then two pairs of green eyes quizzed Red Mond.

'But, here, indeed, is a strange caravan to cross our wild country. Some are ordinary men, like the Children of Mordecai, or others are like the despised offspring of Phineas. In fact, you have friends amongst this Race who have saved you from instant death.' Leef nodded towards the hill of watchful Keepers. 'Yet one of you is a hated wife of the Prophets. One of the Prophets' wives who sent us away. Tell me, why does this woman travel with you and is treated as a friend?'

'Is it true the city of Little Jerusalem has fallen and the Twelve Tribes of Canaan wander lost upon the land?' the boy asked and his eyes lit up in a fierce joy. 'For if it *is* true then sweet will be their cries for mercy when I meet them with my stones, just as they threw stones at my mother and me. The mercy they shall have is the mercy they gave to us!'

'We go together to fight a common foe,' Red Mond Star Light said quietly. 'In this cocoon behind me lies a Goddess, a child of the moon. She leads us all to where the King of the Bats lies in his cave and then we shall kill him and all his evil kin.'

The giant and the little hunchback looked at each other once again, with a bright intense light in their eyes, while there was a muttering from the crowd around them. Slowly Leef's luminous green eyes swivelled around, taking in Nanny, Surrey Anne, Port Rial, Akar Black Head and Laelia, huge glowering Cudjo Accompong and finally the youth in front of him.

'You go to fight the Night Bats?' he said at last.

'No,' cried Akar Black Head. 'We go to *conquer* them and put an end to their reign of terror!'

'Then we, also, shall be a part of this revenge. For revenge is something *all* Outsiders can understand.'

There was a look of consternation on the faces of the Ilkari and their friends, but Leef did not see it as he turned to his followers.

The crooked, twisted boy embraced one of the dwarves, a stumpy, bristle-headed, red-bearded fellow. 'Red Fin can be in charge now. He always was the wisest of us all. He will look after you, my brothers,' he said and his oversized companion agreed.

'Yes. Make your way to Little Jerusalem and gather any of us up on your journey. If it is true it has fallen, then you can make it a safe refuge. The food in the gardens will be succulent indeed.'

As quickly as they had come the gang of deformed men and boys left—silent as always. As silent as this windswept land they called their own. The dwarf known as Red Fin was the last to leave, waving farewell, his orange beard aflame in the sun's light.

Then they were gone. Over the dunes and out of sight.

Only the four dead bodies, the shaven-haired giant and the boy remained. The Keepers also retreated. They settled down in the lee of the dunes to wait, with the infinite patience of their people, for the white man's affairs to be settled.

'We will camp away from the rest. The smell and sight of so many women will only confuse our thoughts. We have been womanless for a long time,' Leef said abruptly.

'Won't you bury your dead?' a shocked Red Mond asked.

'Why? The dead have no feelings. They are only bits of meat, already rotting,' the boy spoke, stooping to pick up his slingshot. 'They are probably glad to be dead. At least they are quiet and at peace now. That is burial enough,' he threw over his shoulder as he limped away.

The giant shrugged his substantial shoulders and the hint of a smile glinted in his eyes. 'It seems we are in civilised society, Leef-shadow. These wanderers, too, have their Goddess and their funeral rites,' he said, then turned. 'Aaah, well, each to his own as a wise man once said,' he rumbled, as he slouched over to just beyond the perimeter of the camp.

Now the others gathered in a furious, curious group. They wanted to know why there was no vote on including this dangerous duo into the caravan. The giant had been about to kill Port Rial. Others had been about to rape Surrey Anne and Laelia.

Red Mond heard them out and then he seemed to deliberate—although actually his mind was already made up. 'They come with us because they will come anyway and we would prefer a peaceful journey. They have the same enemy as we do and they have said they will live away from our camp.'

'Live away from the camp!' growled Akar Black Head. 'They will drink our water and eat our food and sit at our fire.'

'And we will share them as any Ilkari, my beloved,' came Kareen's tranquil voice, startling them all.

Their intense discussion had hidden her approach. She had come swinging, singing over the white sands, festooned in garlands from flowers she had found. The performance to Mother Earth had been her best and most exhilarating yet, as the rough grey water and white-lipped waves and untamed wind had swept her to new heights of enlightenment. Her grey eyes had shone, the very colour of the backs of the waves she worshipped, and her tawny hair, the colour of the sand, had been tossed by her wind—the wind she had been allowed to call her very own. She knew now, without a doubt, that all was at one with her world and nothing could go wrong.

Then, as she had come back along the flat white beach, she had seen the two strangers in the camp and the angry meeting of the others. But today she soared with the seagulls.

'Two more for our quest,' she smiled. 'Isn't that what we are trying to do? Gather up an army?'

'Coo 'pon me, girl. You nevah seen what them do a me man!' Surrey Anne cried out in fear. 'The same-same 'appen to The Baptist, nuh!' she cried out in remembrance. 'This be an evil an' cruel land dey 'bout.'

'We need them strength nuh. I-an'-I watch them soft-soft an' see them cause no 'arm a go Surrey Anne,' Nanny comforted her.

'Yes, we need as much help as we can get,' Red Mond murmured. 'We have hard and dangerous times ahead of us.'

'It seems to me these times have already arrived,' Akar Black Head broke in wryly.

'We need hard and dangerous men. This is their country and they know its ways.' Red Mond pressed onwards. 'If there is any trouble we are more than they, although I will be sad to see blood spilled between travellers.'

The discussion was finished. This was Red Mond Star Light's story, after all, and he must make the final decision. But, as he turned away, he noticed the giant's eyes rest hungrily upon Kareen's golden body and wondered, once more, if he was choosing the right path.

That night they gathered by the side of the ocean, in the shelter of a huge cavern carved out of the cliff by the relentless waves. They were the guests of the Bailer-shell People, and were treated to a feast of seafood such as those from the desert had never tasted.

One of the much favoured dances was from the Dolphin People who lived on the coast. The dance referred to certain of their landmarks and told the tale of how the Bailer-shell People, the Yukana, lived happily on an island in the bay with two of the Amatuana or Dolphin People. There was much food for everyone and plenty of time to play in the warm waters. But one day the murderous Bangudja, or Tiger Shark, came swooping into their happy little world. After a long and violent chase he finally caught and killed the peaceful Amatuana man. So terrified were his wife and their friends, the Yukana, that they fled and turned into a long low boulder on the coastline and a towering magnificent column nearby. And, the old men of the Dolphin Totem would tell their listeners, if you went to where the tragedy took place you will see a large red stain on the cliff in the shape of the murderer and his victim in the shape of a rock awash at low tide.

Here dark eyes speared the uneasy Outsiders and Red Mond Star Light wondered at the hatred the eyes of the Keepers held. So he was uneasy as well.

But at last the dances were over, the stories told and the fires died down as children lay down in peace to sleep. The caravan also slept by their own fires and Red Mond slept with his woman. Of all the people they had thus far met the Bailer-shell Totem were the only ones not to ask any questions as to who S'shony was. They were more interested in the Visitors, believing them to be Spirit Creators come down from the sky as they had done in a time forgotten by all but the Keepers.

In the morning when Red Mond and his companions awoke the Bailer-shell People had gone, as silent as a receding wave. Only the smouldering embers of their fires, the remnants of their feast and a gift of some ten large fish remained.

CHAPTER THIRTEEN

The enormous man and the crippled boy soon proved their worthiness when, three nights later, the little caravan was attacked by the Nightstalkers.

They came in the early hours of the morning. From out of the blackness burst the Keepers', Ilkari's and Outsiders' old foe with a familiarity which, in these unusual times and events, they had almost forgotten. It was S'shony who first sensed their greedy minds, as they crept up through the earth, and she woke a slumbering Red Mond, her eyes wide with terror.

'They're coming. My people. I saw them in a dream. You have only moments to warn the rest,' she hissed breathlessly.

The youth stumbled, half asleep from the warm skins around him, all the old fears leaping to the fore and clearing his mind. He grabbed up his killer's club, for now here was an enemy he *could* understand. This time there would be no sorrow at causing death and destruction.

He bumped into Akar Black Head who kept guard at the door. 'Nightstalkers, cousin-brother,' he yelled.

'At last! Let them taste my wrath.' And the warrior was almost happy at the thought of coming conflict.

'There is danger! Gather into a group!' Red Mond called to the rest. 'Nightstalkers!'

Then the little white monsters burst out into the middle of the camp.

Stand up and take the war
The hun is at the gate!

Red Mond Star Light heard the wheezy old voice of the crazy man. Then he was facing two whirling naked white ghosts, one of whom he crushed like an insect with his wicked club. Akar Black Head, laughing madly, charged into another group of sibilant, scuttling warriors while Kareen leapt to his side, eyes and sword flashing. Over at their own campfire the two Outsiders also engaged in battle.

The pounding of a fighting heart and the rush of adrenalin was soul music to any Ilkari and they sang their song well. Being warned saved their lives though, for so swift and silent were these hungry beasts that they surely would have been taken in their sleep.

The four Visitors, who had never seen a Nightstalker in the flesh, were taken by surprise, despite hearing the Ilkari's bloodcurdling stories. Two of the little men had grabbed Surrey Anne with their cold, rough hands and were beginning to drag her away while another wiry little woman stabbed Cudjo Accompong in the shoulder where he had been wounded before. But the giant West Indian threw her into the air and, pulling the knife from his shoulder, stabbed it into the throat of another who rushed towards him. Port Rial snatched up his ever present machete and began hacking to the left and right of him, in defence of Surrey Anne.

Because of the suddenness of the attack, the group had been unable to gather together and Laelia found herself on her own. She, too, had never seen these apparitions and she cowered upon the ground, believing her God's Hell had finally come to earth. One of the Nightstalkers, human skin wings flapping grotesquely behind him and smelling of death, came creeping towards her. Already, her warm blood was a sweet taste in his mouth and her screams a joyful tune to his ears when, with a terrific crack, the knobbly staff of Prince Michael of the Ants laid his head open and he sank spluttering blood and brains at the feet of the terrified woman.

'One by one, and two by two, He toss'd them human hearts to chew,' the old man quoted quietly and bent down to lift her up. There was a gentleness in his eyes and it was the first time he had touched her willingly since they had met.

Away, away, from men and towns
To the wild wood and the downs

he said softly and, holding Laelia to his withered body, he led her out of danger, over near the cocoon. In both their eyes there shone a memory that was at once both beautiful and sad.

Amidst the turmoil that was being played out upon the sandy middle of the camp, Cudjo Accompong had finally managed to get his weapon ready and loaded. Now he snap-shot from the hip at a group of charging shrieking men and turned them, in an instant, to a mass of broken bodies and torn limbs.

At this show of power, there was a moment of stunned stillness on the part of the Nightstalkers before they quickly slithered away.

Straight away the two Outsiders strode over to the mass of dead and dying Nightstalkers. Calmly, without fuss, Leef began snapping the necks of those still alive, while Leef-shadow stared warily at Cudjo and his smoking weapon. For a second Cudjo was going to complain at this brutal murder but Port Rial breathed that the ways of these barbarians was their own affair.

Leef glared over at Laelia as he lifted a feebly struggling little woman above his head. '*This* is what you drove us into, witch! Do you like the

Hell your God has made?' he called out, then broke the Nightstalker's back with a twist of his mighty hands.

The Prophet's wife hid her face within her tattered blue veil and turned her frightened eyes away from such violence. Leef-shadow cackled like an old crone at her fear and disgust.

Then the old man put his arm around the woman. His wild blue eyes beat the angry olive eyes of the giant down so he turned his scarred shaven head away. Prince Michael's voice was soft as he spoke to Leef.

The world is weary of the past
Oh, might it die or rest at last!

'Uncle, sometimes your songs are the roaring of waves in the ocean and sometimes they are from the very throats of birds. But—once in a while—they are hurricanes to destroy and violate the earth we walk on,' Leef-shadow said, his bright eyes piercing the wrinkled brown face of the old man. And he laughed his horrible cackling laugh again.

Teach us delight in simple things,
And mirth that has no bitter springs,
was the old man's reply.

Leef-shadow seemed about to make a sullen reply but Leef's huge hand rested upon his shoulder.

'Hush, Leef-shadow. Keep quiet and think what the old man says.' Leef admonished.

'He says we should forget the past when you know as well as I do, it is the memories of the past that keep us alive!' the boy spat contemptuously. He casually snapped the necks of two more Nightstalkers then walked back to the Outsiders' fire. Leef killed the last survivor then looked around the campsite.

'It is done!' he said, his usual brusque self again. 'Don't think they would give you any mercy. In fact, if they caught you alive you'd soon wish you were dead.' He stared at the group of Visitors and Surrey Anne, remembering those cold clammy hands upon her skin, had to agree with him. These apparitions were the most scary and worrying thing she had experienced. She wished she had a house with a door so she could leave some grain on the doorstep to be counted, or a broom upside down or a needle with a broken eye to be threaded: all of which were protection against the vampires of her people's true homeland in the sacred as yet unfound haven of Africa. But she had none of these simple things, so felt much afraid of these tiny creatures that had burst from the sandy soil and into her existence.

Still . . . there was Nanny, and Port Rial, whose shaking fingers even now rolled them a smoke from his special bag, and Cudjo Accompong, who methodically cleaned his rocket-launcher. But as Surrey Anne looked at her leader she saw a glint of fear in her almond eyes. Knowing that the Maroons were afraid of nothing mortal on this planet made the healer nervous again.

For the rest of that night a vigilant watch was kept by the members of the caravan but no trouble came. No doubt the Nightstalkers were sending telepathic messages to the rest of their kin about the new monster that roamed with the living dead upstairs, who could kill twenty of their number with a roar that sounded like a distant cave-in.

Yet it was not the last attack by the Nightstalkers. As they wended their way into this land of the Outsiders they were set upon at least once a week. All the skills of the Ilkari and Keepers, so long laid to rest as they had grappled with unknown and unaccustomed enemies, came to the fore. The four West Indians quickly became accustomed to the new foe. Because they were so alert, but more so because they were warned by S'shony's sonar (which she had to insist were dreams or premonitions), none in the caravan was killed, although several sustained minor injuries that were soon healed by either Kareen, Surrey Anne or, quietly, by the mind of Laelia. Sometimes Laelia would help the other two with medicines of her own devising, gleaned from the knowledge of life in Little Jerusalem. The two Outsiders refused to have anything to do with the Prophet's wife and she dared not tamper with their minds. They would know what she was doing and would kill her for it. So Leef and his companion tended their own wounds. Weerluk also was wary of the white woman touching him but Mungart was happy to be close to one he found so interesting.

When Prince Michael was slashed across his thin, withered arm one night, Red Mond observed how gentle the woman was to him in her administrations and wondered at the mystery these two held. He heard the crazy man say:

'Does the imagination dwell the most
Upon a woman won or a woman lost?'

And he wondered at the tears that crept into Laelia's sad eyes. He watched as her hand lingered upon his thin, sunburnt arm.

The country now became heavily wooded. There was an uncanny silence, and a great misery seemed to seep from the very ground. Even the occasional camping places of the Outsiders were seldom seen now. Indeed, their two Outsider travelling companions had to admit they hardly knew this country. But the two Keepers had an affinity with this land, even though they had never been here. Their people's laws and stories of Creation were crisscrossed forever over the vast terrain, joining communities in song, story, dance and law.

In fact the only people—aside from the Nightstalkers—who occupied this area *were* Keepers of the Trees. But they were a different kind of Keeper to the ones the Ilkari knew. They were of large frame, with arms often as big as an ordinary man's leg and, unlike the Keepers from the desert, these men were very hairy with thick bushy beards and thick matted hair on their chests. They also wore kangaroo or intricately designed possum-skin cloaks to keep them warm in this cold climate. The women were taller than other Keeper women and elegant as rare birds. But the strangest thing about these dark people (which the twins informed Red Mond were mainly the Koala Totem) was that almost all had blue or green eyes.

They performed a dance for their guests the first night they arrived; one that showed they were warrior Totems. Then there were the stories of the Totems almost extinct and rarely seen. They were fabulous stories made special by the fact that there would be no one left to recount them as the Totem died out. Like the Heron Totem gathered here now, who were kin to the Platypus Totem. Even in the Creation time this Totem was small and harassed by its neighbours. That is why they changed themselves into Herons and hid in a swamp. But still they were badly treated because the grass was too short and they could be seen. So the only way to get some peace and live in safety was to pull the grass up bit by bit until it was over their heads. If you look today you can see by the nodules on the reeds how far they stretched the grass up to protect themselves.

They told of many fierce battles with the Djanaks and warned the twins that this was truly the land of the Djanaks and they lived here in great numbers. Only the very fit or very alert would survive. They had been there when the Djanaks had taken away Gurrewe and Dongkarak and the rest, losing some people of their own. They wished the Keepers all the best in their quest for revenge.

Weerluk told of the amazing dreaming powers of this white man's Goddess, by which she could tell of trouble before it erupted and this was much discussed. Mungart told their new friends about the journey so far.

The Keepers enjoyed a good story and here was a fantastic one indeed. So all the way through the forest and up into the foothills and luscious green plains that dotted this area the caravan was accompanied at all times by members of the powerful and beautiful Koala Totem.

The two Outsiders welcomed their presence grudgingly. There had always been cautious relations between the Keepers of the Trees and the Outsiders. But it was not infrequent for the two cultures to clash violently. It was well known among the Keepers that the unloved ones were a lawless, womanless Race, with no love and little respect for any but their own kind.

Then, one day, two came who were not of the Keepers nor of the deadly Nightstalkers.

They had just settled down for the night, each to their own camps, when Laelia, who slept beside her friend Surrey Anne, detected the presence of the two standing in the shadows of the trees. Akar Black Head, following her transfixed gaze, stiffened and laid a hand on Red

Mond Star Light's shoulder as the Moon-talker was engrossed in studying the fire. All three stared at the two who walked out of the shadows and into the uncertain flickering light of the smoky fires set about the camp.

From the Outsiders' camp came a sharp cry. 'It is the witches. The bewitchers of the moon.'

Two women stood before the Moon-talker. One was short and squat, olive faced with brown, green-tinted eyes and a sensual mouth. But a thin angry white scar slashed right across her face, stretching from below her left eye and ending on the right side of her chin. Her fluffy hair was cut short and was a dull brown in colour. She was older than the other female, being perhaps in her mid-twenties.

Her friend had long orange hair—really orange like the sun in a spring sunset or the very end of a summer's day. What could be seen of her skin was as white as the sun's glare, while the eyes that peered from over her veil were mauve like an early morning in autumn. Although she was younger—being in her late teens—she was the taller of the two, having a willowy gracefulness. Her body was well-formed, from what could be seen of it through her robes, and her lips, seen faintly through the red gauze that covered most of her face, curled in disdain and her eyes were contemptuous of the people around her.

She walked this earth, untouching and untouchable, for she and her friend considered themselves Goddesses representing Sister Sun and Sister Earth, a sect which scorned men; who needed only themselves for all of life's pleasures, just as Sister Sun needed only the love of her Sister Earth and took it long ago. The forbidden licentious kiss she had first given her sister that had started her incestuous affair and broken her husband moon's heart, turning all the world white, burning up all the water and killing almost all of stupid Mankind who had become too cruel and indifferent towards women.

'Sisters!' breathed Akar Black Head, all his strength evaporating before the ethereal power of these females. 'If they know of your Goddess of the moon they will kill her as surely as they broke Father Moon's heart,' he told Red Mond.

'Be wary, cousin,' Kareen muttered from the other side of him. 'I am an Earth Mother and a Priestess, but these women have powers I can not even imagine.'

'My name is Wunda,' said the hazel-eyed woman. Her voice was surprisingly gentle, deep and calming.

'And I am Jynni,' said the orange-haired one. She had a strange accent, modulated and refined, not harsh like the Ilkari. 'We would ask for a piece of your fireside.'

'Fire is free,' Red Mond murmured, while his cautious eyes studied the girl before him. Wrapped as she was in orange and yellow and red robes, with a type of red trousers wrapped around her legs, she could only be from Sister Sun and so was the more dangerous of the two.

'Why ask for a kiss from your only son, witch?' cried Leef. 'Was not fire born screaming from your own mouth?'

'Choose your words carefully,' Jynni said. 'I have killed bigger men than you.'

Even though the words were softly spoken there was a coldness in them that went to the heart of all there and the look in her bleak eyes stopped any reply from the bearded, sullen giant.

Wunda sat down beside Red Mond and stared intently into his averted face. 'We would talk to the Moon-talker, son of my brother-in-law and therefore my nephew,' she said.

'Is it true one of the tears the moon weeps for us has turned into a Goddess that leads the children of Sister Earth to certain death?' Jynni scoffed.

'What is it to you?' growled Akar Black Head, the unbeliever. As he guarded the cocoon's entrance in the place of Culvato he had formed a curious bond with the unseen woman he sometimes talked to. 'There is no love between you and any of the moon.'

'Perhaps we would see this Sister of ours who fell from the moon and now controls nine men. Who has seen this Goddess?'

'I have!' said Akar Black Head, surprising himself again. But it was true. Even though he had seen her only briefly in the half dark of a desert night. Yet there was the time in the Silver City when that vague thought overtook his brain—and saved his life.

'We would like to see this Sister of ours. Perhaps our magic combined would be of great benefit,' Wunda, the more composed of the two, said.

'No one can see her. You, least of all,' Red Mond Star Light spoke, although he could not look them in the eye. 'It is known you are enemies of any gift of Father Moon. You even despise the Children of the Moon.' He looked at them then, his eyes smouldering. 'I would sooner put a rat in a kennel of dogs than let you see my . . . Goddess.'

'My Goddess,' Jynni said, catching the slight hesitation in Red Mond's voice. 'Perhaps she is just a woman upon whom you perform your animal acts of sex, as all men must do to prove they are men!' Jynni sneered, then concluded. 'I will see this Goddess. *Now!*'

She flowed up off her feet and moved towards the entrance of the cocoon rapidly, catching everyone by surprise. Except for Kareen, who leaped across the fire and placed her big-framed body in the path of the willowy girl. Her grey eyes flashed with real anger.

'You say you are the Moon-talker's aunts? Well, I am his true cousin. No one goes into this cocoon who is not connected to the affairs of Father Moon!'

Jynni's hand crept toward her sword, strapped to her waist, and the javelin held in Kareen's hand was adjusted to a more comfortable position for battle. Grey and purple eyes locked in a preparation for conflict—just as grey and purple clouds often heralded a storm of great turmoil.

Then Wunda was beside her Sister. 'An Earth Mother, Sister of the Sun. She is blood of our blood and we cannot harm her.'

The orange-haired girl visibly relaxed and drifted away to the fire.

Wunda rested a hand on Kareen's shoulder. 'We have travelled far to meet you. You do not know the sensation you are creating in these forests and mountains. All over the countryside, around all manner of fires, your story is being told. You go to defeat the King of the Bats. The King of the Crooked Cross,' she said proudly.

'No, my cousin goes,' Kareen said gently. 'I only follow to make sure the rites of the earth are properly adhered to, as no man knows the secret songs needed. Also, I am a warrior for my clan's brothers.'

'We have come to illuminate you as to your importance. There are, indeed, people all over the land waiting to see the result of your adventure,' Jynni said to the fire, not wanting to look at the despised Moon-talker. She glanced across at the fire where the two Keepers sat, silent and watchful of this further development among the white people they called friends. 'It is the Keepers of the Trees who tell these stories mainly. So, of course, now everyone in the country must know. No white woman—or man—has ever travelled as far as you have.'

'That is adventure enough. But the real adventure is when you go into the caves. We must come with you to record your fate for these hundreds who wait to listen,' Wunda said, joining them at the firelight.

'No. We have no need of witches, you bitch from Hell!' cried Leef and even Akar Black Head looked worried at the thought of these two for company.

'You have other women,' sneered Jynni, looking around. 'And a mere boy with the back of a camel,' she laughed. Then, with an astonishing dexterity, a knife appeared from nowhere. She sent it spinning with a whistle of air and with deadly accuracy, even though it was murky twilight now, into a cancerous growth, the size of a large hand, on a tree not fifty paces away.

'Can any of you do that?'

Then another knife sliced past her ear and slammed into the butt of *her* knife, smashing it to pieces.

'I am no "mere boy", witch. I am Leef-shadow, companion of Leef and friend to none.'

He turned his penetrating eyes onto the girl-woman. 'There is your boy!' Leef-shadow snarled. 'While you were wetting your bed in a nursery I was whetting my knife with the blood of Night Bats.'

'He is a Devil. We say this is true,' Wunda murmured and she remembered the old saying passed down to her from her mother. 'But better the Devil we know than the Devil we don't.'

Jynni looked at her shattered knife then glared at Leef-shadow who stared sullenly back. 'It is decided then. We will come with you and your Goddess. We will camp alone, just as the Outsiders and Keepers do. That

246

way you will not feel threatened by our presence,' Jynni told the assembled company.

Before anyone could protest the two moved sedately away to the opposite edge of the camp from the Outsiders and began to prepare their resting place.

As they walked past the Visitors' camp Jynni stared hard at Nanny and Laelia, then she stopped, stillness freezing her body as she spied Surrey Anne's necklace glinting purple in the firelight.

'She wears the crystal stones, my Sister,' she breathed to Wunda who also stared with suspicion at the Islander woman. Surrey Anne's hand crept to her necklace.

'Their hair, also, is like that of the Prowlers. It is as we were told,' Wunda murmured, gazing at Cudjo Accompong and his awesome weapon. 'When our Sister Sun has gone from our world it also is as black as their skins. How do we know these people are from her womb?' Cold hazel eyes glared at the surly black giant, who glared back, disliking this attention from a despised white person. Then they went towards where they would set up camp.

One night, while they sat around the communal fire, telling stories and singing songs, the wild old man came gliding in from the dark and sat silent and crazy-eyed on the edge of the wavering light. When Kareen played her harp with loving fingers his eyes softened and he murmured along with the sweet notes.

Afterwards, as always when Kareen finished playing her instrument, there was a moment's quiet as everyone let the music make their own images in their own heads. Then, unusually, the old man began to speak in a normal tone.

'There is a certain plant of this planet that is a most magic plant,' he began. 'A small dose of its root juice will produce vanity in one's appearance. It is known to have aphrodisiac powers as well.' He looked at Surrey Anne, 'and renders a human sleepy and lazy with its narcotic.' He looked at Port Rial whose smiling face was lost in a pungent blue cloud of ganja smoke. 'A large dose would turn you into an idiot.'

There was a muttered comment from Jynni that they all knew what portion *he* must have consumed.

'The root itself,' the old man carried on, 'would often split in two and appear in the rough image of a man and any who pulled this root from the ground would surely die. So they would tie the plant to the neck of a dog; then, when chased, the dog would pull the plant out and the dog would die. The Mandrake screamed when it was pulled out of the ground. This is because it comes from the seed of a criminal put to death for a murder.'

There was a deeper silence around the fire at the end of this little tale. Most there, being children of Sister Earth, knew that flowers or trees or rocks or so on *could* have a life of their own. But they could not see the message behind the story and what was the use of a story without a moral. Kareen noticed he kept his crazy eyes fixed upon Akar Black Head though and she worried for her lover.

Prince Michael of the Ants began to quote:

Go and catch a falling star,
Get with child a Mandrake root,
Tell me where all past years are,
Or who cleft the Devil's foot
Teach me to hear Mermaids singing.

'Oh, yes!' he cried, the eternal madness swirling in his eyes.

But such a form as Grecian goldsmiths make
Of hammered gold and gold enameling
To keep a drowsy Emperor awake;
Or set upon a golden bough to sing
To lords and ladies of Byzantuim
Of what is past, or passing, or to come.

He turned and stared long into the face of Laelia. 'The artificial bird singing in a golden tree with silver leaves. Have you ever seen anything so beautiful—so frivolous?' Bitterness and a deeper, unfathomable emotion waged a war in his blue eyes. He whispered, barely heard above the crackling of the fire:

I heard the old old men say,
'All that's beautiful drifts away
Like the waters.'

A spark of intelligence glinted in his eyes for a moment, then, in his erratic way, he abruptly rose from the fire and stalked off into the night, throwing over his shoulder in a hoarse angry voice:

And what rough beast, its hour come round at last,
Slouches towards Bethlehem to be born?

Laelia shuddered and hid her head from the harsh, reverberating words that tore out the quiet heart of darkness. A single tear trickled down her pale cheek.

'He remembers,' she whispered also. 'Sometimes it is lucky that the way we structured our mind was that we had no room or time for memories.'

But that is all she said before lowering her head and allowing herself to be comforted by Surrey Anne, while there were snorts of contempt from where Jynni and Wunda sat.

From the Outsiders' side of the fire, though, came a murmur from the small misshapen youth. 'It seems, my companion, that tonight is a night of storytelling,' and he laid one of his strange hands on the burnt, scarred thigh of his friend.

'Why, so it is,' the giant rumbled. 'The stars call out for more words from our brothers. Shall we tell them the story of Leef and Leef-shadow?'

His hard glowering eyes passed slowly around the people gathered at the fire, then he began.

When the boy, later known as Leef, had been sent stumbling out into the desert with the others who had different bodies as the mark of Cain, or who had been mind destroyed—or whose mind thought differently from the others—he had been only seven years old. His mother, naked and bleeding, staggered behind. The roar of the jeering crowd sounded to his young ears like the cry of the ocean, near where he had lived as the son of a sacred fisherman. He, too, had been going to be a fisher of men. Except a Devil had touched him when he was born and where the Demon's lips had touched the pale skin there lay the purple mark across his chest.

As soon as they walked past the Gate of Shame he was terrified of the vast, red emptiness, but not as much as some who had been used to the towering buildings and narrow streets. He, at least, had been accustomed to the view of the rolling, peaceful ocean that stretched right to the horizon. His father had told him it was a place of no end, just as was this desert. But at least its emptiness had waves to catch the light of the sun, or seaweed under the pale-blue water, moving ethereally to some dance of its own, or darting swooping schools of fish of all kind and shape. Or dolphins, occasionally.

He turned to his mother, who represented everything of love and security in his small life. But when he saw the confusion and fright in her eyes he really did know fear.

He was to survive those terrible years by losing his fear and grasping life in his two young hands. It was he and not his mother who cared for them in their trek across this new, bleak, unfriendly world.

Those who came from the privileged ranks of Little Jerusalem were not prepared for the cruelty of Sister Sun and her daughter or the wild animals of Sister Earth. But it was the Night Bats that held for them a special horror. When the fierce little men and women burst out upon them that first night they were in total shock at these Devils. They had no weapons with which to defend themselves and many had no minds with which to appreciate the danger. It was mostly these unfortunates who died that first cruel night.

The People of the Caves had long since discovered that there was a certain area where a veritable reservoir of food was available, as easy as plucking a bug off the cave walls. So a great many of them had settled beneath the raw, blood-red sands of the desert lands. They soon learnt when to expect another group of stumbling, frightened, succulent carcases that they assumed were some kind of sacrifice to keep them appeased.

Only the strong, the brave or the determined survived to arrive into the relative safety of the mountains. He was to watch in horror as a pack of yelping, snarling dogs tore his screaming, pleading mother apart. It was on *that* day he was to learn hatred for the ones who had sent them out the Gate of Shame.

The boy was christened Leef because he had eyes as green as a leaf and he held onto life as a leaf will hold onto a branch, even in the most violent of storms. Now, in the mountains, they had food and water, skins for clothes and tents, wood for fire and weapons.

When Leef turned seventeen he had already begun to show his unusual size. He was a hard and cruel man by now and sported numerous scars from close encounters with the Night Bats and animals. He was able to kill with just his bare hands, as well as use the sword he had got from a Night Bat. He looked after those weaker than him but his heart had turned to granite and any kindness in him was well-hidden. So when their leader was taken in a night raid the huge youth became their next leader.

Not long after this, he and several others were down in the desert on a recruiting survey where they searched for shocked survivors of any recent walk through the Gate of Shame and took them back to their place in the hills. As they ambled through a deserted camp, that had been the recent scene of mass murder, a cry drifted across the sound of the eternal wind.

They crept forwards warily, ever mindful of some new danger in their world. When they gathered around the bush from whence the cry came and peeped down through the leaves, what a surprise they all got!

For here, wrapped in an old blue rag, lay the ugliest little creature they had ever seen, these abominations of the Human Race. In fact, none, except Leef, had ever seen a baby before. All the animals they ever saw were grown and the few women who survived soon found they could not give birth. Nothing grew in this infertile land, not creatures of the earth nor fish of the water. The women would die of sunstroke or broken heart and no babies were ever born to comfort them in their loveless existence. So all four men stared in amazement at the tiny baby who was only about six months old.

When the four faces, burnt black and covered in scars, with their unkempt hair falling like the skins they wore around their bodies, came into the baby's vision he stopped his tears and stared up at them in curiosity with wonderful, bright-green, intelligent eyes.

One of the men, a misshapen dwarf, reached out a hand to touch this thing, new to his life. But another, a great, heavy-shouldered man who, nonetheless, had only one arm (the other being just a hand that flapped uselessly at his shoulder) reached out his one good arm and picked the baby up. His eyes shone with a black madness and his malevolent mouth dripped venom. 'Soft meat to satisfy my hunger!' he growled.

The baby, oblivious to the seriousness of his predicament, was able to look the man in the face and gurgle a laugh of welcome.

It was the smile that did it for Leef.

He back-handed the huge, one-armed man and tore the baby away. Even though the man only had one arm it was a powerful arm and Leef, who was still really only a boy, sustained many a blow as he laid the baby at the feet of the dwarf. He was to receive many another before he hurled the man, twisting in the air, to land with a sickening thud on the rocky ground. He lay there, whimpering softly, his back broken. It was where the other three left him to his certain fate.

When Leef took the baby from the dwarf, it was crying again. His hard eyes softened for just an instant, as memories of his younger sisters came flowing back. His thin lips lifted just a fraction as he stared into the distressed face. This was another surprise because it was the first time any could remember the boy smiling.

From then on, the baby never left Leef's side and from a baby he grew into a child—although the word child was not adequate enough to describe someone growing up as an Outsider. By the time he was five years old he had become an expert at knife warfare and the use of the slingshot. Despite his twisted body he had a remarkable eye and pinpoint accuracy that earned him respect and saved band members' lives many times. This was enough to earn him a place in the band even if he had not been the companion of their leader. He was known to all and sundry as Leef-shadow and, as the years rolled by, he became as feared yet as liked as the giant for his violence towards his enemy and respect towards his friends.

It was a hard life growing up among men. The few women had all died now. They had been a soft, domesticated breed in Little Jerusalem, used to their women's quarter, their sacred pools, their gardens and their quiet conversations. Women were now treasured only for the relief their bodies gave to men.

Leef's eyes burned around at the other members of the caravan. 'That is why a woman is much searched for. It is why we—all of us who have any feelings left—keep a companion for comfort and relief. As well as friendship.' His eyes speared Wunda who sat close to Jynni. 'Just as does Sister Sun and Sister Earth.'

When his eyes rested upon Kareen, though, Red Mond Star Light felt a twinge of unease. He did not fully trust this angry giant from this angry, barbarous land. Especially when he stared at his cousin like that. A woman could turn his mind if the last woman's comfort he had known had been that of his mother. Besides, the Moon-talker didn't have to read the moon to know what Akar Black Head would think of that look and what he would do.

They moved further into the wild tangle of bushy hills. Most of the days went now with bickering and arguing between the Outsiders and the two Sisters. It was seen that, as with every work of beauty, Jynni had one flaw—and that was that she was incredibly clumsy. She was always bumping into things or tripping over. This was a great source of delight to the two Outsiders and many a joke was had at Jynni's expense.

S'shony set about probing the minds of the four newcomers.

She was afraid of these people and their vicious thoughts that were always on war and death. They reminded her of her own cruel people. But at least she had her friend Laelia with whom she could escape into a world of calm and serenity.

The two Sisters proved to be expert fighters. Like suns around a moon, the campfires of the Keepers, the Outsiders and the Sisters gravitated around the main camp of the Visitors and the Ilkari, often being the first attacked in the dark, early morning raids made by the little Demons.

Coming as she does from a civilised people and being a student of history, she is amazed continually by these people's beliefs and lifestyle. Her country's history is simple: there was a Nation of Islands, some rich, some poor. Trade and Tourism had been important industries. People would come from the Northland, now the dead land, in aeroplanes and boats and take the best the Island had to offer. These were the white people, not the copper-skinned people who came these days in their big canoes once in a while, to talk and dance and trade.

Her Island's history is steeped in violence and Revolution against white people. Her own people, the feared and respected Maroons, fought the British, a Race of white people, and so gained their freedom. Other Uprisings were not so successful.

But that was only the start of the wars on her Island. In the early years of the next century a man named Marcus Mosiah Garvey came along and preached a unification of the black Nations. There were more Uprisings against the despised white people, although this was more a revolution of words and ideas. The great man started a movement called the 'Back to Africa' movement. It was the hallowed ground for most of her countrymen and women, this place called Africa. It is the main reason she and her crew set off from their Island after the last war there. To find Africa, more specifically the birthplace in Africa of Haile Selassie, the Ras Tafarians' champion and a descendant of Solomon, the Lion of Zion.

Norman Washington Manley became the first black Prime Minister of their Island of Springs. A champion athlete in his day, as well as a champion advocate who never lost a murder case. He was a Rhodes scholar, which was a high honour indeed, and a soldier and hero of the British Army.

The Island was not untouched by the massive nuclear war that devastated the planet some three thousand years ago. The Island was again almost completely destroyed some thousand years ago when a series of giant tidal waves, the biggest ever seen, swamped the Nation of Islands. Some of the smaller Islands were absolutely washed away, trees, houses, people, everything and, even today, remained barren, desolate patches of sand and rock.

Scholars and scientists had surmised that the tidal waves were caused by a large asteroid slamming into the side of the earth, causing massive waves, volcanoes, earthquakes and other similar disasters, as the fragile crust of the earth splintered under the awesome power of the collision. Also, some scientists said with trepidation, the planet had been knocked off kilter. Only a few inches it was sure, but enough to bring it that much closer to the sun. Every year, by a fraction of an inch, the earth, in its continuous circling of the life-giving sun, moved a little closer to her fiery flames. In another million—or billion—years earth would be no more than just a dry, dusty shell.

That is her history—stark and bare. Even with all their knowledge and progress the Nation of Islands still has not learnt the meaning of peace. She wishes she could be like these simple people, with their endless stories and songs. They would only gape at her in astonishment if she tried to explain radios, television, automobiles, computer technology—or any type of technology at all. They would laugh out loud and think it the best story they had ever heard.

Yes, these are an ignorant, primitive people. The most primitive she has ever met. Even the intelligent ones like the big woman, Kareen, and her cousin, the Moon-talker, are naive to the point of stupidity about worldly affairs.

In her country the power had gradually passed from the white people; not to the African descendants but to the new Capitalist class of Indian, Chinese, Lebanese and other assorted shopkeepers and other Landowners. Her people were still unemployed and oppressed. It was what the last war had been about when the ones they now called the Muslims had tried to enforce their code of life more stringently upon the unemployed, predominantly Ras Tafarian inhabitants of the Island. Once again her people, the proud and independent Maroons, who only desired the peace of their Cockpit County, had been involved in the bloodshed and violence that periodically ripped their beloved Island of Springs apart. They had gathered together, nine different people—even The Syrian, who was a hated coolie-rial—and set off to find the tranquillity of Africa. Just as their hero Marcus Mosiah Garvey had done those thousands of years ago.

They have not found Africa but they have found an Island that, even though harsh of landscape, is peaceful compared to her home. The petty fights these people have, even with the hideous hordes from beneath the ground, are nothing compared to modern warfare, with tanks, rockets, guns and rifles of all description. They have evolved over the years in that respect, she thinks ironically, in that their wars are fought purely for survival, and not for spite or power. She would live here among these people and teach them the good things from her world. If they wanted to call her a Goddess then that was all right too. For they were a people with great loves and great hates and a huge compassion for the world they knew.

But she would not enlighten them about the world she had come from.

One night when the crazy old man sits down beside her at the fire, Red Mond Star Light calls out for another song, for the youth seems enraptured by his poetry.

Most wretched men
Are cradled into poetry by wrong;
They learn in suffering what they teach in song,

*the old man begins in ominous tones. She is reminded of the better storytellers
of her home when they begin a story about Anancy, the spiderman trickster
of so many of their tales. They, also, have the same knack of using words to
draw their listeners in.*

*Now he has everyone's attention, he glances around the fire. He seems to
reserve special attention for the two glowering Outsiders, sleepy-eyed Wunda
and sullen Jynni . . . and herself.*

*Her black eyes stare into the eyes of the white madman. On her Island
there are no white men, just fair black people occasionally, like Porky with her
blue eyes and blonde hair. They have been taught since birth—especially the
Maroons—to have no love or trust for white people. She herself is part of the
nyabhingi movement—a legendary worldwide sect once led by their hero Haile
Selassie that is devoted to the end of white domination. 'Death to whites' is
their code. She knows that Cudjo Accompong is a Nyaman, a Ras Tafarian
warrior of the sect.*

But these *white people are a friendlier, kinder people than she has been
used to. Even this old insane man, in his tattered cloak, huge knobbly staff
and long white hair held back with the dead bones of animals, has a type of
sensitivity that is often lacking in the greedier blacker people of power back
home.*

*He begins his song now, quietly . . . in a whisper so everyone has to lean
close to hear, the orange flames of the fire bathing their faces and turning them
into other beings just by proportioning light and shadow:*

I never was attached to that great sect,
Whose doctrine is, that each one should select
Out of the crowd a mistress or a friend,
And all the rest, though fair and wise commend
To cold oblivion, though tis in the code
Of modern morals, and the beaten road
Which those poor slaves with weary footsteps tread
Who travel to their home among the dead
By the broad highway of the world, and so
With one chained friend, perhaps a jealous foe,
The dreariest and longest journey go.

*He stares into her face for a moment and she thinks, 'How did he know
my feelings for Culvato? He didn't even know him!' She is a little spooked by
his reading her intimate thoughts. It is time to put Culvato aside. He is gone
. . . just as have Haile Selassie, Marcus Mosiah Garvey, Norman Washington
Manley, Robert Nesta Marley and all their other heroes; just as her father and*

brothers are now only names. It is time to move on and live her own life. She looks up at him but he is staring at Laelia.

Under bare Ben Bulben's head
In Drumcliff churchyard Yeats is lain,

he says to her in a soft-spoken voice and there is a gentility there he has not shown the Blue Woman for some time.

Then he got up and moved stiffly off into the whistling wind with only the dancing, windswept trees for company.

'He was always my favourite,' Laelia whispers after he has gone. 'William Butler Yeats. He is dead but his words live on.'

She raised her face and her eyes looked over the company, even the ones she was normally afraid of. The savagery of the Outsiders, the scorn of the two Sisters hating her subservient nature, the tranquil peace yet strong energy of the Earth Mother, Kareen, and the courage of Akar Black Head and the serene wisdom of the young Moon-talker were all there to see.

'The time has come,' she said, 'for *me* to tell a story to the fire.' She paused, gathering her thoughts. 'The one you call Prince Michael of the Ants was once known as Michael, God-like, and he was a Prophet—just as those you hated were Prophets. He was from the Tribe of Benjamin and a great and powerful man was he. You ask how I know all this? Because he was my husband.'

Then the story crept from her hesitant lips.

The father of Michael, God-like, was called Jehiah and he had been a follower of Jehovah. Now Jehovah was tolerated but a close eye was kept on his followers, for all knew there was only one Yahweh.

Jehiah had an older son named Joel and he taught both children a love for words that was strictly forbidden in this city of unusual and wonderful minds. Only the Scribes could write the sacred books and memorise their passages. But Jehiah had a very dangerous gift that had been passed down from father to son for many generations.

The gift had been three slim volumes by three famous men who had lived even before there was any thought about ending the world. Thus were they the seeds from whence the Devil's rats had come, pitting their meagre minds against the one and only all-powerful God. Questioning his very existence and arguing about or discussing things they could not possibly comprehend. Poets, like Bards, were a dangerous and disturbing people and the three heretics that gradually turned from volumes to dust as the ages went by and only became memorised words to the family of Jehiah were: Rudyard Kipling, Percy Bysshe Shelley and William Butler Yeats.

The followers of Jehovah, although few, were extremely powerful. His younger son was chosen as a Prophet, yet none in that deadly fraternity could get past his mind shields to see the heretic—although beautiful—words his mind held, swirling like silver colourful fish in a rich, deep, dark-blue ocean of wonderful thoughts.

Mainly due to a Pogrom against the Jehovahs, that happened every once in a while when other, more normal, victims were scarce, the family of Jehiah was torn asunder. His father and brother Joel were great entertainment for the Snake Queen in her white sphere, for their superior minds were a fabulous challenge. His mother and sister were turned out as Daughters of Delilah and he was only to see his sister once more. In the distance, a shambling, staggering woman, old before her time.

Michael was spared because he was a Prophet and had, presumably, seen the folly of his family's beliefs and ways.

The torments of hearing in his mind the screams for mercy of Jehiah and Joel and watching the shame of his mother and sister stripped naked upon the pink marble steps of the Palace; of hearing their sobs and shrieks and smelling the burnt flesh as the cross was branded on them, were terrible to bear. The only way he could survive, was to repeat the gentle, powerful or angry words of Kipling, Yeats or Shelley over and over in his secret mind. He fell more and more into a world populated only by those three—and his beloved wife.

He even, under cover of mind shields and darkness, in the privacy of their own bedroom, quoted her poems so she too could enjoy the love and thoughts of a past civilisation.

'See,' he would marvel, 'look at the power of words. These people have been dead for some thousands of years and still yet can their voice be heard. Is that not a glorious thing to contemplate, my sweet Laelia?'

And she would softly murmur passages of poetry with him, perhaps not understanding the full meaning of the words but often just enjoying their rhythm and sound.

Of all three of her husband's friends she had loved William Butler Yeats the best. He came from a place called Ireland, or Erin or Eire. A type of green heaven—as green as the women called their own Garden of Eden—populated by remarkable beings such as giants who flung whole countries around at each other in terrible war, of the little people who could give you a gift of fairy's gold or trick you as well, of handsome heroes and gorgeous queens and a man who lived a thousand years at a time—each time as a different animal, or a magical horse with one wonderful horn growing from out of its soft white forehead.

There were names and ideas that she could not even begin to visualise but somehow the ideas the words conveyed were as clear as water.

It was about then also that she began using the powers given to her by the unclean one, now known as Simeon. She began to search out—carefully—her husband's mind to see if he too could become part of the growing army of dissidents. It would be grand indeed if they could have both a Prophet's wife and her Prophet in the underground movement.

And so she brought about her husband's downfall.

She was not to understand that, even in the elite company of the highly trained Prophets and their wives, such mundane emotions as jealousy could still prevail. The Prophet Joash secretly coveted Laelia. He was an ambitious man and knew what he wanted, so he began casting sly mind probes upon her, to influence her to leave Michael, God-like, and become enamoured of him. So unassuming were these probes, so subtle and delicate, that she could not hope to sense them. While she concentrated on probing Michael's mind she let her defences down, and the cunning Joash, laying a trap for a canary, caught an eagle instead because he caught just a whiff of her love for Ireland that puffed out through a tiny crack in her usually reliable shield.

It was enough of a whiff to realise there were alien thought patterns swirling in either her or her husband's head. As it was Laelia Joash wanted, it was the husband he accused.

None other than the Highest of the High, and her two apprentices, came floating out of the purple sky one evening when the pair of them sat under a willow in one of the many quiet parks around the city, watching the fish in the shallow green pond and being happy in each other's solitude. When questioned by these forceful three she very soon betrayed the one she adored.

She had to! If they had broken her resistance and shattered her shields completely then the whole of the underground army would have been in jeopardy. All the years of work Ivy and Rockstone had put into destroying this evil place would be wasted and hundreds of people would be destroyed. She could not allow that to happen so she gave up her green Ireland and William Butler Yeats and it was through them the three women were able to get past Michael, God-like's, elaborate defences and into his fertile mind.

The look in his eyes—the last free look he would ever give—snapped her heart in two and she had to hide her head in sorrow as they lifted him up from their special, quiet spot in the city and all four flew off. At last her husband had become the bird he had so often dreamed of becoming, so he could fly above the walls of this oppressive city. But what a bird! A poor, pitiful, crying bird, who flopped and flapped uselessly in the incredible power of the women who controlled everything in the city. He had gone, indeed 'to this tumult in the sky' . . . to use the words of her favourite poet.

Thus, the gift that had been passed down from generation to generation for thousands of years was destroyed—or so they thought. They played with him for many days, milking all these curious thoughts from his head as he suffered in the white sphere. But Michael, God-like's, mind was perhaps the strongest of any man's they had yet encountered. They likened him to Samson and his mighty strength and how he, too, had been betrayed by a woman.

When they drove him from the city, with curses and rocks falling all around him, he had not lost all the songs of the Poets. But he had lost almost everything else. The strain of fighting against the corrosive powers of the Snake Queen and her companions had aged him considerably and all but driven him completely insane.

'Now you see why he hates me so—and yet has the same old love for me as before.' Another tear drifted from her eye. 'I do not deserve that love. You can see what they have done.' She looked over at Red Mond Star Light. 'You all think he is an old man. Well, he is only some ten years older than you, Moon-talker,' she breathed, then rose up abruptly and headed for her little bed where it lay beside Port Rial and Surrey Anne's camp. They heard her cry in a rare burst of emotion. 'You can *see* what my Sisters have done!'

There was a deep silence around the fire after she left, with only the popping and crackling of logs as they protested their devouring by the orange flames and the mournful cry of the wind in the trees. It was a story they all knew—of a love betrayed by love.

CHAPTER FOURTEEN

Red Mond Star Light read Father Moon one night, as they were camped in a stand of tall trees forming a quiet grove. They were grey-spotted and very regal. The moonlight filtered down between the leaves and all was silent in the world. It being a full moon there would be no Nightstalkers tonight so every one was relaxed. He had gone a fair way from the camp and it was one of those nights he was able to reflect upon all the events that had thus far happened. It was a most potent, peaceful reading of the sky. When Red Mond Star Light read the moon he was surprised to see that in such a violent part of the country there were mainly signs of love. And one of treachery, although he was prepared for that with two of the Sisters who were his natural enemy right in the camp with him.

Footsteps sounded behind him and a voice breathed:

Kings are like the stars—they rise and set, they have
The worship of the world, but no repose

and a withered old hand rested on his shoulder.

'Greetings, Prince of the Ants. The moon talks much of love this night,' the Moon-talker said softly.

Cross that rules the Southern Sky
Stars that sweep and turn and fly,
Hear the Lovers' Litany:
'Love like ours can never die!'

came the croaking answer. 'Because love is the strongest, strangest . . . most certainly the cruelest and absolutely the most misunderstood emotion in the human mind,' he added a few rare thoughts of his own. Red Mond Star Light knew now there was a hidden message in all his bursts of poetry from those singing Gods of a far past time, in a time before the stronger Gods came to walk upon earth once more.

'So . . . who do *you* love, Michael?' the Moon-talker asked.

For he had seen, earlier on tonight, a weird, hazy light, the second such light he had seen in these unfamiliar skies. It had floated across a part of the sky seldom read it was so dark and devoid of light. It was a star he had never seen in the old days of last year, so he knew it had to be one of the strangers who had recently joined them. It had denoted a virile love, but a forbidden and lost love. When the hazy star—if star it had been and not some illusion—had vanished, it had headed for some of the stars with a more sinister connotation, so he knew there was possible danger there as well.

It almost seemed as though the wizened, tortured face smiled for once, as the piercing blue eyes stared up at the sky for a long, long time. 'I carry the sun in a golden cup, the moon in a silver bag,' he quoted gently at last, then burst into a demented cackle, and drifted away.

It was the next day, after that delightfully quiet night, which was a solitude amongst so much violence, that the small caravan, with its accompaniment of blue- or green-eyed Keepers of the Koala Totem, came out of the forest of tall, serene, grey-spotted gum trees and gazed upon a sight that would take their breath away.

Just as the first sight of the Silver City, with all its writhing aluminium and plastic towers spearing into the sky, had stunned their brains, so too did their first true sight of the broken-backed mountains before them cause their minds to stall at the enormity of what they saw. There was only one mountain in their desert home—the rooftop of the world. But that was a mere rock to these great, grey-green-blue monsters that erupted from the earth almost with a life of their own.

The Keepers knew that they did, indeed, have a life of their own. Some of these mountains were sisters turned to stone and every one of them was of sacred significance. Even the Visitors were struck by the vision of the great rocky wall in front of them. Though they were some distance away they could see they were of great height. They had mountains back home, the John Crow mountains. And the great Blue Mountain that was as tall as these here. But the rest of their mountain range was only half the size of these monolithic monsters. Their shadows seemed to reach out for them across the wide, yellow-green plain. The silence of these mountains was terrible and their craggy heads were hidden in swirling black cloud.

'The wet season is upon us already. It is not good to cross the mountains when the Gods lay their blankets across Sister Earth's back,' Jynni said.

'We could follow the tracks of the Old Ones, who were here before the Gods came down,' Wunda suggested.

'It is best we make our own trail, Sister. We know these are called the death mountains for good reason. Only you and I have been through them.'

'Why should we follow your path when it is known your lying words have destroyed many a man!' Leef shouted.

'Perhaps because we are going to the top of the known world, so close to our Sister Sun. So close to Father Moon,' Jynni sneered and her violet eyes stared into the brown ones of Red Mond Star Light. 'We are curious to see our relation—this moon "Goddess".'

He felt uneasy again. He had not read in the stars about these two coming into his and S'shony's lives. He could not understand how he had missed such a sign of trouble and wondered if they had put a curse on him that blinded him from Father Moon's truths.

But his face remained calm as he gazed into Jynni's angry eyes. 'Just as the moon, our Father, hides his face in sorrow so does his daughter hide, until the time is right to appear. Like moonlight drifting through mist she will come and a fantastic sight she will be. *Then* you will see our Goddess and leader. As for this path you say you will take, it is up to the words of our Goddess and no one else as to which way we will go,' he said quietly.

'We will take you to the city of man-made mountains. It is there you will find the gates to go into the caves,' Wunda broke into what looked like becoming a dangerous argument.

'I have been once into a city and liked it not—' cried Akar Black Head.

'And I have been driven from a city through a Gate,' Leef-shadow snarled. 'All this talk of cities is a sign of evil these witches wish to cause us!'

'Could it be that you are angry that you can never have my body?' Jynni crooned and moved seductively closer to Wunda, caressing her face with her fingers. 'I know that I am as gorgeous as the sun—the giver *and* taker of life.' Now she danced seductively near the boy, her orange hair drifting in the breeze. 'I am all-powerful woman, the taker and breaker of men's souls,' and she laughed as she turned herself away, not seeing the look in the emerald eyes of the one she tormented.

'One thing is certain,' Kareen broke in. 'We must cross these mountains of death. Although,' she added in awe, 'I can see no death there. Only a great and wondrous gift of Sister Earth.'

Thus the argument ended and the ill-assorted army set forth across the huge, grassy plain towards the distant, towering mountains. But there was suspicion and foreboding among the group. S'shony sensed it and tried to warn Red Mond Star Light about the hatred that festered in the camp.

But there was passion as well, just as Red Mond had predicted in the stars.

It was Prince Michael of the Ants who first realised the blossoming of the forbidden love between the club-footed, hunch-backed boy and the girl Jynni.

Increasingly, as they moved across the wide expanse of soft grass, the boy found himself moving closer to the orange-haired girl. There was nothing but scorn for him in her demeanour and he still abused her with his harsh words. But, when no one was looking, a new light shone in his eyes. They would follow her slim, supple body and her clumsy footsteps with an intensity that worried him, for she had no part in his comfortless, lonely world.

Once, as they camped beside a quiet creek, that meandered over the plain, her malicious eyes spotted the boy limping up the slope with his water for the Outsiders. She gave a harsh laugh before flaunting her begowned body in front of him.

'Better you catch the sunlight on the water, freak! It would be an easier task than kissing these lips of mine. And you *do* want to kiss my lips. Just like Father Moon, that stupid, weak man you all worship,' she sneered and to further frustrate him she kissed Wunda long and deep on her full lips.

The boy quietly gathered up his pails of water and went back to his camp. This was unusual for usually he traded insult with insult. The giant realised something was wrong. He laid a gentle hand on the boy's dejected shoulder. 'Shave my head for me and I will comb out your hair,' Leef says.

There was a particular ceremony the two were wont to participate in. It involved mixing a concoction of oils and herbs into an ointment and then the boy would shave the giant's head with his lethal, sharp knife. Leef would rub Leef-shadow all over with the sweet-smelling compound. The shaving and the massaging was a shared moment and one of the few times they laid their hostility aside.

But the boy's green eyes stare out across the plain as he has a dream he will share with no one.

'What is it, little shadow, that makes you so glum? Is it the size of these mountains we must cross soon?' Leef tries again.

'I have a bigger mountain in my heart,' the boy said, and instead of returning the affection the giant offered him, he got up abruptly and went off on his own.

O wild West Wind, thou breath of Autumn being,
Thou, from whose unseen prescence the leaves dead
Are driven, like ghosts from an enchanter fleeing,
Yellow and black, and pale and hectic red,
Pestilence stricken multitudes

Prince Michael said from where he huddled beside his own little fire.

Leef appraised the songman, with troubled eyes. Who was the wild West Wind, himself or someone else? The song spoke also of dead leaves dripping like blood from strong trees and disease. It was a disturbing and sad song. And the enchanter from whom the ghosts fled, he could guess who *she* was!

He followed his companion's departure with the same worried eyes. Could it be that the witch had cast a spell on his little friend? He knew of a tale, told by those men who lived in the hills beyond the sea of grass, about a woman who turned men into pigs after making love to them and serving them up as a banquet for her female friends. It had been told by one of the survivors of the great war, these people had tried to wage upon Little Jerusalem, and who had been sent out into the desert for his efforts, and it was a story that stuck in his mind. This woman of the sun would do similar things he was sure.

Akar Black Head had fallen in love as well.

He had renewed his interest in the curious weapons of the Visitors and spent most of his spare time around Port Rial or Cudjo Accompong. Nanny had warned the two that on no account were the Ilkari to be taught the devastating firepower of their guns and grenades. It was better, she said, that they leave this country innocent of high-tech warfare. But she could not stop the bushy-haired warrior from squatting beside her countrymen as they lovingly cleaned their weapons. He watched as he would track an animal out on the Purple Plains, following every little sign until he was absolutely sure of victory. The more dangerous the animal the more cautiously he tracked. His eyes took in the Visitors' movements and he daydreamed of the time when Akar Black Head, the most powerful warrior of all the Tribes of Ilkari, would lead his people to a better life.

Kareen and Surrey Anne were the happiest they had been throughout the whole trek, as they scouted the lush pastures for herbs and medicines and revelled in the joy their Mother Earth gave them. They often took the lonely Laelia with them, to keep her away from her husband's cruel jibes.

She enjoyed being in the company of the two women. When she was with Surrey Anne or Kareen out on the wide green plains, her eyes lost some of her shyness and a smile or two would find its way to her solemn lips. This was a wild garden, nothing like the cultured fields she was used to. But it was a garden nonetheless and she felt welcome here. At everything else she was quite useless and often earned the scorn of Wunda and Jynni for her dependence on men and her abhorrence of violence.

Occasionally they came across a place of habitation from the old civilisation, marked by the huge, gnarled fruit trees that once would have been someone's garden. These were very old trees indeed but their fruit was often still bountiful and succulent. So the menu included such delicacies as round rich peaches, ripe black mulberries, quinces, apples or apricots. Luxuries the people of the desert had never seen before their journey.

As for game, there was plenty, with scores of kangaroo, deer and a great heavy creature identified by the green-eyed Keepers as Warreen the wombat. There was a story told of how the two friends Mirram the kangaroo and Warreen the wombat had a falling out over shelter during a storm, so the kangaroo's tail was really a thrown spear and the wombat's head was flat from a hurled club; so the kangaroo loved the wide open spaces and the wombat a burrow in the ground. And the two of them were never seen together after the violent break-up of their friendship.

The moral here was to always share what you've got. And so they all did, making it a time of joy, with Kareen's harp and the Moon-talker's flute being heard with the drums of the Visitors and the didgeridoo of the Keepers. There was dancing and plenty of Port Rial's sacred smoke. There were stories and jokes to be told. The little pirate began collecting furs from many exotic animals found on these plains of plenty, so he was happy with his treasure.

There was not a smell of the Nightstalkers anywhere. It seemed as though this land was too splendid and too serene for them. There were not even any predators among the animal kingdom upon these plains. No bears or dogs or giant cats of any description.

And ever closer the huge mountains reared up into the grey sky, while a benign sun shone through the slowly rolling clouds.

In the calendar Nanny kept, and which Red Mond Star Light had begun to grasp the rudimentaries of, it was October the fifteenth. Therefore it was National Heroes Day on the Island of Springs, although that, of course, meant nothing to those not West Indian. The only heroes they knew were the ones from the tales their mothers told.

But for the occupants from the Island of Springs it was a special day indeed. Surrey Anne had spent the night before preparing some delicacies from her homeland, using the last available resources from supplies brought off the aeroplane. Port Rial and Cudjo Accompong had gone fishing and caught some fish they were glad to see were a type of cod. Salted cod was a favourite dish of the Island. Surrey Anne had found a patch of sweet potatoes as well as carrots, pumpkin, turnips and cabbages in what once must have been a town. From her special bag she brought dried chilli peppers and coconut oil, which she had kept just for this day—as well as the onions and ginger roots she had found a week ago and had kept for this day also.

Then she began to fuss around the fire and the sweat shone on her black body as she was transformed into what she was best known as among her community—a famous chef. She made lashings of the dish known as 'Rundown', which was fish boiled with onions and pepper into a mush with coconut oil. She made 'Stamp and go', which was salt fish dropped into hot fat to form fritters. She would have liked to have made her favourite dish which was 'Matrimony'—a concoction of orange sections and star apples or guavas in coconut cream and guava cheese made by boiling down strained ripe guavas in sugar. But there were no guavas or star apples to be had and not enough coconuts to make sufficient cream. She made do with what fruit she had though and kept several huge pots of wild pig, goat, deer, rabbit or kangaroo simmering into curries only she could make. Buried and cooking beneath the ground she had two emus the Keepers had caught, four turkeys unlucky enough to be spotted by the Outsiders, and several wild ducks trapped by Akar Black Head and Kareen when they had learnt a feast was on its way. For there was *nothing*, apart from storytelling and singing, that an Ilkari liked more than a fantastic party.

So Surrey Anne was in her ultimate heaven. The only worry she had was that the national food of the Island—ackee—didn't grow in this land and that meant the flavour could never be entirely true. But, still, they were in a new land and the flavour of kangaroo, deer, emu and rabbit would be more than a challenge for her cooking and their flavours would more than make up for the loss of her favourite ackee.

While Surrey Anne cooked, the two men prepared their jonkannu costumes—and spared a thought for their dead comrade of the same name, who had been the best performer of this particular traditional dance. Of course, on the Island of Springs it would have been done properly, with elaborate costumes in a grotesque parody of Tudor days from the distant past. But here they made best use of the wood, leather and other odds and ends the land had to offer.

The Keepers were most interested and greatly excited at these preparations for a corroboree. The green- and blue-eyed Keepers sent out messengers to gather the families to see this dance of the new black Tribe who had no Totem. By the time the day dawned a large number of these shy people had gathered from the plain and even the mountains. The elders had met and decided that tradition could be dropped for once and the Totem of the Koala People, as well as some of the Platypus and other smaller Totems, could participate in the feast as it had been prepared by black hands.

Nanny herself had disappeared to go and work out the songs that were sung especially on this day. This was an important National Heroes Day for her. She and the remainder of her flight crew had for company a whole new array of heroes and heroines and she must write a good song about all of them. She wished for Culvato's soft voice and the strings of his beloved guitar. That would have made her holiday extra special. But that was not to be. Tears shed over something that could not be brought back were wasted water and water was sacred. That much she had learnt from these 'simple' Ilkari. So, dry eyed, she composed the memory of her lover, intertwined with the other amazing and interesting people she had met on her journey through this land. The land she would remember forever as the land of the golden clouds.

In the old days, events on National Heroes Day would have been different. In these times many children were named after past heroes, so names like Washington, Manley, Bogle, William, Gordon, Vivian, Marcus, Richard, Garvey, Lara, Nesta, Marley, Bunny, Tosh, Livingstone and so on and on abounded. Tradition now, therefore, was that each person dance his or her name out in mime and movement. When National Heroes Day was properly celebrated with some five or six thousand dancers in Kingston or some two or three hundred dancers in the country towns then the whole of the Island's history would come alive.

Accompanied by Keeper men, who softly clacked boomerangs together and played on three didgeridoos at the same time, producing an eerie, haunting noise, Port Rial set out a beat on his bongo drums and the dance began.

First came Surrey Anne, swirling into the circle made by the watching guests. She was dressed in leaves, grass, strips of bark and her short body became fluid and graceful as she represented the parish she had been named after, the gentle, rolling, green hills of her home. Then Cudjo took over the drums as Port Rial swayed on, representing the sea that ravaged the land and the men who came upon that sea—fierce, bold, unruly buccaneers and smugglers.

Now the Keepers of the Trees kept the rhythm up as Cudjo Accompong joined the dance as the mighty Maroon warrior brothers he was named after, who fought the British to a standstill and forced them to sign a treaty. He also danced about the Ras Tafarian religion that he, above all the others, adhered to with all its laws. Because the religion of the Rastas preached a moving away from white dominance and a finding of a black identity, many younger men took on only the shell of the Rasta. But he believed in it most explicitly. He believed that he could only eat certain food—never fish that crawled on the bottom of the sea or other food associated with filth; that he could only eat what he prepared himself or which had been prepared by another Rasta. He even believed that women were superfluous in his society, though he was not as strict as some of his brethren, who banned women altogether from their camps. He believed that Haile Selassie was Jah incarnate. Like every Ras Tafarian he believed God—or Jah—was a Lawgiver, a Judge and a King that had a will beyond mortal understanding and only those equipped with 'art' could comprehend this incredible will and so be enlightened. By smoking ganja this truth could be found and the wisdom was given to tell the truth from a lie.

For one so tall he also was graceful, as well as fierce and proud, as he danced. Last he was joined by Nanny as she lived those long ago heady days of conflict when her namesake had been a great leader and thorn in the side of the white oppressors.

So the four of them floated around the circle while the gentle drone of didgeridoo and hand claps, along with the tapping of boomerang against boomerang, reverberated across the watching, waiting plain.

Then came Nanny's special song. Port Rial went back to his drums and Kareen, moved by the beauty of the words, plucked sweet notes upon her harp, lending substance to the song. She had not thought the hard tough woman could have such a soft heart and she looked upon her differently from then on. After the song there was a deep and thoughtful silence before Surrey Anne called out to come and join in the feast.

It was the first time everyone from their various camps came together as one. Even Wunda and Jynni relaxed enough to dance together in the circle alongside the Keeper twins and the Outsiders, whom they had previously ignored.

The food was wonderful and plentiful. There was more than enough for the caravan and their dark guests from the mountains and plains.

But the best was yet to come. Port Rial, on crossing the sea of grass that had so terrified them, had learnt that some of the grass was in fact sugar cane. He had extracted a quantity of juice and formed a rough base for an alcoholic beverage. Now, several months later, it was well on the way to being a potent brew.

So they filled up their jugs and drank to all their heroes. After a few nips and a story or two, Red Mond took a half jug and some tantalising titbits into the cocoon so S'shony could join in the party as well. There was much laughter and ribald comment from the Outsiders and Akar Black Head. Kareen had only a sip of the fiery drink before deciding the drink was not for her. She set off to perform a tribute to the mountains she knew they would soon be climbing. The two Sisters, who knew what alcohol could do to men, and the Keepers of the Trees abstained as well.

So only the four Visitors, the two Outsiders and Akar Black Head remained to drink and perform contests of song, story, poetry or games. Prince Michael of the Ants remained a while, joining in the poetry and sipping a jug, as each of the others sang songs and told lies—each one bigger than the last. Then he, too, went off on one of his lonely journeys.

The games they played throughout the day were games of strength. But the main game was how much drink each could consume and still be able to stand. The Ilkari were not averse to a drink or two and many a still was to be found scattered over the Purple Plains, and at trade time each clan's best brewer would be in great demand to sell their special brand of the Demon brew. So Akar Black Head, who had travelled all over the Ilkari Kingdom, was a great drinker.

'Aaaaah!' he cried, draining his jug again and beating a fist on his heavy stomach. 'I love this drink of the Gods!' he grinned and held out his jug for more.

But he had met a formidable competitor in the wiry Port Rial, who was also smoking the last of his green tobacco that so changed him. These two drank all day and rivalled each other in the stories they told. One by one the others dropped out to fall asleep or just lie back, giving the drink a rest and enjoying the intense competition between these two entirely different people.

It was towards evening when the stars were just coming out, while the whole sky was covered with a soft blue film as the moon, full and ripe, crept up over the dark mountainous wall. Now was the time for special song. The little pirate began with a tune they had often heard the giant Cudjo Accompong murmur in his deep voice as he swung along the path.

Na-na-na-na-na
We're the survivors; yes the black survival
I tell you what
some people got everything
some people got nothing
some people got hopes and dreams
some people got no aim it seems
Yes, we're the survivors like
Daniel in the lion's den survivors
so my brethren, my sisthren
which way will we choose
we better hurry, oh hurry woe now
'cause we got no time to lose
some people got plots and schemes
some people got ways and means
some people got the facts and claims
some people got the pride and shame.

Then the heavy-shouldered Akar Black Head staggered to his feet and waved his jug about. 'A song from the clan Violet Lynx Foot, of the Tribe Elk,' he shouted.

In the cocoon, a drowsy Red Mond Star Light heard the roar. It had been so long since he had heard that name that a host of memories came pouring into his head: the young, flaxen-haired Chief, the Moon-talker's mother, Kala, with the Moon-talker's hair . . . and his sisters; the cripple Durrilau, who would never see his brother again; the children Odi and Oka, who might even now carry another name and have their own story and wear their Traveller's braid with pride. Would they think of their friend Joda—or would they have forgotten about those few who left many moons ago? Would they be dead—as dead as Joda—and rotting in some lonely grave? Baba. What had become of him?

From purple sand and deep blue sky
I was made in the shape of man.
My heart is red as scorched red rocks
I bend my back like a gnarled grey tree.
Thus do I travel with adversity;
Warrior, that I am.
Nothing do I fear until I die.
Then I shall clasp a Devil by the hand
and laugh into his face with manic glee

Akar Black Head sang lustily.

Red Mond Star Light gently traced patterns over S'shony's extended stomach. Soon she would have the baby and all pretence must be abandoned.

'You think of home, sweet butterfly. Is it the drink you consumed that makes your memories come back?' came his woman's sibilant whisper.

'I see you think of the butterfly that flew into your world one day,' he smiled.

'It was the most beautiful thing I have seen. So small, so delicate and yet a thing of wonder.'

'And you? Do you think of home?' he asked.

'Never!' she said vehemently. 'This cave is all the home I need and my family I have around me.'

'A family that may yet not want you,' the youth sadly reminded her.

They listened to the two drunkards join in a song together and smiled at each other in the soft darkness of the cocoon. It had been a happy, contented day.

Outside, the stars shone down brightly away from the light of the moon, so the whole blue-black stratosphere was spangled with light. Almost as though a giant fire-cracker had gone off, lighting up the sky, Port Rial idly thought. And Port Rial conceived the idea of a joke in his stoned mind.

He would show this man that the Visitors' awesome weapons could also be used for pleasure—and give him a fright he would never forget. He ambled unsteadily over to his horses and went to the spot where most of the ammunition was stored. He would get the gunpowder out of a couple of bullets and throw the contents into the fire, making a minor fireworks explosion. That will make the hairs on the big bear-rial's hairy chest stand out in fright. Port Rial grinned at the image.

He turned.

Then froze.

Just behind him Akar Black Head staggered with two of Nanny's grenades in his hands.

Bravery from the bottle had overcome his shyness in grasping the High Ones power. He was only a warrior, a simple and humble man of great strength. These Gods carried remarkable power in these tiny shapes. He, too, wanted that authority to control and rule and tonight he had no fear.

So he held a grenade in each hand and laughed out loud at the stunned pirate. 'Now I am a High One, too. We are brothers, you and I!' he cried.

He did what his alert eyes had seen Nanny do before destroying half a dozen Nightstalkers in one instant. Before Port Rial's horrified eyes he pulled out the two pins and tossed them away. Now he had the magic in his hands.

The slim pirate had three seconds to make a decision. He knew that when the grenades went off so close to where all the ammunition was stored there would be a chain reaction disastrous to the unprotected people lying around their fires. He acted on instinct.

269

His slight brown body cannoned into the solidly built man so they both fell down and rolled away from the horses. He shouted at them to get away and they, smelling the fear that emanated from Port Rial's body, were already moving in the opposite direction.

One of the grenades fell out of Akar Black Head's hands and dribbled over towards the astonished group of Keepers, who were beginning to rise up from around their fire as they saw what seemed to be a fight between the black spirit and the white man who had been singing and friendly all the day.

Port Rial pounced upon the grenade, with a desperate cry. His eyes looked up into those of a blue-eyed Keeper girl, who stared at him wide-eyed, so his last thought was of his friend, Porky.

Akar Black Head sat up, staring at the other grenade in his hand. Realisation dawned on him and he tried to throw it away, out into the dark silent plain as far as he could. But he was too late. It had just left his hand when, with a shattering roar, it exploded into the placid night sky. A split second later the other grenade exploded, with a terrific thump, sending the thin figure of Port Rial hurtling up into the sky, so his shattered body resembled something like the scattered stars, peering down haughtily at Mankind's small stupidities.

There was immediate confusion. Some of the Keepers, fearing white man's Devilry, ran off into the plain with the bucking, pig-rooting horses. Others gathered their weapons and stood beside their fires ready to fight. They could scarcely believe the Djanaks would attack on a night of the full moon but there was a first time for anything. Amongst the shouts and yelled enquiries a wounded horse screamed like a woman.

Surrey Anne, when she realised what had happened, screamed like a Demon possessed. Screamed and screamed until a hard slap from Nanny stopped her. Then she collapsed and sobbed into her Captain's breast while Nanny's arms encircled her and she murmured calmly into the distressed girl's ear. Immediately, Surrey Anne's hands clasped the purple crystal necklace her lover had made for her those ages ago. It was all she had of him now.

At the sound of the explosions Red Mond burst from the cocoon, club in hand, to stand bewildered while people rushed everywhere around him. Then he ran towards where the horses had been and a crowd was now gathering. He pulled up short when he saw what was left of Akar Black Head.

'Oh, no,' he moaned. 'Not you, my cous-cous. Not my cousin-brother,' he gave an anguished whisper.

He knelt beside the big man. The black bushy hair and beard were flecked with blood and all his side was torn away as though by a giant cat. From the legs down there was nothing but a mess of blood and raw red meat. Yet, surprisingly, the warrior lived. He raised a bloody hand, minus thumb and two fingers and beckoned to Red Mond to come closer.

'I have fought my last fight,' he rasped. 'I fought a God and yet still live.' He paused and coughed up a globule of rich dark blood. 'But not for long, I fear.'

'Stay until the healers come. They have magic that we men know nothing of. Remember how they healed Kareen?' the Moon-talker whispered.

'Tell Kareen my last thoughts were with her,' Akar Black Head murmured, then gave a broken smile. 'It is best to leave affairs of the Gods *with* the Gods. Now,' he pulled Red Mond Star Light closer so only he could hear, 'tell me one thing before I die. Is the woman we carry with us a true Goddess of the moon?'

The youth's dark eyes gazed into the warrior's deep blue ones. Then he patted him gently on the shoulder not damaged by the blast. 'She is my woman and I am the Moon-talker. She leads us to a better world,' he said.

'I shall never see her but I believe she is most beautiful. When I am a rock or tree, then I shall feel her father's arms around me when the moon shines bright.' Akar Black Head smiled again. 'A warrior sees many things in his troubles and travels but I can think of no one who has seen a true Goddess of the moon we all love.'

'You *shall* see her then, my cousin-brother,' Red Mond said on impulse. For what difference would it make now for him to see that, although she was one of his enemies and only a human, she was, indeed, beautiful; that she was only a girl who was having that most precious gift in these turbulent times—a baby.

'No,' Akar Black Head whispered and died.

Unbeknownst to any of them, the Prophet's wife Laelia had used her skills to creep into the injured man's mind and blanket his pain with an aura of calmness so his death would be comfortable.

As the life left the eyes of his clansman and companion, Red Mond Star Light sent forth a loud keening and pulled viciously at the braids hanging down about his face. The most to suffer on this journey were members of his own clan.

Yet, every time the stars had told him nothing or else he had not read them right. Was he just another ordinary human with no gifts at all? A young man led on by his mysterious woman's whims, who killed his clansmen one by one for no purpose?

Sacred water flowed without cease from his eyes even as the moon he had always believed in sailed benignly overhead. Then a scent of wildflowers assailed him and soft arms encircled him and he looked up to see Kareen's grief-stricken face. Flower garlands were around her neck and arms and in her hair for she had been in the middle of a ceremony when a sonar message from S'shony had entered her head and she had raced home.

'Cousin-true, his last words were for you,' the Moon-talker sighed.

'We must not cry for him. It is not the way he would be remembered,' Kareen said brokenly, holding her tears back. She, of all of them, knew how precious were the tears of Father Moon that kept Sister Earth green and alive.

'Come,' she said softly. 'Let us away from here, out into the plains where Father Moon can comfort his children of the earth. Then we shall bury our comrade, before Sister Sun comes up to claim him,' and she led Red Mond away.

Of the laughing Port Rial there was not much to be found at all. Only a boot with a bloody foot in it, part of an arm and a twisted, hot haunch of meat that resembled the slim pirate not a bit. But his three friends gathered these remains up and, in a daze, prepared for his funeral also.

Red Mond Star Light cut off a lock of the bushy black hair to entwine with that of his young cousin and Joda in his bracelet. It did not go past his thoughts that, with the honey-blond hair of Joda and the dark red of Ilki, he had the three sacred colours of the Keepers and truly was one with them now.

Kareen also took a lock of hair to make a love-knot to put in her soul bag hanging around her neck so he would be with her always. She would have no more man, she knew. She had lost two lovers in the space of a year and she could have no children anyway, so from now on she would dedicate herself to the duties of an Earth Mother. But she would not forget the vital, passionate love of her huge, hairy, somewhat stupid, but always gentle, man.

With the help of the Keeper twins, they dug a hole and gathered rocks to place around it. He was humbled into remembering the belief of the Ilkari and the keepers that everything goes around in circles—a thing he had forgotten of late. Once again there was no Baba to say the sacred prayers but Red Mond Star Light cut off Akar Black Head's Traveller's braid to give to the priest when next they met.

Proud Akar, warrior of our clan.
All of Violet Lynx Foot can say he was a man.
But more! He was our brother.
There can never be another
to take the wandering footsteps of our friend.

Thus Red Mond started his eulogy. Then he sang, long and heartfelt, of all the deeds Akar Black Head had performed and others some said he had performed, while he threw clumps of grass (there being no sand in this fertile place) to every direction of the wind and scattered it on the cold body of his clansman. While he sang, Kareen and the two Keepers threw dirt back into the hole, so he was covered before the first warm rays of the sun could crawl over the mountainous horizon and carry him away.

Afterwards Red Mond was physically and emotionally exhausted and went into the cocoon to lie down beside the woman he adored, who took him into her arms and nursed him as though he were the baby she was soon to have. His last coherent thought that night was that poor Kareen would only have nightmares to keep her company.

Cudjo Accompong comes to her and says they cannot afford the usual nine days needed for proper burial ceremonies. When have they ever, she thinks, as she remembers the other five dead bodies of her crew. Then the giant goes away to dig a grave, a lonely figure away out on the plains, while she comforts Surrey Anne. But as she looks into her sisthren's eyes she sees that the great light that burned there—the happy glistening light that made the girl's eyes seem so alive—has gone and they are the eyes of a zombie.

One by one, the dead come back to visit with the living, even though she performed the purification ceremonies each time to avoid that. But she was not Saint Catherine or The Baptist, each of whom had the necessary religious powers to perform the death ceremonies. Besides, nine days before burial were needed to prepare the spirits for the other side. Now The Baptist, Clarendon Jon Cannu, Saint Catherine, Porky, The Syrian—and soon—Port Rial all come to accuse her for not looking after them. She reminds herself that they all chose to come. She did not pressure them to leave their villages, jungles or fields of green plenty to come with her. But she had hinted at treasures untold and, especially as most had some form of Ras Tafarian belief, the finding of the Lion of Judah and his country, the land of Haile Selassie—the spiritual land of every Ras Tafarian.

But all she has brought them is death in lonely places.

Cudjo Accompong is by her side, slowly, sympathetically leading her towards the grave where she must perform, once again, the sad ceremony, bereft of all its feasting, games, dancing and stories. At home, a funeral is generally a jolly time as well as sad, with whole families gathering to tell of the good, funny and even wicked things the deceased has done. In fact, it is only surpassed by a wedding and there are few enough of those on the Island of Springs, for living together is often construed as being married anyway.

But here, on this wide, open plain, surrounded by strangers, it is a miserable affair indeed. Surrey Anne, being a Zionist in religious matters, has gone into a religious trance and even now is moaning and shaking her body into a frenzy. Cudjo Accompong grabs the girl, ready to stop her from biting or swallowing her tongue, while Nanny quietly says the words of purification that will keep Port Rial's spirit here on the plain, not following and tormenting them for the rest of their travels.

Although she knows he will.

What a stupid way to die. The others, at least, were killed by treachery or by an element of unpredictable nature, but he is dead from the hand of a friend, from one of their own weapons. And it was her *decree that forbade the teaching of any of their armoury to these unsophisticated people. If she had taught the warrior Akar Black Head (who was, after all, a soldier just as was she) then he would have known of the danger and they both would be alive today.*

To die on National Heroes Day, a long long way from home and family. This is surely the most upsetting thing to happen to her on this doomed trip. Even the murder of her beloved Baptist cannot surpass this.

She stares up into the bleak mountains. Mountains such as these claimed the lives of the attractive Syrian and the enigmatic Clarendon Jon. Would they all go to their graves never to see the plains and jungles and mountains of their home again?

From beside her a gaunt figure materialises out of the mist, to stare at the newly dug grave.

Till the Future dares
Forget the Past, his fame and fate shall be
An echo and a light unto eternity!

the lunatic old Prince says quietly and throws a clod of earth upon the soil.

Of all the stories that could have been told about Port Rial perhaps that is the one she will most remember. 'A light unto eternity.' That is how he will be remembered. She turns to smile her thanks at the young man who has been turned into an old fool, who gathers words of wisdom to his threadbare clothes like gems of the utmost glory. But he is gone.

There is only the night and all that dwell in it to stare back at her impassively.

Book Five

Into the Mountains

CHAPTER FIFTEEN

The range towered above them, cloaked in trees or showing large patches of bare, dull, grey rock that went silver in the sunlight. Far above their heads the skyline was jagged and raw, with upturned rocks or tall, sparse trees clawing with wooden talons that tore at the blue belly of the sky.

The Keepers of the Trees, who had travelled across the plains with them, left them at last. This was not their Totem's country and, besides, it was dangerous. Many was the countryman who had wandered over the range but none had ever come back. Before they left, however, some of the elders called Weerluk aside and talked to him for about an hour. When he caught up with the caravan that night he would not tell Mungart anything but, rather, kept his own counsel.

'I thought we were brothers!' Mungart sulked.

'Sometimes it is best to keep a secret even from a brother. I will tell you when the time is right.'

'Do what you like. I'm going to get one last fat plains kangaroo before we go into the mountains,' Mungart snapped, in an infrequent bad mood, and stalked off.

As he was crossing the camp he heard muffled weeping and glanced towards the site of Surrey Anne's bed. Just then, she sensed his staring and looked up, the firelight catching her dull black eyes. They held each other's stare for a minute, before Mungart turned away. But in his mind was another pair of eyes that had looked just like that—Gurrewe's, before a huge club had smashed her face into the emptiness that had been his life from then on.

When he continued on his way out to the deep dark plains it was not to hunt a kangaroo but to pursue his own thoughts, as the blue-black twilight of Father Moon shone in splendour around him, making everything larger than life and clearer.

He knew the story of the Ilkari about their Father Moon, a man betrayed by love. Some of the stories of the Keepers were about Japara who through illicit love of Bima, wife of Purukupali, caused the death of Jinini—the first death in all the world. After a fight with Purukupali, Japara went to the sky to become the moon, scars from the fight still visible on his face. So . . . the moon was a lover and sent his lover's light to cover the solitary hunter and seep into his brain with thoughts like Japara had for Bima. Such thoughts were dangerous in a dangerous country like this, where all thoughts should be centred on survival. Besides, she was not of the Keeper people. It was best to leave her alone, Mungart knew.

On his way back from his travels that night he found a clump of she-oak trees and gathered up a number of the knobbly brown nuts with which to make a necklace. Just as a gift to comfort her in her loneliness, he told himself.

With typical Aboriginal ingenuity, he also made her a cunning pair of ear-rings from bird bones, tree gum and some bright feathers, on nights beside his fire. These gifts he left by her bed in the dead of night, creeping silently to her side so that neither she nor her constant companion Laelia awoke.

She would not wear them but he watched from afar as she found them and smiled to himself when he saw her put the gifts carefully in the carry bag she called a 'bankra'.

He did not see his brother Weerluk glance up and scowl in his direction.

The mountains they moved into rose sheer up into the now-grey sky. The slopes were covered in short, hardy trees or else were slippery, bare patches of rock. The soil was crumbly and loose with stones and full of potholes that were treacherous to the horses' hooves. In fact, on the very first day, they lost a horse and some of Port Rial's hard-earned treasure when the beast slipped and fell screaming and tossing in the air to its death some two hundred feet below.

The air became heavier and colder the higher they climbed and often the clouds would pounce upon them, covering them in damp mist. The silence from the forest was eerie and ominous and they were forever on the alert.

They crossed one range of the mountains only to face a higher one. Now it became unbearably cold to those used to the Ilkari desert or the Island climate. Laelia, in particular, suffered in her thin blue gowns and her city-softened skin and her friend Surrey Anne found her some furs out of her man's treasures. S'shony, who had no clothes at all, wrapped herself in Akar Black Head's great bear skin. So the unbeliever kept one whom he would have killed in an instant, alive and in comfort. The gifts the two Keepers had been given by their countrymen were two intricately patterned possum-skin coats. The two Sisters and the two Outsiders cared not for the cold, their whole life having been one of hardship.

They made a curious procession as they climbed the silent cliffs and ravines of the land around them. Just as the enormity of the plains made them insignificant so too did these great heights and cruel ravines.

Surrey Anne kept very much to herself, having time only for Kareen who, herself, had suffered a loss. Besides, she shared the Islander's joy for the plants of this land. At night she would lie down beside Laelia and the Silver City woman would spread a blanket of calm over her troubled thoughts. It was what Laelia's mind and the minds of her people had been trained to do over the centuries and so, once again in secret, she comforted one of her new friends in distress. No one knew of her use of power, of course, except S'shony—who felt a slight uneasiness as she sensed the Blue Woman's mind at work. The doings of the Silver City were not to be forgotten in a hurry and what if this woman dominated each and every one of the caravan—as she certainly had the power to do? What would become of her man then . . . and his friends?

One dark day cold sheets of rain fell in blinding torrents; as they crawled across a steep ravine Weerluk, who was in the lead picking out the safest path, suddenly gave a warning yell. It was a red-bellied black snake, made slow and sleepy by the cold weather, which, nonetheless, was still able to raise its head in a defensive stance. Weerluk knew this was one of the deadlier snakes, so he shouted and leapt away as his brother sprang forwards and sent his boomerang whizzing through the air, smashing the small, evil, diamond-shaped head. But the abrupt movement frightened one of the horses which reared up and back, over the cliff. Its flailing feet knocked the two Sisters flying—Wunda to sprawl upon the ground and Jynni to sail over the cliff with the screaming horse.

At once Leef-shadow, who had, as always, been keeping near her, charged as fast as his club foot would allow him to the ravine's edge, crying out in anguish. The girl clung with one desperate white hand to a jagged piece of rock. The ground waited hungrily for her some two thousand feet below.

With the grace and tenacity of a spider, the little twisted form of the boy crawled down the sheer cliff. If his club foot impeded him, then his extra finger may have helped his descent. Certainly his courage and love of this orange-haired girl helped him forget all the dangers.

His green eyes met her mauve ones. Mauve eyes that were terrified for once and barren of all hate or mockery. 'How like a fish wriggling on a line is the woman who needs no man. How like a moth trapped in a spider's web—and I am that spider,' he said. But the smile—always scarce on his hard face—softened the jibes.

His deformed hand crept out and grasped the slim, pale forearm, and with seemingly little effort (although in truth his heart was near bursting), he hauled the girl up, bit by bit, over the slippery wall of rocks while the rain streamed down. He pulled her over the top of the cliff and into the waiting hands of Wunda. Before the stocky, tousle-haired woman led her lover away, Jynni cast a shy glance in Leef-shadow's direction. It was as much thanks as she would give but that glance was to keep the boy's heart beating for many a day.

As soon as they had gone and the rest were busy quietening the remaining horses, Leef angrily grabbed his companion by the shoulder and swung him around. 'You have touched a Sister of the Sun, fool! Why couldn't you let her die? Of what use is she and her Devil and their spells to us? We are men, you and I, and have no part in their world,' he cried.

'Yes, we are men,' Leef-shadow agreed. 'More—we are Outsiders, where there are *only* men . . . and boys,' Leef-shadow murmured back. 'But now we are in the company of civilised humans and we can put aside our habits of old.'

'Then you will surely die, Leef-shadow. Shadow of the leaf is what I named you and it is *I* who kept you alive until you were old enough to survive.' A great sadness came over the bearded face of the shaven-headed man. 'It is the way we have always lived. You are my companion,' he said gently.

'Can you not see that there is more to life than killing,' the boy said quietly and walked away. Puzzlement and sorrow crept into the giant man's eyes as he watched his friend disappear.

But that night the small figure curled up beside the giant's massive chest and his hand crept around the hairy neck of his companion so they kept each other warm and safe in their dreams—just as they had done as far back as the child could remember.

There came a day when they set off at dawn in the grip of the swirling grey clouds that, this day, seemed alive with malevolent spirits. It was so dark and misty they had to keep shouting to each other to make sure none wandered off and became lost. Although Red Mond was the closest to Father Moon he had ever been, he was terrified. He could no more see the moon than the sun—or anything. Only this cold, clinging, white stuff that deadened the senses and blinded the eyes. The howling wind buffeted their puny bodies—even the giants, Leef and Cudjo Accompong.

And then they came upon a phenomenon none but the three Visitors and the two Sisters could understand. For what they had found were patches of snow lying on the ground. Even as Kareen tentatively touched the ice-hard substance a snowfall crept out of the mists to welcome her. The woman lifted her face to the sky, as the delicate crystals drifted down, and she smiled as they softly touched her skin, melting at once into water.

'The stars have come down to visit us, cousin,' she murmured in delight to Red Mond Star Light, her grey eyes sparkling in the gloom.

'What strange gift is this from the Gods?' Leef called out in the mist. 'Is it a gift of Father Moon's or Sister Sun's?' he said suspiciously.

'It is only the clouds putting their blankets on the ground,' Jynni said, coming up close beside him, her orange hair and bright clothes even brighter in this cold, grey world. 'Now the place becomes dangerous—as you shall see. How many of you brave and fearless men will come through to see our beloved Sister Sun again is amusing to predict.' She giggled maliciously.

The two Keepers had heard of this flying ice but never seen it, so they squatted together excitedly examining it.

The Visitors had heard of snow and knew what it was but they, too, had never seen it before. Even Surrey Anne lost her sadness for awhile as they laughed and played in the snowdrifts, like little children.

But it was Wunda who brought them all back to harsh reality. 'We must get to some shelter, for tomorrow the real storm will begin. We told you this was the wrong time of the year to cross these mountains. Now it will be only luck if we survive.'

They made their way into the snowdrifts that rapidly became deeper and harder to negotiate. Then the snow began to fall in blinding sheets of ice-cold sleet. Wunda took charge, ordering everybody into a close-knit circle and getting them to dig deep into the snowbank to form a sort of cave. She made them all cuddle up to each other. She tried to get Red Mond to let them all cram into the cocoon but he, of course, refused and crawled in himself, to give his body warmth to S'shony.

The dancing, drifting snowstorm tossed and eddied in swirling patterns as the low moaning wind ran like a child at play among the falling flakes. For two days and two nights it fell and completely covered the land. On the third day, with the suddenness that this new disaster had befallen them, then so it ended. The clouds peeled away to stand back in the new blue sky and assess what damage they had done and Sister Sun shone down, a cold white ball in the sky; the Queen in this catastrophe she had caused, yet again, to Sister Earth. The snowfields shone for many miles around. They blinded the eyes of the travellers as they stumbled from their hideaway.

All changed, changed utterly:
A terrible beauty is born

Prince Michael of the Ants droned and his voice was the only sound in a world gone suddenly white and quiet.

Some forty-eight hours spent rubbing shoulders with one's traditional enemy had somewhat smoothed relations between the caravan. Once, Mungart and Weerluk would have thought the wadjullung were all of the same Tribe, but they now knew there were as many different Tribes as there were Totems among their own people.

The thoughts of Mungart, whose sojourn in the caves brought him close to the musky, exciting body of Surrey Anne, were only of a budding romance.

But Weerluk was more practical and eyed this new world with

suspicion. His sixth sense warned him there was something wrong, but he could not work out what.

Of the seven horses remaining from Port Rial's herd and the four horses used to pull the cocoon, one had disappeared and two had died of exposure. This upset Surrey Anne because the horses and the skinny pirate had become one and the same. Cudjo Accompong mourned the disappearance of the third horse, because it was carrying the bulk of ammunition for his rocket-launcher. Without the force of his weapon behind him he was just another giant in an untamed land, with no real skills of survival.

Gathering up the remaining horses and securing S'shony's cocoon to the wagon, they trudged across the desolate landscape, finding it difficult going in the loose piles of snow. In this part of the mountains there were few trees. Mostly there were pinnacles and clumps of rocks. There were no animals to be seen at all.

It was mid-morning on that first day in the snow when Weerluk's fears were realised.

As they struggled through the snow, around a towering grey outcrop of rock, there was a warning cry from Jynni. When Weerluk looked up in startled surprise, his feet entrapped once more in the clinging snow, they were surrounded and it was useless to try and use his weapons.

From out of nowhere they had swooped, like birds of prey, silent as the last thought death allows everyone. On their feet they wore unusual stick-like shoes that enabled them to glide over the crisp white surface with ease. There were eleven males and they were all dressed in white robes so they were hard to see against the surface. Of more interest to the beleaguered travellers, entirely at their mercy as they floundered in the snow, was the fact that they all carried weapons in the shape of heavy clubs or lethal-looking javelins. If it were not for the sun shining down from above, it would have seemed their aggressors were Nightstalkers, for their skin was as white as their hair and eyes were black.

'Well bowled, sir,' cried one, as they came to a swishing halt. 'Caught them in the slips. Howzat, I'd say!'

'Out for a duck!' grinned another.

'There are some Maydinova's here, Cap Tan. Shall we add them to the score board?' a third muttered, eyeing the women lasciviously.

The smallest of the men slid forward on his curiously-shaped shoes and glanced at the members of the caravan, in close scrutiny. Especially did he study the three Visitors from the Island of Springs, who regarded him with equal scrutiny. He stared at Cudjo Accompong's rocket-launcher.

'A Battah,' he murmured. 'Garfield Sobers,' he muttered to himself, then he slid away again and turned to face them all.

'Who is the Keepah amongst you? Who guards the wickets?' he called, and when there was no answer, 'Who leads you in the run rate?'

'I am the leader if that is what you mean,' Red Mond Star Light replied, believing he had fallen into the midst of a cluster of fallen stars. Although all outside signs showed that these people were sane. But then, so it had appeared with the Prophets and their wives . . . and the Hill People . . . and the Outsiders . . . and even the Sisters were sometimes crazy in their thoughts. He sometimes thought that the only really sane person among the lot was the mad Prince of the Ants.

'If you won the toss would you choose to bat or field?' the small man asked, while his comrades moved imperceptibly closer and minutely adjusted their weapons in readiness for the answer. So the Moon-talker guessed this was an important, if seemingly inane, question. Yet he could not know the correct answer as he did not understand it.

And if he got it wrong then many of his companions—even he— would die.

S'shony, in her cocoon, had sent out mind probes to these strangers and now she surreptitiously passed on the answer to her confused beloved.

'Field,' he said.

'Then we will pause for drinks,' the small man replied and they lowered their weapons. 'I am the Cap Tan of the side,' he introduced himself then two others. 'My Bowlah and my Keepah . . . and the rest are either Battahs or Fieldahs.'

'Let us retire hurt,' said the one who was called the Keepah. 'It is surely stumps on the first day.'

Only by the fact that their escort began moving off did it dawn on Red Mond and the rest that they were being invited to join this unintelligible group.

Jynni disagreed loudly, as was her custom. 'Foolish man . . . to trust other men. Do you want to see the end of your adventure?'

'If not, then abandon these people, for they are death to all they meet up with!' cried Wunda.

Some of the white-robed men eyed the two women, with angry black eyes, while others licked their thin pale lips and smiled at each other, like cats over a big, fat, helpless bird, so easy for the kill. One of the Fieldahs skated close to Laelia and stared at her pale face and yellow hair. Her large, frightened blue eyes peered at his mongoloid black slits from over her blue veil.

'A Sun woman,' he hissed. 'What brings you into my cold dark world?'

These were the first words Red Mond Star Light could understand and his heart faltered. How many times had he heard his woman talk of her lover and the other Sun People who had been feared by their darker-haired kin. Could this band indeed be members of the Nightstalkers, who had become immune to sunlight? But it was too late now. They were trapped in the icy wastelands of these people's world, threatened on all sides by vicious-looking weapons.

He passed a message with his eyes to Kareen to beware. She, of course, found no hidden meaning in those snarled words. There were many Sisters of the Sun on this land. Jynni walked beside her even now, sullen and sour, tight-lipped beneath her veil. She could not know of the secret world beneath the ground, where 'Sun Woman' took on a wholly different meaning.

But he was vigilant now and ready for any betrayal. He clutched the heavy club he had taken from the dead Nightstalker those many moons ago, and kept his eyes alert for ambush. The only others to follow his example, he noticed, were the two Keepers of the Trees. They talked together agitatedly in their language and this made the Moon-talker even more anxious. After all, they should know best the troubles in this land.

They progressed at a slow rate towards a massive jumble of rocks, that stood like some ancient ruin on the near horizon. Occasionally one of the Fieldahs—distinguished from the Battahs only in the weapons they had, the former having only javelins while the Battahs carried clubs—would help one of the travellers who were in difficulty. However, mostly there was wariness and distrust between the two groups.

They arrived in a small compound by the rocks, where a number of young boys and youths huddled around two fires or tended a wild herd of small, hairy horses. The snow here had been trampled into a muddy brown sludge, enabling people to walk more freely. Indeed, here it was the eleven men removed their shoes. Everywhere there was activity, as boys cooked food, tended fires, mended clothes or fed the horses. Red Mond was suspicious when he saw that these people lived in the caves dotting the rockpile. No one he had met—and by now he had met a host of unusual people—ever lived in or around caves. The small hole on the rooftop of the world was hardly a proper cave and, besides, it was the special place of Father Moon. Real caves such as these were the sole domain of the hated Nightstalkers.

The boys, as had been the Cap Tan, were greatly excited by the presence of the West Indians and gathered around to touch and stare.

'Them porkys dey nevah see Dreadie before? Me tired fe fuss-fuss given me body all dey time. We got no peace but be monkey fi me zoo,' Cudjo Accompong complained.

'Them different from other white people, me seh. Be wary like tiger dey 'bout grass, Locksman,' Nanny warned. 'Him not jus' our colour either but something me don't quite follow.' She turned to Surrey Anne. 'Coo yah, no women, dereso!'

'De man he touch me him dead!' Surrey Anne snarled and her normally placid face was taut with violent thoughts so Nanny nodded to the giant to watch her. A spark could cause a roaring fire, they knew. She was prone to fits of rage or deep, dark silence these days she was 'deggeh gal'—alone.

Indeed, the boys became most excited again when they saw Surrey Anne's purple crystal necklace. They pointed to it, talking in their barely understandable language and called the Keepah over, who stared at it and made to touch it. But the angry girl pulled away and dared him to, with her fiery eyes, so he stepped back, smiling strangely.

The Cap Tan ambled up to Red Mond and stared languidly into his eyes. His ten men gathered behind them and the boys behind the men.

'It is not often a team comes to play us in either a One Day International or a Test,' he said. 'But it is sporting of you. Do you come from the Gabbah, the Wakkah, or the Emceegee? You cannot come from the Essigee for that is where our pitch is and we have not seen your form in any innings *we* have played,' he conversed genially.

'Yes. This is their Test debut,' called out the Keepah. 'Never have we seen such a line-up.'

There were mutterings among the boys of Garfield Sobers, Viv Veeyan Richards, Desaynes, Jefdujon, Curt Leeambrose, My Cool Holding, Richie-Richie Arrdson, Iron Lara and other incomprehensible words. Looks of confusion and surprise began to appear on the faces of the Visitors. Indeed, it had seemed to Red Mond that Nanny had understood some of the drivel being spoken. He had noticed a look of dawning comprehension come over her face as the eleven had spoken among themselves on the short journey to their home.

'We have to be careful of the short ball placed well outside the off-stump for if he plays it down the ground he could well be out caught in the long-off boundary,' the one called the Bowlah said, looking at the mighty frame of Cudjo Accompong.

'Yes, that would be a good delivery. Perhaps the leg-spinner might play the wrong-un,' said another, also staring and making the man uneasy.

'Let us hope the batsman just beats the outside edge then,' said the Cap Tan, coming up between them and smiling grimly at Cudjo.

Then the one called the Bowlah moved up to Laelia, perhaps sensing that here was the weak link in the chain. He suddenly reached out and ran his pale fingers through her pale yellow hair.

'An innings can be won or lost by a Maydinova. Surely a Maydinova does no harm to the Bowlah.'

The same Fieldah, who had scared her before, sidled up to the Bowlah's side. She was so terrified of their cruel black eyes that she could not bring her mind to use her power over them.

'Often it is the Fieldah who prevents the runs coming and so causes a Maydinova,' he whispered.

'The Maydinova is a disaster for the batsman and is no use to the side on strike,' growled one of the men who wielded a heavy club.

'Reaching out my hand and sliding along the turf I was able to prevent a certain four runs and so also was it a Maydinova,' the Fieldah whispered again in his hissing voice.

And he *did* reach out and, before anyone could react, he cupped Laelia's breast, which heaved in horror.

Then he leapt backwards with a curse and a cry of pain as Prince Michael's knobbly staff crashed down on his fur-covered boot.

Then ye returned to your trinkets; then ye contented your souls
With the flannelled fools at the wicket or the muddied oafs at the goals.

The other white-gowned men moved forward ominously and Nanny reached for her grenades before the shabby man croaked out again, pointing a shaking finger at the Cap Tan: 'An old, mad, blind, despised and dying King,' he quoted.

'A good knock, sir! A Cap Tan's innings!' the Cap Tan cried and motioned his men back. His hard eyes warily watched the insane blue pools swimming in the wrinkled brown face.

Prince Michael put an arm gently around Laelia's shaking shoulders, ignoring Wunda's snorts and Jynni's giggles. Once again he surprised his companions at the caring and kindness he showed his wife, whom he usually hated in a manner that truly *was* insane.

The two Keepers moved to her side, weapons ready in capable brown hands. They had a friendship for this woman they had found and brought into the camp and who constantly amazed them with the silky whiteness of her skin. But, mainly, they disliked anything to do with warlike white men who used their aggression without reason. They knew many stories of past atrocities perpetrated upon their people, that lost none of the horror just because they were only stories now. Their eyes darted about the encampment and their hands held tight to their weapons that were second arms for them. If they saw the irony in being about to die at the hands of the whitest men they had ever seen, protecting a woman just as white, in a country unbelievably white, their scarred ochre-stained faces did not show it.

'You have a good wicket,' the Cap Tan said to Red Mond Star Light, then gestured towards the cocoon. 'What manner of ball are you bowling now? An off-spinner, a googly . . . a chinaman? A bouncer? A wrong-un, a leg spinner? I cannot pick which way the seam will land.'

'If you are talking about the house of skins then you can't go in. It is the hallowed ground of our Goddess of the moon. Only I, the Moon-talker, may converse with her.'

'Goddess of the moon?' the Cap Tan smiled smugly, arching his eyebrows at his Keepah. 'There is no God or Goddess. Only the crimson orb and we devote our lives to finding it again.'

So saying, he stepped back further and made a signal with his hand—by raising one finger—so the group behind him dispersed. His opal black eyes stared once more at the three Visitors.

'Gentlemen, our rivals of the great game in life exist in reality,' he said to the assembled boys. 'After three thousand years their deeds of valour live even now in our memories.'

He smiled once more at the assembled caravan, but it only made his face appear more evil. 'We will send a Fieldah to guide you out of the Essigee, and to go with you in your Test Match to record the Great Ones' innings for the scoreboard. Let us hope none of you get out for a duck!'

With these cryptic words the men and boys all drifted away and went back to doing whatever they had been doing.

Red Mond stared after them until Kareen softly tapped him on the shoulder.

'It is obvious we must stay alert. Do you notice there are no women in this camp?' Kareen murmured.

'Have you not noticed the colour of their eyes and hair and the whiteness of their skin?' came Leef's rumble from behind her.

'The only time I have is when I have squashed a Night Bat like the insect it is,' Leef-shadow said from beside him, eyes glaring incredibly green amidst all this white. 'And I will kill these insects with as much mercy if they bother me.'

'If they wanted to kill us they would have, back in the snow. Even Prowlers don't play games with those who are about to die!' Jynni sneered.

Each and every one went to their own campfires and each campfire surrounded the cocoon, so there was no chance of one of the white-robed men sneaking past. The two Keepers kept guard by the door of the cocoon and Red Mond lay sleepless by S'shony's side. She whispered into his ear, amused and yet a little worried too.

'These men are called the Cricketeers and they believe in a being that is a crimson ball, a shining red light. They are fanatics, believing they can find this crimson orb even in death. They come in four classes: the Keepah, who has the history of the cult in his head; the Bowlah, who is the chief warrior and organises attacks; and the Fieldahs and Battahs are the soldiers. The boys are called 'the twelfth men' for there can only ever be eleven. If someone dies, a boy is apprenticed to the team. That is what the group is called,' she said, enjoying the crazy joke that had been her pleasure to mind probe. 'There is something else too—'

But she was given no chance to say what that was, for the look in Red Mond's dark eyes, as he turned to stare at her, frightened her for the first time since she had known him.

'How do you know all these things?' he murmured wonderingly. 'You have not even seen them.' Then he raised himself on one elbow and gazed down at her in shock. 'You can read minds like the flying woman of the Silver City,' he gasped and shuddered at the memory that image conjured up.

'Sweet butterfly! It was my mind that saved you! Don't be afraid of me,' she whispered. She had thought to share an entertaining piece of buffoonery with her lover and realised—too late—that she had let her secret loose, tired and weary as she was from her difficult pregnancy. She could not take it back now.

'Anyone who can do that to a man like Prince Michael is worthy of fear. If at any time you tire of me . . . or if I upset you in some way . . . Why, Prince Michael was betrayed by the very woman he adored!'

The Moon-talker reared backwards, away from the woman. Her pregnant belly disgusted him and he loathed to touch her pale white skin. Her black plaited hair disappeared into the shadows around her like so many evil, coiled snakes. 'How do I know if you are not, even now, twisting my mind—and have been ever since I first met you. Leading us all into a trap! So the murder of Joda and the disappearance of my cous-cous Culvato and the death of Akar Black Head and the High One was all worthless!'

'My butterfly,' she pleaded. 'Can you not yet trust me as I trust you? Is the hatred between our two peoples that great a rift?' she sobbed.

'I must get away from here to think,' a distressed Red Mond said brusquely. He pointed a finger at her threateningly. 'Don't come into my mind, cave woman! It is only my word that keeps the others out. But if I decide my mind is being tampered with, I shall let the Outsiders and the Sisters and the Keepers in here and they will tear you apart!'

'Sweet Ilgar. I love you,' she murmured tearfully the unfamiliar word Willum had taught her—a lifetime ago it seemed.

There was hurt and confusion in his eyes as he faced her at the door. More—a deep sense of betrayal. And he remembered the message he had seen on the plains at the last reading of the moon.

'Through mind power such as yours I lost my paal. I have seen what the people of the Silver City do to their victims after their games. You have surely felt the hatred of the two called Outsiders, but I saw people like them *before* they became Outsiders. I went to the dungeons to see the last of Culvato—who loved you unto death,' he breathed.

'I know,' she cried.

'Oh, yes, you *would* know. You would know everything about us,' he snarled at her. Then, before she could explain herself, he wheeled around and swept out the door, bumping into Weerluk, who had been listening to the hot foreign words in interest. He supposed even a Goddess could get a man annoyed. But as he listened further, he wondered whether a Goddess could cry. For there was now a muffled weeping from the confines of the cocoon.

Back in the cocoon, S'shony lay upset and frightened. The power she had over Red Mond—if power it was—had vanished. But something else frightened her almost into forgetting this argument and misunderstanding with her lover. As she had innocently probed the minds of those newcomers outside, she had sensed a great void behind their banal chatter and idle conversation. As wide and deep as the King of the Bats' Cave and gaping as hungry as a monster's mouth ready to engulf herself and all her guardians. There was a huge secret emptiness that the

Cricketeers kept and she could not discover it, no matter how hard she probed.

Not knowing this secret was frightening enough but knowing that the Cricketeers possessed a stronger power than she did was, truly, a worrying and frightening thing.

The next morning, after a long sleepless night, the caravan set forth again into a grey, cold, dark world with icy snow flurries dancing around them. The guide chosen to lead them out of the snow country was none other than the Fieldah who had frightened Laelia so much the day before. He was lean of frame with bony capable hands and agile feet. His long black hair fell wild and free over his narrow shoulders. His dark eyes, squeezed to slits against the brightness of the snow, and his cruel, thin mouth were as different from her wide, quiet, blue eyes and round, soft, lush lips as could be. But his skin was as white as hers. He kept close to her, as they trudged through the snow, and sometimes he even helped her out of the drifts she stumbled into. But, all the time, his eyes watched her, studying her with malicious concentration.

His name, he informed them in one of his few bursts of conversation, was Aybee, the name of a famous Cap Tan of old. One of the last Cap Tans before the end of the match, when all the wickets had fallen.

It took three days to cross the snow-covered mountains. Aybee would wheel and float ahead on his special shoes, graceful as a white bird, finding the best path for them. The white fragile crystals drifted down and settled on the traveller's shoulders and in their hair. It was cold and gloomy but Red Mond Star Light went not once into the cocoon to seek instructions from his Goddess, Kareen noticed. In fact, his miserable, musing attitude seemed to soak into everybody, so the company became sullen and irritable. Any moment an argument would flare forth between the Outsiders and the Sisters over some small thing. The Keepers kept to themselves during the day and even Laelia and Kareen lost some of their good nature.

Then, on the third night, the Nightstalkers attacked and brought them all back to reality. Because Red Mond had been sleeping with his cousin by her fire and not with S'shony, the first warning given was by Prince Michael who called out:

Swiftly walk o'er the western wave Spirit of the Night!

Then the beasts from below burst out amongst them, from out of the frozen pale ground, as white and as cold as though the earth itself had come alive.

It was lucky that Cudjo Accompong never let go of his weapon, even in repose, for he was on full alert as they exploded from beneath his feet with furious yells, and one blast of his rocket-launcher wiped out half the attacking force. By then, Nanny and Surrey Anne had their machine guns firing.

Even so, injuries were sustained by the beleaguered group. Surrey Anne was hit across the head with a glancing blow of a hurled club and she dropped to her knees, concussed. Wunda suffered a damaged, possibly broken nose in a scuffle while both Kareen and Nanny were slashed across the chest and back respectively for yet another scar. Leef-shadow was stabbed in his hunchback and Red Mond got a painful slice through the thigh, falling moaning to earth in the last moments of battle.

It was not only surprise that caused so many injuries. These Mountain Nightstalkers were bigger and fiercer than any before encountered and not so easily scared. Also, their feet had curiously adapted to the environment, becoming wider and flatter, so they were able to negotiate the terrain with more dexterity than their opponents.

The Keeper twins had been fighting on the flank near Aybee when, suddenly, they realised they were alone. From out of the shadows and falling snow came three of the Djanaks running towards their unprotected back, their footsteps stifled by the snow. It was only their highly tuned sixth sense that warned them in time. With a cry, Weerluk spun around, running one through with his swiftly flung spear. Even as Mungart hurled his trusty boomerang at the head of another, a sharp javelin came whizzing through the snow-blurred air and thudded into his side, so the orange-ochre-locked youth doubled over with a grunt of pain, coughing up red blood all over the white ground. Weerluk sprang at the last of the murderous trio and, with the strength of rage at his brother's pain, he smashed his stone kodja down on the snapping, frothing white man's head.

S'shony, alone in her cell, felt the red-hot thread of pain go through her head when her lover fell and she was afraid. Any moment her countrymen, whose evil minds had squirmed like maggots in her own as they crawled upwards for a feast, might rip open her flimsy curtain of skins and what would their reaction be then? Would they embrace her as a sister, despite their natural scorn for women? Or would they kill her as a traitor? Thus would end all her small dreams. Alone on a windy, icy mountain top a long way from the jewelled caves of Nimbelyung; even a long way from her lover, whose soul had shied away from her inner strength and who now lay comfortless and bleeding in the cold snow.

But instead, with a mighty whoosh! and the rattling of the Visitors' strange weapons; with the wild yells of Leef and Jynni, for once united in their anger at the beasts who had caused their loved ones injury, the last of the savage men were driven away.

There was only the hush of gently drifting snow covering the blood and bodies and muffling the moans of the wounded. Jynni kissed Wunda's ruined face, already going purple and black, and ran slender fingers through her tangled, brown curls, muttering condolences just as did the mighty Leef, tender in the care of his stricken companion. The Islanders comforted each other and inspected each other's wounds while it was

Laelia who went to Red Mond Star Light, who gritted his teeth in agony and stared in wonder at the ugly gash down his upper leg. Carefully the Blue Woman used snow to wash away the blood and her powers to calm the shock waves that were just beginning to affect him. Kareen administered to her own wound, which was only slight compared to others she had received.

Weerluk let out a cry of sadness, a keening howl of sorrow, and Surrey Anne, stunned though she was, came clambering through the snow. She knew what that cry meant. She had sent one forth from her own mouth to the uncaring moon not one month before.

Mungart was in a bad way, the javelin having shattered his ribs and dug deep into his body. His eyes were glazed and dull from shock and blood coughed steadily from his slack mouth, that once had been curved wide in joyous laughter.

'He hit in he lungs,' the healer said. 'Me a go heal fi you bredrin but me think him dey pon dying.'

At once her hands went to work, choosing and mixing herbs from the bag carried always at her side. Cudjo slowly and carefully pulled the wicked ironstone head of the javelin out of Mungart's body and Surrey Anne just as slowly and carefully pushed the herbal mixture into the gaping wound.

'For a stop bleedin', irie man!' she gently explained to an agitated Weerluk, who prowled the snow as though it were red hot, restless and nervous at the attention so many strangers were giving his brother.

Laelia now came across to help in this more serious problem, having left Red Mond in the care of his cousin. When she laid her white hands on the shaking brown body of his brother, Weerluk was clearly upset. Then he recalled the many times Mungart had shyly touched her white skin in constant wonder. This woman, of all the white people, could place her abominably coloured hands upon the body of his brother. He was glad there were no other Keepers to see this, though.

Mungart let out a cry that made Weerluk stiffen. Laelia's white fingers brushed his quivering lips that were yellow with pain. 'Sshh! dark son of Phineas. Do not be afraid of me. You are closer to me than a tree's shadow is to the earth,' she whispered and sent her calming waves into his—and so also Weerluk's—mind.

Surrey Anne's busy hands prepared to bring healing to a man she considered a friend. They had met at the very beginning of the journey and she would not let him die as they came to the end.

Just then, from out of the mists, the figure of Aybee swooped, only to come to a startled halt. Before anyone could stop him, an irate Weerluk leapt upon him and hurled him to the ground. He raised his deadly stone axe already bloody and would have ended Aybee's life there and then, had not Red Mond Star Light called out and Laelia sent a burst of her calming power into his turbulent mind.

Now Red Mond hobbled over to Aybee, supported by Kareen. One by one the others came over also, to stare with hostile eyes at the Cricketeer sprawled on the ground.

'Why did you leave the side of our friends here?' the Moon-talker asked and his voice was cold and stony.

'I did not—' Aybee began to protest.

'You ran away! I saw you!' came Leef's harsh snarl.

'As soon as your true friends arrived. Is that not the truth?' Leef-shadow joined in, hard green eyes piercing the empty black ones of their guide.

'The Cricketeers are friends only to those of their own creed,' Aybee snarled back.

'We should kill him now,' Jynni shouted.

'Then the mountains will kill us,' Wunda quietly reasoned.

'Wait!' Red Mond said. 'I will seek the wisdom of the moon Goddess in this question.'

Weerluk stared at the fire-headed leader in surprise because for the last three nights he and Mungart had kept guard on the door and the Moon-talker had not gone near his woman once. Both he and his brother had heard her cry on several occasions during this time.

Weerluk pointed at Aybee with his lips, his eyes on Red Mond Star Light's face. 'I will kill this wadgula if my ngoonie dies,' he said in the language of the sacred ones.

'I know, my brother. But let us see what the moon, the first man to cause a death, will tell us before we cause another death.'

It did not surprise Weerluk that this quiet youth should know of the stories about Creation. He merely grunted and nodded his head slightly. But he stood menacingly over the cowering, white-gowned figure of the Cricketeer.

Red Mond limped into the cocoon. He was reminded with a sharp pang of the first time he had crawled through the skin door. When his clansmen and women had shouted, laughed and sung all around him and she had huddled in the dark, alone and frightened. And his heart had been so full of devotion.

As soon as she saw his wounded leg, she let out a sob and reached for him but he gently held her away.

'Use your mind to reach into the one called Aybee, the Cricketeer. Tell me what secrets you see there.' he said quietly.

'I can already tell you that. There is something there but I cannot grasp it. His mind, even on his own, is too strong for me.'

'Is he a friend?'

'Oh yes, I believe so. I can see nothing in his mind that would betray us. He hates my people as much as do you.'

Red Mond Star Light reached out a hand and ran it down her face. 'I cannot hate you. I was confused and afraid of the power the flying woman had. But I should have known you use your power to protect—not hurt—me and our friends.' He brushed his lips against hers in the unfamiliar caress he called kissing and one that she so much enjoyed.

'I'm sorry,' he whispered.

'Sorry,' she hissed in her sibilant tongue in the language of the Sun People. 'There is no need to be sorry, my butterfly.' Then she raised herself up on one elbow. 'Soon we will be on the plains. We are nearly there—at our destination. I have been using my sonar to lead us there and is that not what you say. The moon Goddess leads us on?' She beckoned him closer and breathed. 'Soon also I will have this child. I will need help with the delivery.'

Her black eyes looked into his and he understood the dilemma. He must reveal her to the others—or at least to some of the others—sooner than he wanted to. 'Not yet,' he answered her unspoken question. 'We have suffered terrible injuries. One of the Keepers might even be dying. Now would be a bad time to draw aside the curtain of your home.'

She lowered her eyes in sadness at what her people had done. This would be the first of her guardians to die from her people's hand. She looked at the blood trickling down his leg. What harm had they done? Even to him.

'Well,' he smiled. 'The Goddess of the moon has spoken. We must heed her warnings.' Then he limped out of the cocoon to deliver his verdict.

They spent an extra four days there while their wounds healed. Aybee showed them how to make a type of house out of frozen blocks of snow so they could keep relatively warm and, thus, he began to win the trust of the caravan for otherwise they would have died of the cold.

During those four days Kareen, Laelia and Surrey Anne stayed in a separate snow house with the badly wounded Mungart. Even during a second fight with the Mountain Men they stayed close to his side, killing any who came through the door or floor of their dwelling with knife or gun while Laelia huddled close to the comatose Keeper, useless in this violent situation.

On the morning of the fourth day Mungart stumbled forth, grey about the face and still with a nasty wound . . . but alive.

His brother embraced him and they talked in their own language until Weerluk loped away to get him a feed of much-missed bush tucker.

It was Surrey Anne's medicines that healed up his wound and her scent that was always in his nostrils. Once or twice, when he reached out to her, she clasped his fingers tightly with her own and her black, mysterious eyes regarded him with a calm, untroubled gaze. It did not matter that his ribs were still cracked and he had a damaged lung. The wound in his heart had at last been healed.

Perhaps, more than anything, it was the flock of swift, silent, white cockatoos, that flew like a flurry of snow across the green of the trees, that told him Gurrewe was letting him go.

When Weerluk brought back a small bird, Mungart had already got the fire going and sat in a dream beside the glowing wood. The angry eyes of Weerluk clouded over for a moment while, unobserved, he watched his brother watching Surrey Anne. Then he silently went about preparing the meal.

'Tjurditch also, once he set his mind on something would never let it go,' he said at last. 'Why else does he now hunt at night and have such a ragged tail where once it was so pretty?' he murmured over the crackling of the flames.

'Because, my brother, our kin the green parrot and koolbardi attacked him for insulting our other kin, waitj. It is why he also has a spotted coat from the sharp beaks of koolbardi,' Mungart as softly replied. For when his family talked in the stories of Creation then they were worried indeed.

'Wildcat had no right to go with that emu woman. See all the trouble he caused. When he murdered her husband he caused old man emu's neck and head feathers to go white to remind us never to travel with strangers. When he attacked the woman he tore all her breast feathers out—as can be seen today,' Weerluk muttered and stared morosely into the fire, prodding the cooking meat.

'The possum is always chasing emu woman,' he said abruptly at last. ' Why does kelang have red on his cheeks and face? Because he has no respect and so the sacred wilgie we put on for courtship holds no sacred meaning either.'

'She saved my life. You have gone with women amongst the Koala People. I have seen you. But I have not touched a woman since the death of Gurrewe.'

'Her man is not long dead. She should belong to the brother of the dead man, the giant with the stick of thunder. The laws *cannot* be broken!' Weerluk said angrily, loudly, so heads at other fires turned.

He stood up. It was the first time these two had had a serious argument and he did not know how to react.

'It is as I said. The wildcat, once his mind is made up, never lets go. But remember the fate of possum from the stories of our grandfather. He never wins the woman but only gets beaten—often killed.'

So saying, Weerluk stalked away from the fire. For the first time since their quest for vengeance began the brothers slept apart that night; Mungart by the fire with his dreams of Surrey Anne, and Weerluk by the cocoon, near the sleeping form of his friend, the Moon-talker. Here was one of the white people he could trust and even allowed to touch him during conversation. But he was not in love with him as his brother was obviously in love with the young foreign black woman. The youth's mouth set in a straight line and his eyes, as dark as any of the native animals upon his land and in his stories, were sad and worried at the coming of the ending of his world.

The most important way in which Aybee won their trust was when the Mountain Men, as Aybee called them, attacked again in greater force. This time the caravan was warned by S'shony and they were ready to gain revenge. Even though they were fierce and strong, the Mountain Men were driven back by the sheer force of anger the various members of the caravan felt at the wounds sustained by their friends and kin.

In the midst of the fiercest fighting, Leef felt a puff of air blow past his cheek. He swung to see a huge Night Bat, the biggest he had ever seen in his many dealings with this Race, about to swing once more the club that had missed him by a whisker. Then a glistening white stick was thrust through his killer's naked white chest. The big man looked at it in surprise before sinking to his knees. He tried to pull it out with his hands, but it was slippery with his blood. Behind his stricken face loomed the slim, white-robed figure of Aybee who gave Leef a raw look of savage contentment, before pulling his weapon from his dying victim. His black eyes fairly gleamed with vicious joy at the death of an enemy.

'Nicely placed off the edge of the bat,' he grinned at the giant. 'But you—a bit of a turn and you nearly holed out at long run. So near to your century, too.'

Then he twisted away, wielding his bloody weapon, killing more of the shrieking, screeching, naked creatures, both men and women. There was no doubt in the giant's mind that here was a worthy comrade on this violent, unpredictable trail.

CHAPTER SIXTEEN

During the four days while the women performed their healing rites, the two Sisters set up camp away from the rest and Jynni looked after Wunda's bruised face. One day she passed close by the camp of the Outsiders, with a container of snow to ease the bruising on her partner's face. She paused for a moment and set her bucket down, then folded her arms while she stared at Leef who glared balefully back at her. Then she cast her curiously coloured eyes onto Leef-shadow.

'Your wound must hurt you more than you say,' she said.

'And why do you say that, witch? If it is any of your business to ask in the first place,' Leef snarled.

'Where are the knives you throw so adroitly into your conversation with me?' Jynni said to the boy, ignoring the man. 'Could it be your injured shoulder has spoilt your aim in bitter language? I know that I miss your words of malevolence.'

She raised her veil to wipe at her cheeks and Leef-shadow saw the beauty of her oval white face as she stared boldly at him. A smile pulled at her sullen lips.

When she smiled it seemed to the boy she was as gorgeous as a delicate, brilliantly patterned gecko hiding in the decaying bark of an old log. The boy, who had watched the many small wonders of Nature and knew them as glorious, was able to think this about the girl.

A small smile skittered across his own lean face. 'One raindrop not make a storm, yet also heralds a hurricane. A mighty wind can tear the tree down but it cannot tear the leaf from that tree. It is why my shadow still dances on the ground.'

His eyes met hers and for a long time they locked forces and neither was afraid of the other anymore. The spell was only broken when Leef wrapped a large arm around the misshapen shoulders of the boy.

'Begone, bitch. Leave us alone as we leave you and your harlot alone,' he growled, like an angry dog who senses he might lose his favourite bone.

'How small a heart has this giant of a man!' Jynni sneered, 'Shrivelled and corrupt, as most men's hearts are. Greedy for what he wants and thinks is his own.'

She picked up her bucket of snow and flounced off to her own camp. As she began to put snow on her Sister's face, Wunda's short-fingered hand reached out and grabbed her wrist with such suddenness that she was surprised. The normally placid hazel eyes of her Sister burnt with an intensity and she used her other hand to draw Jynni's face down to her own. Then she licked the pale cheek with her warm red tongue and kissed Jynni's lips with a hunger she had not shown in a long time.

No words needed to be spoken. The emotion was there for Sister Sun to see. Sister Earth was hurting.

They change their skies above them,
But not their hearts that roam

Prince Michael quoted as he drifted out of the silent white landscape like a spectre.

'Away, foolish man!' Wunda cried. Pushing the slender girl from her and springing to her feet, she snarled, 'Keep yourself out of our way or I will make you sorry.'

The wizened figure seemed to float over to the short woman. Before anyone could do anything his thin fingers stretched out and ran through her hair and gently caressed her face.

I arise from dreams of thee
In the first sweet sleep of night

he said, untroubled by her shock at having a man touch her.

She made to strike him but Red Mond Star Light called out from where he had been watching beside the cocoon. 'He is a fallen star and the words he speaks are only star dust. Although sometimes his words are as true as a moonbeam.'

'We have no need of any such illusions the moon may throw at us,' Jynni called back. But Wunda lowered her hand and glared at Prince Michael ominously.

'Touch me again, idiot, and I will kill you!'

Our England is a garden, and such gardens are not made
By singing 'Oh, how beautiful!' and sitting in the shade

the Prince said, apparently vacantly.

'Simple man, this is not England. Do you think we are stupid desert people not to know and understand your raving drivel?' Wunda raged. But, in her heart of hearts, she knew full well he was talking about her and Jynni's love.

So love, that gentle yet confusing and soul-destroying emotion, set up camp with them all. Golden arrows fell like sunbeams, leaden arrows like the snow, until all were affected even if they did not know it.

Two who were smitten with the golden arrows of virtuous love were Nanny and Cudjo Accompong.

297

She wonders why she did not follow his affections sooner. Ever since Saint Catherine died he has been alone, with only his weapons for lovers, his desire to protect the others his burning flame. One by one her followers into her adventure lie mouldering beneath foreign soils and—yes!—she is as alone as any of them. She tells herself it is because she is lonely that she falls into the brawny arms of her fellow Maroon—even though he is a true Ras Tafarian and as alien to her Baptist upbringing as any other stranger. She tells herself that she is a woman, with a woman's needs and that the giant West Indian is lonely too. But, in reality, she knows it is time to forget about Culvato and to start thinking of home.

It is as Cudjo Accompong said in one of the many talks he enjoys after a heavy day's travel. Surely in a land so vast there must be deposits of petroleum somewhere. Then they would fill up their empty barrels and go home to the Island they all missed.

Some would miss it forever.

Was it all her fault their adventure had ended in disaster? All her friends dead and she still alive? She had been blinded by the passionate love of a wandering lawless Gypsy and then by a golden-haired King, who had stolen her mind. Yet, all the time the giant, her countryman and fellow Maroon, has been beside her like a shadow.

The crazy, white-haired man is not as silly as he seems. His words come to her now from his babbling as he talked (if talk is the right word) to the impassive giant.

I pray—for fashion's word is out
And prayer comes round again—
That I may seem, though I die old,
A foolish, passionate man.

A foolish, passionate man. Is that not the exact description of her lover? Her Cudjo is the river and she is the current that carries it along. He is her raft and she drifts down the river, safe and secure . . . the Black River, the only true navigable river. She sings out loud a song of fruit and sun and dancing, leaping fish—and he! He is carried along with it and becomes part of the green, blue-fringed Island again. He also sings a song—from the very heart of the Lion of Judah—and their songs make the Island ring. Oh! how grand it is to be in love again.

And Cudjo Accompong, despite his huge frame, was considerate and kind when he embraced her. They took a subdued, sad and sorry Surrey Anne under their aura. Port Rial and Surrey Anne's love had been a form of love as well for the two lonely people. Now that was all over while their love began and they made sure the last of their followers was safe and at peace with herself.

It was why Cudjo Accompong told Nanny about the infatuation of Mungart towards the healer. But she could see no real harm in it because she could not see with Weerluk's eyes, that laws were being broken.

298

On the day that the Cricketeer led them out of the snowfields known to him as Essigee and announced in his cryptic language that 'the field was spread wide so there was room for lots of twos and singles', desire dealt another blow to the goodwill of the caravan.

The boy, Leef-shadow, had long spent his days wandering, a lost soul, beside the girl who still mocked him unmercifully. His green eyes, once full of violent hatred, were confused as he watched the liquid movement of her body beneath her orange, yellow and red robes; or how she tilted her head in arrogant splendour as she was about to deliver another barb to him. He especially adored the way the sun caught her orange hair and turned it into molten fire that ran down the sides of her pale face.

He could not understand this new feeling that fluttered in his heart. He only knew that he had to possess her just as, when a small child, he had chased the illusive, rare butterflies or chirping crickets that sometimes got lost on the desert winds, so were carried to the rocky hideaway that was Leef's band's home. Now he had another butterfly to catch, a soft, warm, orange and mauve and white one, whose whirling body sailed just out of reach of his two deformed hands.

But he still shared the fire and bodily comforts of his protector for it was the only life he knew and the only friendship he had ever known. He would rub the ointment onto the scarred bristled head and shave it with his knife tenderly, as he had always done. And Leef also would massage his body, so they gave each other the only pleasure they knew.

He still had a vague memory, however, of a face bending over him, smiling and murmuring and gently laughing. He can still vaguely remember the feel of a firm, velvet-skinned breast and, he thinks he can remember this, the taste of sweet, life-giving mother's milk.

Now he thought that he had found it, the love that his mother had tried to give him before cruel, white Demons had erupted from the red dust and dragged her away screaming—with all the rest of his almost-forgotten memories.

Leef's behaviour towards the two Sisters became more vitriolic as they passed over the mountains. Once or twice there was nearly a savage fight, stopped only by Kareen's lenient words. The two women were wary of the Earth Mother, as they were afraid of no man. And, as for Leef, his eyes would flicker away from her grey gaze and he would shuffle his feet and tug agitatedly at his beard before stomping off.

At last, however, things came to a head.

They were crossing over a terrain of small hardy trees and short sharp ravines, backed by the jagged mountain tops they had just traversed. It was tough going and tempers were frayed. For three nights in a row they had been harassed by Nightstalkers. It was almost as if they knew where they were heading and Red Mond, at least, could believe this for he now knew what mind powers these creatures possessed. The constant fighting was wearing them all down, even the giant Leef, who liked nothing better than to fight. The other giant was fast becoming aware of his vulnerability as his depleted ammunition slowly ran down.

On this day as they trudged monotonously through the grey-green bush with the black-grey clouds rolling above them, the last thoughts in Leef's great shaven head were romantic as he slowly steamed into a temper.

'Another sunbeam has crashed to earth,' he said to no one in particular as Jynni's clumsy feet once more caused her to stumble and land on her knees.

'Can't you *ever* leave her alone? She does not bother us anymore,' Leef-shadow said from beside him.

'What are the words she called you this morning then if not bother-some? She bothers me, anyhow,' Leef growled

'The words of this morning are this morning's matter. It is the afternoon now,' Leef-shadow stubbornly said.

Leef stopped and turned around, hands on hips, to stare down at his little companion. 'I think Sister Sun has boiled your brain and burnt your eyes so you are blind. Whatever you say of Sister Sun, therefore, has to be untrue because you cannot see the truth.'

Leef-shadow also adopted a war-like stance, one hand near his lethal slingshot, the other straying by his knife. At *this*, the other members of the caravan stopped.

'I am not so blind as not to see your lust for the Earth Mother—my companion. Why you live this lie when you know nothing about women or their ways I could not tell—' Leef-shadow started.

'We—all of us—know a little of the women's ways. And we all miss the touch of a woman. But *you* are dancing with a Devil,' Leef shouted.

'There are no Devils here. Only the Devils in your mind,' the boy shouted back.

Then Leef swept Leef-shadow up, before the boy could bring his weapons to bear, and he held him hovering between his mighty arms. 'We all know when Sister Sun creeps into a woman then she is made barren and can have no child. But if she creeps into a man then she takes his mind and he can have no ideas of his own. She *is* a Devil and has turned you into a Devil also,' the giant breathed in a voice that sounded too small for his huge, heaving chest. 'Leave my side, Devil worshipper, or I will kill you as I would a snake!' he suddenly roared and hurled the boy away to roll down the hill until he came to a stop against a tree.

Surprisingly it was the moderate Laelia who reacted first. She sprang at the giant with a cry of 'Monster!' and raked her hand down his startled face. Then she scurried down the hillside to cradle the groaning boy in her blue-gowned lap. Leef was so shocked at getting struck by one he openly despised, that he could only stand there, mouth agape.

Wunda burst into laughter and only stopped when Jynni glared at her from behind her veil.

Red Mond Star Light was still musing over the words the boy had spoken—'lust for the Earth Mother'—and was glad Kareen was not there to hear it. She had gone with Surrey Anne that day, on a herb-gathering expedition. He hardly heard Wunda say, 'The men will kill each other with no help from us,' before he heard the scream from Laelia.

A groggy Leef-shadow had awoken in the arms of his enemy, one from Little Jerusalem who had turned his mother and himself out. Still only half conscious he had slashed out with his knife, cutting her across the arm, and staggered to his feet. Now he was performing a zig-zag charge towards his giant adversary.

As fast as his damaged leg would allow him, Red Mond half limped, half hopped forwards to throw himself into the path of the irate youngster. 'There is one law, cous-cous, that we all must follow,' he gasped as he struggled with the blood-crazed boy. 'Never try to kill another clansman or woman of our Tribe.' He looked around at the gathered people. 'And this is our Tribe. It is the only reason we have survived so long by following this one law. It was the last law broken that brought the High Ones down to walk upon the earth with all the Devils yelping at their feet.'

'I hear you,' the boy hissed. His light-green eyes, glaring up at Red Mond Star Light, lost their blood-lust and he relaxed.

When he stood up Jynni stood beside him. But her face was white and pinched with anger. 'You truly *are* a man, to hurt a woman who was only trying to help you!'

Leef-shadow glanced sullenly around at a sobbing Laelia, who was being comforted by Wunda. He sensed all the angry glances he received from everyone in the camp, for the Blue Woman was a favourite of them, if only because she was so useless at everything. But all he knew was fighting and death. He had no time for remorse.

'This is a woman you hate and despise as much as I!' he barked at the enraged girl.

Her hand slapped him hard across the face so he rocked backwards, and again and again. Then she stood near him, nostrils flaring like a wild horse's and mauve eyes wild as smoke from a bushfire, daring him to hit her back.

Normally anyone who touched an Outsider violently died a sudden brutal death. That was *their* law because there was no place for forgiveness in their world. And—for a brief second—murder shone forth like a pale green beacon from the depths of his eyes. But then he spun around abruptly and loped away from the confrontation.

For almost a week after that they saw no sign of him. But Weerluk, on his own solitary hunting or scouting forays, sometimes spotted him roaming like some wild creature so there was no great fear in him being taken in a Nightstalker raid or wild animal attack.

When he came back he made his camp as far from Leef as he could. He also ignored Jynni for a while but, such is the power of the laughing Demon called Love, that soon his eyes would wander after her small slim clumsy form, with all the old signs of adoration.

As for Leef, his green eyes often strayed to the big-boned, voluptuous body of Kareen as she went about her business of soothing this sad piece of the country. And sad it was. Even the unbelievers like Laelia could feel the spirits crying out from among the cracks of the mountains.

But one day—one glorious day—they crested a steep hill and, spread out before them for miles and miles, was another vast and seemingly endless plain. This one was dotted with clumps of trees and blue lakes and the odd blue hill in the distance. But it was flat at last.

'Now the bowling is straying off stump, giving the batsmen plenty of room to use the bat,' Aybee said to Red Mond, who sensed the relief the others felt at the fact that there were no more mountains to climb. The last month had been horrendous and they had been extremely lucky not to lose anyone. As it was, Mungart often wheezed to a stop, with grey face and troubled eyes, while others, who had wounds less serious, were exhausted and strained.

'Soon we will be at Emceegee, the greatest shrine for the Cricketeers. I myself have only heard of this place, although our Cap Tan was there as a twelfth man.' Aybee smiled and his lean face softened and seemed almost kind. Then he turned to Red Mond.

'Soon also we will be at the place of departure of this world.' He saw the look in the Moon-talker's eyes. 'How do I know this, you ask? Because the Cricketeers have long been the guardians of the mountains and it is our business to know where not to tread or else we would—all of us—be dead by now. Prepare yourself, red hair, for you have a month at the most to enjoy life and loving and laughter.'

His black eyes shone with a strange excitement.

The day they came out onto the plains it was as if the very earth had decided to turn against them. An icy wind came down off the mountains and brought with it the heavy black clouds that had hovered over them for so many days, like birds of prey. Now a fierce biting rain drenched them to the bone, as they crouched at the foot of the mountain range. Violent bolts of lightning streaked across the sky in jagged motion or, with a tremendous crash, lit up the whole sky in a flickering, eerie blue light while thunder reverberated all around them. For the Ilkari, the Outsiders and Laelia, who had never really seen a serious storm before, it was most frightening. A vicious wind howled morbidly through the leaves of the few trees that waited to welcome them with shelter and wood for a much needed fire.

Red Mond Star Light and even Kareen knew that this storm was a sign of bad times. He cuddled up to S'shony, at least dry from the driving sheets of icy water that whipped around them. The cocoon shook with the forces of an angered Sister Earth and he wondered what sacred law he had broken now. His story so far was turning out to be a disaster. Only the regard for his woman and the company of his cousin kept him going. But it was true he had broken nearly every rule he knew, so perhaps he had broken one that he did not, he thought wryly. He fingered his soul stone given him by Baba and caressed the hair bracelet of his dead clansmen. *Here* was something he understood.

Kareen went out into the downpour and, although pelted vindictively by cold, hard rain, that at times was so cold it became pellets of ice, she performed a soothing ritual. By morning the sky was a dirty grey and the storm had passed over. But the message of warning was there for all to see.

Weerluk found his brother dreaming under a tree away from the main camp. 'Did you hear the stories our ancestors brought us last night or were you thinking of the black stranger? The woman whose skin is as black as those awesome-shaped clouds that brought the rain. The rain that will be tears in your eyes. Did you listen to them as you don't listen to me? Do you remember that a thunderstorm means the Waugal is upset?'

'I heard only rain on the roof of our miah and saw only lightning that I have seen a thousand times before,' Mungart said gently.

'This woman is taking away your spirit, brother,' Weerluk said sharply. But he could not be angry—only sad and confused. He rose up and walked away from the tree, alone as he had never been before.

This plain was different from the plain on the other side of the ranges. For one thing there was no sign of any Keepers of the Trees. This fact did not become obvious to any but Weerluk for quite a time. There *were* more signs of the white man's occupation than anywhere the two Keepers had been. Vast herds of cattle and horses, wild and untamed. Flocks of sheep, shaggy-coated and nervous, roamed the green, grassy wastelands. Groups of pigs snorted and rooted amongst great patches of vegetables or forests of old fruit trees. Turkeys, geese, ducks and chickens wandered everywhere and the larders of the caravan were never empty.

Surrey Anne would go for long walks by herself, spurning the companionship of even her two friends, Kareen and Laelia. She spent more time away from the camp than in it these days as she came to terms with her grief. Unbeknownst to her she was always safe because Mungart would shadow her wherever she went.

His chest wound was still worrying him, so he could no longer hunt as well as his brother. Like Leef-shadow, all reason had left Mungart's mind, and all the old laws went scattering to the wind.

There came a day when Sister Sun crept from behind the grey clouds upon the fast receding mountains and, once again, looked over her domain, with a watery, pale kind of power that was nothing like her fierce dominance of the northern country. The people in the caravan could have been the only people in the whole world, yet the presence of something evil—something that still lurked about from the Old Time—kept them alert and tense.

This place of dark splendour seemed also to have an air of great sorrow and abomination so it was no surprise when they came upon a huge pile of jumbled human bones that, even three thousand years after the event, still dotted the green plain in hideous, gleaming, white patterns.

They decided to camp the day, while Kareen performed a cleansing ritual to lay the spirits at peace. Even though the souls of the dead had long been taken by Sister Sun, it did not seem right to just leave the bones lying there.

Surrey Anne, as with the other two Visitors, had seen enough bones lying unburied and forgotten to really be upset by this scene. She took the opportunity to go out on her own, to where she had seen an old garden some two miles back. She was running low of some herbs and the tumbled-down remains of the building, with its garden and fruit trees, had seemed a likely place to find them.

She did not see Mungart creep off after her on dark silent feet, a dark silent look of desire in his eyes. But Weerluk's fierce gaze watched with a white intensity as his brother slid out of sight amongst the tall green grass and dotted eucalypts.

So they wandered over the undulating land until they came to the ancient remains of the farmhouse. As a rule, any Keepers kept away from these remains of European civilisation, not only because of the law that forbade associating with any of the white people, but also because often uneasy, restless spirits frequented the ruins of their home. Mungart paused while he watched Surrey Anne's figure melt into the cool shade of the foreign trees. A flurry of brilliant green parrots flew from the purple leaves of the twisted, old, flowering plum with a burst of wings and raucous shrieks. So, he thought, brothers and sisters of my Totem live here. It must be safe for me to follow. He knew there was no such thing as coincidence. Everything had a sign and a place in the life of a person and the sign here was interpreted by the youth as being good.

He crept closer to the young woman, following the path of her travels by the crackling of twigs and the murmuring of her song—soon broken by the short exclamations of delight, as she found the herbs she desired. The terrain here was dark and shadowed and the ground was covered with great, broken, gnarled boughs choked in tangled throngs of grass. But underfoot was soft from the layers of dead yellow grass and everywhere were the signs of civilisation dying from the relentless hands of time.

The youth followed the remnants of what had once been a wall around the fruit trees, keeping low and out of sight. In a break in the wall, made by the roots of one of the huge old trees, he settled among the crumbling, moss-covered bricks to watch the foreign black-woman spirit.

A shaft of sunlight had pierced the armour of the tough old trees and illuminated a patch of garden with yellow warmth. A host of brilliant butterflies played in the soft glare while Surrey Anne knelt in the middle, placing branches of a bush into her shoulder bag.

In certain places of the vast, unruly garden it could be seen that herds of the grass-eating animals of the plains had browsed. Yet none had come close to the ruins of the house. Hiding behind the erupting root of the twisted old tree, Mungart could also sense a foreboding about the place and he shivered.

Then his sharp eyes noticed a small blue wren, a brilliant speck of sapphire, become agitated from its perch in a branch of a small tree a little way behind Surrey Anne. At the same time he was able to discern a slight movement of grass, that went against the breath of the wind.

With a shout he rose from his spot of concealment, startling Surrey Anne. He could not yet see the source of danger but charged forward nonetheless, boomerang raised in readiness. His pounding feet took him past the confused woman and on to where he had seen the grass move.

Suddenly, just under his feet in the shadows and tangled grass, a slippery sleek black body rose in the air, orange belly afire from the sun's rays. It was the offspring of a snake whose ancestors had slithered down here from the mountains, centuries ago, and who had finished up in this dilapidated farmhouse. As each generation lived and died so they had grown in stature and cunning so that the gargantuan reptile, which faced Mungart now, reared some five feet in the air, with a fair proportion of its body still hidden in the grass.

The youth, terrified by the unexpected apparition swaying in front of him like some Demon from the dark earth, skidded to a halt and instinctively hurled his boomerang at the hissing black head.

He missed!

Then the monster struck, flashing through the air. Mungart was prepared this time and hurled his upper body sideways, spinning on his feet to face the giant snake who had disappeared into the grass as fast as it had appeared. From under his springing feet it whipped out its head and portion of its body again . . . and again. And Mungart, not as fit or agile as he had been, got caught up in the long skeins of grass and tripped. The gleaming, coiled body reared upwards, in preparation to strike downwards with its mighty fangs, when its small brain was distracted by a bag flying through the air and hitting it. As it turned its attack on this new enemy, Mungart sprang, and grabbing it around the neck, grappled with it for some hectic minutes before being able to snap its powerful neck.

He stood shaking beside the long, twitching orange and black coils of the biggest snake he had ever seen. He had a fear of snakes, as many of his people did. Always, in the Creation stories, the snakes were the ones never to trust. A snake could be the spirit of a dead person or the soul of an evil person. A snake was their Creator—but, more often than not, a snake was only the creator of bad luck and evil and was best avoided.

His frightened eyes went up to Surrey Anne's stricken face. She was not used to snakes on her Island. The few non-poisonous varieties were seldom seen. A tiny, timid Boa not eighteen inches long had been a sort of pet of hers. Her friend Porky had been bitten by a snake just as small and had died only a quarter of an hour later. But a vicious creature such as this was another trauma to be faced in this harsh land.

Mungart felt a rasping pain in his chest and doubled over coughing as his damaged lung took the brunt of all the activity. The young woman moved to him when the cruel coughs erupted from his mouth, shaking his chest. Her gentle, soft fingers touched his scarred body.

'You fine, Dreadie? Snake him duppi, me seh! But you tallowah man, yaah? Cho, he snake stand no chance, bwoy!'

He could not understand her lilting language but he was able to follow her meaning. He touched the hand upon his chest and gave the sign of everything all right as he formed a smile from the grimace on his face.

Then their eyes met properly for the first time since he had been injured. She remembered the many small gifts of feathers and pieces of coloured stones and the necklace made out of the lovely nuts, that she had found when she awoke in the morning after another dreamless, loveless night. She understood now why she had sometimes sensed herself not alone when she was out in the bush.

Here now stood a man just a little younger than Port Rial, with skin just a little lighter and hair in the same coiling dreadlocks—even though they were an unusual orange colour. The look in his ebony eyes was the same as her man had given her time and time again. A look of unadulterated admiration.

Her other hand reached out and tenderly traced the scars on his face, while his whole body and being went still at the closeness of one he had cherished from afar for so long. He felt a great warmth coming from his belly as he experienced feelings he had not felt since the death of his much loved Gurrewe. He went to say something—to tell her she was a black swan, a beautiful bird who came from the sky—but she raised a hand to his lips and smiled a quiet, contented smile while her eyes shone with an inner light.

'Hush now, yah. I-an'-I dey pon rhygin fi you. Me no dey pon un'erstan' what you seh,' she whispered.

Then her hand slid seductively down his hard flat stomach to his crotch. Here was what she *could* understand and her smile was wicked now. The scents of the two of them mingled as did their tranquil mutterings of desire and, finally, their bodies, as they sank to the soft earth. Strands of green grass fluttered over their sweat-shining, dark bodies and touched them as gently as the sun's rays—for even Sister Sun could not deny love when she saw it. Insects of many colours and shapes flew above their pounding bodies, butterflies hovered in the warm blue air, and crickets and cicadas echoed the passionate beating of their hearts. She opened up her soul to this shy silent youth and all of his vast silent land slid in with him as he became a part of her.

For a moment she could believe she was back in one of the many glades she and Port Rial had visited on their journey across this land, as her short but exquisitely formed legs locked around the back of her new lover. The thought was gone. This was her new life now. She had saved this youth from certain death and now he had saved her. She moaned in sheer delight as her new man possessed her and her fingers dug into his back while she claimed him for her own.

They stayed in that garden all afternoon and only left when the sun began to sink and the cold crept in over the plain. The last thing she did was cut off the giant snake's head and deftly skin its long length. It was her intention to make her new man a gift and she was so happy—so satiated after her long time barren of love—that she did not see the worried look flash across his face, before her peaceful smile made him smile too—such as he had not done in a very long while.

When they arrived back at the camp, Surrey Anne was not slow in telling her two companions about the giant snake, for it made a fine story. She did not need to tell Nanny and Cudjo Accompong about the new love this snake had inadvertently sparked and made fertile by its death. The look in the Keeper's eyes was enough.

Leef-shadow gave a rare grin and his hoarse whisper croaked out across the clearing. 'It looks as though the hunter has caught more than a kangaroo this time. I think he has caught a bundle of trouble.'

'Neither can understand the other, though. What use is a mate if you can't talk to each other?' Leef wanted to know.

'One is man and another woman. That is all that is needed to be known,' the boy said.

'A lot you would understand about that!' Wunda sneered from her and Jynni's fire. But her fingers rested protectively on the orange-haired girl's thigh.

All this Weerluk heard as he sat by his own fire and he knew they were talking about his brother. He also had watched them come in, hand in hand, across the plain and he felt a great emptiness in his chest. Now his angry eyes burnt into those who had spoken, so the Outsiders were reminded of the hostile protectiveness these aloof people held for their kind, and the two Sisters of the dark secrets of the land and all its laws this youth possessed. He ignored them, as only a Keeper could, and stood up, addressing his brother.

'You see already she has broken one of our laws. To leave the people of the snake alone. But if you *must* kill one, leave it where it lies, unless you eat it. Now the snake's partner will come to you for the skin of its companion,' he called out in his language.

Only Red Mond could follow most of what he said and his eyes were troubled as he pondered on what further calamity could occur. He might read signs in the cast of the stars and the light of the moon but he knew now the true signs were down here on Sister Earth. He had seen that, in all his travelling and meeting these strangers with their different beliefs. And who knew the land and her signs better than those who had been formed out of the land—the Keepers of the Trees.

As for Weerluk, he remembered another time and another snake on the mountain when the boy had rescued the orange-haired girl and all the friction it had caused and was still causing. There were no such things as coincidences, he told himself dourly and spat bitterly into his lonely fire.

The general feeling in the caravan was one of unease. The only one apparently happy was Aybee. Even the gentle Kareen could offer no comfort to the land all around her. It was in great pain, she told her cousin. There were certainly enough signs of the turmoil that had erupted here at the time the High Ones had walked upon the earth.

Often the remains of whole villages were found, with the bones and belongings of the dead scattered all over the ground.

It was even more disturbing as it became obvious, the further they moved south, the more recent the massacres: within the last hundred to fifty years even. The three Visitors, who knew about armoury, were surprised to notice no weapons had been used. No spear or sword, slingshot or axe such as these primitive people fought with. No bullet or grenade or modern weapon either. How these people had died was a mystery to the West Indians, who had travelled to many countries and seen more mysterious things than the rest could cram into their various lifetimes.

One day they passed close to an enormous blue lake, that lay still and serene under the turbulent grey sky. The Ilkari were getting used to the sight of so much water now. But, even so, it was Kareen's sacred duty to bless the water, so they decided to rest a day or two. It was one of the few places on this plain that they felt real peace. And S'shony, with her ungainly burden, was increasingly in need of peace now.

They made their various camps as usual, roughly keeping the cocoon in the midst of a circle. Mungart, Weerluk and Leef set out in various directions in search of meat for the evening meal. Surrey Anne and Laelia went down to the lakeside to search for wild-fowl eggs.

The two Sisters set up their camp on the lake side of the cocoon, in a small glade of paperbarks where there was privacy and plenty of wood.

'It has been weeks since our bodies have tasted water,' Jynni said softly and ran her slender fingers down Wunda's moonlike face. It was a special pleasure of theirs to bathe together and wash each other's bodies. The act of washing each other had always been the most sensuous of their love-making, when their fingers and mouths and limbs had explored each other and the cool water had caressed their entire bodies with a calm devotion.

'Perhaps I will join you later on,' Sister Earth replied.

The sunlight glinted off Jynni's orange hair, so it shone like fiery gold, and the sun's rays melted around her in loving kindness, so her lissom form was hinted at through the swirls of orange, red and yellow gossamer material that covered her body. Truly, she was a Sister of the Sun and the sun loved her as it loved no other.

Leef-shadow needed some firewood anyway, he told himself, and what harm could come from one so sweet and beautiful, his infatuated mind said. Her hard words could only cause him to walk away and he knew of no law that forbade a man—or woman for that matter—to look upon the other sex in admiration.

He waited until Wunda disappeared into the shadows of the trees before he hobbled off towards the lake. Just in case anyone was watching, he made his way towards where Surrey Anne and her friend were laughingly gathering up some of the dozens of eggs. He could hear their magnified voices from across the water as they splashed through the swampy edges.

He caught a far distant glimpse of Leef, as the giant waded knee deep through the water in search of food. Then, close by, he heard the soft lilt of a lullaby being sung.

He crept through the rustling reeds, as silent as a snake. Like the others, he sensed the serenity of this place. The feathery heads of the rushes nodded to him in friendly accord and made the journey easy for his crippled, clumsy body. And it seemed to the boy that, for the first time in his short life, everything had come together to make it his most perfect day. Birds were lazily winging overhead or calling out from the reeds about him; the sun shone down in benign splendour, robed in fleecy white clouds that lessened the intensity of the heat, and the girl he loved was singing just a few paces away.

Then he came upon the narrow beach made by the hard-packed grey mud, that was the lake's foundations. The reeds that kept this beach a secret from the rest of the world were tall and thick, taller even than Leef or the giant black man.

The girl had unwrapped her orange, red and yellow robes and veils like some wondrous creature emerging from a cocoon. He knelt spellbound in the sticky black mud as she shook her body out of her clothes.

How pale she looked in the white light of the sun. His mesmerised eyes could not move from the thatch of curling red hair between her thighs that burnt like the heart of the sun, into his mind. Once, in the desert, Leef and his band had come across a limestone mountain hurled into the air. Against the red desert and with the full glare of the cruel sun upon its face, its whiteness had nearly blinded him and made others of the band cry out in fear at such intensity and sharp beauty. But he knew now that her skin was even whiter than that cliff and the hair that covered her sacred place was even redder than the sands of his desert home—redder certainly than the hair on her head. He gave a soft cry at the newness and elegance of it all.

She paused from tying her hair up and her purple eyes glanced around for a moment. But she returned to her toilette and resumed her murmured lullaby, padding softly over the mud to the water.

She ducked her head under the water then came up, swishing her long wet hair into the sun while her face burst into a radiant smile and a gale of laughter broke away from her. A type of rainbow materialised briefly above her as the sun's rays caught the droplets flung from her hair.

He lay amongst the reeds and watched her duck and dive, float on her back or swim languidly. A feeling of warmth grew in his stomach and groin. A feeling he had not felt before—not even when Leef's huge hands had gently caressed him and his lips had kissed him. This was a feeling akin to the vague memory he had of his mother and the soft breast she had pushed into his hungry mouth.

At last she came out of the water, fully satisfied with her bath. As she rose her hands up into the air, giving her whole body to the sun, she sensed someone was watching her, with a fire that burnt into her back as bright as Sister Sun's.

Her mauve eyes turned and stared directly at where Leef-shadow lay hidden. For a moment, he was afraid, knowing the powers of these two women. Would she burn him to a crisp, with the special look it was said Sister Sun reserved for her carefully chosen victims, or would she torture him first?

She made no move to cover herself and a faint mocking smile played about her pink lips as she swayed seductively forwards, the mockery and seduction broken a little when she tripped on a piece of slippery mud and stumbled slightly. She still held her hands out to him, just as she had held them out to Sister Sun moments before.

'Where is the shadow of a leaf when there aren't any trees?' she breathed.

He crept out from hiding, his bright alert eyes downcast and confused for once. He felt ugly and useless in the clear gaze of her purple eyes.

'Look at me, Outsider! Tell me what you see,' she whispered.

He glanced briefly upwards but the sight of her wet naked body, so close, frightened him so that he started to shake and looked away.

She stepped up closer and ran a cool white hand down his face. He looked up now, straight into her eyes, with unflinching stare. Without the fluttering veil to hide them he saw how incredible the colour of her eyes were—and the look in them.

She had thought to humiliate him once again; to tease him with the promise of her body that she would give to no man ever again. But when she had lured him out into the open she had looked upon his smooth face and golden curls and remarkable eyes and had known a spark of desire she thought she would never feel again. Perhaps it was the magic of this place or the loveliness of the day or the feeling of raw sexuality that came upon her whenever she bathed, but the feeling of desire stirred in her.

'Don't be afraid, little one. You touched me once before, remember, and you saved my life. You did not burn then, did you? Touch me now and I will give you the life I owe you.'

Her lips were so close that her breath was upon his cheek in a soft wind. When she brushed her mouth against his, somehow it smelt of apples. She pulled away with a wicked smile.

'Come! Come, taste the sacred water, which I doubt you have for some time,' she laughed, dragging him towards the lake's shore.

He still could not speak, letting his eyes do all the talking as he tried to come to terms with this new emotion. They drifted all over her slim perfect body, noticing the drips of water in her hair and the freckles on her arms and legs and the moles on her left breast and thigh; and the faint healed scar that ran across her stomach and hips. This girl, whom Leef had called an evil witch, the most dangerous of any human; this girl, whom once he would have enjoyed killing. Leef would have growled that that was the first trick witches learnt—to disguise their true self under a cloak of gentility. And perhaps he was right! But, to the boy, as he allowed her pink-tipped fingers to undress him, Leef did not matter any more.

The undressing was swift since all he wore was his goatskin vest and a loose type of trousers. He did not feel deformed in front of her—not now. Disgust for his six-fingered hands, the hump on his back and the ugly lump of meat that was his foot did not exist in the clear light of her eyes.

He limped with her into the cool water until they were waist deep. She sensed he was uncertain in this new terrain, with new ideas and feelings swirling like currents in his head. It was new to her too, having a naked male so close . . . being invited by her to be so close. It went against all the laws of her Sisterhood and, yet, ever since the day he had rescued her from dropping off the cliff face, she had, little by little, let him *near*—but not into—her life. She had often wondered, as she mocked and scorned him, what it would be like to be loved by him.

She came to him now and wrapped arms as light as feathers around him, drawing him to her. He felt her pubic hair against his leg and, even in the water, sensed the heat from her body.

'Is it not curious, Outsider, that we are no strangers to love and—yet—we have never *really* loved any other of the opposite sex,' she murmured huskily.

'Was it love we had for our companions or only the need of a friend,' Leef-shadow muttered, speaking at last. He put his hands upon her smooth buttocks that shimmered yellow in the water. Never had he touched such a sensitive body before and, having touched, his mind exploded.

She stroked his damp curls and, with her fingertips, carved intricate patterns on his face and hairless chest and narrow, though heavily muscled, back. Especially was she fascinated by his hump and his six-fingered hands. Once it would have upset him to have someone pay so much attention to what had got him shunned from the safety of Little Jerusalem, but now he was almost proud of them.

'It's time,' she said softly. 'Time to see if all the stories our partners told us and we believed are true. Will you tear out my heart and eat it raw, in front of my dying eyes? Will I burn out your mind and so make you as weak and foolish as the talker to the ants?'

'I don't think so,' he murmured just as softly back.

She led him out onto the dry, hard, grey shore. But the mud was also soft as she laid him down upon it. With an elegant movement she swept the hair from her heart-shaped face and smiled down at his naked body. She gently sat down astride his body, her hair glowing like a second sun above his enraptured face and her eyes staring into him with a bright elation.

As far as love-making went perhaps it was not the greatest in history, for both had to explore and discover aspects of themselves they were nervous of, or unused to. But the feeling of true love far outreached that of carnal desire. The feeling that emanated from them could not have been any less than that which was commemorated in the legends of the Old Ones. Cleopatra and Mark Anthony, Romeo and Juliet, Nelson and Lady Hamilton, Samson and Delilah were all just ghosts of names from stories whispered to them by ghosts of family they no longer knew. This love, the love story of Jynni the Sister Sun and Leef-shadow the Outsider, would be passed down from mouth to mouth for centuries to come, so they believed as they rose in united passion. The relaxing rhythm of Jynni's body as it moved with his in the act of sexual pleasure—such as neither had known the act of sex to be—was *their* story. The craving mounted in their young bodies, to emerge at last in a throbbing, heart-rending climax that left her laughing and him crying and both one and happy and whole.

Jynni rolled off the satiated Leef-shadow with a deft movement, slipped herself into the water to cleanse herself, then began to dress, ignoring him. But she stopped to smile down at him slightly. 'The leaf has got a stem as well as a shadow, we see. Now I have given the gift of life to you in return for saving mine. But we must not let Wunda know of this. The rage of Sister Earth is terrible indeed—and unpredictable.'

'If I must share you with Sister Earth that does not worry me at all. Remember, I am also from the children of the earth and I love her for that,' Leef-shadow said.

'We shall see, shadow of the leaf. And if the leaf finds out that the shadow that he thought his own is that of another tree, what would he do then?' Jynni laughed.

'Who makes the shadows but the sun?' the boy countered, a smile playing upon his own face, then watched as her robed body tripped through the reeds.

He lay for a while upon the warm earth, letting the sun warm his body. This time he was not afraid of her warmth. He had just lain with a Sister of the Sun and was not dead. He was very much alive. He felt at ease with himself and with the world he had just discovered.

At last he roused himself and had another swim, then dressed himself lazily as he hummed snatches of the song he had heard her sing. He wandered off through the reeds, away from the camp. He wanted to retain the images of himself and Jynni in his memory so they would be with him forever.

So the boy did not hear the thrashing of the reeds as a weary Leef strode through the rushes, only wishing to get home as quickly as he could with the four dead ducks that dangled from his belt. He did not see the giant burst unexpectedly onto the small beach and, kneeling down by the water for a cool, refreshing drink, see the familiar and highly unique footprints of his companion in the mud by the shore. Then, seeing the footprints of a woman—and he knew which one straight away—beside them, Leef followed them slowly up the beach to where they had lain. He was an expert enough tracker to know what had probably happened.

He raised his shaven head and sniffed the breeze and told himself it was not what he scented that lingered there. The boy had only followed her, as he was wont to do and even followed her tracks down to the water. He would not be foolish enough to break the one law of the Outsiders and kiss a Sister Sun. Surely he knew that meant certain death, Leef tried to tell himself. But there was a deep pain in his green eyes when he rose from the crumpled mud, and there was an emptiness in his heart as big as the deserts he had left behind when he stumbled away.

CHAPTER SEVENTEEN

One day, far on the distant horizon, there appeared misty blue shapes—the same misty blue as the mountains now unseen behind them. Aybee was happy and even allowed himself a cruel smile that twisted his thin lips.

'Well,' he announced, 'it's been a good knock. I knew if we came down the track and used our feet the bowler would give us some loose deliveries.'

'It is another city,' Kareen murmured. 'Just like the Silver City.'

'You should give the batsman the benefit of the doubt,' Aybee retorted. 'This is Emceegee, our most sacred pitch.'

The white-robed Cricketeer had talked of little else as they crossed the plain. Now they were to see his cult's shrine. Perhaps they would see his God as well. And the jagged towers on the horizon looked safe enough. Certainly not as imposing as the mountains or as impressive as the towers of the Silver City.

Red Mond Star Light wished Akar Black Head were still alive to give a warrior's advice. Uneducated in the ways of the world, Akar Black Head had never been wrong when it came to the intuition of pitfalls. Culvato, too, would have known the meaning of the dark thoughts that nagged him in the back of his mind.

'We go on,' the Moon-talker said to his cousin. 'Besides, it is where the moon Goddess wants us to go. Soon we will face our enemy!'

'And who is our enemy?' Leef whispered, almost to himself although he was looking at Leef-shadow. 'Remember the city we once all left? Now we are to walk into another, like beasts with no knowledge of the terror within cities,' he spoke out loud to Red Mond. 'As well there are other things, smaller than cities,' he said to his young companion, who turned and limped away.

Every day they came closer to the city, that stood so silent and grey against the rushing black clouds, and the feeling of uneasiness grew in everyone's mind. It did not help that the fruitful green plain began gradually to give way to foul-smelling swamps and stagnant, algae-covered pools of filthy water and barren sandy patches. An icy wind blew in from the south and few animals could be seen or found by even their most skilled hunters. But the piles of human bones were still around.

The three Visitors had come across this scenery before, in the Northlands across from their Island, and they knew a nuclear strike had destroyed this city. Even after three thousand years they were sure there would still be radiation around and they were worried. But how could they hope to explain to the others what a nuclear explosion was and what it could do? The only good that could come of this, Nanny said, was that they might find some petrol in the ruins of this city and so go home to sanity and civilisation.

There was no time for love now.

Mungart still kept an eye on Surrey Anne and slept with her at night sometimes, by her fire. But he kept close to Weerluk too. This was their land, after all, even though they had never been here. They kept an eye out for signs of their people, but it was as though the Keepers of the Trees had never existed in this morbid place.

'Why must we stay? This could be one of the evil places on the land where no one, not even the elders, would dare go!' Mungart said one night.

'We must go on. It is something the elders back beyond the mountains told me. You will see,' his brother answered cryptically.

'Why go into this white man's place? Even here I feel the spirits screaming out in pain.'

'Because it is where our journey ends and our new world begins. Long I talked into the night with the Old Ones and they have shown me a dream. We must go into the city to make this dream come true.'

'Tell me what this dream is, brother.'

'Why? You dream only of one who snores beside you and keeps you warm and happy. What more dreams could you want?' Weerluk muttered.

In their worry they had come closer together again. But Weerluk insisted when Mungart came with him, hunting or scouting, he leave his much adored snakeskin belt with his woman.

The swamps now gradually turned into massive, tangled semi-jungle but the trees and shrubs were such as they had never seen before. *These* trees were not of this land at all, but trees the High Ones had planted from their own grotesque garden.

That this was nothing like the Silver City soon became obvious. Where the Silver City had been decorated by rearing, twisted, wonderful shapes all created from fertile, mighty minds, here there was only the remains of rubble underneath the overflowing greenery. That this had been a huge village, even bigger than the Silver City, could not be mistaken. But the masses of people who must have lived here were dead and gone. Not even birds dwelt in the abundant flowers of the many trees. It was quiet except for the noise of the caravan's erratic journey as they manoeuvered the horses and S'shony's wagon around the piles of fallen buildings.

Finally the jumbled rubble transformed to areas clear of trees, and with huge decaying remnants of once fantastic buildings. Everywhere the precious jewel known as glass was to be found, much to the Ilkari's surprise and delight. Kareen collected some lumps of the prettier colours to take home as gifts. Her eyes lit up as she thought of the favours she could get for some of these brilliant jewels in all shades of a rainbow. But she was not a greedy person and only kept a few.

The Islanders were the least worried by this dead city. They had come from their own Capital City that had also been destroyed by nuclear war. Then the other factional wars that had converted Kingston into its present ruined state: the Uprisings against the rich Middle Classes and the Army, the Ras Tafarian Wars and—last—the one that had driven her and her friends out of the Island—the great Muslim War. They knew that people could and did live in places like this.

As they came into the place where the crumbling buildings leered down at them with countless empty black eyes, Prince Michael stated:

My temptation is quiet
Here at life's end
Neither loose imagination
Nor the mill of the mind
Consuming its rat and bone,
Can make the truth known.

His cracked voice reverberated up and down the streets and thereafter they called the place, The City of Bones, for they felt they had indeed reached life's end and the buildings resembled nothing but a pile of bones and no-one seemed to know the truth anymore.

Now that they were in the centre and the misty, blue shapes, they had seen on the horizon, rose high and brown or grey around them, there was no sign of bones at all. Indeed, here it seemed almost clean and liveable.

The first place Aybee took them to, a place he recommended as safe from any evil souls, was just out of the canyons and ravines of this man-made landscape, down beside a wide stream that ran, dirty yellow-brown, through the city.

This area was huge in proportion and round of shape. Once they stepped inside, they were dwarfed by its aura, and history seemed to swamp them. The spirits of so many people seemed to call out to each of them in different ways. Massive walls kept the rest of the world out and tier after tier of what appeared to be seats looked down at them as they stood in the middle of a flat green ground that had been kept meticulously tidy by someone over the centuries. But what amazed them most of all was that, around the ground, huge towers soared up into the sky and on top of each tower was a mighty square that was as silver as the moon seen during the day; but when caressed by Sister Sun's hands they seemed to burn with a liquid white fire that turned them into pieces of the sun themselves.

She looks around at the awe-struck company—even Laelia—gaping about and staring with wide-eyed wonder and feels saddened by their ignorance and primeval lifestyle. How could they hope to succeed against their enemy, unless the enemy were as savage as they were? Even then they were vastly out-numbered. She looks at the one called Aybee with his dark eyes alight with worship. All she could see was an abandoned cricket ground in an abandoned city. A fine and spectacular cricket ground she knew, able to seat up to a hundred thousand people she guessed at a glance—but just a cricket ground all the same. Her people had been fine cricketers too, centuries ago, before more worldly affairs had forced the abandonment of such trivial pastimes. But these people are entirely ignorant of the game, or, like Aybee and his cult, worship it as a religion.

She turns away to talk to Cudjo Accompong, then the hairs on the back of her neck stand up as she hears the ghostly refrain of a chant and hears a mighty roar go up as from the mouths of thousands of people. She knows her giant friend hears it as well because his hands tighten on his rocket-launcher and he swivels uneasily around.

'This place is green with grass,' Leef suddenly rumbled to break the respectful silence, 'but it feels as dead as the deserts of our home. Why is that?'

'This place can never be dead,' Aybee said, in one of his rare normal speeches. 'This is hallowed ground, where the spirits of my ancestors walk. When we find the crimson orb, we shall bring it back here and they shall rise to walk on earth again. This is Emceegee, the most famous of our four sacred sites and the only one I have never visited even though it is so close to our mountain home.'

'It is a piece of grass in a building in a city,' Leef-shadow growled, in a parody of Akar Black Head that made the Moon-talker smile to himself. A dire smile gleamed on the boy's face.

'Outsiders have no Gods—or Goddesses either for that matter,' he muttered, glaring at Red Mond Star Light. 'We have only ourselves.'

'Yes, you are struggling to hit one off the square. Always attacking just off-side the leg stump,' the Cricketeer sneered.

'Why are we safe here?' Red Mond intervened to stop a fight.

'Sister Sun has sent guardians down to watch over us,' Wunda said, pointing at the towers. 'Never have we seen such power as this, have we, my Sister?'

'No, it is a gift from the sun,' Jynni said, but she did not seem so convinced. She darted a glimpse at Leef-shadow, then withdrew it quickly before Wunda noticed.

'I tell you it doesn't matter why this is safe. I *know* this is the last safe place you will see before you go to your deaths in the caves,' Aybee snarled, then wheeled away. 'I have played my innings as told by my Cap Tan. Now I will head for the dressing room.'

Jynni sprang forwards then and, swift as always, a knife appeared from nowhere in her hand. 'If it is so safe, why leave?' she purred.

'We think we would like you to stay for a while longer. Your conversations amuse us,' Wunda said, coming up on the side, her vicious sword swinging.

'Of course, as you wish,' Aybee demurred. 'A good aggressive stop at cover, that.' He turned to Red Mond Star Light. 'But I must go to pray now. Soon it will be stumps and we must organise a nightwatchman.' He pointed towards Prince Michael. 'Perhaps the twelfth man might be brought in to bat.'

As usual the Moon-talker found it difficult to follow Aybee's rhetoric but he assumed the Cricketeer wanted the songman to stand guard over the caravan. Why pick on the weakest one here, the one whose mind wandered as much as his feet so therefore was useless as a watchdog?

'We need no guards if we are safe as you say,' he replied, worry sharpening his reply.

'As you wish,' Aybee said again. 'No batsmen.'

Red Mond Star Light watched him walk away into the gloom of the coming night and wondered what would happen now. He sensed there was trouble and he had not even read the moon. These structures rising all around him reminded him of the buildings in the Silver City. He had decided long ago he hated this word city and here they were—in the City of the Bones.

That night they all camped on the green, flat ground. Once again, as various of them moved around the camp, they heard a muted roar or a chant and Mungart was sure he saw a section of the tiers erupt into a ghostly conflagration of figures, as they leapt to their feet and flung up their arms in some white man's form of celebration.

The next day, Red Mond took the two Outsiders and the two Keepers out to explore the city. Last night he had felt the baby in S'shony's womb move more vigorously than ever before and she had told him soon would be the time for its birth. The time for its birth and the time for them to go and face her people. Therefore he wanted to be absolutely certain that they were as safe as could be. So close to the caves. So close to the King of the Bats—the nemesis of the Ilkari that was a story *every* Ilkari knew. Soon he would see him face to face in the place where the moon never went. Of all that he had so far encountered on his travels, this was the most terrifying to imagine.

Leef strode out in front, the two Keepers warily scouted the sides and Leef-shadow brought up the rear. It was quiet and unsettling as they made their way through the city. Ostensibly this was a food-gathering expedition, but he was watching out for signs. This was, after all, the Gateway to the King of the Bats.

All morning, with hardly a word passing between them, they meandered through the city. Some parts were under water, where once there must have been land, for only the tops of the taller buildings stood out above the waterline, like so many small islands in the distance . . . or the heads of monsters creeping up onto the land to devour them at night.

We're poor little lambs who've lost our way,
Baa! Baa! Baa!
We're little black sheep who've gone astray
Baa—aa—aa!

came the echoing tones of Prince Michael, although he himself could not be seen yet. Then he appeared, as wild as ever, at the far end of a wide, though damaged, street.

Gentlemen rankers out on the spree,
Damned from here to Eternity
God ha' mercy on such as we.
Baa! Yah! Baa!

His feet were bare and his clothes were in tatters, Red Mond realised and felt sorry that, on the quiet part of the journey across the abundant plain before the mountains, no one had taken time to fix his clothes. Prince Michael of the Ants had spent enough time giving them advice and love and knowledge in his own way. Now he looked old and cold and ready to die.

As he came close to Leef he tripped and almost fell but the giant reached out a hand and steadied him in one of his gestures of affection and gentleness that constantly surprised the Moon-talker.

'Rest easy, old friend of the desert,' the giant breathed and he sat him down, courteous for one so huge and mean.

All at once, from all points it seemed, silent figures, as silent as the buildings and all dressed in garments as black as the gaping holes in the buildings, stood up from their places of concealment. There were dozens of them, imperceptible, indomitable and completely in control.

They moved swiftly down the broken hills of rubble. They were all small, slight people, as tiny as the Nightstalkers the Moon-talker thought uneasily, wondering if he had led half his force into a trap. They were only half Leef's height but when the giant reverted to his usual violent disposition, at this new threat, and took a swing at two of the figures, with his sword, another surprise was in store for the caravan.

For, in an effortless motion, one of the small figures tossed the giant over a slight shoulder sending his sword clattering. When he tried to rise, another flew through the air and kicked him in the head. The figure landed lightly on his feet and appeared about to send a hand crunching into the thick neck of the Outsider, but Prince Michael of the Ants staggered to his feet and pointed a wavering finger at the offender.

Your new-caught sullen peoples
Half-Devil and half-child.

Another voice broke the tension and the crowd of quiet, still, black forms shuffled back to let through a figure dressed in white, with yellow braiding. He seemed to float across the ground, he was so silent and there were those who remembered the flying women.

The white-gowned figure came up to Red Mond Star Light and he could see two fierce black eyes watching him—and that was all. There was a moment when he thought again they had met some form of cave person who could withstand the sun's rays. Maybe that was why they were clothed so heavily, he was thinking—when the figure undid his headscarf. He unwound it slowly without taking his eyes off Red Mond and then the Moon-talker had his first glimpse of a true Child of the Moon.

Even though the man before him was old, for the thin moustache above his lips was as grey as the fur of a wolf, his yellowish-brown face was unlined and his slits of eyes were full of a proud aliveness. The story about the Children of the Moon went that their skin was the same colour as the moon's yellow light and their hair was as black as the night around it. As were their eyes squeezed shut against the cruelty of Sister Sun who had banished them to live as outcasts, jealous of their creation at the hands of Father Moon. But Sister Earth had no love for them either, so they remained a hidden, reclusive Race, heard of only in story or song.

No wonder no one had heard of or seen them and treated them like a myth, if *this* was their Home Ground. A desolate place of death and emptiness—as desolate as their father, the moon, was said to be.

'Stranger, it is as well you come with women and old men. Has no one told you of the danger you are in?' the small man said, in a curious, lilting voice.

'We don't welcome strangers here, as you don't welcome us in your homes,' one of the black-gowned figures cried.

'How do we know they are not agents for the King of the Crooked Cross?' another called.

'My people forget their manners,' the man in front of Red Mond murmured. 'It is not often the barbarians from behind the ranges visit us and the only round eyes we see are the ones from under the ground.'

'They come with one of the white-gowns and even now camp in the Holy Ground of those people!' one of the black-robed figures said, stepping over to Prince Michael of the Ants and removing the headscarf. Upon which it was obvious that she was a woman. 'They bring one who wears the scars of death in his eyes. All this tells me they can be trusted.'

'Ho-Hsien-Ku speaks true. Long have been the poems passed down to our children's children that a band of strangers will one day come to our land to bring peace once more to our two Nations. Have you forgotten this poem already?' a taller figure said calmly.

There was a noticeable relaxation amongst the figures then. They came, chattering and whispering, down from their hills of rubble and crowded around the six travellers, wonderingly touching their clothes, faces and hair.

'My name is Han-shan and I am the poet of this city,' the tall one, who had spoken before, said to Red Mond. 'This is our Emperor, Fu-hsi,' he indicated the white-gowned man. 'I see by your eyes that you, too, are an Emperor. And the old man here is your poet,' he smiled as he unwrapped his scarf.

'Come. We shall eat in this honour of a poem coming true,' Fu-Hsi said. 'For this also is a hard task. To see a poem we recite in hope for centuries come true before our very eyes.'

As they picked their way amongst the rubble, Fu-Hsi told the story of the Children of the Moon.

Many hundreds of years ago this derelict place had been as fine a city as any the Gods could make. Unimaginable things of aesthetic form could be found here. But, under the surface, like maggots hiding in good meat, there had crawled and spawned much evil. So, when the Gods walked upon earth, this was the first place they destroyed . . . and destroyed completely.

Afterwards the humans gathered themselves, aimless and demoralised. Absolutely ruined in faith and esteem, they fell into three main groups.

The first main group left the ruins of their homes and lives and set off to start a new life across the ranges. This was by far the greatest group and, of course, they did not all leave together, but trickled away as adversity became too great for them. These were the ancestors of Red Mond Star Light and the other barbarians.

The second group elected to stay in the city and try to patch up what had once been a great civilisation. But gradually it became clear that these people would rather destroy the city further. Instead of soaring with the High Ones again they, like rabid rats left to themselves, would rather dance with the Devils in the dirt of the ruined old world. They thrived on hate and violence and their leader was known as the King of the Crooked Cross.

The third group—and the second that elected to stay in this poisoned city—was predominantly of Asiatic decent, those people now called the Children of the Moon by the barbarians. It was the dream of every Asian that they would one day return to their own land. It was why they waited by the water because that was where their journey would begin.

It was unfortunate that the minions of the King of the Crooked Cross vented most of their hatred against any who were not white-skinned and, especially, any Asians.

These two groups had been at war ever since the ending of the Old Time and the hatred each held for the other was unparalleled. The Children of the Moon carried few weapons, because they had no need of them. Over the centuries they had passed down certain disciplines and forms of defence once known only to a few monks or privileged ones.

Every form was based on the principle of using your body, or the other person's body, to defeat your opponent. Every child began learning these methods almost as soon as they could walk and it was a secret held only by the Children of the Moon.

The story had been passed down from family to family of the great poets that a man from the north would come one day with a collection of heroes and heroines infamous in stature, to descend into the caves and defeat their lifelong enemy. It was now only left to Fu-Hsi to choose two of his own people to follow with them into the depths of their Nemesis' home. For this also was mentioned in the poem. It was, in fact, the last stanza and the one every child among the Children of the Moon dreamed of—that they would be one of the two to go with the men and women of the poem and so bring honour to their family. The moment the King of the Crooked Cross was dead they were to rise to the top and tell the others waiting to join in the final battle.

Thus would the poem and history be completed and life would go on as it had before the Gods let loose this particular Devil upon the earth.

As Fu-Hsi finished his narrative the procession arrived at the huge circular structure so worshipped by the Cricketeer. Here the Children of the Moon halted.

'The Holy Ground of the white-gowned ones. We do not go in here just as they do not enter our temples. Only once a month a chosen few from among us clean the lawn and keep it tidy for any of the white-gowned ones' arrival,' Han-shan the poet said. 'For this life is balanced by good and bad, day and night, man and woman, sweet and sour and especially different beliefs from different Races. This is our most funda-mental belief and the one that keeps all wheels of the Universe turning. We call it Yin and Yang and so we go in circles of peace.'

'Or war!' the woman Hu-Hsien-Ku hissed in a voice not unlike S'shony's, so that Red Mond looked at her twice.

These people were very like the Nightstalkers he had seen: dark haired, dark eyed and small. They had association with the Cricketeer, whom he did not fully trust and they covered themselves from the sun. He didn't like this place. He could feel the death and decay that lived in the silent, stagnant city. Yet they had one belief that all Ilkari held—that the circle was an important emblem.

A hand rested on his shoulder and he turned to see the Emperor of the Children of the Moon studying him with quizzical eyes. 'Could you be the one the poets talk about? Already, one such character from the poem has come alive in our eyes.' He pointed at a glowering Leef. 'A giant, shaven-haired soldier of the King of the Crooked Cross, who joins the other side for the love of a woman and performs many deeds of valour.'

'We have watched you from the beginning of your arrival, waiting for a sign and re-studying the poem,' Hu-Hsien-Ku said. 'We are not a strong people anymore and soon our Race will be overwhelmed by our lifelong enemies.'

'It is told in the poem that help arrives in our darkest hour,' the poet interjected.

'But the poem is not yet finished. We do not know what happens when they go into the caves,' Fu-Hsi reminded Han-shan.

'Let us go and meet our poem. It is an honour to be present when words leap off the page in life and colour so we can touch them,' Hu-Hsien-Ku laughed and her hand went out to touch Leef-shadow's curly blond hair.

But when the boy jerked away and made to unsling his slingshot, there was a swift and remarkable change among the Children of the Moon. At once their relaxed attitude turned into one of defence. Their hands moved into stiffened attitudes of war and their feet took on a balanced stance. Just like snakes in the far-off deserts of the Ilkari, they moved slowly and menacingly, eyes watchful on the boy.

'My cous-cous has sharp reflexes,' Red Mond said quickly, to avert trouble. 'I am named Red Mond Star Light and in my religion I am a son of Father Moon—just as you are my brothers and sisters in my belief. You said a while ago that one of your wheels in your Universe was the acceptance of many different beliefs. We come in peace to do battle with our common enemy. Even though we all have different beliefs we all have the one enemy.'

'This, too, is mentioned in the poem!' Han-shan eagerly said.

The Emperor chose three to go into the sacred Holy Ground and meet with these barbarians. The first chosen was the poet Han-shan, then the slight Hu-Hsien-Ku, and one who was taller and more powerfully built than the rest, a man known as Yi, who carried a bow and quiver slung over his shoulders. His build, and the fact that he was one of the very few to carry a weapon, caused him to stand out from the crowd. He did not wear a scarf around his face. His eyes were calm yet cold and his face looked as though it were made of chiselled marble, like the faces of the Gods in the Hall of the Hill People. Attached to his belt was a golden instrument not unlike the trumpet of Gabriel, the Silver City's Gatekeeper, and this also put him apart from the others.

The first to see them was Cudjo Accompong who called out to Nanny. Here were a people, not even they, in all their sophistication, had seen. Anything unknown was a threat in Cudjo's eyes and he would not be taken by surprise like most of his dead countrymen had been on this flight into unheard of worlds.

The women gathered together, subconsciously taking strength from each other, and Aybee stayed hovering in the background, his eyes glittering and alert to any danger. For, even though this was his Holy Ground, trouble and mistrust were close friends in this city.

Jynni and Wunda fingered their swords, not even fully relaxing when they realised one of the strangers was a woman. Laelia gently probed the newcomers' minds and saw a whole new world there that frightened her because of its curious ideas and mighty hatreds. S'shony also retreated from their minds. She was too tired to grapple with new concepts now and, besides, *her* world was kicking at her womb, demanding to get out.

The only one not afraid was Kareen, who knew these people as Children of the Moon and therefore kin to her cousin.

The first meeting between people in a poem and people in a story was tentative and shy, each staring at the other and remembering all the words spoken about these mythical events that now had come true.

Then Fu-Hsi bowed down to the giant West Indian and opened his arms in embrace. 'The poem tells of a Thunder God who came with fierce black clouds and much lightning to tear open the earth and drag the King of the Crooked Cross out like a white wriggling worm. Now I know this poem to be true and these people to be true, for here, beside me, is the Thunder God and,' he indicated the two Island women, 'his two clouds.'

'We are saved from death and destruction,' breathed Han-shan, still not quite believing that he would be the poet to find words for the ending of the poem that had been handed down for centuries.

In a milling, noisy, excited procession they left the mighty building with its attendant huge towers. The dying rays of Sister Sun, orange and red in the cloud-filled sky, touched these towers and they flared as orange as fires. In some, it was a sign of foreboding but to the women Jynni and Wunda it was a sure sign of success and they relaxed their taut suspicions.

They moved through the dead city, skirting dark pools of black water, crouching in an awful silence, and the ruins of once impressive buildings. As they went on their way, more of the shrouded figures joined them, emerging from murky shadowy places, to follow hushed and muted in their wake. At last they reached the shores of this land of the Children of the Moon. Unlike the endless ocean that vibrantly caressed the edge of Little Jerusalem, with sparkling, blue, clean waves and the cry of seagulls constantly in the ears, this ocean was flat and empty—ruined as the city before it. The wrecks of buildings stood half buried in the lifeless smooth water. Here was where the main living area for the Children of the Moon lay, in a great entanglement of tents and dilapidated humpies. There were countless boats out on the water, also where people lived. All around, the destroyed city—empty except for memories of violence and catastrophe—looked down at this hive of activity.

But tonight was a celebration and the Children of the Moon were delighted with their guests. Fu-Hsi made them most welcome in the largest of the tents, with goatskin rugs and cushions.

It was a refined affair, with twirling graceful dancers and extraordinary acrobats. They were treated with awe and much respect. If this part of the poem was coming true then so would the other part be fulfilled: when they sailed back to the country of Asia.

Once again Han-shan told the poem passed down to him, while dancers took on the part of the characters. It was a moving and intricate piece of storytelling. Red Mond knew his friend, Akar Black Head, who enjoyed a good story almost as much as a good fight, would have delighted in it. He clasped Kareen's hand and smiled at her briefly. She was all he had now of his much-missed clan.

Some of the characters were hard to place. Leef was definitely there, a huge, angry ex-soldier of the one the poem called King of the Crooked Cross. Also there was a Dwarf—who could only have been Leef-shadow—with a slingshot as his chosen weapon. And both fall in love with a woman who changed their cold cruel ways. Red Mond glanced at his cousin, but she did not seem to notice the significance.

The Thunder God and his clouds were there and a character who was either Mungart or Weerluk. There was a songman like the crazy Prince Michael of the Ants. There were some women characters, too, who might have been Laelia, Jynni, with her orange hair as the girl had in the poem, and Kareen. But there were a lot of discrepancies between the poem and real life.

After the poem, a number of young men and women came out and gave a display of such dazzling speed and skill as none of the travellers had ever seen before. Twisting and turning and parrying each other's lethal blows, they were a great army in action. An army with no weapons yet with the ability to maim or kill.

'This is only to show you we are not a lost people,' Fu-Hsi explained politely. 'We prefer to do our drawings, tend our gardens and contemplate the intricacies of life. But,' he added ominously, 'if we are forced to fight for survival then we can do so.'

'The battle has been long and costly and we are glad to see the end in sight,' Han-shan said to Red Mond Star Light.

'We have chosen two to go into battle with you,' Fu-Hsi said. He stood and clapped his hands together, which brought the feast to a standstill.

He called out to the expectant throng. 'After much thought I have chosen the two who will go into the caves. Step forth now and into immortality, Hu-Hsien-Ku and the bowman Yi!'

There were hushed gasps and whispers and polite clapping as the two chosen ones stepped proudly, if a little shyly, forward and bowed their thanks to their Emperor, then fixed black emotionless eyes on Red Mond.

'They will follow you unto death, for, like you, death is no stranger to us and we embrace him most warmly. Why fear the inevitable?' Fu-Hsi faintly smiled. Then he spread his arms again into the air.

At once, there was a great cacophony of sound as coloured lights exploded in the sky and a number of cymbals and drums exploded into noise. The whole village—some eight thousand or so—began to move forward.

'It is time to go. Destiny awaits!' Han-shan called out above the festivity and the occupants of the tent were swept off their feet. Willingly or unwillingly they were hoisted onto shoulders and fell in behind a giant, gyrating, paper snake or lizard that wormed its way through the shouting, exuberant crowd. The face upon the creature was most fierce indeed and, every now and then, fire burst forth from its mouth, so it reminded some of the pirate Port Rial and the smoke that often trickled from *his* mouth.

Above the noise Mungart called to Weerluk, 'It is a snake, like the Creator of our land!'

He ran fingers over the snake-skin belt his woman had so lovingly made him. To him, it was a good sign, something concrete he could believe in amongst this world of strangers, but Weerluk remembered another snake and the woman from a different place who had stolen his brother's heart. The same woman who, only a pace or two away, swayed above the milling crowd, her black face shiny with amusement and joy. His eyes were troubled as he was swept along by this river of Asians.

Another who recognised a sign of good luck was Leef. He knew it was not a snake but a dragon, like the one tattooed on his chest, near his incriminating birthmark. It was one of the memories of his father, the sailor, who had had one on his arm, and it had been the desire of the boy to make his own dragon on his skin. He had done so, using the juices from different plants. Then, he knew, he would never forget his father and the good life he had led before being torn away.

The feast had taken up most of the night and the journey to their destination, with its dancing and ceremonies, took up the rest and most of the morning. By the time they arrived it was past midday and Sister Sun was sliding down the sky, to vanish beyond the far horizon.

Soon the buildings diminished and there was only wild garden, although it could be seen there had once been houses here. There were the remains of a river between two large cliffs and here the people stopped, suddenly all silent and expectant in the cold evening air.

Fu-Hsi moved forward. 'It is down there in the banks of the river the Gateway lies. It has been known for many years but we have waited for you to arrive. You must go alone now, with Hu-Hsien-Ku and Yi as your guides. Our people shall wait here for a message to say you have succeeded. Only then can we join in your victory for the poem must be adhered to, word by word.'

Red Mond Star Light and the others glanced down into the deep dark ravine and each felt the cold pulsating vibes that emanated from there.

A lone duck cried out and the sound drifted up from the rustling shadows of the trees. Kareen shivered and the thought crossed the Earth Mother's mind that she would never have dreamed of not being happy to see the sight of sacred water. But there it was! The still black water seemed like an open mouth to her, ready to swallow her body and spit out the bones, so they stood white and bare like the chalky white bodies of the trees beside the bank. *They* were draped in strangling green vines that slithered like snakes over their bare smooth torsos—like the hands of the cave people over her naked body before tearing her apart.

She turned and smiled a wan smile at her cousin and the look in her usually calm, grey eyes frightened him. She was the last of his clan. For all he knew, the entire clan of Violet Lynx Foot could have been wiped out and they were the only two left of that family, in all the world. Now this look in her eyes told him that she thought soon they, too, would be dead and gone, forgotten except in a dirge sung by any who may remember.

Then a hand touched his shoulder and he turned to see the craggy face of Prince Michael, who then set off down the narrow track that cut between the rocks and trees studding the hillside. One did not have to guess whose feet had made that track and, even to walk upon it, gave a thrill of fear, as if one had suddenly come across the fresh tracks of a wild tiger in a gently swaying, sunny field of tall grass.

These were our kin. These were the men who laid
Their lives down for a friend and for the world;
Who, in the darkest hour, their challenge hurled
Into the face of Fortune, undismayed.
Their youth was lovely as a shining blade
Swung singing in the sunlight to the skies,
And courage as a flame shone in their eyes,
Who met Death in the morning, unafraid.
The sharpest sword shall rust within the sheath,
The wind of age shall dim the brightest flame.
What is our life? It passes as a breath
Into nothingness from which it came.
But these are they who, dying, conquered death,
And live forever in the house of Fame.

Cracked and reedy his voice spiralled up out of the dark ravine and rang like the gloomy bell of the dead, that Red Mond vaguely remembered from one of the Ilkari women's tales.

'Let us go and crack some Night Bats' heads so their brains will spill across their black evil world like the Milky Way across our own,' grunted Leef. Which, for *him*, was quite lyrical. His shambling form followed the thin, shabby figure of the mad poet, his old friend.

Then, one by one, the others disappeared into the ravine, whilst the vast crowd above watched in total stillness and silence like the city that, in turn, watched over them.

327

Book Six

The Battle

CHAPTER EIGHTEEN

She watches with her black eyes, as they go down into the cleft of the earth. Cudjo Accompong, beside her, emanates apprehension in almost visible rays. They are going with hardly any weaponry to face an enemy and she knows he now feels he is just another human with very little left to give. They have seen this land can be as treacherous as their own. Yet, just as there is loveliness peeling back from the Blue Mountain to the green rolling hills of Surrey Anne's Parish, or the short, sharp, green rush of the Rio Cobre, or the more gentle surge of the Black River, then there is beauty here in this new land. A rugged, often violent beauty it is true, with mountains leaping out of the earth or huge red-purple patches of hot desert. The jewellery in this land, though, comes in small things: a red flower growing in a flat, dead environment, a small multi-coloured bird flitting across an empty blue sky, a smile on a green-eyed Keeper child. These small things will stay in her memory far longer than any of the more substantial wonders she has seen on her travels.

Surrey Anne has bid a tender leave of her horses and she has seen the girl caress each velvet nose in fondness. Thinking, no doubt, of Port Rial, who will be sorely missed on this sojourn.

Now Surrey Anne's comely hips sway ahead of her, her dreadlocks rocking from side to side. She, of all three, has taken most to the dress of her friend Kareen and wears now a fur vestkin. She lets her breasts flow free, like the Earth Mother. A blue veil from Laelia flutters around her face.

There was a time when she was shy and coy, saving her giggles for her man, Port Rial. She would have laughed at any who dressed as she did now, calling them Bo-bo or bongo or monkey-rial or quashie. How the ways of this land creep into us, like its fine red dust, so we are a part of it at last. How curious that we should be a part of this adventure when it really has nothing to do with us. Nanny wonders how her new companions would have handled landing in the middle of Kingston, during one of the Muslim Wars. How on earth would they have coped?

She hears Surrey Anne softly sing one of Port Rial's favourite songs, so even he is with them in this dangerous if exciting time. It is an ironical song given the circumstances.

Ambush in the night
All guns aiming at me

Ambush in the night
They opened fire on me
Ambush in the night
Protected by his Majesty.

The huge form of Leef brusquely brushes branches aside, his angry eyes ever wary for trouble. Beside him Leef-shadow nonchalantly farts as he hobbles along, the ever ready slingshot swinging from his hand. Mungart tries to suppress a laugh and says something to Weerluk, so even he grins at the back of the boy. The two women, Wunda and Jynni, seem to slide over the ground. Even so Jynni's clumsy feet find a rock and she tumbles forward, to be caught by Kareen. Wunda places a hand upon her arm in a gesture of closeness. Red Mond leads two horses that drag a smaller version of the wagon carrying the cocoon with the unseen woman inside. The two newcomers, these Children of the Moon, glide silently along beside him, keeping to themselves.

As they descend this final pathway it seems to her that for the only time on this entire trek every little thing becomes magnified: Cudjo Accompong coughing, Surrey Anne singing, Wunda burping, Leef-shadow farting, the body language of the two brothers as they converse with each other, the way Laelia runs a finger across her delicately formed nose when she is worried, Aybee's scratching of his spiky black hair, as though he had not a worry in the world. They are all humans and can die tomorrow, yet they are all so different. When they die they take their mannerisms and beliefs with them but the world rolls on. She allows herself a thought of Culvato and his flashing black eyes and flashing white mouth, both expressing his wild philosophy in thought and word. He had no beliefs except for himself. What would he have been doing now? Grinning like a Demon, devouring this sombre scene with his shining eyes, maybe singing a song to keep the mad Prince company in his rambling, or joining Surrey Anne in a duet?

Contrary to first impressions, this valley was actually quite peaceful in the afternoon light when they arrived at the bottom. There were many of the trees known as willows growing along the banks, drooping their feathery arms into the river. The water was not black. It was only the looming shadows of the cliff that made it appear so. In fact, it was quite clear and sweet to the taste. There were numerous grassy knolls and small beaches of pebbly pink sand. In all the places of the city this was—curiously enough as it was so close to the Gateway of the underground world—the only place they had seen birds. Several ducks were on the banks, near some reeds, and small birds flitted through the leaves of the trees. Out on the water three swans floated in serene grandeur. Weerluk's eyes lit up when he saw them and he grasped his brother in joyous embrace.

'See! Spirits watching over us.'

'And, look! Our own family . . . . Kawar,' Mungart smiled. He pointed at a purple-crowned lorikeet that watched them with bright black eyes and croaked a greeting through its wicked-looking black beak. Surrey Anne, watching their happiness together, saw this and almost believed that the parrot was talking to them. More so when Mungart mimicked its whistle perfectly. Then she shook her head. She was a Ras Tafarian and a Zionist . . . not an obeah like Saint Catherine had been. Only in the West Indian stories of her childhood, about the trickster Anancy the spider, could animals or birds converse with each other and humans.

She glanced again at Mungart, who wrestled playfully with his brother. She *did* love this youth and she knew he loved her. It was not a case of lust, either. Sometimes she thought it might be safer to kindly break apart the relationship now, before they got too close, for their two lives were so different. She really *did* have feelings for him and thought she could live with him in his country. He would die of a broken heart for his land, if she took him back to her Island. Would she also pine for her green land and blue, crashing seas? Just lately she had begun to say no, to herself. There was nothing there for her to go back to. But there was something heart-wrenching to know it existed. To know—and to know you would never see it again.

She decided to go and gather some herbs for her medicine bag, as she was sure they would need all the medicine they could carry. Besides, she wanted to be alone for a while with her confusing thoughts.

Again, she wanted to perform a little magic of her own for herself and for her man. She was not, in any way, involved in voodoo, but, like almost any woman in her part of the Island, she knew a little magic and she would use it now. She fingered her purple-pink crystal necklace and wished she could have used magic to protect her other man. Then she shook her head. She must not become like The Syrian, whose brilliant eyes had become lack-lustre at the loss of her man, Clarendon Jon, and so she had not been prepared for the wildcat that tore out her throat.

She smiled and waved at Mungart who, for a joke, mimicked her rolling, sway-backed walk and laughed after her. Weerluk seemed relaxed too, now that they were finally getting into the battle, for he smiled after her and even raised a hand in the gesture she knew meant 'see you later'.

The rest began setting up their camps. Although it was still daylight in this narrow valley, the sun had already lost her power. On the distant buildings, that pawed futilely at the sky in their tarnished splendour, Sister Sun still hurled golden lances, illuminating them so they appeared bleaker than ever. Red Mond Star Light was reminded of the decaying bones of some giant creature. Even more than the magnificent towers of the Silver City, these ruins made him feel as insignificant as an ant. With the soft twittering of birds around them here, though, there seemed to be an uneasy peace.

The Moon-talker looked up sharply at the sound of a soft footfall. The tall Child of the Moon stood before him, impassive and stolid.

'Tomorrow we go into the Gateway of Hell. It is but a short walk away,' he said.

'Then tonight will be our last night in our world,' Red Mond Star Light murmured back.

'Will you talk to your stars to find the pathway?' the woman Child of the Moon said, as she emerged soft and silent from the shadows.

'Perhaps.'

'Why do you not talk to this moon Goddess?' Yi asked.

He knew then that some plan of theirs was afloat and became uneasy.

'Even a Goddess needs her sleep,' he replied.

'You call us Children of the Moon. Might we not see our sister?' Hu-Hsien-Ku said softly, but there was a hard look in her eyes.

Kareen wandered over from her and Laelia's fire, to stand beside her cousin. She didn't need to be able to read minds to know there was trouble here.

'In our poem everything has come true, except for this one thing,' Yi said, his face stoic as ever. 'A cocoon that hides a hidden part of our story. No one knows how our poem ends. And, for now, our poem has ended. Tomorrow a new song will be sung.'

'We wish to know how to begin our first stanza,' Hu-Hsien-Ku breathed.

'It will begin with the rising of our other enemy, Sister Sun, and end with the beginning of a new world,' Kareen said mildly, although her body was tense.

'No one can enter this cocoon, for to do so would be to destroy us all.' Her grey eyes stared down at Red Mond Star Light and her callused fingers ran through his auburn braids. 'We, like you, are of the same clan and are the closest to each other in all the caravan. We have lost good friends in coming here but we are here, like you. Our Gods are different to yours and the Gods of those we face are different from both of ours. Let us go into battle as brothers and sisters of the flesh and not as Children of the Moon and Ilkari,' she concluded quietly.

By then, others had gathered about the little group.

'Let there be no secrets now!' Wunda said aggressively. 'In the light of her father, this last night, let her come forth in all her glory!'

'She is the one who led us here. Now let us praise her for the deaths we will inflict and the blood that will flow,' Leef rumbled, while beside him Aybee stared into the Moon-talker's eyes with his own merciless black eyes, a smirk fixed upon his pale face.

'I must go and speak to my father, the moon, and read the book of the stars,' Red Mond Star Light said and hurriedly made to move off.

'You do not mean those words, even as you speak,' an astute Jynni growled from the outskirts of the crowd. 'I love Wunda because I hate men, not because she is Sister Earth and I am Sister Sun. The fleshy temple of a woman's body is my desire and my domain. The moon and the sun are only dead rocks—as are the stars. The earth is the dust of our dead bodies.'

After this blasphemy, she bent and picked up a handful of dirt and threw it on to Red Mond's fire. 'Go and talk to your dead rock, you foolish man.'

'The moon is my father. I was born under his rays on the highest place in our land, the rooftop of the world.'

'Now you know it is *not* the rooftop of the world, though. What else can only be illusion?' Jynni laughed.

'He came into my body as I was born and the light of his wisdom shines through my eyes,' Red Mond said as he walked away, but the orange-haired girl's derisive laughter ripped into him.

As he made his way through the trees, he sensed someone else fall in beside him then heard the rasping voice of Prince Michael:

The intellect of man is forced to choose
Perfection of the life or of the work,
And if it take the second must refuse
A heavenly mansion raging in the dark.

'Leave me!' he cried. 'You are a foolish old man and I have much to do!'

Yet he knew that, once again, the man's rambling had hit upon a truth. Who was he if he was a Moon-talker and the moon *was* only a dead rock? Maniacs talked to rocks out in the deserts when the sun fried their brains.

Everyone thought they were led by a Goddess when they were led by a girl younger than Jynni, who was heavy with an unknown man's child and whom they—every one of them—would enjoy killing. Then the words that Jynni had just spoken were true as well. All the wondrous, amazing and—yes!—cruel things he had seen made him realise the Ilkari were an ignorant people and all their great beliefs and stories *were* as dust of dead bodies. Nothing could ever be the same again.

Back in the camp the Children of the Moon, Wunda, Jynni, Leef and Leef-shadow stood in a group, tense and uncertain.

'Let us visit the cocoon of our friend,' Aybee called, in one of his few understandable comments, and glided forward.

Behind Kareen there appeared the two Keepers. They could not understand all that was said, but, in the not so distant past, the red-haired one had the seed of their people in him so that made him a brother and they moved now to protect his female relation.

They, at least, held strongly to their stories and they knew the moon and sun were not dead rocks at all. Nothing in this land was dead, even the ghosts who walked upon it were alive as spirits. If there was a tear from the moon in this cocoon then they would defend it—and their brother's possessions—with their lives.

Their wild black eyes bit into Aybee's own. But the Cricketeer gave his strange smile that carried no warmth and moved back, so the others also drifted to their fires.

Leef-shadow squatted down beside his own small fire and lovingly caressed his knife with a whetstone. His hard eyes lit up at the thought of all the killing tomorrow. Then he heard again the call of ducks off in the reeds and his thoughts turned to more urgent matters. A nice fat duck would make a change for his last meal above ground. He had not had duck since . . . since he had met with Jynni on that beautiful lake.

An emptiness filled his belly. He wondered if he would ever again taste her body and all the delights it held.

He gave his knife one last wipe across the stone, enjoying the slick sound it made. Then he tested its sharpness on his finger and licked away the blood. He put it in its sheath and moved off towards the river.

Using all the skills he had honed in a lifetime of constant expectation of peril, he moved through the gently rustling reeds. There was nary a sound despite his dragging club foot. His six fingers grasped his ging in an ever ready capable hand.

There! Sitting complacently upon the water in the blue twilight, dreaming whatever dreams ducks had. In an instant he had loaded and fired, the round hard pebble smashing those dreams bloodily into the still, quiet water. Frogs croaked their applause at a job well done. He waded out and gathered up the still warm body.

As he made his way back through the reeds, he tensed suddenly at a slight sound that was neither bird nor animal. He dropped his prize, spinning around, loaded ging in one hand and knife in the other.

'A little warrior to the very end,' Jynni murmured as she stepped out of her hiding place.

'It is my life,' he answered simply.

'And such a young life to have such violent thoughts.'

'You, also,' he countered, 'are young to have such a hate of this world.'

'It is what this world has done to me. That is the nature of our world. We either die—or we live as violent as the whole world and all its cruelties,' she breathed as she floated towards him, her bright robes brushing the ground.

He was still not sure if she was playing one of her hurtful games, for she had scarcely spoken to him, even in spite, since the lake. She lifted her veil and stared at him with eyes the colour of the darkening sky. She reached out a pale, long-fingered hand and brushed his face in the way he had dreamed of so many nights.

'The time has come, would you not say, for love to once more creep into this world of ours?' she whispered.

Then she put her arms around his deformed shoulders and drew him to her. Tantalisingly she moved her lips forward slowly and softly—moistly—kissed his hard mouth. She was more composed than before and made every moment last longer as she kissed him on the mouth, cheeks, his eyes and then his neck, nibbling at his ears. His whole being burned with the want of her. He wrapped his arms around her slender waist, breathing rapidly with desire. Then she pulled away and smiled down at him, her eyes alight with a mischievous fire.

'You men are all the same, with only one thought inside your head. To breed more men so you can be all powerful. But that is the gift of a woman. We only need you for a certain time but you desire us forever.'

She laughed softly as she slowly undid her robes so her shoulders and breasts fell free of the cloth.

'Is your tongue melting, little one? Don't you know to kiss Sister Sun is death for any man? They shrivel up inside and their brain drops out their arsehole,' she giggled and moved sensuously in front of him.

'Why did you say what you did to Red Mond Star Light? Can they be true words and Sister Sun was never the wife of Father Moon nor the sister to earth?' Leef-shadow said at last.

'Does it matter? We are here, that is all. Tomorrow we might be dead.'

'Then why were we cast out as imperfect? And how do you explain the black ones who fell from the sky?'

'How do you explain the patterns on a butterfly's wings that become a face? How can you explain the birth of a perfect flower or the death of a star?'

She moved towards him then and nibbled his ear again, while he felt the heat from her body and her firm hot breasts rub against him.

'There is only one thing that I can know,' he whispered. 'I was born to kill the Night Bats—and to love you as I have only loved Leef before.'

'Then let us go to a place where only love may be found,' she whispered back.

She led him away through the reeds, hand in hand. The twilight songs of the birds rang drowsily in their ears and the distant noise of the camp was another song.

'If it were true that Sister Sun loved Sister Earth more than her husband and, thus, any woman loving another woman was cursed forever from the sight of man, then do you think you would still be alive, little warrior?' Jynni smiled quietly back at him. 'Love is love and a very powerful emotion indeed.' She caressed his cheek with her fingers, in her own particular way of devotion.

They stepped forth onto a tiny secluded beach, watched over by a huge, gnarled, old willow tree that protectively threw haphazard shadows over the grainy sand.

'This is a place I found earlier on today,' she said and slipped out of the rest of her robes. Even in the dark, her skin gleamed with a vibrant energy.

He, too, divested himself of his meagre attire and they closed in upon one another, all thoughts centred on the pleasure they knew was about to come. As he laid her down on the cool sands, she flung out an arm.

She touched something and half turned her head. Then she was up on her feet in a flash, while her head snaked around and her nostrils dilated as she sniffed out any sign of peril. Leef-shadow fumbled for his knife, uncertain of what was happening; his mind still befuddled with more peaceful notions than battle.

They both saw it at once.

The sand was scuffled with splashes of bright red blood mixed stickily with the smooth pink stones of the beach and there were drag marks leading to a dark opening under the archway made by the grotesque roots of the enormous tree, looking like the legs of a giant spider. One of Surrey Anne's boots and her bag of herbs were all that were left of her. Even her precious weapon, that could not save her this time, was gone.

Leef-shadow shuddered, horror flooding his mind rather than hatred. Even in the midst of this bliss, that this new feeling love could give him, there was death and murder. What, he thought desolately, was the use of it all?

Jynni's arms were around him again. This time not as a lover, or a woman who demanded love, but as a friend who could see that, for all his vicious ways, here was just a boy who could feel pain as any other child could.

'We must go and tell the others in case they come again. She has not long been stolen, you can tell,' she whispered kindly.

When Red Mond Star Light came back from his lone walk he entered a silent camp and knew at once there was something drastically wrong. Everyone was gathered to meet him, with cold faces and accusing eyes. Only Kareen seemed saddened and confused.

It was Mungart who broke the silence, speaking in the language both understood. 'You walk with death as your brother. All who were close to you have died or disappeared, except the Earth Mother. When we first met, you were burying your brothers and it was not long after *that* that death visited my sister. Now the healer is gone and you could not even see it in your stars!'

It was the very quietness of Surrey Anne's death that was the most shocking of all. She had been within sight and sound of the camp but they had heard nothing. They were used to wild shouting melees with screaming and yelling and lots of noise. But this peaceful—yet hazardous—place had taken away a friend, with the stealth of a creeping monster from one of the Ilkari women's tales. It was impossible to believe her last sound on earth would have been a horrified gurgling squeal or that her plump torso, even now, was being bloodily torn apart, to be shared as food.

The look in Nanny's eyes as she stood under the protection of her huge companion told it all. He made to move towards her, to comfort her. But she shrank from his touch, nestling back into the man mountain beside her, who also stared down at him with hate in his eyes. This hurt him more than any physical wound he had endured on this journey.

'Why couldn't your stars tell of the healer's death?' Jynni scoffed, eyes dark with scorn. 'Why couldn't your Goddess tell about the woman who flew down from the sky and yet was eaten by the earth?'

Laelia moved up to the red-haired youth and put a pale arm around his shoulders. 'Let us rest while we can. It does no good to fight among ourselves. My friend and our sister is dead and we will avenge her death soon. Many of us will die before this battle is over and those of us who live must bond together all the more strongly than before. This is what my comrade, Surrey Anne, would want.'

Her soft voice murmured over the company and Red Mond Star Light was reminded of the Silver City and the welcome they received. Laelia stood for everything that that city could have been. Her calming influence was not strong enough for *this* grief, though.

Mungart stared the Moon-talker down, with angry black eyes. 'You are not my brother,' he said at last and stalked off to his lonely fire.

'She gel grow fe like unu life, maan. She love-love man yah. Do you see what 'appens if you forget who you are?' Cudjo Accompong's bass voice rumbled and he placed a huge hand over Nanny's shoulder. 'Rasta help unu. But we coo pon fe I-an'-I first.'

'We nah be Gods. Me only human an' can die jus' like unu, yaah?' Nanny said sharply and loudly.

The Moon-talker made his way to the cocoon, where S'shony waited. He was not only distressed at Surrey Anne's death and Mungart's hatred of him, he was worried that during his time away he had not been able to read one message from the stars. A huge blanket of cloud had swept away the pages of the book of the moon and there was just a swirling grey mass above him on this, his last chance to read their destiny. Far off, amidst the discarded buildings, the flicker of lightning had trembled and there was the faint cry of thunder. Just before the heavy rolling clouds had blotted out the sky, a falling star had revealed that death by cowardice would be the lot of one, but he had not been able to tell who.

He ducked through the skins and into his little world. The familiar smells engulfed him and the sight of the mundane objects soothed his eyes. The woman he worshipped and who had become his whole life lay on the bed of skins and furs. But now her sloe eyes gazed up at him with fear—an emotion he had rarely seen in those dark depths. She was curled into as small a ball as her pregnant stomach would allow and sweat shone on her white face.

'I tried to warn her. I tried to get into her mind but I was too late. It happened so fast. I called to those outside, but they did not understand.' She stared in agony up into his face. 'It is dreadful to live someone's death. Especially when she was killed by my own people. I never want to live that again for it will surely destroy me,' she gasped. 'Now they really *will* hate me and we shall all die!' she moaned.

He put a hand to her trembling shoulder. 'Tomorrow the Children of the Moon say we will arrive at the caves.'

Her eyes looked bleakly into his from out of her tear-stained face. 'Tomorrow something else will arrive and one of the women I needed to be here is gone. Hatred is here now—for you as well as for my people. Is *this* a world to bring a child into?'

His eyes were subdued as he stared at her. The birth of a baby was a truly wonderful thing for the Ilkari, being as it was such an infrequent event. On all his travels he had hardly seen any small babies and they had mostly been Keeper babies. He had known there would be difficulties faced when the rest found out who S'shony was, but he had counted on the miracle of birth to stay their anger. Now a young woman, also with the gift of motherhood, had been taken, maybe even by another woman, to be eaten in the caves of the walking dead.

Another thing bothered him as well. The people this caravan now numbered, after the death of Surrey Anne, was sixteen and in the Ilkari beliefs there were three unlucky numbers. These were sixteen, twelve and ninety-nine because it was on the sixteenth day of the twelfth moon of the ninety-ninth year, three thousand years before, that the High Ones had walked upon earth and all of life had changed. This was an unequivocal truth and could not be denied.

They were going into the greatest risk of their lives with the most unlucky number. For tradition predicted the first was the worst. He was the clan's Moon-talker and this was *his* journey, *his* story, and nothing had gone right from the very beginning. Why should he hope for anything to go right now?

He sank into a fit of depression not even his woman could comfort him out of. She was just as upset as he, for different reasons. All around the camp, that last night, was unhappiness. There were those who checked and rechecked their weapons, those who mourned the recent death of their friend, those who kept a sharp-eyed look out for further enemy.

And everyone wondered what tomorrow would bring.

The morning brought the sun, a little more watery than usual as it had to battle through a mass of heaving, squirming grey clouds that cluttered the horizon. And any who knew would have said this was unusual for this time of the year—another ominous sign.

The clouds glowed red and orange and lesser shades of pink or purple, all the way across the sky. Many wondrous shapes and patterns were thus obtained but no one had any inclination to study or admire them.

The river wound under the cliffs, amongst the tall twisted trees, and they followed it closely, subconsciously falling into a battle formation. The two Children of the Moon led the way, flanked by Jynni and Wunda on one side and Mungart on the other. Weerluk, after some argument, helped carry the cocoon, since it was too narrow and slippery a pathway for horses. There was the distinct feeling that no one cared if they left this *'Goddess'* behind. Today all trust in Gods and Goddesses seemed to have faded altogether. But Weerluk had whispered to his brother that he could smell the scent of motherhood on this Goddess whom their white brother so protected. Babies in their world, as in Red Mond's, were most precious.

'If she's having a baby, we should leave until she has it,' Mungart had whispered back, knowing the laws of his people meant only women could be present at birth.

'When she has it. It will not be long now and we shall not leave, but just move away. I would live forever before seeing a baby born from a God,' Weerluk had replied, his eyes lighting up in an uncommon spark of merriment.

So Mungart moved moodily along, his whole body tensed for war. Roving on the sides were Leef-shadow and Nanny, since their two giant companions also carried the cocoon, rocking on their broad shoulders. Kareen walked behind with Laelia, the blue-robed woman sending out mind probes, and Kareen probing with her sharp grey eyes. They both missed their happy companion very much. Kareen was also worried about her cousin, who was the fourth bearer of the cocoon. Aybee glided everywhere as did Prince Michael of the Ants, who seemed to spend a lot of time this day talking to his little ant friends. So they were a tight-knit group as they made their way through the whispering trees, along the bank of the chuckling river.

As the sun rose higher, so the clouds, bunched up on the horizon, spread out across the sky—as though trying to hide the violation of Sister Earth's most secret womb from the eyes of Sister Sun. The day loomed hot, humid and heavy. The dark water looked inviting and yet unsafe, and there were no more birds to be seen or heard.

It was Mungart who first sensed them, followed closely by Laelia who let out a little gasp.

There was a whistle from up-river and a bird call from behind. Then, as though being born from the rocks and trees whose shadows they stepped from, about a hundred Keepers of the Trees surrounded them silently. Another hundred or so appeared up ahead and behind them as well.

The leader greeted Weerluk with a shout of recognition, for it was none other than Arakui of the Platypus Totem. But the others came from different regions. Even as far back as the desert of the Ilkari, Red Mond Star Light noticed, for one had the feathers of a bird found only there in his hair. Then there were darker Keepers that came from the coastal plains, with coloured shell necklaces. There were some from the brothers' own land whom they greeted with smiles and familiar language. They were young men from all over the land and from many Totems. The sacred colours of the Keepers, the red, black and yellow splashes of brilliance, were everywhere to be seen. The leader carried a green branch in his hand as a sign of peace.

'The fires have told many stories, my brother,' Arakui spoke to Weerluk. 'But the most interesting story is of two of our brothers, who yet are one, who follow the white men on white men's business.'

'We knew you would come,' Weerluk said. 'It is as the old men told me would happen. We have left the same story at every camp. We go to kill the Djanaks for whom—not one of us—have forgotten their pain.'

'Then, you see, we have listened for here we now are—every one of us have ghosts of our dead to find and we have gathered a great force, that waits, even now, where none of us have waited before. Although some of us knew about this place. It is one of the Creation stories of our Totem.'

'It is an evil place where not even spirits dwell. A dead place,' one from the coastal plains said.

'Yet we have come to be with the purple-crowned lorrikeet,' called another who was close kin to the twins. 'How could the smoker parrot not fight alongside his old friend. My name itself is Kooraa.'

'We shall bring you to our camp and to the gates of the underground world,' Arakui said. 'I see you still have the gift I gave you those many days ago.' He smiled at Weerluk.

'And many is the Djanak who has felt the poisoned spur of the Platypus,' Mungart answered.

The great crowd of warriors swept noiselessly through the bush, often casting shy glances at the white people. The Outsiders were notably nervous at this vast gathering of their old enemies for there were some from their own part of the country, who might set about paying back old grudges. Like Mungart and Weerluk, the other Keepers were at first apprehensive and then curious at the paleness of Laelia's, Jynni's and the Cricketeer's skin. Every Keeper was apprehensive to be in the company of white people, at a spot many of their stories told was a cold and perilous place upon their land.

Then they arrived at a huge, jagged gap in the cliff face. The rocks that had belonged there were strewn in great grey piles among the trees, the shore of the river, or in the river itself. It was as though a High One's hand had reached out into the cliff and torn out the innards. An almighty cave snaked back into gloomy obscurity and the waters of the river flowed into the cave. No trees grew here and on the desolate grey beach camped perhaps another eight hundred Keepers from every Totem ever mentioned. Their dark eyes washed over the members of the caravan as they made their entrance onto the beach. Some had never before seen a white person, so there was hardly friendship. They had come only at a Keeper's request and the wishes of their various elders.

It seemed to many they were breaking every single law of their strictly coded life and they were not happy. However, the common enemy was the one that went under many names, but who loved fresh warm flesh, be it Keeper or white man's meat, and they plucked that flesh like berries from a bush. They had also all heard of the other black Tribe, not Keepers of the Trees, who carried thunderous, incredible weapons and this was a story they desired to see.

'Let us dance, brother, to welcome you and drive away bad spirits and also bring you luck,' Arakui said.

It was not only a dance but an intricate part of structured life. A dance was their way of telling a story and there was no thought in the Moon-talker's mind of refusing it.

Besides, there was a more pressing problem. As he had carried the cocoon along through the forest, S'shony had sent a mind message to him. She was about to have the baby.

The dance of the Keepers of the Trees at the gateway to the bastion of death and destruction, that had been their Nemesis for three thousand years, was probably the greatest dance ever performed. It was certainly the first *sacred* dance any of the travellers had ever seen, so that in itself made it special. It was the first and last really great dance performed by these people, so close to the land . . . so aloof to other humans, because never again would so many Totems gather together from such diverse regions. For once, all were united and they united in this magnificent dance.

Every man took on the persona of his Totem. It was a graceful dance, as they leapt and gyrated upon that empty shore. It seemed as though every bird and animal in this land had gathered at this lifeless place as kangaroo, emu, dingo, possum, wombat, lizard, crocodile, scores of birds and fish and other animals descended onto the beach, with the thudding of feet, dirge of didgeridoo and clacking of boomerangs the only sound.

In the midst of this dance, Red Mond Star Light knew that the time for his woman had come. He called his cousin softly to his side. Few noticed them as they made their way to the cocoon. Red Mond touched Kareen on her arm and ran his fingers lightly over the scars there.

'She is about to have the baby. All I can tell you is don't believe everything you see. A drop of rain does not make a storm you once told me, remember, cousin-true.'

Then Laelia joined them. The blue-gowned woman had had a mind probe from her distressed friend in the cocoon, as the pain brought her barriers down. Now Laelia hurried over to help Kareen.

The tall, tawny-haired woman crouched down at the entrance, in awe at entering the domain of one she, at least, still believed to be a sort of Goddess. She tentatively pushed aside the skin covers, musing over what her cousin had just said. She crept forward, soft and shy, the first of them all to meet the Goddess they had protected and wondered at for so long. Laelia crept behind.

It took a moment for her grey eyes to adjust to the gloom. Then, over in the corner, spread-eagled on a bed of skins and furs, lying on Akar Black Head's bear skin, she saw her.

At once, Kareen's eyes dilated in shock and fear at this massive trickery and her hand sprang for her sword. But Laelia saw the movement and sent out a calming vibration that lulled the warrior woman's mind just long enough for her to see this girl was in labour and great pain. So she became the Earth Mother again, where it was her duty to ensure all living things had a chance to survive.

Even so, her fingers recoiled at touching the cold white skin of the grunting, sweating girl and she could not look into the black depths of the Nightstalker's eyes. Laelia went out to fetch some water and the two were alone.

'You are the cousin in blood to my man and he has told me much about you,' S'shony gasped. 'He has told me you are the greatest healer in your clan and you would help me in my trouble.'

Kareen hesitantly touched her long black braids, the first time she had touched a live Nightstalker. 'Your man was right,' she murmured back.

So was *her* man right too, she thought wryly. The only one to be so and yet everyone had thought him slow-witted. Akar Black Head, would you laugh heartily at the joke the Moon-talker has played on us or would you have chopped off her head with your mighty axe? Would you see as I do that here lies not a Goddess, not an enemy, but a girl who is just that—a girl who is small as her people are and frail from lack of exercise, who is about to have a difficult birth? It would be hard to save both her and the baby's life but she would try. These were the thoughts of Kareen as Laelia came back with her bowl of water.

As Laelia went through the entrance, Wunda noticed and nudged Jynni. 'The blue-robed fool who fell into the lying love of a man has dared enter another man's castle. We think we should also invade this man's domain and visit our sister of the moon at last!'

They glided towards the cocoon, only to be met by an agitated Red Mond Star Light. 'No one goes into the cocoon.'

'Laelia went there,' Jynni said.

'She is a healer and a woman. Both are needed now.'

'We are women also. More so than Laelia, who fouls her mind with thoughts of men. We are pure women,' Wunda said.

'You are warriors,' the Moon-talker said. 'You are Sister Sun and Sister Earth and not welcome in the eyes of Father Moon.'

'And you are a fool, as I have said before,' Jynni sneered then squatted down. 'We will wait. The sun has yet a long journey to make this day and the earth has nothing to do but lie underneath.'

But this small altercation had alerted the rest of the caravan and others now ambled over. They could all plainly hear the cries that came from the cocoon and the soothing tones of Kareen and Laelia.

'What is wrong with your Goddess? Will she die just when we need her the most?' Leef grumbled. A derisive snort from Jynni bought a scowl to the giant's face.

Weerluk took Mungart aside and they talked quietly in their language before fading away back to their people. Softly yet swiftly the word passed around that huge throng and gradually the dance stopped and they stood, silent and expectant, at the birth of a new Creator—from one who was supposed to be a mighty spirit.

It *was* a troublesome time and took a long time. It was late afternoon when Laelia emerged from the cocoon, holding a bloody, wet, crying little bundle in her blue robes.

'A girl child,' she smiled out into the crowd.

An exhausted but happy Kareen came out beside her.

'It was a troublesome time but both have lived.' She breathed a sigh of relief.

'Good! Then we can all go and visit the Goddess!' Wunda cried.

Before anyone could do anything the short squat woman had leapt up and burst through the skin covers, Jynni going after her. Then there was a short scream and a triumphant cry. Even as Red Mond charged forward they emerged from the cocoon, dragging S'shony behind by her long braids—out into the dying daylight.

'Behold! Your tear from the moon. A liar like all Moon-talkers are,' Wunda shouted.

Jynni forced S'shony's head up so she had to close her eyes against the feeble rays of the sun. But even this was too much for one used to a dark world. She whimpered and squirmed and tried to talk but Wunda slapped her hard across the mouth, so she gave a little squeal and was mute as she faced her tormentors.

She looked pathetic. Blood from the birth still stained her body, which was seen to be even more frail in the harsh light of day. The months in the partial light of the cocoon had made her somewhat immune to the harmful effects which light had on her people. But her pale, naked body wriggled like an insignificant maggot. She mewed in pain and her hands reached out blindly for her new-born baby or her man. Blood ran from her broken mouth.

'Leave her alone!' Red Mond Star Light cried and leapt to be at her side, but he was caught from behind and hurled backwards.

'You have forsaken all right to speak. A Devil has a hold of your mind,' roared Leef, who sprang forward with Leef-shadow beside him.

But in the path of the raging giant and his vicious little companion stepped Laelia, her blue eyes calm, her pale face expressionless.

'Look! Would you kill her baby as well?' she whispered.

The two reared up, agitated, with the blood-lust of the Outsiders already boiling all reason out of their heads. But Leef glanced down at the now quiet baby and was reminded of sixteen odd years ago when he stood in another clearing, bloody and empty as this clearing was full, and looked down at another small, smiling baby. He remembered he had killed a man who had dared try and harm the little body.

Of course he could not kill a baby, he thought.

But Leef-shadow shouted, 'She is one who turned us out! She was in a safe world. Indeed, is probably connected to the Night Bats. She uses magic to bewitch you!' and he moved forward purposely. 'I will kill this other witch whom we *know* is a Night Bat enemy!'

'Wait!' Laelia tried to use her calming influence on the boy but her power was drained, as she had used much of her energy on comforting S'shony. 'I do know what the Night Bats look like, as do you. Is this the child of a Nightstalker?'

She thrust the baby into Leef-shadow's face.

'Her eyes are as green as yours and your companions and nearly like the eyes of the Earth Mother.' And it was true because the eyes of the little human who blinked their first glimpse at its new world were a brilliant green, flecked with the grey of Kareen's clear eyes. She glanced across at Leef. 'Can you kill the mother of your brother, little friend of all the world?'

'I am friend to no one,' the boy hissed.

'There are three here who would call you a liar. Your companion, the poet who calls you "little friend of all the world" and another . . .' Laelia smiled a tired smile at the look that crossed the young face. 'Yes, it *is* true I possess my magic but, you see, I only use it to heal my new friends. If I can change from an enemy into a friend, then so can others.'

Aybee called from the back in quite normal language, except for the trembling of anger in his voice. 'She is a Devil woman who uses trickery to confuse you people. Has she ever raised a hand against the Night Bats? No, for she is one of them in disguise. See how fair-skinned she is! Do her people not live in huge caves that reach to the sun, but never let the sun inside? Did not her people send others out into the desert to be food for her kin living under the desert? Do not be taken in by her spells!'

As soon as he saw the naked, white, wriggling girl dragged struggling through the door, the Cricketeer had gone pale with anger and hatred. 'Kill her and the one she loves. Before she can trick us further let her die!' he cried.

Surprisingly, Nanny stepped up to the group then and Cudjo came behind, confused and unsure, but backing up his Captain, his lover and the only one of them left now. The others who knew of their awesome weapons stood back, including the Cricketeer.

'She woman live wid I-man since unu start on journey. Me wonder at times if she duppi or human. But she nah kill Surrey Anne. I-an'-I don't believe in unu God. She only woman she live with Moon-talker yah an' we nah seh him enemy. Let 'er live, me say!'

There was a brief pause broken only by the cracked voice of Prince Michael of the Ants.

When the lamp is shattered
The light in the dust lies dead—
When the cloud is scattered
The rainbow's glory is shed.

'And what stupidity is that the old fool dribbles from his penis now?' growled Wunda, still keeping a tight hold on S'shony's hair.

'Why, can't you see?' Leef said in one of his gentler moods. 'If we kill the woman we must kill the baby too.' He gave an evil grin at the brown-haired woman. 'Any who try to kill the baby will die by *my* hand. So I think the woman is safe.'

Wunda let go of S'shony so the cave girl grovelled blindly in the dust.

'What do *I* care?! See your *Goddess* now!' She pointed in derision at the slumped figure. 'Has she perhaps led you all to Father Moon?' She spat at the pitiable figure. 'All we see is a Prowler who we can kill as easily as another. We go now to kill her brothers and sisters and perhaps we will kill her as well if she does even the smallest thing wrong.' As they stalked off, she kicked S'shony viciously in the side.

Red Mond Star Light moved to intercept the two women. His normally placid face was pinched with anger and his eyes were alight with a fury never before seen in them that gazed dreamily at the moon. 'You will *not* go into the caves! I will go with my beloved S'shony. I don't need *any* of you to come. This is *my* story and I will end it now. But you . . . you have listened to your hatred and let it blind you.'

As quick as a striking snake he snapped out a hand and slapped Wunda across the face. 'I will *not* have you beside me as a friend.'

When the Moon-talker slapped Sister Earth everyone had gone still. Wunda's eyes glittered and her hand strayed to her sword. Then she shrugged her broad shoulders and smiled icily. 'You have touched me. Now, according to your beliefs, you will die. I would not walk beside a dead man,' she muttered, stepping away.

Red Mond covered the naked, cringing body of his woman with his old kangaroo-skin coat, as he had done many months before in the race against the sun to the rooftop of the world. Once again she clung tightly to him, as he strode towards the cave. Except for the two Sisters, the others followed reluctantly after him. Laelia stood alone for a moment holding the baby, her blue eyes pools of fright, until a withered arm wrapped itself protectively around her narrow shoulders.

What were all the world's alarms
To mighty Paris when he found
Sleep upon a golden bed
That first dawn in Helen's arms?

When she looked up into his blue eyes there was a bright clearness there. Then his dry, cracked lips bent down and kissed hers. As he moved away his fingers brushed her yellow hair.

She could almost have wept when she saw he still remembered his devotion for her. She could not let him go in there alone, she knew. Not now he had almost found her after years of mental torture. She clasped the new-born baby to her breast and hurried after the others.

Leef-shadow tarried a few seconds looking back at Jynni and wondering if he would ever see her again. But she had reverted back to the old Sister Sun of before the mountains, aloof and cruel.

'What do you stare at, little shadow? It is I who make you what you are, a patch of disappearing blackness on the ground. A mere shadow of a leaf that soon will die!' she laughed heartlessly. 'The sun and the earth live forever!'

'They are just two dead rocks!' he called back, stung by her remarks.

'They are more useful than two balls,' Wunda retorted and, on impulse, she embraced the laughing figure of Jynni in a passionate kiss. 'Here are your two dead rocks!' she cried.

The boy followed the shambling big figure of his companion. Here, he knew, at last, was a true friend.

As Red Mond moved into the shadows of the cave mouth, Mungart stepped up to him, Weerluk by his side. 'You are no longer my brother. If we were not on sacred ground I would kill you *now*,' the orange-haired keeper rasped.

'We go to kill the Djanaks to set our people free. Our business with you is over. You are a liar like every other white person,' Weerluk growled.

'Can you not see, ngan ngooni, that there is good and bad in everyone. This is the woman I love,' the Moon-talker said sadly, for he cared for these two young men who had shared so much of his story with him.

'The women my brother loved are all dead. Speak not of love to me—nor of friendship,' Weerluk snapped, then dragged Mungart away. 'Wait here, my people,' he called. 'Beside the waters until we return. We shall give the call of the bush to show it is us and then there shall be much killing.'

Then they were with the others beside the dark waters, staring down at their reflections that glimmered murkily in the yellow-brown depths. In their own way each and every one of them said goodbye to themselves as they stared down at the gurgling waters.

And I may dine at journey's end
With Landor and with Donne

Prince Michael whispered.

Then he stepped forth off the bank, thus breaking the waters and the images there. One by one the others followed. There was a rush of bubbles and the cold clammy water all around, then the silence of the underwater world. They looked like a school of strange fish as they swam the short journey, clothes and hair drifting around them. The huge Cudjo Accompong was dragged down by his weapon and Nanny had to help him carry the one box of ammunition he could afford to carry. He hoped it would be enough. By all accounts this was going to be one battle to end all battles.

In front, the naked body of S'shony seemed most at home in this environment. Soon she *would* be home, the only one comfortable in her world. Then they would all see she was their friend. She had her rope tied around her middle and it was to this that Red Mond Star Light clung. He carried the Beacon's mighty club in one hand, and the other Beacon's sword strapped to his side. His whole body sang in expectation of what lay before him.

They disappeared in their short journey underwater. There was no sound and they moved as if they were asleep.

It was almost as though they were in a dream.

CHAPTER NINETEEN

They tear up out of the water that forms a small pool, their heads smashing open the surface and causing noise to tinkle and reverberate around the close darkness of this first cave. Even under the water some sunlight has filtered through, but here there is a solid, thick blackness. Red Mond Star Light feels S'shony grab his hand and, using her sonar powers and mind probes, she hauls him from the water. He hears and senses others grunting and gasping and splashing around him but can see nothing. He is absolutely terrified.

As he stands up on the rocks, his feet, slippery from the water and the pain from his wound, cause him to stumble. It is this that saves his life.

First he feels a sharp, burning pain in his shoulder and he is sent tumbling backwards almost into the water again. He hears the rustle of sibilant voices and can sense forms around him. There are cries and shouts from around him as well and loud splashings, as of someone wrestling in the water. He feels the wet sticky blood trickle down his shoulder, then the giant Visitor gives a roar of anger and defiance and there is a flash of light, as one of his eggs is laid with devastating effect in the small cavern. Red Mond is tossed to the ground again and sees in the flickering light of the explosion a Nightstalker poised over his helpless body, cruel smile on his face and javelin raised.

This is when I die, he thinks. Not on the purple plains amidst friends but in this evil, sunless land. The thought that this is how his story is to end is the bitterest of all.

Then, where there had stood his killer, there is only black space and S'shony stands beside him, the rope that broke his killer's neck coiled around her arm. 'Come, sweet butterfly. We must make our way to where there is light from the green mushrooms, before others come.'

Others, too, in that brief light have seen what she has done: saved the life of one they all knew and admired in different ways. There is a faint glimmering of trust as they make their way down the passage. Red Mond is wounded—but no one is dead—as they pour forth into a larger passage. Now along the walls, luminous mushrooms give out a type of light. Now they see each other as green ghostly forms, as if already dead.

Their nostrils dilate at the curious scent of decay and their eyes take in the hideous beauty of their new world.

'Stick together,' he calls. 'Our only hope is to stick together.'

Even as he says this, he notices Prince Michael of the Ants wander up another passage but there is no time to grab him, for already a squealing horde of small, naked, white bodies is upon them. On his left, Leef and Leef-shadow leap forward with equally wild cries, challenging them in fierce glee. On his right, Kareen and the two Children of the Moon join in. The battle has really begun and it is each to their own.

The weapons of Cudjo Accompong and Nanny send swathes of death amongst the on-coming crowd and none can get near them, so the Nightstalkers fall back, leaving many dead or dying, broken bodies behind.

But here there comes a Beacon S'shony knows is a famous warrior. It is not until he triumphantly holds up what is in his hand that she knows what it is.

He carries the gun of Surrey Anne. Around his neck the purple-pink crystals flash. Crystals are a sacred stone to the People of the Caves and they can ward off death. He wields the gun like a club, as he and his followers, assured of the magic of this incredible weapon, leap forward with him. It is at one of those moments when both Nanny and Cudjo Accompong are desperately reloading so they wash over the caravan and it is up to primitive weapons and the strength of fear to drive them back.

Mungart and Weerluk have hurled their supply of boomerangs with lethal effect and now stand side by side, heavy stone axes cracking heads like eggs. Now Mungart is confronted by the gun-wielding Beacon, yelling his warrior's song and, with sick horror, he realises the tiny white Djanak has two sets of hair both black and in dreadlocks but only one his own. He notices the greyish garment flapping around his body, like grotesque wings of some evil bat, as the skin he once touched and caressed with love—the skin that had been on the warm vital body of Surrey Anne, keeping her vibrant spirit within.

He freezes in shock and is almost run through with a wicked javelin. The Beacon, quite by accident, pulls the trigger of the gun and the bullet zooms through the air smashing into Cudjo Accompong's shoulder. He curses and drops the rocket-launcher, reeling away from the shock. He has a thought that this is truly bad luck—to be killed by an ignorant savage in a strange black place, by his friend's own weapon, in a war that really had nothing to do with him.

There is a great cry at the fall of the huge man, as the Nightstalkers realise their magic is strong. So they pour forth en masse, stabbing and clubbing and cutting. Kareen receives a gash on her arm and a cut to her head. Cudjo Accompong is stabbed in the fleshy part of his thigh before he breaks the stabber's neck with his one good arm. Red Mond Star Light is slashed across his face, almost losing an eye, but he hardly feels the pain in his terror. Laelia at the back, numb with trepidation, clings to the baby, protected by her old enemies, Leef and Leef-shadow, who are in their element.

Nanny finally gets her gun loaded and sends a close-quarters' burst into the charging mass. White-hot pieces of lead rip into the slight bodies and then she hurls two of her grenades for good measure. One of the first to fall is the Beacon, and the others, seeing their power is only an illusion, dart back the way they came, to recuperate and count their losses.

After so much noise, there is an ear-exploding silence. The Moon-talker checks on the others and sees they are all right, except for Cudjo Accompong who spits up blood and curses mightily. There is nothing they can do now and he can still walk, so they must go on. Leef is the only one who can support the huge West Indian's weight so the two giants, cramped in these narrow tunnels, go first, keeping alert to danger.

They come out of the passageway and into a massive honeycomb of caves, eerie in their silence and emptiness.

'Is this the castle of the King of Bats?' Red Mond asks S'shony.

'No, it is further on. But this is a main nest. I cannot understand why no one is here.'

'I am glad no one is here,' Leef grunts, but as he speaks, from the walls and roofs of the cave, just like the green slime that grows all over the walls, Nightstalkers ooze from everywhere.

Mungart is still in shock over seeing the skin and hair of Surrey Anne. He had reached down to touch her as they hurried by the dead Beacon, but Weerluk had angrily pulled him away.

'Do you want to die?' Weerluk had called. 'There have been too many rules broken already.'

But Mungart scarcely hears. He strays, in a dream, from Weerluk's protection. Into his mind comes an image of Surrey Anne on top of him, warm wet legs around him and brown purple-nippled breasts swaying above him as butterflies cartwheel around her ecstatic face in the sunny meadow of their first meeting. Surrey Anne bending down to skin the snake and holding the skin up so it shines like jewels in the dying sun. His eyes focus as he hears his brother scream.

'Mungart! Nooooo!'

The last thing he sees, shining like jewels in this new yellow-green sun, are the shards of glass embedded in a heavy club before it smashes into his surprised face.

Weerluk can only watch his brother's death. The Nightstalkers, buzzing like angry bees in their hissing language, are everywhere. The pain of Mungart's death numbs him, as his brother falls and is torn to pieces by the advancing crowd. Of all the ghosts who walk in the sun above, none are more hated than the Keepers of the Trees. Weerluk, flattened against the wall, sees his brother's bloody head torn off and swung around in the air by its long orange-ochred locks.

He runs amok, feeling a huge part of him has died and he simply does not care anymore. All his siblings have been injured or killed at the hands of the Djanaks. He would rather join his twin in death, as they were together in life. He swings his axe again and again and grabs up a javelin from a dying Djanak's twitching hand, stabbing and thrusting with a rage that sends his foes falling back from him. Then one larger than the rest, another Beacon, charges in with a club similar to the one that killed his brother. The first swing sends his axe flying from his hand and the next is aimed at his defenceless head.

But he decides in that instant that he will *not* die. That he will live to fight and kill until every one of his brother's tormentors and killers are dead dead *dead*.

His hand closes around the descending club and he does not feel the pain as the glass cuts into his palm and fingers—indeed so much so that his little finger is completely decapitated. He halts the downward flight then viciously, with a white mirthless grin on his blood-streaked face, he sends the javelin into his victim's stomach, with such force it shatters the vertebrae as it comes out the other side. He tears away the club from his would-be killer's clutching fingers and kills the Beacon with his own highly prized weapon. Yelling his Totem's war-cry he sets to, as the bloodlust rushes to his head, and charges forward to twist and turn, maiming and killing. There is no stopping him *now*. Any Nightstalkers who saw the killing of their Beacon know this was a charmed man and fall back from his onslaught.

Kareen fetches a more serious wound on her leg. She falls to one knee and would have died had not Leef materialised at her side, wielding his huge, blood-slippery sword.

Laelia is grabbed from behind and has her blue cloak torn from her, before her attacker lets go with a curse at the sight of her yellow hair and blue eyes. 'Sun woman,' he hisses, before Leef-shadow runs him through. The boy grabs up the cowering woman and shouts in her ear, 'Stay close with me!'

Then there is a commotion from behind and the two Sisters charge out of the passage. 'It is better she stay with us women, we say!' Wunda cries.

'We cannot have the men get all the glory,' Jynni laughs beside her.

They have followed the caravan and now are most welcome in their fresh warrior state. But for every Nightstalker killed, another two seem to take their place in never-ending lines of whispering sibilant hatred. The members of the caravan are weakened by their wounds and from the pressure that doesn't seem to ease. Red Mond Star Light wipes the blood from his eyes and risks a glance at his beloved S'shony. At least they would all die together, he thinks, and maybe someday someone would make up a song about this battle—even though they would not be around to hear it.

But now there occurs a strange thing.

There are sudden squeals of pain from further up the passages where the Nightstalkers wait. Also a curious shuffling sound and a noise that is not unlike the rapid clapping of wood pieces.

From out of the passageways the Nightstalkers pour. Not to annihilate the desperate members of the caravan but to face a new enemy. Then, following the tumbling, confused bodies, a living mass of the biggest ants they have ever seen. They are all as big as a large dog, with red, shining bodies and clacking mandibles. Their dead black eyes stare out at the huddled members of the caravan, with some kind of intelligence.

Cudjo Accompong looks to Nanny for some advice. He has never seen such creatures except for the smaller ones on the plain of the whispering grass. And he would never forget the agonising sting of *their* bite. Yet these ants have just attacked their enemies. But, he thought, if they are going to die he would prefer it to be by human hand. He raises his rocket-launcher at the nearest mass of insects, but Nanny's hand on his blood-drenched shoulder stops him.

'It is Prince Michael,' she gasps.

There he is! Coming behind with another army of ants that crowd the wide corridor they are in. He rides upon the foremost, that is itself as big as a small pony, and no longer does he seem frail and useless to his fellow travellers. His body is powerful and his eyes a clear blue colour—and dead of all emotion like his new friends . . . his true friends.

He calls out in a voice that once must have been his own, before the Prophets and their wives destroyed it. It is soft and gentle and entirely sweet, almost wistful: 'I am Michael, Prince of the Ants. I know that you could not believe I speak to these creatures of God, but I do. Now we go forth to destroy these humans who dared to think they are the ants of this world. Fear not the ones I leave behind to protect you. They are your friends too and I have planted an image of each and every one of you in their minds. It was why I travelled by myself, passing on the message to my Kingdom. Even now every ant, all over this land, descends into the caves.'

Then he reverts back into his old ways:

Down to Gehenna or up to the throne,
He travels fastest who travels alone.

And he is on his way with his rustling, clicking army, up one of the side passages.

As the ants surround them, Laelia walks about using her healing powers as best she can. There is nothing she can do for Cudjo Accompong's horrific shoulder wound except pack it with the herbs Surrey Anne had taught her to use. But she eases the pain of some of the slighter wounds. One or two she heals altogether. They are in a bad way, with over half the caravan injured seriously. They tie up their bleeding wounds and gather themselves for the next assault.

During this brief rest, S'shony sends out probes to see where her people are hiding and which is the safest way to the King of the Bats. She is confused that they are being so cleverly ambushed, for her senses have not picked up any readings of her people. Perhaps she has been too long up in the sun and her powers are fading. Her mind probes and sonar had not felt that last ambush that would have finished them were it not for the ants' arrival.

They set off and come with great abruptness into an enormous cavern that is studded with stalactites and stalagmites of wonderful shapes and colour. For a bewildered moment S'shony thinks she is in the Cave of Jewels of the wizard Nimbelyung, where she and her lover had found such joy. But then she realises it is an illusion. This cave has a darker grace—an evil loveliness that lulls one into a sense of peace before destroying one.

'Be careful,' she hisses to Red Mond Star Light. 'Something is wrong.'

'We are safe at the crease,' the Cricketeer Aybee cries. His white gown is spattered with blood and his black eyes shine with a cruel relish. 'This Innings has been expensive for the batsmen and the fielding has been atrocious.'

'Such stupid things these men say,' Wunda sneers.

'It has been a pleasure to be in your ridiculous company and see at first hand how idiotic the male can be,' Jynni joins in.

'Sister Sun, you are a long way from your kin and I have noticed amongst those you kill are women. Does that not make you as foolish as us?' Leef growls, but there is half a smile on his battered face. His long beard is streaked with blood, not all of it the blood of enemies. He enjoys this killing, Red Mond thinks, and he does not care if he lives or dies. The Moon-talker wonders how Akar Black Head would have acted and he glances over to Kareen, who smiles painfully and hobbles onward.

'We should go this way. Let us go forth to score more runs,' Aybee says and sets off down a passageway.

'Wait! We are only here to kill the King of the Bats. Then we can convert these people into our way of life,' Red Mond Star Light calls out.

In the second of confusion that this small argument causes, as some head off after Aybee and others wait for S'shony's word, there is a sudden rumble and, from behind and above, a trapdoor opens and boulders rain down upon them. Nanny has her gun knocked out of her hand, as she is sent reeling to the ground, and Leef-shadow is temporarily winded when a boulder the size of his head slams into his stomach. Kareen screams in agony, as a large boulder crushes her already wounded leg, and she is pinned to the ground, helpless. After the boulders, Nightstalkers drop from the roof, stabbing and grabbing at their enemy.

In that second, S'shony gets a clear message from the mind of one she has probed so long without result. She cries out, 'It is the white-gowned one from the white land. He is stopping my mind probes with his own images of safety so I get no warning of danger. He is a cowardly traitor!'

She leaps upon him but he throws her off and stabs her in the breast. A malignant smile crosses his face. 'It is *you* who are the traitor. We hoped to keep you alive a little longer, but now it cannot be,' he says almost sadly. 'The pleasure your pain would have given us was greatly desired by myself and my brethren—the People of the Caves who live in the world of the sun and keep an eye on our flock of flesh.' He laughs maniacally.

Then his cruel head goes sailing from his shoulders and his white gown is drenched with his own pumping blood. His body collapses at her feet and Leef looks down at her, bloody sword in his hand. 'He was a cunning and clever foe, and merciless, killing his own kind with as much pride as killing us would have given him,' the giant murmurs, for here is an emotion he can relate to.

As soon as the Cricketeer's head departs his body, his power over S'shony's mind is released and she can see clearly what lies in front— indeed, even above. She almost faints.

'Prepare yourselves, the cave of the King of Bats is not far and even now his special soldiers come,' she cries above the din. 'If we are almost dead now, we will be dead in a few moments.' Then she turns and, amidst all the commotion, she caresses Red Mond Star Light and whispers, 'I love you, red hair. Ilgar, my sweet butterfly.'

She lets all the memories of her time with him flood into both of their minds, so they can share a tender moment before death can take them in his hands and carry them away. They hope it will be quick as they hear the resounding war-cries of the King's own soldiers come to kill and eat of their flesh.

The Nightstalkers who leap, with their chilling war-cries of laughter, through the gaps in the slimy walls, are taller and heavier than their predecessors and almost all are armed with vicious clubs, axes or swords. Predominantly flint or ironstone they are virtually unbreakable.

Leef bears the brunt of the attack, with the two Children of the Moon beside him kicking and cutting with their fast moves. Behind this formi- dable trio the two West Indians have time to reload. For a moment the yelling crowd of Nightstalkers is kept back, but they have no fear whatsoever—and are possessed of a bloodlust as strong as the Outsiders. They break through and the fierce fighting begins again. Red Mond leaps to protect his cousin, pinned to the earth. Weerluk stands beside Laelia, the stone club a blur in his hands. S'shony, the ugly wound in her breast pulsing blood, charges into the midst of her advancing kin, the sword of 'The Secret-maker' flaying the air.

As Jynni rushes to join one she would have called an enemy, her clumsy feet cause her to trip—right in the path of a charging group of the King's soldiers!

With a fiendish cry, Wunda leaps forward. 'No man may touch the flesh of Sister Sun.'

She wields her sword with stunning effect, allowing Jynni to get to her knees, then the short, brown-haired woman is run through with a javelin. Her hazel eyes widen in shock and her precious blood flows from her mouth. She tries to speak but only a gurgle comes forth.

'My darling!' Jynni yells and tries to embrace her.

Leef-shadow hears this cry, as he is engaged in despatching two more of the many enemy he has killed this glorious day. He spins around just in time to see a huge Night Bat looming over his lover, who holds the dying Wunda in her arms. As fast as a cat, he unleashes his deadly knife and sends it hurtling across the cavern to sink into the white throat. Then, unfurling his dangerous slingshot, he leaps and twists to join her. Pulling her up onto her feet he says, 'The number of times you fall to earth you should have been Sister Earth instead of Sister Sun.'

'Here there is no earth, no sun. Only rocks and darkness.'

'So . . . it seems you are just a woman, after all,' he returns with a twisted smile, then the charging, insane group are upon them, tearing and slashing and ripping them to pieces. But even as they die, they take more enemies with them.

Leef cries out in agony at the death of his companion. He had warned him. The High Ones were never wrong. Touch a Sister and there can only be misfortune and death, if you were a man. Cudjo Accompong groans too and turns to Nanny, 'Me down to me las' rocket fe launcher yah, gel!'

'Me on'y got two lousy deggeh clip, maan!' she calls back, horrified.

'Deh too many fe kill, Nanny.'

'So, me sweet. Make him bullet count, tallowah-man.'

'Jah lives. Irie. One love, gel.' The giant says goodbye and faces the enemy of his last battle.

They stand grimly side by side and wait for the heaving mass of naked, cruel humanity to come close. Then Nanny cuts a swathe of destruction with her chattering machine-gun while Cudjo Accompong steadies himself, to make his last bomb have maximum effect. There is a final reverberating crash as the whole tunnel lights up and bodies are tossed everywhere. Cudjo Accompong tosses away his still smoking, but useless, rocket-launcher and snatches up a double-headed flint axe. He can still find time to laugh bitterly at this final irony—to die with a weapon in his hands he has only seen used in the movies back home, in the Kingston cinemas.

He calls out a Ras Tafarian oath and turns to face the enemy that, despite this latest blast of explosive destruction, have rallied again and, like wild dogs who sense the fox's demise, come baying and growling with the scent of blood in their nostrils.

Nanny picks up a fallen sword and stands at the giant's back. She can think of no words good enough for a final farewell, so she waits silently for her death.

But now another strange thing occurs.

Laelia has been left alone for a moment and she cringes against the far wall, gripping the crying baby to her bosom.

In another passageway, on the back of his giant ant, Prince Michael senses his wife's despair. From the depths of his mind he dredges up one of her favourite poems.

How many loved your moments of glad grace,
And loved your beauty, with false love or true,
But one man loved the Pilgrim soul in you,
And loved the sorrows of your changing face.

The placid words of the gentle Irishman, from thousands of years ago, drift through this turbulent atmosphere and curl around her numbed brain. All at once the whole of the green Island, Eire, Erin, the most magical land known to her who is supposed to know everything, opens up in her mind and all her old power is back. The power she had as a wife of a Prophet, but which this vast land had gradually whittled away until it was almost gone.

Her whole body seems to glow a pale luminous blue, as blue as her eyes and the blueness of her gown. She floats some inches off the ground. Her eyes become a blur of blue as her pupils expand and she floats even higher.

The whole battle stops. For those of her company who have never seen a flying woman before, like Weerluk who stands beside her, and the giant Leef, there is awe and fear at this unknown power. But to the horde of Nightstalkers there is nothing *but* fear and horror at the despised Sun Woman bathed in the hated colour of blue light that hurts their eyes. There is also another subtle weapon that Laelia applies, for she sends forth a wave of calmness over the tumultuous multitude that numbs the cruel and evil thoughts of the cave people, confusing them.

As one, they back off, wary, awkward and nervous at this throbbing light and the new minds they now seem to possess. Once again, unforeseen events have saved the damaged little band. In this respite the others gather their wounded. There is no time to mourn the dead. Laelia floats above them, glowing with a soft vibrating light, their greatest weapon right now. Leef rolls the boulder from Kareen's leg, which is not a pretty sight. He heaves her up into his massive hands, like a baby. S'shony has received a wound to her arm but she cannot stop now, despite her serious chest wound.

'Come,' she gasps. 'Follow the Blue Woman. We are almost there!'

They leave the cave with the wonderful stalagmites and stalactites and follow through a twisting, narrow tunnel, that is frighteningly quiet after all the noise of fighting. Laelia floats in front, a soothing blue glow, like some sort of Goddess.

With the suddenness of water pouring over a waterfall they pour out from the narrowness and confines of the tunnel, into the awesome emptiness of a giant cave. They cannot see either wall or roof in this huge hollow of the earth. They can only hear a dull booming as hundreds of voices call out a chant and thousands of feet and hands stamp out a rhythm or clap out a resonating beat. Yet there is not a body to be seen, which makes them all the more apprehensive. In this immense openness they all seem as tiny and insignificant as the smallest ant.

'The cave of the King of Bats,' S'shony gasps, in great pain.

The enormous void turns Laelia's brilliant blue light into a mere speck. Each and every one can hear the rustling of the Nightstalkers, Night Bats, Djanaks, crawl down the wall. The victors they think, as they huddle around the aura that is Laelia and the circle of clicking, stinging ants.

'They are never-ending,' Red Mond Star Light cries out in despair.

Hu-Hsien-Ku turns to Yi and whispers—for she is much afraid of this vacuum. 'It is time to go and gather the others. Bring them to this place.'

Then a javelin rushes soundlessly out of the darkness and pierces her side, so she is swept away by the momentum. She turns stricken eyes towards her countryman. 'Run! Run and blow your horn. They will hear you from the river. We cannot die for nothing and you can lead them here!'

Yi is upset at his countrywoman's pain, but he knows the poem of his people must live on. He unsheaves an arrow and fires blindly into the darkness, more out of defiance than accuracy, then turns to run. Weerluk, realising the Child of the Moon's intentions, joins him and the pair run silently and swiftly back the way they came.

At the same time, the others gather quickly into a circle, with their seriously injured in the middle and their allies the ants on the outside. This time the attack comes in the form of hurled javelins, as the People of the Caves keep well away from the dreaded blue light. Laelia starts to falter. It has taken a lot of energy to keep up this light and, even though she is a Prophet's wife, she is alone. The minds of the cave people are as powerful as hers, in their savagery. She can sense herself going and she knows when she does she must self-destruct and so take as many as possible of the Nightstalkers' minds with her—just as her sisters destroyed countless other minds in their time of power. Her body vibrates with a clear, deep, purple light, her eyes darken and she floats some twelve feet above the crowd. She will take this baby with her, she thinks. It is no world for children.

No javelin, no matter how accurately thrown, can touch her. She shines like a sun. But first she sends out a message to her lover, husband and friend who is somewhere in the caves.

Was it for this the wild geese spread
The grey wing upon every tide?

Then her mind starts to go and she cannot remember the rest of the verses until:

Romantic Ireland's dead and gone,
It's with O'Leary in the grave.

And thus, she thinks, it is with me. I go and join William Butler Yeats in whatever heaven his words have given him.

Prince Michael has been in another tunnel with his army of ants and, now, has almost arrived at the Cave of the King. Hearing that faint message awakens in his memory the remnants of the power that once was his. He casts out his mind net and is hit by a wall of fear and terror. What he feels most of all, though, is the flickering soul of Laelia as she bids him goodbye.

'No, it cannot be!' he cries and, using all his power in one huge blast of energy, he sends out a mind message to Laelia, giving her all the images of love he kept for her, that no amount of torture from Zoheletha and her helpers could take from him.

As soon as this is done he feels an emptiness descending upon him. It is as though he is caving in from the inside and his mind crumples in upon itself.

Oh, lift me as a wave, a leaf, a cloud!
I fall upon the thorns of life! I bleed!

he whispers, before all his world goes black and he topples lifeless from his curious steed, as the ant army pours like liquid fire out into the huge cave and amongst the hated enemy of their friend.

At the instant the mind-power ball sent by Prince Michael envelops Laelia, she is shaken by its aura and awakens again. She is revitalised and is able to send out a powerful message of calm to halt the advancing unseen army. Then she falls out of the air like a shot bird, her light extinguished and her body weak. She would have broken her neck or back on the hard rocky ground, but Leef catches her and gently lowers her down beside a moaning Kareen.

'You have saved our lives for now, Blue Woman. Rest, for you have done all you can,' he says softly, and kindness shines in his deep green eyes.

She has given them the respite they need. The ants that were with Prince Michael attack and, as they do, above them there are whoops and cries.

S'shony is suffering a great deal but she is still able to use her mind and sonar skilfully. Now she cries out in delight and wonder, 'It is the Sun Children. Fear not these people for they are my friends.'

Then a ladder made of the strange rope material flops down beside them. Leef prepares to run through the first person who climbs down it, but is stopped by S'shony's words. She has proven to him this day that she, although a traditional enemy, is a *true* companion.

He has never seen a blue-skinned person before and he wonders briefly if this is some sort of Cave God. The blue apparition rushes over to S'shony and embraces her briefly in welcoming arms. 'We have been trying to reach you with our sonar but could not get through!' the young blue-painted man cries.

Then she realises it is Radi, Willum's brother, who holds her with loving arms and stares at her from warm green eyes. The last time he had spoken to her had been with hate, but now she has returned with an army to defeat their enemy.

'Tell your friends not to hurt anyone in the colours of the earth above or the sun. They will see that the Sun Children are their comrades in this battle,' Radi yells above the din, then he is away, leaping out into the darkness as more of his kind scramble down the ladders snaking from the walls. They are painted in various ochres of blues and greens, reds, oranges, purples and pinks and yellows. One, a woman in red paint and with red hair, stops in front of S'shony.

'You must send out a message to the black and yellow ones. They are killing our people. Already the black one has killed my husband who only wished to guide him to the river cave.'

Then she is gone with a fearsome battle cry, as the years of oppression are swept aside for her people and the tables turned. Who would have believed that the Children of the sun would dare invade the Cave of the King of the Bats? This is just one of the last old beliefs to flee howling down the corridors of time.

Even now, Weerluk leaps over a pile of fallen bodies, Yi just behind. He sees a shadowy shape in the perimeter of his vision and he raises his bloody club to send it crashing into the body of his enemy. Then an image seems to come into his head that is one of fellowship. Three women step forward, equally cautious. They are green or purple-skinned and two have hair as blond as the Blue Woman while another has eyes just as blue. Weerluk remembers how that woman had helped save his brother's life and the innocent enjoyment Mungart had from her company, and the image becomes stronger in his mind that these different-skinned people are compatriots.

The three women leave them but, periodically, shadowy figures join them in their run. Apart from them, they might be the only people left in the caves.

The two warriors arrive in the dark cave where they had first arrived but by now their eyes are used to the gloom. Yi props his bow against the wall and reaches for his horn that is slung to his side. He blows a pure note, long and true, so it reverberates around the cave like the crash of the Visitors' awesome weapon, and seems to shatter the darkness with its melody.

But no one comes. No one at all.

Back in the Cave of the King of the Bats the battle is turning at last, although Red Mond Star Light, Leef and Nanny are the only ones left standing and in any fighting spirit. Kareen has fainted from loss of blood and Laelia lies exhausted beside her. S'shony kneels by Red Mond's side, coughing up blood, as does Cudjo Accompong beside Nanny. Hu-Hsien-Ku slides slowly away into unconsciousness as she tries in vain to remove the javelin in her side.

It is *then*, as the Moon-talker's eyes grow used to the dark, that he notices the huge stone throne and great flat area near the middle of the cave. There stands the biggest Nightstalker Red Mond has ever seen—as tall as Leef. Around his massive neck, the youth can see, is a necklace of tiny skulls and he knows without a doubt that here stands the Creator of evil, the mythical King of the Bats, or King of the Crooked Cross. . . who must die if they are to win this battle.

Although Red Mond, too, is weak from loss of blood, he struggles across the uneven terrain with murder in his heart. But he is not as fast as the giant Outsider, who is possessed with the exhilaration of bloodlust, and leaps to his destiny. Already around the throne lie the broken and bloody bodies of many of the Sun Children in ghastly postures of death.

Leef reaches the tall Night Bat first and parries a blow with his cut and chipped sword. But the next blow from the huge axe in the big King's hand smashes his sword to pieces. In the King's other hand he wields a short javelin and it is this he thrusts into Leef's side, sending a thrill of white-hot pain shuddering through his body. Leef, however, is in a frenzy and does not heed the pain. Instead, he turns his powerful body, tearing the javelin from the King's grasp. He pulls it with a grunt of suppressed agony from his side and turns it on the owner but the King of Bats is no longer there, having twisted away to deal with two Sun Children who have come to help. Then, like a wild erratic hurricane, he is back in Leef's path and as the Outsider thrusts with his javelin the axe comes down with unerring accuracy onto the hand that holds it severing the thumb and pointer finger. The javelin drops with a clang onto the stony floor and Leef waits to die.

Then Red Mond Star Light is beside him and the brown eyes of the youth stare into the malignant black eyes of his worst nightmare. He has time to notice this Nightstalker is different from the others. Not only is he gigantic, but his fingernails have been filed to sharp points. He has never had to dig his way through rock or soil to get his gruesome meals. He waits, just like a huge spider, for meals to be brought to him.

Now Red Mond Star Light will kill him just like a spider, so the Moon-talker's story will be remembered for ever more.

'You carry the weapon of "The Creeper"—my most famous warrior. It will be good to eat of your cringing flesh. Perhaps I will eat you alive.' The King speaks, in a language now familiar to the youth.

Red Mond has no strength to answer back but instead swings the club at the head of the King. It is met by the downswing of the axe and there is a resounding crash throughout the cavern.

In the other cave, Yi gives forth another blast on his horn. He is confused, for in the poem his people sing, it is after the first blast the caves are filled with light. But the only person to come through is another Sun Child, this one painted in a luminous purple.

But something is not right!

Too late Weerluk sees that this Sun Child's eyes are as black as his hair that falls around his knees. It is a trick and, with a cry, he leaps forward.

He cannot stop the javelin that tears into the uncomprehending Yi, ripping out his throat. Even as the Child of the Moon sinks to his knees, his precious horn useless beside his lifeless fingers, Weerluk hurls himself upon the lone Beacon, who has hovered here in a rear-guard action that seemed hopeless but has almost succeeded.

The fight is fierce but brief and Weerluk emerges the winner. The many times he and his brother had wrestled together has saved him. He uses skills acquired then, to toss the small but hardy man onto his back and snap his neck.

He looks at the mellow, yellow, beckoning light at the mouth of the cave and knows what he must do. All his life he has lived apart from others except his own kind and adhered strictly to his laws. But this is *his* land and it is crying out for him to save it now. Grabbing up the foreign horn, he leaps noiselessly into the waters and heads for the outside world. It will be *his* lips that summon the Asian people, foreigners—and yet friends—of the Keepers.

Red Mond Star Light strikes again. And again. But each time there is no one there. The King cackles with hideous joy, for he knows he is the better of the two. Red Mond's wounded leg goes stiff. He cannot move as fast as he would like. He is tired and 'The Tearer' is heavy in his grip. He falls to the floor, letting the club fall beside him and feels sad for all the people he has led into the caves and to their deaths. He only hopes their torment will not be long. He spits blood at the leering face of the King in a final act of defiance.

Then there is a movement from the shadows and suddenly the King's eyes bulge as he drops his axe and his hands go to his neck. He dances a mad dance, as his feet whirl around the platform, then his feet leave the ground and he is flying in the air like Laelia from before. But he is nowhere near as graceful as she. He cries out in a croaking voice, but the only person to hear is S'shony who staggers forward, leaning on the other end of her rope that she has slung over a rocky crag. Leef stumbles to help her pull on the rope and Red Mond crawls to his feet.

In an instant, he has the sword all Nightstalkers know as 'The Whispering Death' in his hands—the sword his injured beloved has dragged across for him. With one terrifying scream he severs the wriggling King's head from his shoulders. Even as the body falls to the ground, along with an exhausted Leef and dying S'shony, he grabs the head by its long black braids and swings it high into the air above him. It shines white and pale, like a dreadful parody of a moon, in this new morbid sky.

'Behold!' he cries. 'Your King is dead. We came like sunlight into your world and never shall we leave it!'

At this moment, into the caves, scores of yelling Keepers and Children of the Moon come like a huge tide of sacred water, wave after wave of warriors washing over the floor.

Red Mond Star Light holds the limp and bloody body of his woman close to him and whispers, 'You cannot die now, sweet moonbeam.'

'No! Goddesses of the moon don't die,' came Leef's growl. 'How can they when they are from the moon and we all know Father Moon always comes back to life again.'

The giant's savage eyes stare into Red Mond Star Light's and a rusty laugh emanates from his bloody and scarred chest.

For them the adventure is over.

Epilogue

Epilogue

The battle ended with the death of the King. That was the turning point anyway, although the fierce fighting in the caves and corridors went on for some weeks. But the People of the Caves were not used to invasion and had no defence against the vengeful packs of Keepers of the Trees, Children of the Moon and Sun Children that roamed their Home Ground. Others throughout the land, who had been tormented for centuries, also joined the fray when triumphant victors emerged from chimneys with the news.

The ants also killed a great number before the powers of their Prince faded and they disappeared. But, from that day on, no ant was ever intentionally hurt. In time they took over as the Gods of this land. But that is another story.

The survivors of the caravan were all wounded, but with the flood of black and yellow warriors came their finest physicians with their vast knowledge of medicine. So the seriously wounded: Kareen, S'shony, Cudjo Accompong and Hu-Hsien-Ku were all carried away by sympathetic, caring Aboriginal or Asian hands. Leef, Nanny and Red Mond Star Light were left to be patched up on the field of battle. Too exhausted to think, they lay back near the throne of the King and reflected on all the death and destruction they had seen these few short hours. Blood dripped freely from their wounds and they could not truly believe it was over. At last, Laelia recovered enough to come and comfort them in her own way. For the first time she was welcomed as a friend by every one of them.

After the slaying of the King, the cave people had fled, chased by the victorious Sun Children. Some of these people gathered to stare curiously at their saviours, but they were too shy to meet with the ghosts from above who, yet, spoke a semblance of the Old Ones' language.

Those next few weeks saw the resistance crushed and the remnants sent scuttling to the deepest darkest depths of their home, almost to the Never World where all their Demons lay. In those weeks also the worst wounds of S'shony were healed by Chinese ingenuity, Aboriginal bush lore and Laelia's magic. She was able to hold her baby for the first time and she vowed that her baby born in such a violent time would inherit a world of peace.

It was with this in mind that she moved to Red Mond Star Light's camp, which he had set up on the throne of the King. Then he sent out messages through all the corridors to collect the roaming warriors and hunters together. To all those gathered he showed the baby. Then the shy Moon-talker made the second important speech of his lifetime.

'The time for war is over. Go forth and bring in the rest of the Nightstalkers unharmed. For the purpose of all this death and the loss of our compatriots was not to continue the killing but to end it all. You see the woman I love—who has saved my life twice and who almost died by my side—is one of the enemy. We see cave people who are hated and despised and killed by cave people. Above, there are many different people, all of whom hate each other, and yet we banded together. So who can say who is an enemy? Let us embrace our enemy and all be friends and I will lead you out of our dark world!'

'All hail, King Red!' shouted the vast crowd of Sun Children.

And that is what he came to be known, with S'shony as his Queen, and his stepdaughter, named Karinsurri, after two women much admired by S'shony, became a very famous person in her own right. Which was only correct for one born so auspiciously.

Of the others, Leef became the new King's right-hand man and settled down with Kareen. With her compassionate nature, yet warlike ways, and his savagery, they made a formidable pair. But their fighting days were really over now, with the loss of the use of his right hand and her left leg. They were able to advise the King and Queen fairly and honestly—a cousin and a good friend.

The two West Indians never did find their petrol and they stayed with Red Mond Star Light as well. They hid what was left of their weapons in a sealed cave and brought more peaceful technology to this savage, primitive world. They kept the memory of their Island of Springs in the back of their minds. Cudjo Accompong devised a system of giant mirrors to bring the sunlight down via reflection into the dark damp world of the caves and thus use some of the more fertile areas for crops.

Laelia became known as the Blue Light Woman and wandered the caves where her husband had died, healing and curing illness. She was much loved by everyone but she kept to herself, a lonely woman who often murmured strange songs under her breath, it was said.

Hu-Hsien-Ku went back to her people and became immortalised in the poem of her people, and Weerluk . . .

After he led the charge into the Cave of the King of Bats he disappeared like the rest of his surviving warriors. Back to their secret tracks and sacred life and their dedication to protecting their land. But it was said he was a lone man who had no family, no traditional home, who wandered all over. They said he was really only half a man, even though he was whole, for something was missing in his heart and mind and he carried a strange white man's instrument by his side.

The caves were opened up and, where before the chimneys had been places of evil and the openings to stealthy death, now they became highways of safety and trade. The People of the Caves were taught to eat cattle or sheep that lived in the plains of grass that grew now in some of the caves. Never had the Ilkari realised the magic their jewel glass could become, the jewel their stories said had come from Father Moon. Gradually they lost their savage ways and the two peoples could live together, sharing their skills and knowledge to make the caves a bigger and more comfortable place. As the years went by, even the cave people lost their fear of the light and were able to lead a more normal life.

Many Ilkari, Outsiders, and other people from above began to make their homes in the caves, where they were safe from the effects of the sun. They were able to use the huge reservoirs of underground water to irrigate their crops and the caves' walls offered more protection from the wild beasts that had killed so many of them before.

Red Mond Star Light, once known as Ilgar and now known as King Red—clansman and Moon-talker—lived in the cave below, far from the light of the moon. Although when he was alone, some nights, he would wander up and let the soft blue light of his friend wash over him. He did not read the stars, but only admired their beauty and, sometimes, he would ponder on the thought that if he had never gone out to the rooftop of the world to talk to Father Moon, none of this would have happened.

Glossary of general terms

Ando bersch dui chiro, ye ven, ta nilei. O felhegos del o breschino, te purdel o barbal. (Gypsy)
: in the year (are) two seasons, the winter and the summer. The cloud gives the rain and puffs (forth) the wind

Ambról (Gypsy)
: a pear

Amigos (Spanish)
: friends

Aunsos me dicas vriardao de jorpoy ne sirlo braco hinjiri (Gypsy)
: although thou seest me dressed in wool I am no sheep

Balo (Gypsy)
: hog

Bengui—from Spanish Gypsy Bengue i. q. Beng (Gypsy)
: toad, dragon; Devil

Bidit Warda Kadak (Aboriginal)
: ant man of importance

Billah, Bila (Aboriginal)
: tailor fish

Bitchadey pawdel—perda'l on the other side, across (Gypsy)
: sent, transported

Boshomengro (Gypsy)
: fiddler

Cams tu lati (Gypsy)
: Who do you love?

chal devlehi—For Jal from Java (Ja Devle'sa) (Gypsy)
: Go with God. Farewell

chavo'—i.q. cha'bo (tchava) (Gypsy)
: child, lad

chi—tcha'i (Gypsy)
: child, girl, lass

Churi—tchori (Gypsy)
: knife

Coliko—Kaliko—Spanish Gypsy calicaste— (Gypsy)
: On the morrow. In the morning

coumlo chiricli (Gypsy)
: comely bird

371

Damen devla saschipo ando mure cocolai (Gypsy)	give us Goddess health in our bones
deyvil (Gypsy)	God
djanak (Aboriginal)	Spirit
?Donde nos encontramus (Spanish)	Where shall we meet?
gorgios (Gypsy)	non-Gypsies
grasni (Gypsy)	mare; or the stone Jade
gul eray—Hungarian Gypsy (Gypsy)	sweet gentleman
Juva, Juwa (Gypsy)	young woman
kakkaratchi (Gypsy)	magpie
kalo'—kali' plural kale' (Gypsy)	black, dark
Kart warrah (Aboriginal)	lit. head bad—ie, mad
Kaulo ratti adrey leste (Gypsy)	he has Gypsy blood in him
kawar (Aboriginal)	purple-crowned lorrikeet
kek ta'tcho—(tacho') none (Gypsy)	lit. none truth—ie, not true, a lie
Kelang (Aboriginal)	male possum
kirlkirl (Aboriginal)	bullant
kittiupcowra (Aboriginal)	birds singing in the morning
Kooaar (Aboriginal)	smoker parrot
koolbardi (Aboriginal)	magpie
koomal (Aboriginal)	possum
Kral (Gypsy)	King
Kwila (Aboriginal)	shark
Kwoola (Aboriginal)	mullet
La bola (Spanish)	the wineskin
Lens sus sonsi bela pani o' reblandi tere'la (Gypsy)	the river that makes a noise* has either water or stones
lubbeny—lubni' (Gypsy)	harlot

* in the original 'wears a mouth'; the meaning is, ask nothing gain nothing

mabarn (Aboriginal)	magic man
manushi—(Spanish Gypsy) manus . . . manush (Gypsy)	man
mardingu (Aboriginal)	sweet heart, desire someone
?Me permite este baile (Spanish)	May I have this dance?
merel—merava, meresa merela (Gypsy)	he dies
Mi casa tu casa (Spanish)	my house is your house
Mi familia (Spanish)	my family
mi kalo'—hinjiri F. of hinjiro' . . . fr. djandjir—chain (Gypsy)	lit. I (am the) dark executioner
miah (Aboriginal)	house
miduveleskue (Gypsy)	divine or Godly book
mitchi—from minchi (Gypsy)	s.f. pudendum feminae
mumboyet (Aboriginal)	sea
nashkado—nashavdo' (Gypsy)	lost, ruined, hanged
ngan ngooni (Aboriginal)	my brother
ngangk (Aboriginal)	sun, mother
Ngoonies noycha ngoorndiny (Aboriginal)	lit. brothers dead lying down, that is his brothers are lying there dead
ngort (Aboriginal)	horse
Nolka (Aboriginal)	flathead fish
nyinak (Aboriginal)	yours. Is this yours?
paal (Gypsy)	brother
palor—prala' (Gypsy)	brothers
Pacuaro' (Spanish Gypsy)	handsome, pretty
petu'l duvel (Gypsy)	lit. Horseshoe God
Pruebe uno de estos (Spanish)	try one of these
Rom andrees (Gypsy)	Gypsy at heart
Romaneskoenaes (Gypsy)	in Gypsy fashion
Romani' (Gypsy)	Gypsy language
Sastra (Gypsy)	iron

tjitti-tjitti (Aboriginal)	willy-wagtail
tjuk (Aboriginal)	sister
tjurditj (Aboriginal)	wildcat
wadgula (Aboriginal)	white person
wadjullung (Aboriginal)	white people
waitj (Aboriginal)	emu
Wilgie (Aboriginal)	ochre
Winyarn (Aboriginal)	sorry, sorrowful
Yabini (Aboriginal)	stars
yarraman (Aboriginal)	horse
yorgas (Aboriginal)	women
Yuwintj (Aboriginal)	falling star

Glossary of Jamaican Words

a	to, as in 'Go a shop,' from Spanish
a go	going to do as in Me a go tell him
ackee	African food tree introduced about 1778. From Twi ankye, or Kru akee
alias	(urban slang) dangerous, violent
Babylon	Westernized Government and Institutions. Oppressive force, Police
batti	(slang) the buttocks
boasie	proud, concieted, ostentatious. Combination of English Boastful—Yoruba bosi = proud
bredrin	brother or brothers. From the biblical Brethren
bungo	racially pejorative. Crude black ignorant boorish person. From Hausa Bunga = bumpkin, nincompoop
cho	dismissive exclamation
coo'pon	Look! Look upon
coo'yah	look here
coolie	one of East Indian descent as in 'coolie gal'
Deggeh	sole, lonely From Ewe deka = one single
deh	there
dereso, deso	(place, emphatic) there as in Look dereso = Look there
dey	to be, exist as in 'No yam no dey' = There is no yam
dey 'bout	be about, available. 'No ganga dey 'bout
dey 'pon	to be engaged in action or continuing activity as in I dey pon dying = I am dying, I dey pon hurry = I am in a hurry
Faastie, fiesti	impertinent, rude, impudent
fe	'to' as in Have fe go = Have to go, Look fe it = Look for it, Him ready fe kill = He is ready to kill

375

fi	'fi me' mine 'fi you' yours
I an' I, I-man	(Rasta talk) first person singular
ilie	(Rasta talk) literally 'highly' valuable, exalted even sacred
irie	(Rasta talk) powerful and pleasing
Jah	short for Jah Ras Tafari, common way to refer to the divinity. Probably from Hebrew Jahweh = God
kass kass	quarrel or contention. Combination of English cuss/curse and Twi kasa kasa, to dispute verbally
Maas	master. Now freed of its class origin a term of affection and respect as used in addressing an older man
Nah	will not. Emphatic as in 'Me nah do that!'
nuh	interrogative at end of sentence. Literally 'Is that not so?' 'Not true?' or imploringly 'please' as in 'Do it for me, nuh?'
quashie	peasant, country bumpkin, coarse and stupid person. Racially pejorative generic term for blacks. Originally Twi word for boy born on Sunday
Raas	expletive extremely impolite. From English 'your arse'
rahtid	to be enraged—or expression of surprise. From the biblical 'wrothed'
rhygin	spirited, vigourous, lively, passionate with great vitality and force; also sexually provacative and aggression. Probably from English 'raging'
royal (rial)	off-spring of some other race and black as in chinky-rial Chinese-Black or as fun monkey-rial
Tallowah	sturdy, strong, fearless physically capable. From Ewe talala
Tata	father, affectionate and respectful title for old man
Unu	you, plural. In usage close to Afro-American y'awl. From Ibu unu, same meaning
yaah	expletive, emphatic conclusion. 'You hear me,' as in 'Don't do it, yaah.'
Yah	here, as in 'Come yah!'

Glossary of language used in the Silver City

Names in italics denote female origins

Bathsheba	voluptuous
Bethesda	from a place of fountains
Carmela	garden
Clemence	mildness
Danette	the Lord judges me
Darkon	leader, head of Tribe
Delilah	the Temptress
Edra	woman of power
Elia	the highest
Elias	the Lord is God
Elihu	the Lord is God
Elon	mighty oak, invincible
Esau	noted for his hair; long hair
Evadne	life
Gabriel	strongman of God
Ishmael	the wanderer
Israel	the Lord's warrior or soldier
Jaala	wild she-goat
Janan	Grace of the Lord
Jarebb	lively son
Jegar	witness our love
Jehiah	his life is Jehovah's
Jehovah	another name for God. A different type of worship
Jessamine	God is
Joel	Jehovah is God
Johanan	favoured of God

Lilith	Goddess of storms (assyro-Babylonian)
Madeline	woman of Magdala
Melchoir	King of light
Meras	worthy
Mordecai	worshipper of Marduk, God of Babylon
Naomi	sweet, pleasant
Phenice	from a palm tree
Phineas	black (Egyptian)
Raphael	God has healed
Ruth	beauty
Sarah	princess
Shama	obedient woman
Shimona	little princess
Simeon	little hyena
Solomon	little man of peace
Tamara	thought to mean 'palm tree' (Russian-Hebrew)
Tarrsus	from the city of Tarrsus
Zillah	shade
Zoheletha	serpent stone